T4-ADP-183

THE INSULTED
AND INJURED

THE NOVELS OF
FYODOR DOSTOEVSKY
VOLUME VI

THE NOVELS OF IVAN TURGENEV

Translated from the Russian by CONSTANCE GARNETT, in fifteen volumes, foolscap 8vo, price, leather, 3s net; and cloth, 2s net each

RUDIN
A HOUSE OF GENTLEFOLK
ON THE EVE
FATHERS AND CHILDREN
SMOKE
VIRGIN SOIL (2 vols.)
A SPORTSMAN'S SKETCHES (2 vols.)
DREAM TALES AND PROSE POEMS
THE TORRENTS OF SPRING
A LEAR OF THE STEPPES, etc.
THE DIARY OF A SUPERFLUOUS MAN, etc.
A DESPERATE CHARACTER, etc.
THE JEW, etc.

Also a small Limited Large Paper Edition, with 48 Photogravure Plates, in fifteen volumes, crown 8vo, in sets only, price £3 net

NOVELS BY COUNT LEO TOLSTOY

Translated from the Russian by CONSTANCE GARNETT

WAR AND PEACE, 1536 pages, one volume, crown 8vo, price 3s 6d net
ANNA KARENIN, 920 pages, one volume, crown 8vo, price 2s 6d net
THE DEATH OF IVAN ILYITCH and other Stories, one volume, demy 8vo, price 7s 6d

THE NOVELS OF FYODOR DOSTOEVSKY

Translated from the Russian by CONSTANCE GARNETT, Crown 8vo, price 3s 6d net each volume.

THE BROTHERS KARAMAZOV
THE IDIOT
THE POSSESSED
CRIME AND PUNISHMENT
THE HOUSE OF THE DEAD
THE INSULTED AND INJURED
A RAW YOUTH (shortly)

London: WILLIAM HEINEMANN, 21 Bedford St., W.C.

THE INSULTED AND INJURED

A NOVEL IN FOUR PARTS
AND AN EPILOGUE BY
FYODOR DOSTOEVSKY

FROM THE RUSSIAN BY
CONSTANCE GARNETT

LONDON
WILLIAM HEINEMANN

London : William Heinemann . 1915

PART I

CHAPTER I

LAST year, on the evening of March 22, I had a very strange adventure. All that day I had been walking about the town trying to find a lodging. My old one was very damp, and I had begun to have an ominous cough Ever since the autumn I had been meaning to move, but I had hung on till the spring. I had not been able to find anything decent all day. In the first place I wanted a separate tenement, not a room in other peoples' lodgings; secondly, though I could do with one room, it must be a large one, and, of course, it had at the same time to be as cheap as possible. I have observed that in a confined space even thought is cramped. When I was brooding over a future novel I liked to walk up and down the room. By the way, I always like better brooding over my works and dreaming how they should be written than actually writing them. And this really is not from laziness. Why is it?

I had been feeling unwell all day, and towards sunset I felt really very ill. Something like a fever set in. Moreover, I had been all day long on my legs and was tired. Towards evening, just before it got dark, I was walking along the Voznesensky Prospect. I love the March sun in Petersburg, especially at sunset, in clear frosty weather, of course. The whole street suddenly glitters, bathed in brilliant light. All the houses seem suddenly, as it were, to sparkle. Their grey, yellow, and dirty-green hues for an instant lose all their gloominess, it is as though there were a sudden clearness in one's soul, as though one were startled, or as though some one had nudged one with his elbow. There is a new outlook, a new train of thought.... It is wonderful what one ray of sunshine can do for the soul of man!

But the ray of sunshine had died away; the frost grew sharper, and began to nip one's nose; the twilight deepened; gas flared from the shops. As I reached Müller's, the confectioner's, I suddenly stood stock-still and began staring at that side of the street, as though I had a presentiment that something extraordinary was just going to happen to me ; and at that very instant I saw, on the opposite side of the street, the old man with his dog. I remember quite well that I felt an unpleasant sensation clutch at my heart, and I could not myself have told what that sensation was.

I am not a mystic. I scarcely believe in presentiments and divinings, yet I have, as probably most people have had, some rather inexplicable experiences in my life. For example, this old man : why was it that at that meeting with him I had at once a presentiment that that same evening something not quite ordinary would happen to me ? I was ill, however, and sensations in illness are almost always deceptive.

The old man, stooping and tapping the pavement with his stick, drew near the confectioner's, with his slow, feeble step, moving his legs as though they were sticks, and seeming not to bend them. I had never in my life come across such a strange, grotesque figure, and, whenever I had met him at Müller's before, he had always made a painful impression on me. His tall figure, his bent back, his death-like face with the stamp of eighty years upon it, his old great-coat torn at the seams, the battered round hat, at least twenty years old, which covered his head—bald but for one lock of hair not grey but yellowish-white—all his movements, which seemed performed, as it were, aimlessly, as though worked by springs—no one who met him for the first time could help being struck by all this. It really was strange to see an old man who had so outlived the natural span alone, with no one to look after him, especially as he looked like a madman who had escaped from his keepers. I was struck, too, by his extraordinary emaciation ; he seemed scarcely to have any body, it was as though there were nothing but skin over his bones. His large lustreless eyes, set as it were in blue rims, always stared straight before him, never looking to one side, and never seeing anything—of that I feel certain ; though he looked at you, he walked straight at you as though there were an empty space before him. I noticed this several times. He had begun to make his appearance at Müller's only lately, he was always accompanied by his dog, and no one knew where he came from. Not one of the customers at Müller's could make up his mind to address him, nor did he accost any of them.

" And why does he drag himself to Müller's, what is there for him to do there?" I wondered, standing still on the opposite side of the street and gazing fixedly at him. A sort of irritable vexation, the result of illness and fatigue, surged up within me. "What is he thinking about?" I went on wondering. "What is there in his head? But does he still think of anything at all? His face is so dead that it expresses nothing at all. And where could he have picked up that disgusting dog, which never leaves him, as though it were an inseparable part of him, and which is so like him?"

That wretched dog looked as though it, too, were eighty; yes, it certainly must have been so. To begin with, it looked older than dogs ever are, and secondly, it struck me, for some reason, the very first time I saw it, that it could not be a dog like all others; that it was an exceptional dog; that there must be something fantastic about it, something uncanny; that it might be a sort of Mephistopheles in dog-form, and that its fate was in some mysterious unknown way bound up with the fate of its master. Looking at it you would have allowed at once that twenty years must have elapsed since its last meal. It was as thin as a skeleton, or, which is much the same, as its master. Almost all its hair had fallen off, and its tail hung down between its legs as bare as a stick. Its head and long ears drooped sullenly forward. I never in my life met such a repulsive dog. When they both walked down the street, the master in front and the dog at his heels, its nose touched the skirt of his coat as though glued to it. And their gait and their whole appearance seemed almost to cry aloud at every step: "We are old, old. Oh Lord, how old we are!" I remember too that it occurred to me once that the old man and the dog had somehow stepped out of some page of Hoffmann illustrated by Gavarni and were parading this world by way of walking advertisements of the edition.

I crossed the road and followed the old man into the confectioner's.

In the shop the old man behaved in a very strange way, and Müller, standing at his counter, had begun of late to make a grimace of annoyance at the entrance of the unbidden guest. In the first place, the strange visitor never asked for anything. Every time he went straight to a corner by the stove and sat down in a chair there. If the seat by the stove were occupied, after standing for some time in bewildered perplexity before the gentleman who had taken his place, he walked away, seeming puzzled, to the other corner by the window. There he fixed on a chair, deliberately seated himself in it, took off his hat, put it on the floor beside him, laid his stick by his hat, and then, sinking back into the chair, he would remain without moving for three or four hours. He never took up a newspaper, never uttered a single word, a single sound, and simply sat there, staring straight before him with wide-open eyes, but with such a blank, lifeless look in them that one might well bet he saw and heard nothing of what was going on around him. The dog, after turning round two or three times in the same place, lay down sullenly at his feet with its nose between his boots, heaving deep sighs, and, stretched out full length on the floor, it too stayed without moving the whole evening as though it had died for the time. One might imagine that these two creatures lay dead all day somewhere, and only at sunset came to life again, simply to visit Müller's shop to perform some mysterious, secret duty. After sitting for three or four hours, the old man would at last get up, take up his hat and set off somewhere homewards. The dog too got up, and, with drooping tail and hanging head as before, followed him mechanically with the same slow step. The habitual visitors at the shop began at last to avoid the old man in every way and would not even sit beside him, as though he gave them a feeling of repulsion. He noticed nothing of this.

The customers of this confectioner's shop were mostly Germans. They gathered there from all parts of the Voznesensky Prospect, mostly heads of shops of various sorts: carpenters, bakers, painters, hatters, saddlers, all patriarchal people in the German sense of the word. Altogether the patriarchal tradition was kept up at Müller's. Often the master of the shop joined some customer of his acquaintance and sat beside him at the table, when a certain amount of punch would be consumed. The dogs and small children of the household would sometimes come out to see the customers too, and the latter used to fondle both the children and the dogs. They all knew one another and all had a respect for one another. And while the guests were absorbed in the perusal of the German newspapers, through the door leading to the shopkeeper's rooms came the tinkling of "Mein lieber Augustin," on a cracked piano played by the eldest daughter, a little German miss with flaxen curls, very much like a white mouse. The waltz was welcomed with pleasure. I used to go to Müller's at the beginning of every month to read the Russian magazines which were taken there.

As I went in I saw that the old man was already sitting by the window, while the dog was lying as always, stretched out at his feet. I sat down in a corner without speaking, and inwardly asked myself why had I come here when there was really nothing for me to do here, when I was ill and it would have been better to make haste home to have tea and go to bed. Could I have come here simply to gaze at this old man? I was annoyed. "What have I to do with him?" I thought, recalling that strange, painful sensation with which I had looked at him just before in the street. And what were all these dull Germans to me? What was the meaning of this fantastic mood? What was the meaning of this cheap agitation over trifles, which I had noticed in myself of late, which hindered me from living, and taking a clear view of life? One penetrating reviewer had already remarked on it in his indignant criticism of my last novel. But though I hesitated, and deplored it, yet I remained where I was, and meantime I was more and more overcome by illness, and I was reluctant to leave the warm room. I took up a Frankfort paper, read a couple of lines and dropped into a doze. The Germans did not interfere with me. They read and smoked, and only once in half an hour or so communicated some piece of Frankfort news to one another abruptly in an undertone, or some jest or epigram of the renowned German wit, Saphir, after which they would plunge into their reading again with redoubled pride in their nationality.

I dozed for half an hour and was waked by a violent shiver. It was certainly necessary to go home.

But meanwhile a drama in dumb show which was being enacted in the room stopped me again. I have said already that as soon as the old man sat down in his chair he would fix his eye on something and not remove it the whole evening. It had been my fate in the past to be exposed to that meaningless, persistent, unseeing stare. It was a very unpleasant, in fact unbearable sensation, and I usually changed my seat as soon as I could. At this moment the old man's victim was a small, round, very neat little German, with a stiffly starched stand-up collar and an unusually red face, a new visitor to the shop, a merchant from Riga, called, as I learned afterwards, Adam Ivanitch Schultz. He was an intimate friend of Müller's, but as yet knew nothing of the old man or many of the customers. Sipping his punch and reading with relish the *Dorfbarbier*, he suddenly raised his eyes and observed the old man's immovable stare fixed upon him. It disconcerted him. Adam Ivanitch was a very touchy and sensitive man, like all "superior" Germans. It seemed to him strange and insulting that he should be stared at so unceremoniously. With stifled indignation he turned his eyes away from the tactless guest, muttered something to himself, and took refuge behind the newspaper. But within five minutes he could not resist peeping out suspiciously from behind the paper; still the same persistent stare, still the same meaningless scrutiny. That time, too, Adam Ivanitch said nothing. But when the same thing was repeated a third time he flared up and felt it incumbent upon himself to defend his dignity and not to degrade, in the eyes of so gentlemanly a company, the prestige of the fair town of Riga, of which he probably felt himself to be the representative. With an impatient gesture he flung the paper on the table, rapping it vigorously with the stick to which the paper was fastened, and blazing with personal dignity, and crimson with punch and *amour propre*, in his turn he fastened his little bloodshot eyes on the offensive old man. It looked as though the two of them, the German and his assailant, were trying to overpower each other by the magnetic force of their stares, and were waiting to see which would be the first to be put out of countenance and drop his eyes. The rap of the stick and the eccentric position of Adam Ivanitch drew the attention of all the customers. All laid aside what they were doing, and with grave and speechless curiosity watched the two opponents. The scene was becoming very comical, but the magnetism of the little red-faced gentleman's defiant eyes was entirely thrown away. The old man went on staring straight at the infuriated Schultz, and absolutely failed to observe that he was the object of general curiosity; he was as unperturbed as though he were not on earth but in the moon. Adam Ivanitch's patience broke down at last, and he exploded.

"Why do you stare at me so intently?" he shouted in German, in a sharp, piercing voice and with a menacing air.

But his adversary continued silent as though he did not understand and even did not hear the question. Adam Ivanitch made up his mind to speak to him in Russian.

"I am asking you what for you at me so studiously staring?" he shouted with redoubled fury. "I am to the court well known, and you known not!" he added, leaping up from his chair.

But the old man did not turn a hair. A murmur of indignation was heard among the Germans. Müller himself, attracted by the uproar, came into the room. When he found out what was the matter he imagined that the old man was deaf, and bent down to his ear.

"Master Schultz asked you studiously not to stare at him," he said as loud as he could, looking intently at the incomprehensible visitor.

The old man looked mechanically at Müller; his face, which had till then been so immovable, showed traces of disturbing thought, of a sort of uneasy agitation. He was flustered, bent down sighing and gasping to pick up his hat, snatched it up together with his stick, got up from his chair, and with the piteous smile of a beggar turned out of a seat that he has taken by mistake, he prepared to go out of the room. In the meek and submissive haste of the poor decrepit old man there was so much to provoke compassion, so much to wring the heart that the whole company, from Adam Ivanitch downward, took a different view of the position at once. It was evident that the old man, far from being capable of insulting anyone, realized that he might be turned out from anywhere like a beggar.

Müller was a kind-hearted and compassionate man.

"No, no," he said, patting him on the shoulder encouragingly, "sit still. *Aber* Herr Schultz asking you particularly not to look upon him. He is well known at the court."

But the poor old man did not understand this either; he was more flustered than ever. He stooped to pick up his handkerchief, a ragged old blue one that had dropped out of his hat, and began to call his dog, which lay motionless on the floor, and seemed to be sound asleep with its nose on its paws.

"Azorka, Azorka," he mumbled in a quavering, aged voice. "Azorka!"

Azorka did not stir.

"Azorka, Azorka," the old man repeated anxiously, and he poked the dog with his stick. But it remained in the same position.

The stick dropped from his hands. He stooped, knelt down, and in both hands lifted Azorka's head. The poor dog was dead. Unnoticed it had died at its master's feet from old age, and perhaps from hunger too. The old man looked at it for a minute as though struck, as though he did not understand that Azorka was dead; then bent down gently to his old servant and friend and pressed his pale cheek to the dead face of the dog. A minute of silence passed. We were all touched. At last the poor fellow got up. He was very pale and trembled as though he were in a fever.

"You can have it stoffed," said the sympathetic Müller, anxious to comfort him in any way (by "stoffed" he meant stuffed). "You can have it well stoffed, Fyodor Karlitch Krüger stoffs beautifully ; Fyodor Karlitch Krüger is a master at stoffing," repeated Müller, picking up the stick from the ground and handing it to the old man.

"Yes, I can excellently stoff," Herr Krüger himself modestly asserted, coming to the front.

He was a tall, lanky and virtuous German, with tangled red hair, and spectacles on his hooked nose.

"Fyodor Karlitch Kruger has a great talent to make all sorts magnificent stoffing," added Müller, growing enthusiastic over his own idea.

"Yes, I have a great talent to make all sorts magnificent stoffing," Herr Krüger repeated again. "And I will for nothing to stoff you your dog," he added in an access of magnanimous self-sacrifice.

"No, I will you pay for to stoff it!" Adam Ivanitch Schultz cried frantically, turning twice as red as before, glowing with magnanimity in his turn and feeling himself the innocent cause of the misfortune.

The old man listened to all this evidently without understanding it, trembling all over as before.

"Vait! Drink one glass of goot cognac!" cried Müller, seeing that the enigmatical guest was making efforts to get away.

They brought him the brandy. The old man mechanically took the glass, but his hand trembled, and before he raised it to his lips he spilt half, and put it back on the tray without taking a drop of it. Then with a strange, utterly inappropriate smile he went out of the shop with rapid, uneven steps, leaving Azorka on the floor. Every one stood in bewilderment ; exclamations were heard.

"*Schwernoth! Was für eine Geschichte?*" said the Germans, looking round-eyed at one another.

But I rushed after the old man. A few steps from the shop, through a gate on the right, there is an alley, dark and narrow, shut in by huge houses. Something told me that the old man must have turned in there. A second house was being built here on the right hand, and was surrounded with scaffolding.

The fence round the house came almost into the middle of the alley, and planks had been laid down to walk round the fence. In a dark corner made by the fence and the house I found the old man. He was sitting on the edge of the wooden pavement and held his head propped in both hands, with his elbows on his knees. I sat down beside him.

"Listen," said I, hardly knowing how to begin. "Don't grieve over Azorka. Come along, I'll take you home. Don't worry. I'll go for a cab at once. Where do you live?"

The old man did not answer. I could not decide what to do. There were no passers-by in the alley. Suddenly he began clutching me by the arm.

"Stifling!" he said, in a husky, hardly audible voice. "Stifling!"

"Let's go to your home," I cried, getting up and forcibly lifting him up. "You'll have some tea and go to bed. . . . I'll get a cab. I'll call a doctor. . . . I know a doctor. . . ."

I don't know what else I said to him. He tried to get up, but fell back again on the ground and began muttering again in the same hoarse choking voice. I bent down more closely and listened.

"In Vassilyevsky Island," the old man gasped. "The sixth street. The six . . . th stre . . . et . . ."

He sank into silence.

"You live in Vassilyevsky Island? But you've come wrong then. That would be to the left, and you've come to the right. I'll take you directly . . ."

The old man did not stir. I took his hand; the hand dropped as though it were dead. I looked into his face, touched him—he was dead.

I felt as though it had all happened in a dream.

This incident caused me a great deal of trouble, in the course of which my fever passed off of itself. The old man's lodging was discovered. He did not, however, live in Vassilyevsky Island, but only a couple of paces from the spot where he died, in Klugen's Buildings, in the fifth storey right under the roof, in a separate flat, consisting of a tiny entry and a large low-pitched room, with three slits by way of windows. He had lived very poorly. His furniture consisted of a table, two chairs, and a very, very old sofa as hard as a stone, with hair sticking out of it in all directions; and even these things turned out to be the landlord's. The stove had evidently not been heated for a long while, and no candles were found either. I seriously think now that the old man went to Müller's simply to sit in a lighted room and get warm. On the table stood an empty earthenware mug, and a stale crust of bread lay beside it. No money was found, not a farthing. There was not even a change of linen in which to bury him; some one gave his own shirt for the purpose. It was clear that he could not have lived like that, quite isolated, and no doubt some one must have visited him from time to time. In the table-drawer they found his passport. The dead man turned out to be of foreign birth, though a Russian subject. His name was Jeremy Smith, and he was a mechanical engineer, seventy-eight years old. There were two books lying on the table, a short geography and the New Testament in the Russian translation, pencil-marked in the margin and scored by the finger-nail. These books I took for myself. The landlord and the other tenants were questioned—they all knew scarcely anything about him. There were numbers of tenants in the building, almost all artisans or German women who let lodgings with board and attendance. The superintendent of the block, a superior man, was also unable to say much about the former tenant, except that the lodging was let at six roubles a month, that the deceased had lived in it for four months, but had not paid a farthing for the last two, so that he would have had to turn him out. The question was asked whether anyone used to come to see him, but no one could give a satisfactory answer about this. It was a big block, lots of people would be coming to such a Noah's Ark, there was no remembering all of them. The porter, who had been employed for five years in the flats and probably could have given some information, had gone home to his native village on a visit a fortnight before, leaving in his place his nephew, a young fellow who did not yet know half the tenants by sight. I don't know for certain how all these inquiries ended at last, but finally the old man was buried. In the course of those days, though I had many things to look after, I had been to Vassilyevsky Island, to Sixth Street, and laughed at myself when I arrived there. What could I see in Sixth Street but an ordinary row of houses? But why, I wondered, did the old man talk of Sixth Street and Vassilyevsky Island when he was dying? Was he delirious?

I looked at Smith's deserted lodging, and I liked it. I took it for myself. The chief point about it was that it was large though very low-pitched, so much so that at first I thought I should knock my head against the ceiling. But I soon got used to it. Nothing better could be found for six roubles a month. The independence of it tempted me. All I still had to do was to arrange for some sort of service, for I could not live entirely without a servant. The porter undertook meanwhile to come in once a day to do what was absolutely necessary. And who knows, thought I, perhaps some one will come to inquire for the old man! But five days passed after his death, and no one had yet come.

CHAPTER II

At that time, just a year ago, I was still working on the staff of some papers, wrote articles, and was firmly convinced that I should succeed one day in writing something good on a larger scale. I was sitting over a long novel at that time, but it has all ended in my being here in the hospital, and I believe I am soon going to die. And since I am going to die, why, one might ask, write reminiscences?

I cannot help continually recalling all this bitter last year of my life. I want to write it all down, and if I had not found this occupation I believe I should have died of misery. All these impressions of the past excite me sometimes to the pitch of anguish, of agony. They will grow more soothing, more harmonious as I write them. They will be less like delirium, like a nightmare. So I imagine. The mere mechanical exercise of writing counts for something It will soothe me, cool me, arouse anew in me my old literary habits, will turn my memories and sick dreams into work, into occupation. . . . Yes, it is a good idea. Moreover, it will be something to leave my attendant if he only pastes up the window with my manuscript, when he puts in the double frames for the winter.

But I have begun my story, I don't know why, in the middle. If it is all to be written, I must begin from the beginning. Well, let us begin at the beginning, though my autobiography won't be a long one.

I was not born here but far away in a remote province. It must be assumed that my parents were good people, but I was left an orphan as a child, and I was brought up in the house of Nikolay Sergeyitch Ichmenyev, a small landowner of the neighbourhood, who took me in out of pity. He had only one child, a daughter Natasha, a child three years younger than I. We grew up together like brother and sister. Oh, my dear childhood! How stupid to grieve and regret it at five-and-twenty, and to recall it alone with enthusiasm and gratitude! In those days there was such bright sunshine in the sky, so unlike the sun of Petersburg, and our little hearts beat so blithely and gaily. Then there were fields and woods all round us, not piles of dead stones as now. How wonderful were the garden and park in Vassilyevskoe, where Nikolay Sergeyitch was steward. Natasha and I used to go for walks in that garden, and beyond the garden was a great damp forest, where both of us were once lost. Happy, golden days! The first foretaste of life was mysterious and alluring, and it was so sweet to get glimpses of it. In those days behind every bush, behind every tree, some one still seemed to be living, mysterious, unseen by us; fairyland was mingled with reality; and when at times the mists of evening were thick in the deep hollows and caught in grey, winding wisps about the bushes that clung to the stony ribs of our great ravine, Natasha and I, holding each other's hands, peeped from the edge into the depths below with timid curiosity, expecting every moment that some one would come forth or call to us out of the mist at the bottom of the ravine; and that our nurse's fairy tales would turn out to be solid established truth. Once, long afterwards, I happened to remind Natasha how a copy of "Readings for Children" was got for us; how we ran off at once to the pond in the garden where was our favourite green seat under the old maple, and there settled ourselves, and began reading "Alphonso and Dalinda"—a fairy-story. I cannot to this day remember the story without a strange thrill at my heart, and when a year ago I reminded Natasha of the first lines: "Alphonso, the hero of my story, was born in Portugal; Don Ramiro his father," and so on, I almost shed tears. This must have seemed very stupid, and that was probably why Natasha smiled queerly at my enthusiasm at the time. But she checked herself at once (I remember that), and began recalling the old days to comfort me. One thing led to another, and she was moved herself. That was a delightful evening. We went over everything, and how I had been sent away to school in the district town—heavens, how she had cried then!—and our last parting when I left Vassilyevskoe for ever. I was leaving the boarding-school then and was going to Petersburg to prepare for the university. I was seventeen at that time and she was fifteen. Natasha says I was such an awkward, gawky creature then, and that one couldn't look at me without laughing. At the moment of farewell I drew her aside to tell her something terribly important, but my tongue suddenly failed me and clove to the roof of my mouth. She remembers that I was in great agitation. Of course our talk came to nothing. I did not know what to say, and perhaps she would not have understood me. I only wept bitterly and so went away without saying anything. We saw each other again long afterwards in Petersburg; that was two years ago. Old Nikolay Sergeyitch had come to Petersburg about his lawsuit, and I had only just begun my literary career.

CHAPTER III

NIKOLAY SERGEYITCH came of a good family, which had long sunk into decay. But he was left at his parents' death with a fair estate with a hundred and fifty serfs on it. At twenty he went into the hussars. All went well; but after six years in the army he happened one unlucky evening to lose all his property at cards. He did not sleep all night. The next evening he appeared at the card-table and staked his horse—his last possession. His card was a winning one, and it was followed by a second and a third, and within half an hour he had won back one of his villages, the hamlet Ichmenyevka, which had numbered fifty souls at the last census. He sent in his papers and retired from the service next day. He had lost a hundred serfs for ever. Two months later he received his discharge with the rank of lieutenant, and went home to his village. He never in his life spoke of his loss at cards, and in spite of his well-known good nature he would certainly have quarrelled with anyone who alluded to it. In the country he applied himself industriously to looking after his land, and at thirty-five he married a poor girl of good family, Anna Andreyevna Shumilov, who was absolutely without dowry, though she had received an education in a high class school kept by a French *emigrée*, called Mon-Reveche, a privilege upon which Anna Andreyevna prided herself all her life, although no one was ever able to discover exactly of what that education had consisted. Nikolay Sergeyitch was an excellent farmer. The neighbouring landowners learned to manage their estates from him. A few years had passed when suddenly a landowner, Prince Pyotr Alexandrovitch Valkovsky, came from Petersburg to the neighbouring estate, Vassilyevskoe, the village of which had a population of nine hundred serfs. His arrival made a great stir in the whole neighbourhood. The prince was still young, though not in his first youth. He was of good rank in the service, had important connexions, and a fortune ; was a handsome man and a widower, a fact of particular interest to all the girls and ladies in the neighbourhood. People talked of the brilliant reception given him by the governor, to whom he was in some way related ; of how he had turned the heads of all the ladies by his gallantries, and so on, and so on. In short, he was one of those brilliant representatives of aristocratic Petersburg society who rarely make their appearance in the provinces, but produce an extraordinary sensation when they do. The prince, however, was by no means of the politest, especially to people who could be of no use to him and whom he considered ever so little his inferiors. He did not think fit to make the acquaintance of his neighbours in the country, and at once made many enemies by neglecting to do so. And so every one was extremely surprised when the fancy suddenly took him to call on Nikolay Sergeyitch. It is true that the latter was one of his nearest neighbours. The prince made a great impression on the Ichmenyev household. He fascinated them both at once ; Anna Andreyevna was particularly enthusiastic about him. In a short time he was on intimate terms with them, went there every day and invited them to his house. He used to tell them stories, make jokes, play on their wretched piano, and sing. The Ichmenyevs were never tired of wondering how so good and charming a man could be called a proud, stuck-up, cold egoist, as all the neighbours with one voice declared him to be. One must suppose that the prince really liked Nikolay Sergeyitch, who was a simple-hearted, straightforward, disinterested and generous man. But all was soon explained. The prince had come to Vassilyevskoe especially to get rid of his steward, a prodigal German, who was a conceited man and an expert agriculturist, endowed with venerable grey hair, spectacles, and a hooked nose ; yet in spite of these advantages, he robbed the prince without shame or measure, and what was worse, tormented several peasants to death. At last Ivan Karlovitch was caught in his misdeeds and exposed, was deeply offended, talked a great deal about German honesty, but, in spite of all this, was dismissed and even with some ignominy. The prince needed a steward and his choice fell on Nikolay Sergeyitch, who was an excellent manager and a man of whose honesty there could be no possible doubt. The prince seemed particularly anxious that Nikolay Sergeyitch should of his own accord propose to take the post. But this did not come off, and one fine morning the prince made the proposition himself, in the form of a very friendly and humble request. Nikolay Sergeyitch at first refused; but the liberal salary attracted Anna Andreyevna, and the redoubled cordiality of the prince overcame any hesitation he still felt. The prince attained his aim. One may presume that he was skilful in judging character. During his brief acquaintance with Ichmenyev he soon perceived the kind of man he had to deal with, and realized that he must be won in a warm and friendly way, that his heart must be conquered, and that, without that, money would do little with him. Valkovsky needed a steward whom he could trust blindly for ever, that he might never need to visit Vassilyevskoe again, and this was just what he was reckoning on. The fascination he exercised over Nikolay Sergeyitch was so strong that the latter genuinely believed in his friendship. Nikolay Sergeyitch was one of those very simple-hearted and naïvely romantic men who are, whatever people may say against them, so charming among us in Russia, and who are devoted with their whole soul to anyone to whom (God knows why) they take a fancy, and at times carry their devotion to a comical pitch.

Many years passed. Prince Valkovsky estate flourished. The relations between the owner of Vassilyevskoe and his steward continued without the slightest friction on either side, and did not extend beyond a purely business correspondence. Though the prince did not interfere with Nikolay Sergeyitch's management, he sometimes gave him advice which astonished the latter by its extraordinary astuteness and practical ability. It was evident that he did not care to waste money, and was clever at getting it indeed. Five years after his visit to Vassilyevskoe the prince sent Nikolay Sergeyitch an authorization to purchase another splendid estate in the same province with a population of four hundred serfs. Nikolay Sergeyitch was delighted. The prince's successes, the news of his advancement, his promotion, were as dear to his heart as if they had been those of his own brother. But his delight reached a climax when the prince on one occasion showed the extraordinary trust he put in him. This is how it happened. . . . But here I find it necessary to mention some details of the life of this Prince Valkovsky, who is in a way a leading figure in my story.

CHAPTER IV

I HAVE mentioned already that he was a widower. He had married in his early youth, and married for money. From his parents in Moscow, who were completely ruined, he received hardly anything. Vassilyevskoe was mortgaged over and over again. It was encumbered with enormous debts. At twenty-two the prince, who was forced at that time to take service in a government department in Moscow, had not a farthing, and made his entrance into life as the "beggar offspring of an ancient line." His marriage to the elderly daughter of a tax-contractor saved him.

The contractor, of course, cheated him over the dowry, but anyway, he was able with his wife's money to buy back his estate, and to get on to his feet again. The contractor's daughter, who had fallen to the prince's lot, was scarcely able to write, could not put two words together, was ugly, and had only one great virtue: she was good-natured and submissive. The prince took the utmost advantage of this quality in her. After the first year of marriage he left his wife, who had meanwhile borne him a son, at Moscow, in charge of her father, the contractor, and went off to serve in another province, where, through the interest of a powerful relation in Petersburg, he obtained a prominent post. His soul thirsted for distinction, advancement, a career, and realizing that he could not live with his wife either in Petersburg or Moscow, he resolved to begin his career in the provinces until something better turned up. It is said that even in the first year of his marriage he wore his wife out by his brutal behaviour. This rumour always revolted Nikolay Sergeyitch, and he hotly defended the prince, declaring that he was incapable of a mean action. But seven years later his wife died, and the bereaved husband immediately returned to Petersburg. In Petersburg he actually caused some little sensation. With his fortune, his good looks and his youth, his many brilliant qualities, his wit, his taste, and his unfailing gaiety he appeared in Petersburg not as a toady and fortune-hunter, but as a man in a fairly independent position. It is said that there really was something fascinating about him; something dominating and powerful. He was extremely attractive to women, and an intrigue with a society beauty gave him a scandalous renown. He scattered money without stint in spite of his natural economy which almost amounted to niggardliness; he lost money at cards when suitable, and could lose large sums without turning a hair. But he had not come to Petersburg for the sake of amusement. He was bent on making his career and finally establishing his position. He attained this object. Count Nainsky, his distinguished relative, who would have taken no notice of him if he had come as an ordinary applicant, was so struck by his success in society that he found it suitable and possible to show him particular attention, and even condescended to take his seven-year-old son to be brought up in his house. To this period belongs the prince's visit to Vassilyevskoe and his acquaintance with Nikolay Sergeyitch. Attaining at last, through the influence of the count, a prominent post in one of the most important foreign embassies, he went abroad. Later, rumours of his doings were rather vague. People talked of some unpleasant adventure that had befallen him abroad, but no one could explain exactly what it was. All that was known was that he succeeded in buying an estate of four hundred serfs, as I have mentioned already. It was many years later that he returned from abroad; he was of high rank in the service and at once received a very prominent post in Petersburg. Rumours reached Ichmenyevka that he was about to make a second marriage which would connect him with a very wealthy, distinguished and powerful family. "He is on the high road to greatness," said Nikolay Sergeyitch, rubbing his hands with pleasure. I was at Petersburg then, at the university, and I remember Nikolay Sergeyitch wrote on purpose to ask me to find out whether the report was true. He wrote to the prince, too, to solicit his interest for me, but the prince left the letter unanswered. I only knew that the prince's son, who had been brought up first in the count's household, and afterwards at the *lycée*, had now finished his studies at the age of nineteen. I wrote about this to Nikolay Sergeyitch, and told him, too, that the prince was very fond of his son, and spoilt him, and was already making plans for his future. All this I learnt from fellow-students who knew the young prince. It was about this time, that one fine morning Nikolay Sergeyitch received a letter from Prince Valkovsky that greatly astonished him.

The prince who had till now, as I have mentioned already, confined himself to dry business correspondence with Nikolay

Sergeyitch, wrote to him now in the most minute, unreserved, and friendly way about his intimate affairs. He complained of his son, said that the boy was grieving him by his misconduct, that of course the pranks of such a lad were not to be taken too seriously (he was obviously trying to justify him), but that he had made up his mind to punish his son, to frighten him; in fact, to send him for some time into the country in charge of Nikolay Sergeyitch. The prince wrote that he was reckoning absolutely on "his kind-hearted, generous Nikolay Sergeyitch, and even more upon Anna Andreyevna." He begged them both to receive the young scapegrace into their family, to teach him sense in solitude, to be fond of him if they could, and above all, to correct his frivolous character "by instilling the strict and salutary principles so essential to the conduct of life." Nikolay Sergeyitch, of course, undertook the task with enthusiasm. The young prince arrived. They welcomed him like a son. Nikolay Sergeyitch very soon grew as fond of him as of his own Natasha. Even later on, after the final breach between the boy's father and Nikolay Sergeyitch, the latter sometimes would brighten up speaking of his Alyosha, as he was accustomed to call Prince Alexey Petrovitch. He really was a very charming boy; handsome, delicate and nervous as a woman, though at the same time he was merry and simple-hearted, with an open soul capable of the noblest feelings, and a loving heart candid, and grateful. He became the idol of the household. In spite of his nineteen years he was a perfect child. It was difficult to imagine what his father, who, it was said, loved him so much, could have sent him away for. It was said that he had led an idle and frivolous life in Petersburg, that he had disappointed his father by refusing to enter the service. Nikolay Sergeyitch did not question Alyosha, since the prince had evidently been reticent in his letter as to the real cause of his son's banishment. There were rumours, however, of some unpardonable scrape of Alyosha's, of some intrigue with a lady, of some challenge to a duel, of some incredible loss at cards; there was even talk of his having squandered other people's money. There was also a rumour that the prince had decided to banish his son for no misdeed at all, but merely from certain purely egoistic motives. Nikolay Sergeyitch repelled this notion with indignation, especially as Alyosha was extraordinarily fond of his father, of whom he had known nothing throughout his childhood and boyhood. He talked of him with admiration and enthusiasm; it was evident that he was completely under his influence. Alyosha chattered sometimes, too, about a countess with whom both he and his father were flirting, and told how he, Alyosha, had cut his father out, and how dreadfully vexed his father was about it. He always told this story with delight, with childlike simplicity, with clear, merry laughter, but Nikolay Sergeyitch checked him at once. Alyosha also confirmed the report that his father was intending to marry.

He had already spent nearly a year in exile. He used to write at stated intervals respectful and sedate letters to his father, and at last was so at home in Vassilyevskoe that when his father himself came in the summer (giving Nikolay Sergeyitch warning of his visit beforehand), the exile began of himself begging his father to let him remain as long as possible at Vassilyevskoe, declaring that a country life was his real vocation. All Alyosha's impulses and inclinations were the fruit of an excessive, nervous impressionability, a warm heart, and an irresponsibility which at times almost approached incoherence, an extreme susceptibility to every kind of external influence and a complete absence of will. But the prince listened somewhat suspiciously to his request. . . . Altogether Nikolay Sergeyitch could hardly recognize his former "friend." Prince Valkovsky was strangely altered. He suddenly became peculiarly captious with Nikolay Sergeyitch. When they went over the accounts of the estates he betrayed a revolting greed, a niggardliness, and an incomprehensible suspiciousness. All this deeply wounded the good-hearted Nikolay Sergeyitch; for a long time he refused to believe his senses. Everything this time was just the opposite of what had happened during the first visit, fourteen years before. This time the prince made friends with all his neighbours, all who were of consequence, that is, of course. He did not once visit Nikolay Sergeyitch, and treated him as though he were his subordinate. Suddenly something inexplicable happened. Without any apparent reason a violent quarrel took place between the prince and Nikolay Sergeyitch. Heated, insulting words were overheard, uttered on both sides. Nikolay Sergeyitch indignantly left Vassilyevskoe, but the quarrel did not stop there. A revolting slander suddenly spread all over the neighbourhood. It was asserted that Nikolay Sergeyitch had seen through the young prince's character, and was scheming to take advantage of his failings for his own objects; that his daughter, Natasha (who was then seventeen), had ensnared the affections of the twenty-year-old boy, that the parents had fostered this attachment though they had pretended to notice nothing, that the scheming and "unprincipled" Natasha had bewitched the youth, and that by her efforts he had been kept for a whole year from seeing any of the girls of good family who were so abundant in the honourable households of the neighbouring landowners. It was asserted that the lovers were already plotting to be married at the village of Grigoryevo, fifteen versts from Vassilyevskoe, ostensibly without the knowledge of Natasha's parents, though really they knew all about it and were egging their daughter on with their abominable suggestions. In fact, I could fill a volume with all the slander that the local gossips of both sexes succeeded in circulating on this subject. But what was most remarkable was that the prince believed all this implicitly, and had indeed come to Vassilyevskoe simply on account of it, after receiving an anonymous letter from the province. One would have thought that no one who knew anything of Nikolay Sergeyitch could believe a syllable of all the accusations made against him. And yet, as is always the case, every one was excited, every one was talking, and, though they did not vouch for the story, they shook their heads and . . . condemned him absolutely. Nikolay Sergeyitch was too proud to defend his daughter to the gossips, and sternly prohibited his Anna Andreyevna from entering into any explanations with the neighbours. Natasha herself, who was so libelled, knew nothing of all these slanders and accusations till fully a year afterwards. They had carefully concealed the whole story from her, and she was as gay and innocent as a child of twelve. Meanwhile the breach grew wider and wider. Busybodies lost no time. Slanderers and false witnesses came forward and succeeded in making the prince believe that in Nikolay Sergeyitch's long years of stewardship at Vassilyevskoe he had by no means been a paragon of honesty and what is more, that three years before, Nikolay Sergeyitch had succeeded in embezzling twelve thousand roubles over the sale of the copse, that unimpeachable evidence of this could be brought before the court, especially as he had received no legal authorization for the sale from the prince, but had acted on his own judgment, persuading the prince afterwards of the necessity of the sale, and presenting him with a much smaller sum than he had actually received for the wood. Of course all this was only slander, as was proved later on, but the prince believed it all and called Nikolay Sergeyitch a thief in the presence of witnesses. Nikolay Sergeyitch could not control himself and answered him with a term as insulting. An awful scene took place. A lawsuit immediately followed. Nikolay Sergeyitch, not being able to produce certain documents, and having neither powerful patrons nor experience in litigation, immediately began to get the worst of it. A distraint was laid on his property. The exasperated old man threw up everything and resolved to go to Petersburg to attend to his case himself, leaving an experienced agent to look after his interests in the province. The prince must soon have understood that he had been wrong in accusing Nikolay Sergeyitch. But the insult on both sides had been so deadly that there could be no talk of reconciliation, and the infuriated prince exerted himself to the utmost to get the best of it, that is, to deprive his former steward of his last crust of bread.

CHAPTER V

AND so the Ichmenyevs moved to Petersburg. I am not going to describe my meeting with Natasha after our long separation. All those four years I had never forgotten her. No doubt I did not myself quite understand the feeling with which I recalled her, but when we saw each other again I realized that she was destined to be my fate. For the first days after their arrival I kept fancying that she had not developed much in those four years but was just the same little girl as she had been at our parting. But afterwards I detected in her every day something new of which I had known nothing, as though it had been intentionally concealed, as though the girl were hiding herself from me—and what a joy there was in this discovery.

After moving to Petersburg the old man was at first irritable and gloomy. Things were going badly with him. He was indignant, flew into rages, was immersed in business documents, and had no thoughts to spare for us. Anna Andreyevna wandered about like one distraught, and at first could comprehend nothing. Petersburg alarmed her. She sighed and was full of misgivings, she wept for her old surroundings, for Ichmenyevka, worried at the thought that Natasha was grown up and that there was no one to think about her, and she lapsed into strange confidences with me for lack of a more suitable recipient of them.

It was not long before their arrival that I finished my first novel, the one with which my literary career began, and being a novice I did not know at first what to do with it. I said nothing about it at the Ichmenyevs'. They almost quarrelled with me for leading an idle life, that is, not being in the service and not trying to get a post. The old man bitterly and irritably reproached me, from fatherly solicitude, of course. I was simply ashamed to tell him what I was doing. But how was I to tell them straight out that I did not want to enter the service, but wanted to write novels? And so I deceived them for the time, saying that I had not found a post, and that I was looking for one as hard as I could. Nikolay Sergeyitch had no time to go into it. I remember that one day Natasha, overhearing our conversation, drew me aside mysteriously and besought me with tears to think of my future. She kept questioning me and trying to discover what I was doing, and when I refused to tell my secret even to her, she made me swear that I would not ruin myself by being an idler and a loafer. Though I did not confess what I was doing even to her, I remember that for one word of approval from her of my work, of my first novel, I would have given up all the most flattering remarks of the critics and reviewers, which I heard about myself afterwards. And then at last my novel* came out. Long before its appearance there was a lot of talk and gossip about it in the literary world. B. was as pleased as a child when he read my manuscript. No! If I was ever happy it was not in the first intoxicating moment of my success, but before I had ever read or shown anyone my manuscript; in those long nights spent in exalted hopes and dreams and passionate love of my work, when I was living with my fancies, with the characters I had myself created, as though they were my family, as though they were real people; I loved them, I rejoiced and grieved with them, and sometimes shed genuine tears over my artless hero. And I cannot describe how the old people rejoiced at my success, though at first they were awfully surprised. How strange it seemed to them!

Anna Andreyevna, for instance, could not bring herself to believe that the new writer who was being praised by every one was no other than the little Vanya who had done this and that and the other, and she kept shaking her head over it. The old man did not come round for some time, and at the first rumour of it was positively alarmed; he began to talk of the loss of my

* Dostoevsky's first novel, "Poor People," and its reception by Byelinsky, is here suggested.—*Translator's note.*

career in the service, of the immoral behaviour of authors in general. But the new reports that were continually coming, the paragraphs in the papers, and finally some words of praise uttered about me by persons whom he revered and trusted forced him to change his attitude. When he saw that I suddenly had plenty of money and heard how much money one might get for literary work, his last doubts vanished. Rapid in his transitions from doubt to full enthusiastic faith, rejoicing like a child at my good fortune, he suddenly rushed to the other extreme and indulged in unbridled hopes and most dazzling dreams of my future. Every day he was imagining a new career, new plans for me, and what did he not dream of in those plans! He even began to show me a peculiar respect of which there had been no trace before. But I remember, doubt sometimes assailed and perplexed him suddenly, often in the midst of the most enthusiastic fancies.

"A writer, a poet. It seems strange somehow. . . . When has a poet made his way in the world, risen to high rank? They're only scribbling fellows after all, not to be relied upon."

I noticed that such doubts and delicate questions presented themselves more frequently at dusk (how well I remember all these details and all that golden time!). Towards dusk my old friend always became nervous, susceptible and suspicious. Natasha and I knew that and were always prepared to laugh at it beforehand. I remember I tried to cheer him up by telling him tales of Sumarokov's being made a general, of Derzhavin's having been presented with a snuff-box full of gold pieces, of how the empress herself had visited Lomonossov; I told him about Pushkin, about Gogol.

"I know, my boy, I know all that," the old man replied, though perhaps it was the first time he had heard these stories. "Hm! Well, Vanya, anyway I'm glad your stuff isn't poetry. Poetry is nonsense, my boy; don't you argue, but believe an old man like me. I wish you nothing but good : it's simple nonsense, idle waste of time! It's for schoolboys to write poetry; poetry brings lots of you young fellows to the madhouse. . . . Granting Pushkin was a great man, who would deny it! Still, it's all jingling verse and nothing else. Something in the ephemeral way. . . . Though indeed I have read very little of it. . . . Prose is a different matter. A prose writer may be instructive—he can say something about patriotism for instance, or about virtue in general. . . . Yes! I don't know how to express myself, my boy, but you understand me; I speak from love

But there, there, read!" he concluded with a certain air of patronage, when at last I had brought the book and we were all sitting at the round table after tea, "read us what you've scribbled; they're making a great outcry about you! Let's hear it! Let's hear it!"

I opened the book and prepared to read. My novel had come from the printer's only that day, and having at last got hold of a copy, I rushed round to read it to them.

How vexed and grieved I was that I could not read it to them before from the manuscript which was in the printer's hands! Natasha positively cried with vexation, she quarrelled and reproached me with letting other people read it before she had. . . . But now at last we were sitting round the table. The old man assumed a particularly serious and critical expression. He wanted to judge it very, very strictly "to make sure for himself." Anna Andreyevna, too, looked particularly solemn; I almost believe she had put on a new cap for the reading. She had long noticed that I looked with boundless love at her precious Natasha; that I was breathless and my eyes were dim when I addressed her, and that Natasha, too, looked at me as it were more kindly than before. Yes! At last the time had come, had come at the moment of success, of golden hopes and perfect happiness, all, all had come at once. The old lady had noticed, too, that her husband had begun to praise me excessively, and seemed to look at his daughter and me in a peculiar way. . . . And all at once she took fright; after all I was not a count, nor a lord, nor a reigning prince, nor even a privy councillor, young and handsome with an order on his breast. Anna Andreyevna did not stop half-way in her wishes.

"The man's praised," she thought about me, "but there's no knowing what for. An author, a poet. . . . But what is an author after all?"

CHAPTER VI

I READ them my novel at one sitting. We began immediately after tea, and stayed up till two o'clock. The old man frowned at first. He was expecting something infinitely lofty, which might be beyond his comprehension, but must in any case be elevated. But, instead of that, he heard such commonplace, familiar things—precisely such as were always happening about him. And if only the hero had been a great or interesting man, or something historical like Roslavlev, or Yury Miloslavsky; instead of that he was described as a little, down-trodden, rather foolish clerk, with buttons missing from his uniform; and all this written in such simple language, exactly as we talk ourselves. . . . Strange! Anna Andreyevna looked inquiringly at Nikolay Sergeyitch, and seemed positively pouting a little as though she were resentful. "Is it really worth while to print and read such nonsense, and they pay money for it, too," was written on her face. Natasha was all attention, she listened greedily, never taking her eyes off me, watching my lips as I pronounced each word, moving her own pretty lips after me. And yet before I had read half of it, tears were falling from the eyes of all three of them. Anna Andreyevna was genuinely crying, feeling for the troubles of my hero with all her heart, and longing with great naïveté to help him in some way out of his troubles, as I gathered from her exclamations. The old man had already abandoned all hopes of anything elevated. "From the first step it's clear that you'll never be at the top of the tree; there it is, it's simply a little story; but it wrings your heart," he said, "and what's happening all round one grows easier to understand, and to remember, and one learns that the most down-trodden, humblest man is a man, too, and a brother."

Natasha listened, cried, and squeezed my hand tight by stealth under the table. The reading was over. She got up, her cheeks were flushed, tears stood in her eyes. All at once she snatched my hand, kissed it, and ran out of the room. The father and mother looked at one another.

"Hm! what an enthusiastic creature she is," said the old man, struck by his daughter's behaviour. "That's nothing though, nothing, it's a good thing, a generous impulse! She's a good girl. . . ." he muttered, looking askance at his wife as though to justify Natasha and at the same time wanting to defend me too.

But though Anna Andreyevna had been rather agitated and touched during the reading, she looked now as though she would say: "Of course Alexander of Macedon was a hero, but why break the furniture?" * etc.

Natasha soon came back, gay and happy, and coming over to

* A quotation from Gogol's "Inspector General." The story is of a history teacher so enthusiastic that he broke several chairs in the course of a lesson — *Translator's note.*

me gave me a sly pinch. The old man attempted to play the stern critic of my novel again, but in his joy he was carried away and could not keep up the part.

"Well, Vanya, my boy, it's good, it's good! You've comforted me, relieved my mind more than I expected. It's not elevated, it's not great, that's evident. . . . Over there there lies the 'Liberation of Moscow,' it was written in Moscow, you know. Well, you can see in that from the first line, my boy, that the author, so to speak, soars like an eagle. But, do you know, Vanya, yours is somehow simpler, easier to understand. That's why I like it, because it's easier to understand. It's more akin to us as it were; it's as though it had all happened to me myself. And what's the use of the high-flown stuff? I shouldn't have understood it myself. I should have improved the language. I'm praising it, but say what you will, it's not very refined. But there, it's too late now, it's printed, unless perhaps there's a second edition? But I say, my boy, maybe it will go into a second edition! Then there'll be money again! Hm!"

"And can you really have got so much money for it, Ivan Petrovitch?" observed Anna Andreyevna. "I look at you and somehow can't believe it. Mercy on us, what people will give money for nowadays!"

"You know, Vanya," said the old man, more and more carried away by enthusiasm, "it's a career, though it's not the service. Even the highest in the land will read it. Here you tell me Gogol receives a yearly allowance and was sent abroad. What if it were the same with you, eh? Or is it too soon? Must you write something more? Then write it, my boy, write it as quick as possible. Don't rest on your laurels. What hinders you?"

And he said this with such an air of conviction, with such good nature that I could not pluck up resolution to stop him and throw cold water on his fancies.

"Or they may be giving you a snuff-box directly, mayn't they? Why not? They want to encourage you. And who knows, maybe you'll be presented at court," he added in a half whisper, screwing up his left eye with a significant air—"or not? Is it too soon for the court?"

"The court, indeed!" said Anna Andreyevna with an offended air.

"In another minute you'll be making me a general," I answered, laughing heartily.

The old man laughed too. He was exceedingly pleased.

"Your excellency, won't you have something to eat?" cried Natasha playfully. She had meantime been getting supper for us.

She laughed, ran to her father and flung her warm arms round him.

"Dear, kind daddy!"

The old man was moved.

"Well, well, that's all right! I speak in the simplicity of my heart. General or no general, come to supper. Ah, you sentimental girl!" he added, patting his Natasha on her flushed cheek, as he was fond of doing on every convenient occasion. "I spoke because I love you, Vanya, you know. But even if not a general (far from it!) you're a distinguished man, an author."

"Nowadays, daddy, they call them writers."

"Not authors? I didn't know. Well, let it be writers then, but I tell you what I wanted to say; people are not made kammerherrs, of course, because they write novels; it's no use to dream of that; but anyway you can make your mark; become an attaché of some sort. They may send you abroad, to Italy, for the sake of your health, or somewhere to perfect yourself in your studies; you'll be helped with money. Of course it must all be honourable on your side; you must get money and honour by work, by real good work, and not through patronage of one sort or another."

"And don't you be too proud then, Ivan Petrovitch," added Anna Andreyevna, laughing.

"You'd better give him a star, at once, daddy; after all, what's the good of an attaché?"

And she pinched my arm again.

"This girl keeps making fun of me," said the old man, looking delightedly at Natasha, whose cheeks were glowing, and whose eyes were shining like stars. "I think I really may have overshot the mark, children; but I've always been like that. . . . But do you know, Vanya, I keep wondering at you: how perfectly simple you are. . . ."

"Why, good heavens, daddy, what else could he be?"

"Oh, no. I didn't mean that. Only, Vanya, you've a face that's not what one would call a poet's. They're pale, they say, you know, the poets, and with hair like this, you know, and a look in their eyes . . . like Goethe, you know, and the rest of them. I've read that in Abaddon . . . well? Have I put my foot in it again? Ah, the rogue, she's giggling at me! I'm not a scholar, my dears, but I can feel. Well, face or no face, that's no great matter, yours is all right for me, and I like it very much. . . . I didn't mean that. . . . Only be honest, Vanya, be honest. That's the great thing, live honestly, don't be conceited! The road lies open before you. Serve your work honestly, that's what I meant to say; yes, that's just what I wanted to say!"

It was a wonderful time. Every evening, every free hour I spent with them. I brought the old man news of the literary world and of writers, in whom he began, I don't know why, to take an intense interest. He even began to read the critical articles of B., about whom I talked a great deal. He praised him enthusiastically, though he scarcely understood him, and inveighed against his enemies who wrote in the *Northern Drone*.

Anna Andreyevna kept a sharp eye on me and Natasha, but she didn't see everything. One little word had been uttered between us already, and I heard at last Natasha, with her little head drooping, and her lips half parted, whisper "Yes." But the parents knew of it later on. They had their thoughts, their conjectures. Anna Andreyevna shook her head for a long time. It seemed strange and dreadful to her. She had no faith in me.

"Yes, it's all right of course, when it's successful, Ivan Petrovitch," she said, "but all of a sudden there'll be a failure or something of the sort; and what then? If only you had a post somewhere!"

"I've something I want to say to you, Vanya," said the old man, making up his mind. "I've seen for myself, I've noticed it and I confess I'm delighted that you and Natasha . . . you know what I mean. You see, Vanya, you're both very young, and my Anna Andreyevna is right. Let us wait a bit. Granted you have talent, remarkable talent perhaps. . . . not genius, as they cried out about you at first, but just simply talent (I read you that article in the *Drone* to-day; they handle you too roughly, but after all, it's not much of a paper). Yes! You see talent's not money in the bank, and you're both poor. Let's wait a little, for a year and a half, or a year anyway. If you get on all right, get a firm footing, Natasha shall be yours. If you don't get on—judge for yourself. You're an honest man, think things over . . . ."

And so we left it. And this is what happened within the year. Yes, it was almost exactly a year ago. One bright September day I went to see my old friends, feeling ill, and sick at heart, and sank on a chair almost fainting, so that they were actually frightened as they looked at me. My head went round and my heart ached so that ten times I had approached the door and ten times I had turned back before I went in, but it was not because I had failed in my career and had neither renown nor money; it was not because I was not yet an attaché and nowhere near being sent to Italy for my health It was because one may live through ten years in one year, and my Natasha had lived through ten years in that year. Infinity lay between us. And I remember I sat there before the old man, saying nothing, with unconscious fingers tearing the brim of my hat, which was torn already; I sat, and I don't know why, waited for Natasha to come in. My clothes were shabby and did not fit me; I had grown thin, yellow and sunken in the face. And yet I did not look in the least like a poet, and there was none of that grandeur in my eyes about which good Nikolay Sergeyitch had been so concerned in the past. Anna Andreyevna looked at me with unfeigned and ever ready compassion, thinking to herself:

"And he was within an ace of being betrothed to Natasha. Lord have mercy on us and preserve us!"

"Won't you have some tea, Ivan Petrovitch?" (the samovar was boiling on the table). "How are you getting on?" she asked me. "You're quite an invalid," she said in a plaintive voice which I can hear at this moment.

And I can see her as though it were to-day; even while she talked to me, her eyes betrayed another anxiety, the same anxiety which clouded the face of her old husband, too, as he sat now brooding, while his tea grew cold. I knew that they were terribly worried at this moment over their lawsuit with Prince Valkovsky, which was not promising well for them, and that they had had other new worries which had upset Nikolay Sergeyitch and made him ill.

The young prince, about whom the whole trouble that led to the lawsuit had arisen, had found an opportunity of visiting the Ichmenyevs five months before. The old man, who loved his dear Alyosha like a son, and spoke of him almost every day, welcomed him joyfully. Anna Andreyevna recalled Vassilyev-skoe and shed tears. Alyosha went to see them more and more frequently without his father's knowledge. Nikolay Sergeyitch with his honesty, openness and uprightness indignantly disdained all precautions. His honourable pride forbade his even considering what the prince would say if he knew that his son inwardly despised all his absurd suspicions, and was received again in the house of the Ichmenyevs? But the old man did not know whether he would have the strength to endure fresh insults. The young prince began to visit them almost daily. The parents enjoyed having him. He used to stay with them the whole evening, long after midnight. His father, of course, heard of all this at last. An abominable scandal followed. He insulted Nikolay Sergeyitch with a horrible letter, taking the same line as before, and peremptorily forbade his son to visit the house. This had happened just a fortnight before I came to them that day. The old man was terribly depressed. Was his Natasha, his innocent noble girl, to be mixed up in this dirty slander, this vileness again! Her name had been insultingly uttered before by the man who had injured him. And was all this to be left unavenged? For the first few days he took to his bed in despair. All that I knew. The story had reached me in every detail, though for the last three weeks I had been lying ill and despondent at my lodging and had not been to see them. But I knew besides. . . . No! At that time I only felt what was coming; I knew, but could not believe, that, apart from these worries, there was something which must trouble them beyond anything in the world, and I looked at them with torturing anguish. Yes, I was in torture; I was afraid to conjecture, afraid to believe, and did all I could to put off the fatal moment. And meanwhile I had come on account of it. I felt drawn to them that evening.

"Yes, Vanya," the old man began, suddenly rousing himself, "surely you've not been ill? Why haven't you been here for so long? I have behaved badly to you. I have been meaning ever so long to call on you, but somehow it's all been . . ."

And he sank into brooding again.

"I haven't been well," I answered.

"Hm! Not well," he repeated, five minutes later. "I dare say not! I talked to you and warned you before, but you wouldn't heed me. Hm! No, Vanya, my boy, the muse has lived hungry in a garret from time immemorial, and she'll go on so. That's what it is!"

Yes, the old man was out of spirits. If he had not had a sore heart himself, he would not have talked to me of the hungry muse. I looked intently at his face: it was sallower; there was a look of bewilderment in his eyes, some idea in the form of a question which he had not the strength to answer. He was abrupt and bitter, quite unlike himself. His wife looked at him uneasily and shook her head. When he turned away she stealthily nodded to me.

"How is Natalya Nikolaevna ? Is she at home ?" I inquired of the anxious lady.

"She's at home, my dear man, she's at home," she answered, as though perturbed by my question. "She'll come in to see you directly. It's a serious matter ! Not a sight of you for three weeks ! And she's become so queer . . . there's no making her out at all. I don't know whether she's well or ill, God bless her !" And she looked timidly at her husband.

"Why, there's nothing wrong with her," Nikolay Sergeyitch responded jerkily and reluctantly, "she's quite well. The girl's beginning to grow up, she's left off being a baby, that's all. Who can understand girlish moods and caprices ?"

"Caprices, indeed !" Anna Andreyevna caught him up in an offended voice.

The old man said nothing and drummed on the table with his finger-tips.

"Good God, is there something between them already ?" I wondered in a panic.

"Well, how are you getting on ?" he began again. "Is B. still writing reviews ?"

"Yes," I answered.

"Ech, Vanya, Vanya," he ended up, with a wave of his hand. "What can reviews do now ?"

The door opened and Natasha walked in.

CHAPTER VII

She held her hat in her hand and laid it down on the piano ; then she came up to me and held out her hand without speaking. Her lips faintly quivered, as though she wanted to utter something, some greeting to me, but she said nothing.

It was three weeks since we had seen each other. I looked at her with amazement and dread. How she had changed in those three weeks ! My heart ached as I looked at those pale, hollow cheeks, feverishly parched lips, and eyes that gleamed under the long dark lashes with a feverish fire and a sort of passionate determination.

But, my God, how lovely she was! Never before, or since, have I seen her as she was on that fatal day. Was it the same, the same Natasha, the same girl who only a year ago had listened to my novel with her eyes fixed on me and her lips following mine, who had so gaily and carelessly laughed and jested with her father and me at supper afterwards; was it the same Natasha who in that very room had said "Yes" to me, hanging her head and flushing all over?

We heard the deep note of the bell ringing for vespers. She started. Anna Andreyevna crossed herself.

"You're ready for church, Natasha, and they're ringing for the service. Go, Natasha, go and pray. It's a good thing it's so near. And you'll get a walk, too, at the same time. Why sit shut up indoors? See how pale you are, as though you were bewitched."

"Perhaps . . . I won't go . . . to-day," said Natasha slowly, in a low voice, almost a whisper. "I'm . . . not well," she added, and turned white as a sheet.

"You'd better go, Natasha. You wanted to just now and fetched your hat. Pray, Natasha, pray that God may give you good health," Anna Andreyevna persuaded her daughter, looking timidly at her, as though she were afraid of her.

"Yes, go, and it will be a walk for you, too," the old man added, and he, too, looked uneasily at his daughter. "Mother is right. Here, Vanya will escort you."

I fancied that Natasha's lips curled in a bitter smile. She went to the piano, picked up her hat and put it on. Her hands were trembling. All her movements seemed as it were unconscious, as though she did not know what she were doing. Her father and mother watched her attentively.

"Good-bye," she said, hardly audibly.

"My angel, why 'good-bye.' Is it so far away? A blow in the wind will do you good. See how pale you are. Ah, I forgot (I forget everything), I've finished a scapular for you; there's a prayer sewn into it, my angel; a nun from Kiev taught it to me last year; a very suitable prayer. I sewed it in just now. Put it on, Natasha. Maybe God will send you good health. You are all we have."

And the mother took out of her work-drawer a golden cross that Natasha wore round her neck; on the same ribbon was hung a scapular she had just finished.

"May it bring you health." she added, crossing her daughter

and putting the cross on. "At one time I used to bless you every night before you slept, and said a prayer, and you repeated it after me. But now you're not the same, and God does not vouchsafe you a quiet spirit. Ach, Natasha, Natasha! Your mother's prayer is no help to you. . . ."

And the mother began crying.

Natasha kissed her mother's hand without speaking, and took a step towards the door. But suddenly she turned quickly back and went up to her father. Her bosom heaved.

"Daddy, you cross . . . your daughter, too," she brought out in a gasping voice, and she sank on her knees before him.

We were all perplexed at this unexpected and too solemn action. For a few seconds her father looked at her quite at a loss.

"Natasha, my little one, my girl, my darling, what's the matter with you?" he cried at last, and tears streamed from his eyes. "Why are you grieving? Why are you crying day and night? I see it all, you know. I don't sleep at night, but stand and listen at your door. Tell me everything, Natasha, tell me all about it. I'm old, and we . . ."

He did not finish; he raised her and embraced her, and held her close. She pressed convulsively against his breast, and hid her head on his shoulder.

"It's nothing, nothing, it's only . . . I'm not well . . ." she kept repeating, choking with suppressed tears.

"May God bless you as I bless you, my darling child, my precious child!" said the father. "May He send you peace of heart for ever, and protect you from all sorrow. Pray to God, my love, that my sinful prayer may reach Him."

"And my blessing, my blessing, too, is upon you," added the mother, dissolving into tears.

"Good-bye," whispered Natasha.

At the door she stood still again, took one more look at them, tried to say something more, but could not and went quickly out of the room. I rushed after her with a foreboding of evil.

CHAPTER VIII

She walked with her head down, rapidly, in silence, without looking at me. But as she came out of the street on to the embankment she stopped short, and took my arm.

"I'm stifling," she whispered. "My heart grips me. . . . I'm stifling."

"Come back, Natasha," I cried in alarm.

"Surely you must have seen, Vanya, that I've gone away *for ever*, left them for ever, and shall never go back," she said, looking at me with inexpressible anguish.

My heart sank. I had foreseen all this on my way to them. I had seen it all as it were in a mist, long before that day perhaps, yet now her words fell upon me like a thunderbolt.

We walked miserably along the embankment. I could not speak. I was reflecting, trying to think, and utterly at a loss. My heart was in a whirl. It seemed so hideous, so impossible!

"You blame me, Vanya?" she said at last.

"No . . . but . . . but I can't believe it; it cannot be!" I answered, not knowing what I was saying.

"Yes, Vanya, it really is so! I have gone away from them and I don't know what will become of them . . . or what will become of me!"

"You're going to *him*, Natasha? Yes?"

"Yes," she answered.

"But that's impossible!" I cried frantically. "Don't you understand that it's impossible, Natasha, my poor girl! Why, it's madness. Why, you'll kill them, and ruin yourself! Do you understand that, Natasha?"

"I know; but what am I to do? I can't help it," she said; and her voice was as full of anguish as though she were facing the scaffold.

"Come back, come back, before it's too late," I besought her; and the more warmly, the more emphatically I implored her, the more I realized the uselessness of my entreaties, and the absurdity of them at that moment. "Do you understand, Natasha, what you are doing to your father? Have you thought of that? You know his father is your father's enemy. Why, the prince has insulted your father, has accused him of stealing money; why, he called him a thief. You know why they've gone to law with one another. . . . Good heavens! and that's not the worst. Do you know, Natasha (Oh, God, of course you know it all!) . . . do you know that the prince suspected your father and mother of having thrown you and Alyosha together on purpose, when Alyosha was staying in the country with you? Think a minute, only fancy what your father went through then owing to that slander; why, his hair has turned grey in these two years! Look at him! And what's more, you know all this, Natasha. Good heavens! To say nothing of what it will mean to them both to lose you for ever. Why, you're their treasure, all that is left them in their old age. I don't want to speak of that, you must know it for yourself. Remember that your father thinks you have been slandered without cause, insulted by these snobs, unavenged! And now, at this very time, it's all flared up again, all this old rankling enmity has grown more bitter than ever, because you have received Alyosha. The prince has insulted your father again. The old man's anger is still hot at this fresh affront, and suddenly now all this, all this, all these accusations will turn out to be true! Every one who knows about it will justify the prince now, and throw the blame on you and your father. Why, what will become of him now? It will kill him outright! Shame, disgrace, and through whom? Through you, his daughter, his one precious child! And your mother? Why, she won't outlive your old father, you know. Natasha, Natasha! What are you about? Turn back! Think what you are doing!"

She did not speak. At last she glanced at me, as it were, reproachfully. And there was such piercing anguish, such suffering in her eyes that I saw that apart from my words her wounded heart was bleeding already. I saw what her decision was costing her, and how I was torturing her, lacerating her with my useless words that came too late. I saw all that, and yet I could not restrain myself and went on speaking.

"Why, you said yourself just now to Anna Andreyevna that perhaps you would not go out of the house . . . to the service. So you meant to stay; so you were still hesitating?"

She only smiled bitterly in reply. And why did I ask that? I might have understood that all was irrevocably settled. But I was beside myself, too.

"Can you love him so much?" I cried, looking at her with a sinking at the heart, scarcely knowing what I was asking.

"What can I say to you, Vanya? You see, he told me to come, and here I am waiting for him," she said with the same bitter smile.

"But listen, only listen," I began again, catching at a straw; "this can all be arranged differently, quite differently; you need not go away from the house. I'll tell you how to manage, Natasha. I'll undertake to arrange it all for you, meetings, and everything. Only don't leave home. I will carry your letters; why not? It would be better than what you're doing. I know how to arrange it; I'll do anything for both of you. You'll see. And then you won't ruin yourself, Natasha, dear, as you're doing. . . . For you'll ruin yourself hopelessly, as it is, hopelessly. Only agree, Natasha, and everything will go well and happily, and you can love each other as much as you like. And when your fathers have left off quarrelling (for they're bound to leave off some day)—then . . ."

"Enough, Vanya, stop!" she interrupted, pressing my hand tightly, and smiling through her tears. "Dear, kind Vanya! You're a good, honourable man! And not one word of yourself! I've deserted you, and you forgive everything; you think of nothing but my happiness. You are ready to carry letters for us."

She burst into tears.

"I know how you loved me, Vanya, and how you love me still, and you've not reproached me with one bitter word all this time, while I, I . . . my God! how badly I've treated you! Do you remember, Vanya, do you remember our time together? It would have been better if I'd never met him; never seen him! I could have lived with you, with you, dear, kind Vanya, my dear one. No, I'm not worthy of you! You see what I am; at such a minute I remind you of our past happiness, though you're wretched enough without that! Here you've not been to see us for three weeks: I swear to you, Vanya, the thought never once entered my head that you hated me and had cursed me. I knew why you did not come! You did not want to be in our way, and to be a living reproach to us. And wouldn't it have been painful for you to see us? And how I've missed you, Vanya, how I've missed you! Vanya, listen, if I love Alyosha madly, insanely, yet perhaps I love you even more as a friend. I feel, I know that I couldn't go on living without you. I need you. I need your soul, your heart of gold. . . . Oh, Vanya, what a bitter, terrible time is before us!"

She burst into a flood of tears; yes, she was very wretched.

"Oh, how I have been longing to see you," she went on, mastering her tears. "How thin you've grown, how ill and pale you are. You really have been ill, haven't you, Vanya? And I haven't even asked! I keep talking of myself. How are you getting on with the reviewers now? what about your new novel? Is it going well?"

"As though we could talk about novels, as though we could

talk about me now, Natasha! As though my work mattered. That's all right, let it be! But tell me, Natasha, did he insist himself that you should go to him?"

"No, not only he, it was more I. He did say so, certainly, but I too. . . . You see, dear, I'll tell you everything; they're making a match for him with a very rich girl, of very high rank and related to very grand people. His father absolutely insists on his marrying her, and his father, as you know, is an awful schemer; he sets every spring working; and it's a chance that wouldn't come once in ten years. . . . Connexions, money . . . and they say she's very pretty, and she has education, a good heart, everything good; Alyosha's attracted by her already, and what's more his father's very anxious to get it over, so as to get married himself. And so he's determined to break it off between us. He's afraid of me and my influence on Alyosha. . . ."

"But do you mean to say that the prince knows of your love?" I interrupted in surprise. "Surely he only suspects it; and is not at all sure of it?"

"He knows it. He knows all about it."

"Why, who told him?"

"Alyosha told him everything a little while ago. He told me himself that he had told him all about it."

"Good God, what is going on! He tells all this himself and at such a time?"

"Don't blame him, Vanya," Natasha broke in; "don't jeer at him. He can't be judged like other people. Be fair. He's not like you and me. He's a child. He's not been properly brought up. He doesn't understand what he's doing. The first impression, the influence of the first person he meets can turn him away from what he has promised a minute before. He has no character. He'll vow to be true to you, and that very day he will just as truthfully, just as sincerely, devote himself to some one else; and what's more he'll be the first person to come and tell you about it. He may do something bad; but yet one can't blame him for it, but can only feel sorry for him. He's even capable of self-sacrifice, and if you knew what sacrifice! But only till the next new impression, then he'll forget it all So he'll forget me if I'm not continually with him. That's what he's like!"

"Ach, Natasha, but perhaps that's all not true, that's only gossip. How can a boy like that get married!"

"I tell you his father has special objects of his own."

"But how do you know that this young lady is so charming, and that he is already attracted by her?"

"Why, he told me so himself."

"What! Told you himself that he might love another woman, and demands this sacrifice from you now?"

"No, Vanya, no. You don't know him. You've not been much with him. You must know him better before you judge of him. There isn't a truer and purer heart than his in the world. Why, would it be better if he were to lie? And as for his being attracted by her, why, if he didn't see me for a week he'd fall in love with some one else and forget me, and then when he saw me he'd be at my feet again. No! It's a good thing I know it, that it's not concealed from me, or else I should be dying of suspicion. Yes, Vanya! I have come to the conclusion; *if I'm not always with him continually, every minute, he will cease to love me, forget me, and give me up.* He's like that; any other woman can attract him. And then what should I do? I should die . . . die indeed! I should be glad to die now. But what will it be for me to live without him? That would be worse than death itself, worse than any agony! Oh, Vanya, Vanya! It does mean something that I've abandoned my father and mother for him! Don't try and persuade me, everything's decided! He must be near me every hour, every minute. I can't go back. I know that I am ruined and that I'm ruining others. . . . Ach, Vanya!" she cried suddenly and began trembling all over; "what if he doesn't love me even now! What if it's true what you said of him just now" (I had never said it), "that he's only deceiving me, that he only seems to be so truthful and sincere, and is really wicked and vain! I'm defending him to you now, and perhaps this very minute he's laughing at me with another woman . . . and I, I'm so abject that I've thrown up everything and am walking about the streets looking for him. . . . Ach, Vanya!"

This moan broke with such anguish from her heart that my whole soul filled with grief. I realized that Natasha had lost all control of herself. Only a blind, insane, intense jealousy could have brought her to this frantic resolution. But jealousy flamed up in my heart, too, and suddenly burst out. I could not restrain myself. A horrid feeling drew me on.

"Natasha," I said, "there's only one thing I don't understand. How can you love him after what you've just said about him yourself ? You don't respect him, you don't even believe in his love, and you're going to him irrevocably and are ruining every one for his sake. What's the meaning of it ? He'll torture you so as to spoil your whole life ; yes, and you his, too. You love him too much, Natasha, too much ! I don't understand such love ! "

"Yes, I love him as though I were mad," she answered, turning pale as though in bodily pain. "I never loved you like that, Vanya. I know I've gone out of my mind, and don't love him as I ought to. I don't love him in the right way. . . . Listen, Vanya, I knew beforehand, and even in our happiest moments I felt that he would bring me nothing but misery. But what is to be done if even torture from him is happiness to me now ? Do you suppose I'm going to him to meet joy ? Do you suppose I don't know beforehand what's in store for me, or what I shall have to bear from him ? Why, he's sworn to love me, made all sorts of promises ; but I don't trust one of his promises. I don't set any value on them, and I never have, though I knew he wasn't lying to me, and can't lie. I told him myself, myself, that I don't want to bind him in any way. That's better with him ; no one likes to be tied. I less than any. And yet I'm glad to be his slave, his willing slave ; to put up with anything from him, anything, so long as he is with me, so long as I can look at him ! I think he might even love another woman if only I were there, if only I might be near. Isn't it abject, Vanya ? " she asked, suddenly looking at me with a sort of feverish, haggard look. For one instant it seemed to me she was delirious. "Isn't it abject, such a wish ? What if it is ? I say that it is abject, myself. Yet if he were to abandon me I should run after him to the ends of the earth, even if he were to repulse me, even if he were to drive me away. You try to persuade me to go back—but what use is that ? If I went back I should come away to-morrow. He would tell me to and I should come ; he would call, would whistle to me like a dog, and I should run to him. . . . Torture ! I don't shrink from any torture from him ! I should know it was at his hands I was suffering ! . . . Oh, there's no telling it, Vanya ! "

"And her father and mother ? " I thought. She seemed to have already forgotten them.

"Then he's not going to marry you, Natasha ? "

"He's promised to. He's promised everything. It's for that he's sent for me now, to be married to-morrow, secretly, out of town. But you see, he doesn't know what he's doing. Very likely he doesn't know how one gets married. And what a husband! It's absurd really. And if he does get married he won't be happy; he'll begin to reproach me. . . . I don't want him to reproach me with anything, ever. I'll give up everything for him, and let him do nothing for me! If he's going to be unhappy from being married, why make him unhappy?"

"Yes, this is a sort of frenzy, Natasha," said I. "Well, are you going straight to him now?"

"No, he promised to come here to fetch me. We agreed . . ."

And she looked eagerly into the distance, but as yet there was no one.

"And he's not here yet. And you've come *first!*" I cried with indignation.

Natasha staggered as though from a blow. Her face worked convulsively.

"He may not come at all," she said with bitter mockery. "The day before yesterday he wrote that if I didn't give him my word that I'd come, he would be obliged to put off his plan—of going away and marrying me; and his father will take him with him to the young lady. And he wrote it so simply, so naturally, as if it were nothing at all. . . . What if he really has gone to *her*, Vanya?"

I did not answer. She squeezed my hand tight, and her eyes glittered.

"He is with her," she brought out, scarcely audibly. "He hoped I would not come here, so that he might go to her, and say afterwards that he was in the right, that he told me beforehand I wouldn't, and I didn't. He's tired of me, so he stays away. Ach, my God! I'm mad! Why, he told me himself last time that I wearied him. . . . What am I waiting for?"

"Here he is," I cried, suddenly catching sight of him on the embankment in the distance.

Natasha started, uttered a shriek, gazed intently at Alyosha's approaching figure, and suddenly, dropping my hand, rushed to meet him. He, too, quickened his pace, and in a minute she was in his arms.

There was scarcely anyone in the street but ourselves. They kissed each other, laughed; Natasha laughed and cried both together, as though they were meeting after an endless separation. The colour rushed into her pale cheeks. She was like one possessed. . . . Alyosha noticed me and at once came up to me.

CHAPTER IX

I LOOKED at him eagerly, although I had seen him many times before that minute. I looked into his eyes, as though his expression might explain all that bewildered me, might explain how this boy could enthral her, could arouse in her love so frantic that it made her forget her very first duty and sacrifice all that had been till that moment most holy to her. The prince took both my hands and pressed them warmly, and the look in his eyes, gentle and candid, penetrated to my heart.

I felt that I might be mistaken in my conclusions about him if only from the fact that he was my enemy. Yes, I was not fond of him ; and I'm sorry to say I never could care for him— and was perhaps alone among his acquaintances in this. I could not get over my dislike of many things in him, even of his elegant appearance, perhaps, indeed, because it was too elegant Afterwards I recognized that I had been prejudiced in my judgment. He was tall, slender and graceful ; his face was rather long and always pale ; he had fair hair, large, soft, dreamy, blue eyes, in which there were occasional flashes of the most spontaneous, childish gaiety. The full crimson lips of his small, exquisitely modelled mouth almost always had a grave expression, and this gave a peculiarly unexpected and fascinating charm to the smile which suddenly appeared on them, and was so naïve and candid that, whatever mood one was in, one felt instantly tempted to respond to it with a similar smile. He dressed not over fashionably, but always elegantly ; it was evident that this elegance cost him no effort whatever, that it was innate in him.

It is true that he had some unpleasant traits, some of the bad habits characteristic of aristocratic society : frivolity, self-complacency, and polite insolence. But he was so candid and simple at heart that he was the first to blame himself for these defects, to regret them and mock at them. I fancy that this boy could never tell a lie even in jest, or if he did tell one it would be with no suspicion of its being wrong. Even egoism in him was rather attractive, just perhaps because it was open and not concealed. There was nothing reserved about him. He was weak, confiding, and faint-hearted; he had no will whatever. To deceive or injure him would have been as sinful and cruel as deceiving and injuring a child. He was too simple for his age and had scarcely any notion of real life; though, indeed, I believe he would not have any at forty. Men like him are destined never to grow up. I fancy that hardly any man could have disliked him; he was as affectionate as a child. Natasha had spoken truly; he might have been guilty of an evil action if driven to it by some strong influence, but if he had recognized the result of the action afterwards, I believe he would have died of regret. Natasha instinctively felt that she would have mastery and dominion over him, that he would even be her victim. She had had a foretaste of the joys of loving passionately and torturing the man that she loved simply because she loved him, and that was why; perhaps, she was in haste to be the first to sacrifice herself. But his eyes, too, were bright with love, and he looked at her rapturously. She looked at me triumphantly. At that instant she forgot everything—her parents, and her leave-taking and her suspicions. She was happy.

"Vanya!" she cried. "I've been unfair to him and I'm not worthy of him. I thought you weren't coming, Alyosha. Forget my evil thoughts, Vanya! I'll atone for it!" she added, looking at him with infinite love.

He smiled, kissed her hand, and still keeping his hold of her hand turned to me, and said:

"Don't blame me either. I've been wanting to embrace you as a brother for ever so long; she has told me so much about you! We've somehow not made friends or got on together till now. Let us be friends, and . . . forgive us," he added, flushing slightly and speaking in an undertone, but with such a charming smile that I could not help responding to his greeting with my whole heart.

"Yes, yes, Alyosha," Natasha chimed in, "he's on our side, he's a brother to us, he has forgiven us already, and without him we shall not be happy. I've told you already. . . . Ah, we're cruel children, Alyosha! But we will live all three together. . . . Vanya!" she went on, and her lips began to quiver. "You'll go back home now to them. You have such a true heart that though they won't forgive me, yet when they see that you've forgiven me it may soften them a little. Tell them everything, everything, in your own words, from your heart; find the right words. . . . Stand up for me, save me. Explain to them all the reasons as you understand it. You know, Vanya, I might not have brought myself to *it*, if you hadn't happened to be with me to-day! You are my salvation. I rested all my hopes on you at once, for I felt that you would know how to tell them, so that at least the first awfulness would be easier for them. Oh, my God, my God! . . . Tell them from me, Vanya, that I know I can never be forgiven now; if they forgive me, God won't forgive; but that if they curse me I shall always bless them and pray for them to the end of my life. My whole heart is with them! Oh, why can't we all be happy! Why, why! . . . My God, what have I done!" she cried out suddenly, as though realizing, and trembling all over with horror she hid her face in her hands.

Alyosha put his arm round her and held her close to him without speaking. Several minutes of silence followed.

"And you could demand such a sacrifice?" I cried, looking at him reproachfully.

"Don't blame me," he repeated. "I assure you that all this misery, terrible as it is, is only for the moment. I'm perfectly certain of it. We only need to have the courage to bear this moment; she said the very same to me herself. You know that what's at the bottom of it all is family pride, these quite foolish squabbles, some stupid lawsuits! . . . But (I've been thinking about it for a long while, I assure you) . . . all this must be put a stop to. We shall all come together again; and then we shall be perfectly happy, and the old people will be reconciled when they see us. Who knows, perhaps, our marriage will be the first step to their reconciliation. I think, in fact, it's bound to be so. What do you think?"

"You speak of your marriage. When is the wedding to be?" I asked, glancing at Natasha.

"To-morrow or the day after. The day after to-morrow at the latest—that's settled. I don't know much about it myself yet, you see; and in fact I've not made any arrangements. I thought that perhaps Natasha wouldn't come to-day. Besides, my father insisted on taking me to see my betrothed to-day. (You know they're making a match for me; has Natasha told you? But I won't consent.) So you see I couldn't make any definite arrangements. But anyway we shall be married the day after to-morrow. I think so, at least, for I don't see ho else it can be. To-morrow we'll set off on the road to Pskal

I've a school-friend, a very nice fellow, living in the country not far off, in that direction; you must meet him. There's a priest in the village there; though I don't know whether there is or not. I ought to have made inquiries, but I've not had time. . . . But all that's of no consequence, really. What matters is to keep the chief thing in view. One might get a priest from a neighbouring village, what do you think? I suppose there are neighbouring villages! It's only a pity that I haven't had time to write a line; I ought to have warned them we were coming. My friend may not be at home now perhaps. . . . But that's no matter. So long as there's determination everything will be settled of itself, won't it? And meanwhile, till to-morrow or the day after, she will be here with me. I have taken a flat on purpose, where we shall live when we come back. I can't go on living with my father, can I? You'll come and see us? I've made it so nice. My schoolfriends will come and see us. We'll have evenings . . ."

I looked at him in perplexity and distress. Natasha's eyes besought me to be kind and not to judge him harshly. She listened to his talk with a sort of mournful smile, and at the same time she seemed to be admiring him as one admires a charming, merry child, listening to its sweet but senseless prattle. I looked at her reproachfully. I was unbearably miserable.

"But your father?" I asked. "Are you so perfectly certain he'll forgive you?"

"He must," he replied. "What else is there left for him to do? Of course he may curse me at first; in fact, I'm sure he will. He's like that; and so strict with me. He may even take some proceedings against me; have recourse to his parental authority, in fact. . . . But that's not serious, you know. He loves me beyond anything. He'll be angry and then forgive us. Then every one will be reconciled, and we shall all be happy. Her father, too."

"And what if he doesn't forgive you? Have you thought of that?"

"He's sure to forgive us, though perhaps not at once. But what then? I'll show him that I have character. He's always scolding me for not having character, for being feather-headed. He shall see now whether I'm feather-headed. To be a married man is a serious thing I shan't be a boy then. . . . I mean I shall be just like other people . . . that is, other married men. the hall live by my own work. Natasha says that's ever so much better than living at other people's expense, as we all do. If you only knew what a lot of fine things she says to me ! I should never have thought of it myself—I've not been brought up like that, I haven't been properly educated. It's true, I know it myself, I'm feather-headed and scarcely fit for anything ; but, do you know, a wonderful idea occurred to me the day before yesterday. I'll tell you now though it's hardly the moment, for Natasha, too, must hear, and you'll give me your advice. You know I want to write stories and send them to the magazines just as you do. You'll help me with the editors, won't you ? I've been reckoning upon you, and I lay awake all last night thinking of a novel, just as an experiment, and do you know, it might turn out a charming thing. I took the subject from a comedy of Scribe's. . . . But I'll tell you it afterwards. The great thing is they would pay for it. . . . You see they pay you."

I could not help smiling.

"You laugh," he said, smiling in response. "But, I say," he added with incredible simplicity, "don't think I'm quite as bad as I seem. I'm really awfully observant, you'll see that. Why shouldn't I try ? It might come to something. . . . But I dare say you're right. Of course I know nothing of real life ; that's what Natasha tells me ; and indeed every one says so ; I should be a queer sort of writer. You may laugh, you may laugh ; you'll set me right ; you'll be doing it for her sake, and you love her. I tell you the truth. I'm not good enough for her ; I feel that ; it's a great grief to me, and I don't know why she's so fond of me. But I feel I'd give my life for her. I've really never been afraid of anything before, but at this moment I feel frightened. What is it we're doing ? Heavens, is it possible that when a man's absolutely set upon his duty that he shouldn't have the brains and the courage to do it ? You must help us, anyway ; you're our friend. You're the only friend left us. For what can I do alone ! Forgive me for reckoning on you like this. I think of you as such a noble man, and far superior to me. But I shall improve, believe me, and be worthy of you both."

At this point he pressed my hand again, and his fine eyes were full of warm and sincere feeling. He held out his hand to me so confidingly, had such faith in my being his friend.

"She will help me to improve," he went on. "But don't think anything very bad of me ; don't be too grieved about us. I have great hopes, in spite of everything, and on the financial side we've no need to trouble. If my novel doesn't succeed—to tell the truth I thought this morning that the novel is a silly idea, and I only talked about it to hear your opinion—I could, if the worst comes to the worst, give music-lessons. You didn't know I was good at music ? I'm not ashamed to live by work like that. I have quite the new ideas about that ; besides I've a lot of valuable knick-knacks, things for the toilet ; what do we want with them ? I'll sell them. And you know we can live for ever so long on that ! And if the worst comes to the worst, I can even take a post in some department. My father would really be glad. He's always at me to go into the service, but I always make out I'm not well. (But I believe my name is put down for something.) But when he sees that marriage has done me good, and made me steady, and that I have really gone into the service, he'll be delighted and forgive me. . . ."

"But, Alexey Petrovitch, have you thought what a terrible to-do there'll be now between your father and hers ? What will it be like in her home this evening, do you suppose ?"

And I motioned towards Natasha, who had turned deadly pale at my words. I was merciless.

"Yes, yes, you're right. It's awful !" he answered. "I've thought about it already and grieved over it. But what can we do ? You're right ; if only her parents will forgive us ! And how I love them—if you only knew ! They've been like a father and mother to me, and this is how I repay them ! Ach, these quarrels, these lawsuits ! You can't imagine how unpleasant all that is now. And what are they quarrelling about ! We all love one another so, and yet we're quarrelling. If only they'd be reconciled and make an end of it ! That's what I'd do in their place. . . . I feel frightened at what you say. Natasha, it's awful what we're doing, you and I ! I said that before. . . . You insisted on it yourself. . . . But, listen, Ivan Petrovitch, perhaps it will all be for the best, don't you think ? They'll be reconciled, you know, in the end. We shall reconcile them. That is so, there's no doubt of it. They can't hold out against out love. . . . Let them curse us ; we shall love them all the same, and they can't hold out. You don't know what a kind heart my father has sometimes. He only looks ferocious, but at other times he's most reasonable. If you only knew how gently he talked to me to-day, persuading me ! And I'm going against him to-day, and that makes me very sad. It's all these stupid prejudices ! It's simple madness ! Why, if he were to take a good look at her, and were to spend only half an hour with her, he would sanction everything at once."

Alyosha looked tenderly and passionately at Natasha.

"I've fancied a thousand times with delight," he went on babbling, "how he will love her as soon as he gets to know her, and how she'll astonish every one. Why, they've never seen a girl like her! My father is convinced that she is simply a schemer. It's my duty to vindicate her honour, and I shall do it. Ah, Natasha, every one loves you, every one. Nobody could help loving you," he added rapturously. "Though I'm not nearly good enough for you, still you must love me, Natasha, and I . . . you know me! And do we need much to make us happy! No, I believe, I do believe that this evening is bound to bring us all happiness, peace and harmony! Blessed be this evening! Isn't it so, Natasha? But what's the matter? But, my goodness, what's the matter?"

She was pale as death. All the while Alyosha rambled on she was looking intently at him, but her eyes grew dimmer and more fixed, and her face turned whiter and whiter. I fancied at last that she had sunk into a stupor, and did not hear him. Alyosha's exclamation seemed to rouse her. She came to herself, looked round her, and suddenly rushed to me. Quickly, as though in haste and anxious to hide it from Alyosha, she took a letter out of her pocket and gave it to me. It was a letter to her father and mother, and had been written overnight. As she gave it me she looked intently at me as though she could not take her eyes off me. There was a look of despair in them; I shall never forget that terrible look. I was overcome by horror, too. I saw that only now she realized all the awfulness of what she was doing. She struggled to say something, began to speak, and suddenly fell fainting. I was just in time to catch her. Alyosha turned pale with alarm; he rubbed her temples, kissed her hands and her lips. In two minutes she came to herself. The cab in which Alyosha had come was standing not far off; he called it. When she was in the cab Natasha clutched my hand frantically, and a hot tear scalded my fingers. The cab started. I stood a long while watching it. All my happiness was ruined from that moment, and my life was broken in half. I felt that poignantly. . . . I walked slowly back to my old friends. I did not know what to say to them, how I should go in to them. My thoughts were numb; my legs were giving way beneath me.

And that's the story of my happiness; so my love was over and ended. I will now take up my story where I left it.

CHAPTER X

FIVE days after Smith's death, I moved into his lodging. All that day I felt insufferably sad. The weather was cold and gloomy: the wet snow kept falling, interspersed with rain. Only towards evening the sun peeped out, and a stray sunbeam probably from curiosity glanced into my room. I had begun to regret having moved here. Though the room was large it was so low-pitched, so begrimed with soot, so musty, and so unpleasantly empty in spite of some little furniture. I thought then that I should certainly ruin what health I had left in that room. And so it came to pass, indeed.

All that morning I had been busy with my papers, sorting and arranging them. For want of a portfolio I had packed them in a pillow-case. They were all crumpled and mixed up. Then I sat down to write. I was still working at my long novel then; but I could not settle down to it. My mind was full of other things.

I threw down my pen and sat by the window. It got dark, and I felt more and more depressed. Painful thoughts of all kinds beset me. I kept fancying that I should die at last in Petersburg. Spring was at hand. "I believe I might recover," I thought, "if I could get out of this shell into the light of day, into the fields and woods." It was so long since I had seen them. I remember, too, it came into my mind how nice it would be if by some magic, some enchantment, I could forget everything that had happened in the last few years; forget everything, refresh my mind, and begin again with new energy. In those days I still dreamed of that and hoped for a renewal of life. "Better go into an asylum," I thought, "to get one's brain turned upside down and rearranged anew, and then be cured again." I still had a thirst for life and a faith in it! . . . But I remember even then I laughed. "What should I have to do after the madhouse? Write novels again? . . ."

So I brooded despondently, and meanwhile time was passing. Night had come on. That evening I had promised to see Natasha I had had a letter from her the evening before, earnestly begging me to go and see her. I jumped up and began getting ready. I had an overwhelming desire to get out of my room, even into the rain and the sleet.

As it got darker my room seemed to grow larger and larger, as though the walls were retreating. I began to fancy that every night I should see Smith at once in every corner. He would sit and stare at me as he had at Adam Ivanitch, in the restaurant, and Azorka would lie at his feet. At that instant I had an adventure which made a great impression upon me.

I must frankly admit, however, that, either owing to the derangement of my nerves, or my new impressions in my new lodgings, or my recent melancholy, I gradually began at dusk to sink into that condition which is so common with me now at night in my illness, and which I call *mysterious horror*. It is a most oppressive, agonizing state of terror of something which I don't know how to define, and something passing all understanding, and outside the natural order of things, which yet may take shape this very minute, as though in mockery of all the conclusions of reason, come to me and stand before me as an undeniable fact, hideous, horrible, and relentless. This fear usually becomes more and more acute, in spite of all the protests of reason, so much so that although the mind sometimes is of exceptional clarity at such moments, it loses all power of resistance. It is unheeded, it becomes useless, and this inward division intensifies the agony of suspense. It seems to me something like the anguish of people who are afraid of the dead. But in my distress the indefiniteness of the apprehension makes my suffering even more acute.

I remember I was standing with my back to the door and taking my hat from the table, when suddenly at that very instant the thought struck me that when I turned round I should inevitably see Smith : at first he would softly open the door, would stand in the doorway and look round the room, then looking down would come slowly towards me, would stand facing me, fix his lustreless eyes upon me and suddenly laugh in my face, a long, toothless, noiseless chuckle, and his whole body would shake with laughter and go on shaking a long time. The vision of all this suddenly formed an extraordinarily vivid and distinct picture in my mind, and at the same time I was suddenly seized by the fullest, the most absolute conviction that all this would infallibly, inevitably come to pass ; that it was already happening, only I hadn't seen it because I was standing with my back to the door, and that just at that very instant perhaps the door was opening. I looked round quickly, and—the door actually was opening, softly, noiselessly, just as I had imagined it a minute before. I cried out. For a long time no one appeared, as though the door had opened of itself. All at once I saw in the doorway a strange figure, whose eyes, as far as I could make out in the dark, were scrutinizing me obstinately and intently. A shiver ran over all my limbs; to my intense horror I saw that it was a child, a little girl, and if it had been Smith himself he would not have frightened me perhaps so much as this strange and unexpected apparition of an unknown child in my room at such an hour, and at such a moment.

I have mentioned already that the door opened as slowly and noiselessly as though she were afraid to come in. Standing in the doorway she gazed at me in a perplexity that was almost stupefaction. At last softly and slowly she advanced two steps into the room and stood before me, still without uttering a word. I examined her more closely. She was a girl of twelve or thirteen, short, thin, and as pale as though she had just had some terrible illness, and this pallor showed up vividly her great, shining black eyes. With her left hand she held a tattered old shawl, and with it covered her chest, which was still shivering with the chill of evening. Her whole dress might be described as rags and tatters. Her thick black hair was matted and uncombed. We stood so for two minutes, staring at one another.

"Where's grandfather?" she asked at last in a husky, hardly audible voice, as though there was something wrong with her throat or chest.

All my mysterious panic was dispersed at this question It was an inquiry for Smith; traces of him had unexpectedly turned up.

"Your grandfather? But he's dead!" I said suddenly, being taken unawares by her question, and I immediately regretted my abruptness. For a minute she stood still in the same position, then she suddenly began trembling all over, so violently that it seemed as though she were going to be overcome by some sort of dangerous, nervous fit. I tried to support her so that she did not fall. In a few minutes she was better, and I saw that she was making an unnatural effort to control her emotion before me.

"Forgive me, forgive me, girl! Forgive me, my child!" I said. "I told you so abruptly, and who knows perhaps it's a mistake ... poor little thing! ... Who is it you're looking for? The old man who lived here?"

"Yes," she articulated with an effort, looking anxiously at me.

"His name was Smith? Was it?" I asked.

"Y-yes!"

"Then he ... yes, then he is dead. ... Only don't grieve, my dear. Why haven't you been here? Where have you come from now? He was buried yesterday; he died suddenly. ... So you're his granddaughter?"

The child made no answer to my rapid and incoherent questions. She turned in silence and went quietly out of the room. I was so astonished that I did not try to stop her or question her further. She stopped short in the doorway, and half-turning asked me:

"Is Azorka dead, too?"

"Yes, Azorka's dead, too," I answered, and her question struck me as strange, it seemed as though she felt sure that Azorka must have died with the old man.

Hearing my answer the girl went noiselessly out of the room and carefully closed the door after her.

A minute later I ran after her, horribly vexed with myself for having let her go. She went out so quickly that I did not hear her open the outer door on to the stairs.

"She hasn't gone down the stairs yet," I thought, and I stood still to listen. But all was still, and there was no sound of footsteps. All I heard was the slam of a door on the ground floor, and then all was still again.

I went hurriedly downstairs. The staircase went from my flat in a spiral from the fifth storey down to the fourth, from the fourth it went straight. It was a black, dirty staircase, always dark, such as one commonly finds in huge blocks let out in tiny flats. At that moment it was quite dark. Feeling my way down to the fourth storey I stood still, and I suddenly had a feeling that there was some one in the passage here, hiding from me. I began groping with my hands. The girl was there, right in the corner, and with her face turned to the wall was crying softly and inaudibly.

"Listen, what are you afraid of?" I began. "I frightened you so, I'm so sorry. Your grandfather spoke of you when he was dying; his last words were of you. ... I've got some books, no doubt they're yours. What's your name? Where do you live? He spoke of Sixth Street ..."

THE INSULTED AND INJURED

But I did not finish. She uttered a cry of terror as though at my knowing where she lived; pushed me away with her thin, bony, little hand, and ran downstairs. I followed her; I could still hear her footsteps below. Suddenly they ceased. . . . When I ran out into the street she was not to be seen. Running as far as Voznesensky Prospect I realized that all my efforts were in vain. She had vanished. "Most likely she hid from me somewhere," I thought, "on her way downstairs."

CHAPTER XI

But I had hardly stepped out on the muddy wet pavement of the Prospect when I ran against a passer-by, who was hastening somewhere with his head down, apparently lost in thought. To my intense amazement I recognized my old friend Ichmenyev. It was an evening of unexpected meetings for me. I knew that the old man had been taken seriously unwell three days before; and here I was meeting him in such wet weather in the street. Moreover it had never been his habit to go out in the evening, and since Natasha had gone away, that is, for the last six months, he had become a regular stay-at-home. He seemed to be exceptionally delighted to see me, like a man who has at last found a friend with whom he can talk over his ideas. He seized my hand, pressed it warmly, and without asking where I was going, drew me along with him. He was upset about something, jerky and hurried in his manner. "Where had he been going?" I wondered. It would have been tactless to question him. He had become terribly suspicious, and sometimes detected some offensive hint, some insult in the simplest inquiry or remark.

I looked at him stealthily. His face showed signs of illness; he had grown much thinner of late. His chin showed a week's growth of beard. His hair, which had turned quite grey, hung down in disorder under his crushed hat, and lay in long straggling tails on the collar of his shabby old great-coat. I had noticed before that at some moments he seemed, as it were, forgetful, forgot for instance that he was not alone in the room, and would talk to himself, gesticulating with his hands. It was painful to look at him.

"Well, Vanya, well?" he began. "Where were you going?

I've come out, my boy, you see; business. Are you quite well?"

"Are you quite well?" I answered. "You were ill only the other day, and here you are, out."

The old man seemed not to hear what I said and made no answer.

"How is Anna Andreyevna?"

"She's quite well, quite well. . . . Though she's rather poorly, too. She's rather depressed . . . she was speaking of you, wondering why you hadn't been. Were you coming to see us now, Vanya, or not? Maybe I'm keeping you, hindering you from something," he asked suddenly, looking at me distrustfully and suspiciously.

The sensitive old man had become so touchy and irritable that if I had answered him now that I wasn't going to see them, he would certainly have been wounded, and have parted from me coldly. I hastened to say that I was on my way to look in on Anna Andreyevna, though I knew I was already late, and might not have time to see Natasha at all.

"That's all right," said the old man, completely pacified by my answer, "that's all right."

And he suddenly sank into silence and pondered, as though he had left something unsaid.

"Yes, that's all right," he repeated mechanically, five minutes later, as though coming to himself after a long reverie. "Hm! You know, Vanya, you've always been like a son to us. God has not blessed us . . . with a son, but He has sent us you. That's what I've always thought. And my wife the same . . . yes! And you've always been tender and respectful to us, like a grateful son. God will bless you for it, Vanya, as we two old people bless and love you. . . . Yes!"

His voice quavered. He paused a moment.

"Well . . . well? You haven't been ill, have you? Why have you not been to see us for so long?"

I told him the whole incident of Smith, apologizing for having let Smith's affairs keep me, telling him that I had besides been almost ill, and that with all this on my hands it was a long way to go to Vassilyevsky Island (they lived there then). I was almost blurting out that I had nevertheless made time to see Natasha, but stopped myself in time.

My account of Smith interested my old friend very much. He listened more attentively. Hearing that my new lodging was damp, perhaps even worse than my old one, and that the rent was six roubles a month, he grew positively heated. He had become altogether excitable and impatient. No one but Anna Andreyevna could soothe him at such moments, and even she was not always successful.

"Hm! This is what comes of your literature, Vanya! It's brought you to a garret, and it will bring you to the graveyard! I said so at the time. I foretold it! . . . Is B. still writing reviews?"

"No, he died of consumption. I told you so before, I believe."

"Dead, hm, dead! Yes, that's just what one would expect. Has he left anything to his wife and children? You told me he had a wife, didn't you? . . . What do such people marry for?"

"No, he's left nothing," I answered.

"Well, just as I thought!" he cried, with as much warmth as though the matter closely and intimately concerned him, as though the deceased B. had been his brother. "Nothing! Nothing, you may be sure. And, do you know, Vanya, I had a presentiment he'd end like that, at the time when you used to be always singing his praises, do you remember. It's easy to say left nothing! Hm! . . . He's won fame. Even supposing it's lasting fame, it doesn't mean bread and butter. I always had a foreboding about you, too, Vanya, my boy. Though I praised you, I always had misgivings. So B.'s dead? Yes, and he well might be! It's a nice way we live here, and . . . a nice place! Look at it!"

And with a rapid, unconscious movement of his hand he pointed to the foggy vista of the street, lighted up by the street-lamps dimly twinkling in the damp mist, to the dirty houses, to the wet and shining flags of the pavement, to the cross, sullen, drenched figures that passed by, to all this picture, hemmed in by the dome of the Petersburg sky, black as though smudged with Indian ink. We had by now come out into the square; before us in the darkness stood the monument, lighted up below by jets of gas, and further away rose the huge dark mass of St. Isaac's, hardly distinguishable against the gloomy sky.

"You used to say, Vanya, that he was a nice man, good and generous, with feeling, with a heart. Well, you see, they're all like that, your nice people, your men with heart! All they can do is to beget orphans! Hm! . . . and I should think he must have felt cheerful at dying like that! E-e-ech! Anything to get away from here! Even Siberia. . . . What is it, child?"

he asked suddenly, seeing a little girl on the pavement begging alms.

It was a pale, thin child, not more than seven or eight, dressed in filthy rags; she had broken shoes on her little bare feet. She was trying to cover her shivering little body with a sort of aged semblance of a tiny dress, long outgrown. Her pale, sickly, wasted face was turned towards us. She looked timidly, mutely at us without speaking, and with a look of resigned dread of refusal, held out her trembling little hand to us. My old friend started at seeing her, and turned to her so quickly that he frightened her. She was startled and stepped back.

"What is it? What is it, child?" he cried. "You're begging, eh? Here, here's something for you . . . take it!"

And, shaking with fuss and excitement, he began feeling in his pocket, and brought out two or three silver coins. But it seemed to him too little. He found his purse, and taking out a rouble note—all that was in it—put it in the little beggar's hand.

"Christ keep you, my little one . . . my child! God's angel be with you!"

And with a trembling hand he made the sign of the cross over the child several times. But suddenly noticing that I was looking at him, he frowned, and walked on with rapid steps.

"That's a thing I can't bear to see, Vanya," he began, after a rather prolonged, wrathful silence. "Little innocent creatures shivering with cold in the street . . . all through their cursed fathers and mothers. Though what mother would send a child to anything so awful if she were not in misery herself! . . . Most likely she has other helpless little ones in the corner at home, and this is the eldest of them; and the mother ill herself very likely; and . . . hm! They're not prince's children! There are lots in the world, Vanya . . . not prince's children! Hm!"

He paused for a moment, as though at a loss for words.

"You see, Vanya, I promised Anna Andreyevna," he began, faltering and hesitating a little, "I promised her . . . that is Anna Andreyevna and I agreed together to take some little orphan to bring up . . . some poor little girl, to have her in the house altogether, do you understand? For it's dull for us old people alone. Only, you see, Anna Andreyevna has begun to set herself against it somehow. So you talk to her, you know, not from me, but as though it came from yourself . . . persuade her, do you understand? I've been meaning for a long time to ask you to persuade her to agree; you see, it's rather awkward for me to press her. But why talk about trifles! What's a child to me? I don't want one; perhaps just as a comfort . . . so as to hear a child's voice . . . but the fact is I'm doing this for my wife's sake—it'll be livelier for her than being alone with me. But all that's nonsense. Vanya, we shall be a long time getting there like this, you know; let's take a cab. It's a long walk, and Anna Andreyevna will have been expecting us."

It was half-past seven when we arrived.

CHAPTER XII

THE Ichmenyevs were very fond of each other. They were closely united by love and years of habit. Yet Nikolay Sergeyitch was not only now, but had, even in former days, in their happiest times, always been rather reserved with his Anna Andreyevna, sometimes even surly, especially before other people. Some delicate and sensitive natures show a peculiar perversity, a sort of chaste dislike of expressing themselves, and expressing their tenderness even to the being dearest to them, not only before people but also in private—even more in private in fact; only at rare intervals their affection breaks out, and it breaks out more passionately and more impulsively the longer it has been restrained. This was rather how Ichmenyev had been with his Anna Andreyevna from their youth upwards. He loved and respected her beyond measure in spite of the fact that she was only a good-natured woman who was capable of nothing but loving him, and that he was sometimes positively vexed with her because in her simplicity she was often tactlessly open with him. But after Natasha had gone away they somehow became tenderer to one another; they were painfully conscious of being left all alone in the world. And though Nikolay Sergeyitch was sometimes extremely gloomy, they could not be apart for two hours at a time without distress and uneasiness. They had made a sort of tacit compact not to say a word about Natasha, as though she had passed out of existence. Anna Andreyevna did not dare to make any allusion to her in her husband's presence, though this restraint was very hard for her. She had long ago in her heart forgiven Natasha. It had somehow become an established custom that every time I came I should bring her news of her beloved and never-forgotten child.

The mother was quite ill if she did not get news for some time, and when I came with tidings she was interested in the smallest details, and inquired with trembling curiosity. My accounts relieved her heart; she almost died of fright once when Natasha had fallen ill and was on the point of going to her herself. But this was an extreme case. At first she was not able to bring herself to express even to me a desire to see her daughter; and almost always after our talk, when she had extracted everything from me, she thought it needful to draw herself up before me and to declare that though she was interested in her daughter's fate, yet Natasha had behaved so wickedly that she could never be forgiven. But all this was put on. There were times when Anna Andreyevna grieved hopelessly, shed tears, called Natasha by the fondest names before me, bitterly complained against Nikolay Sergeyitch, and began in his presence to drop hints, though with great circumspection, about some people's pride, about hard-heartedness, about our not being able to forgive injuries, and God's not forgiving the unforgiving; but she never went further than this in his presence. At such times her husband immediately got cross and sullen and would sit silent and scowling, or begin suddenly talking of something else very loudly and awkwardly, or finally go off to his own room, leaving us alone, and so giving Anna Andreyevna a chance to pour out her sorrows to me in tears and lamentations. He always went off to his own room like this when I arrived, sometimes scarcely leaving time to greet me, so as to give me a chance to tell Anna Andreyevna all the latest news of Natasha. He did the same thing now.

"I'm wet through," he said, as soon as he walked into the room. "I'll go to my room. And you, Vanya, stay here. Such a business he's been having with his lodgings. You tell her, I'll be back directly."

And he hurried away, trying not even to look at us, as though ashamed of having brought us together. On such occasions, and especially when he came back, he was always very curt and gloomy, both with me and Anna Andreyevna, even fault-finding, as though vexed and angry with himself for his own softness and consideration.

"You see how he is," said Anna Andreyevna, who had of late laid aside all her stiffness with me, and all her mistrust of me; "that's how he always is with me; and yet he knows we understand all his tricks. Why should he keep up a pretence with me?

Am I a stranger to him ? He's just the same about his daughter. He might forgive her, you know, perhaps he even wants to forgive her. God knows! He cries at night, I've heard him. But he keeps up outwardly. He's eaten up with pride. Ivan Petrovitch, my dear, tell me quick, where was he going ? "

"Nikolay Sergeyitch ? I don't know. I was going to ask you."

"I was dismayed when he went out. He's ill, you know, and in such weather, and so late ! I thought it must be for something important ; and what can be more important than what you know of. I thought this to myself, but I didn't dare to ask. Why, I daren't question him about anything nowadays. My goodness ! I was simply terror-stricken on his account and on hers. What, thought I, if he has gone to her? What if he's made up his mind to forgive her ? Why, he's found out everything, he knows the latest news of her ; I feel certain he knows it ; but how the news gets to him I can't imagine. He was terribly depressed yesterday, and to-day too. But why don't you say something ? Tell me, my dear, what has happened ? I've been longing for you like an angel of God. I've been all eyes watching for you. Come, will the villain abandon Natasha ?"

I told Anna Andreyevna at once all I knew. I was always completely open with her. I told her that things seemed drifting to a rupture between Natasha and Alyosha, and that this was more serious than their previous misunderstandings; that Natasha had sent me a note the day before, begging me to come this evening at nine o'clock, and so I had not intended to come and see them that evening. Nikolay Sergeyitch himself had brought me. I explained and told her minutely that the position was now altogether critical, that Alyosha's father, who had been back for a fortnight after an absence, would hear nothing and was taking Alyosha sternly in hand; but, what was most important of all, Alyosha seemed himself not disinclined to the proposed match, and it was said he was positively in love with the young lady. I added that I could not help guessing that Natasha's note was written in great agitation. She wrote that to-night everything would be decided, but what was to be decided I did not know. It was also strange that she had written yesterday but had only asked me to come this evening, and had fixed the hour—nine o'clock. And so I was bound to go, and as quickly as possible.

"Go, my dear boy, go by all means!" Anna Andreyevna urged me anxiously. "Have just a cup of tea as soon as he comes back. . . . Ach, they haven't brought the samovar! Matryona! Why are you so long with the samovar? She's a saucy baggage! . . . Then when you've drunk your tea, find some good excuse and get away. But be sure to come to-morrow and tell me everything. And run round early! Good heavens! Something dreadful may have happened already! Though how could things be worse than they are, when you come to think of it! Why, Nikolay Sergeyitch knows everything, my heart tells me he does. I hear a great deal through Matryona, and she through Agasha, and Agasha is the god-daughter of Marya Vassilyevna, who lives in the prince's house . . . but there, you know all that. My Nikolay was terribly angry to-day. I tried to say one thing and another and he almost shouted at me. And then he seemed sorry, said he was short of money. Just as though he'd been making an outcry about money. You know our circumstances. After dinner he went to have a nap. I peeped at him through the chink (there's a chink in the door he doesn't know of). And he, poor dear, was on his knees, praying before the shrine. I felt my legs give way under me when I saw it. He didn't sleep, and he had no tea, he took up his hat and went out. He went out at five o'clock. I didn't dare question him: he'd have shouted at me. He's taken to shouting—generally at Matryona, but sometimes at me. And when he starts it makes my legs go numb, and there's a sinking at my heart. Of course it's foolishness, I know it's his foolishness, but still it frightens me. I prayed for a whole hour after he went out that God would send him some good thought. Where is her note, show it me!"

I showed it. I knew that Anna Andreyevna cherished a secret dream that Alyosha, whom she called at one time a villain and at another a stupid heartless boy, would in the end marry Natasha, and that the prince, his father, would consent to it. She even let this out to me, though at other times she regretted it, and went back on her words. But nothing would have made her venture to betray her hopes before Nikolay Sergeyitch, though she knew her husband suspected them, and even indirectly reproached her for them more than once. I believe that he would have cursed Natasha and shut her out of his heart for ever if he had known of the possibility of such a marriage.

We all thought so at the time. He longed for his daughter with every fibre of his being, but he longed for her alone with every memory of Alyosha cast out of her heart. It was the one condition of forgiveness, and though it was not uttered in words it could be understood, and could not be doubted when one looked at him.

"He's a silly boy with no backbone, no backbone, and he's cruel, I always said so," Anna Andreyevna began again. "And they didn't know how to bring him up, so he's turned out a regular weather-cock; he's abandoning her after all her love. What will become of her, poor child? And what can he have found in this new girl, I should like to know."

"I have heard, Anna Andreyevna," I replied, "that his proposed fiancée is a delightful girl. Yes, and Natalya Nikolaevna says the same thing about her."

"Don't you believe it!" the mother interrupted. "Delightful, indeed! You scribblers think every one's delightful if only she wears petticoats. As for Natasha's speaking well of her, she does that in the generosity of her heart. She doesn't know how to control him; she forgives him everything, but she suffers herself. How often he has deceived her already. The cruel-hearted villains! I'm simply terrified, Ivan Petrovitch! They're all demented with pride. If my good man would only humble himself, if he would forgive my poor darling and fetch her home! If only I could hug her, if I could look at her! Has she got thinner?"

"She has got thin, Anna Andreyevna."

"My darling! I'm in terrible trouble, Ivan Petrovitch! All last night and all to-day I've been crying . . . but there! . . . I'll tell you about it afterwards. How many times I began hinting to him to forgive her; I daren't say it right out, so I begin to hint at it, in a tactful way. And my heart's in a flutter all the time: I keep expecting him to get angry and curse her once for all. I haven't heard a curse from him yet . . . well, that's what I'm afraid of, that he'll put his curse upon her. And what will happen then? God's punishment falls on the child the father has cursed. So I'm trembling with terror every day. And you ought to be ashamed, too, Ivan Petrovitch, to think you've grown up in our family, and been treated like a son by both of us, and yet you can speak of her being delightful, too. But their Marya Vassilyevna knows better. I may have done wrong, but I asked her in to coffee one day when my good man had gone out for the whole morning. She told me all the ins and outs of it. The prince, Alyosha's father, is in shocking relations with this countess. They say the countess keeps reproaching him with not marrying her, but he keeps putting it off. This fine countess was talked about for her shameless behaviour while her husband was living. When her husband died she went abroad: she used to have all sorts of Italians and Frenchmen about her, and barons of some sort—it was there she caught Prince Pyotr Alexandrovitch. And meantime her stepdaughter, the child of her first husband, the spirit contractor, has been growing up. This countess, the stepmother, has spent all she had, but the stepdaughter has been growing up, and the two millions her father had left invested for her have been growing too. Now, they say, she has three millions. The prince has got wind of it, so he's keen on the match for Alyosha. (He's a sharp fellow! He won't let a chance slip!) The count, their relative, who's a great gentleman at court, you remember, has given his approval too: a fortune of three millions is worth considering. 'Excellent,' he said, 'talk it over with the countess.' So the prince told the countess of his wishes. She opposed it tooth and nail. She's an unprincipled woman, a regular termagant, they say! They say some people won't receive her here; it's very different from abroad. 'No,' she says, 'you marry me, prince, instead of my stepdaughter's marrying Alyosha.' And the girl, they say, gives way to her stepmother in everything; she almost worships her and always obeys her. She's a gentle creature, they say, a perfect angel! The prince sees how it is and tells the countess not to worry herself. 'You've spent all your money,' says he, 'and your debts you can never pay. But as soon as your stepdaughter marries Alyosha there'll be a pair of them; your innocent and my little fool. We'll take them under our wing and be their guardians together. Then you'll have plenty of money. What's the good of you're marrying me?' He's a sharp fellow, a regular mason! Six months ago the countess wouldn't make up her mind to it, but since then they say they've been staying at Warsaw, and there they've come to an agreement. That's what I've heard. All this Marya Vassilyevna told me from beginning to end. She heard it all on good authority. So you see it's all a question of money and millions, and not her being delightful!"

Anna Andreyevna's story impressed me. It fitted in exactly with all I had heard myself from Alyosha. When he talked of it he had stoutly declared that he would never marry for money. But he had been struck and attracted by Katerina Fyodorovna. I had heard from Alyosha, too, that his father was contemplating marriage, though he denied all rumour of it to avoid irritating the countess prematurely. I have mentioned already that Alyosha was very fond of his father, admired him and praised him ; and believed in him as though he were an oracle.

"She's not of a count's family, you know, the girl you call delightful!" Anna Andreyevna went on, deeply resenting my praise of the young prince's future fiancée. "Why, Natasha would be a better match for him. She's a spirit-dealer's daughter, while Natasha is a well-born girl of a good old family. Yesterday (I forgot to tell you) my old man opened his box—you know, the wrought-iron one ; he sat opposite me the whole evening, sorting out our old family papers. And he sat so solemnly over it. I was knitting a stocking, and I didn't look at him ; I was afraid to. When he saw I didn't say a word he got cross, and called me himself, and he spent the whole evening telling me about our pedigree. And do you know, it seems that the Ichmenyevs were noblemen in the days of Ivan the Terrible, and that my family, the Shumilovs, were well-known even in the days of Tsar Alexey Mihalovitch ; we've the documents to prove it, and it's mentioned in Karamzin's history too, so you see, my dear boy, we're as good as other people on that side. As soon as my old man began talking to me I saw what was in his mind It was clear he felt bitterly Natasha's being slighted. It's only through their wealth they're set above us. That robber, Pyotr Alexandrovitch, may well make a fuss about money ; every one knows he's a cold-hearted, greedy soul. They say he joined the Jesuits in secret when he was in Warsaw. Is it true ?"

"It's a stupid rumour," I answered, though I could not help being struck by the persistence of this rumour.

But what she had told me of her husband's going over his family records was interesting. He had never boasted of his pedigree before.

"It's all the cruel-hearted villains!" Anna Andreyevna went on. "Well, tell me about my darling. Is she grieving and crying? Ach, it's time you went to her! (Matryona! She's a saucy baggage.) Have they insulted her? Tell me, Vanya ?"

What could I answer her ? The poor lady was in tears. I

asked her what was the fresh trouble of which she had been about to tell me just now.

"Ach, my dear boy! As though we hadn't trouble enough! It seems our cup was not full enough! You remember, my dear, or perhaps you don't remember, I had a little locket set in gold—a keepsake, and in it a portrait of Natasha as a child. She was eight years old then, my little angel. We ordered it from a travelling artist at the time. But I see you've forgotten! He was a good artist. He painted her as a cupid. She'd such fair hair in those days, all fluffy. He painted her in a little muslin smock, so that her little body shows through, and she looked so pretty in it you couldn't take your eyes off her. I begged the artist to put little wings on her, but he wouldn't agree. Well, after all our dreadful troubles, I took it out of its case and hung it on a string round my neck; so I've been wearing it beside my cross, though I was afraid he might see it. You know he told me at the time to get rid of all her things out of the house, or burn them, so that nothing might remind us of her. But I must have her portrait to look at, anyway; sometimes I cry, looking at it, and it does me good. And another time when I'm alone I keep kissing it as though I were kissing her, herself. I call her fond names, and make the sign of the cross over it every night. I talk aloud to her when I'm alone, ask her a question and fancy she has answered, and ask her another. Och, Vanya, dear, it makes me sad to talk about it! Well, so I was glad he knew nothing of the locket and hadn't noticed it. But yesterday morning the locket was gone. The string hung loose. It must have worn through and I'd dropped it. I was aghast. I hunted and hunted high and low—it wasn't to be found. Not a sign of it anywhere, it was lost! And where could it have dropped? I made sure I must have lost it in bed, and rummaged through everything. Nowhere! If it had come off and dropped, some one might have picked it up, and who could have found it except him or Matryona? One can't think of it's being Matryona, she's devoted to me heart and soul (Matryona, are you going to bring that samovar?). I keep thinking what will happen if he's found it? I sit so sad and keep crying and crying and can't keep back my tears. And Nikolay Sergeyitch is kinder and kinder to me as though he knows what I am grieving about, and is sorry for me. Then I've been wondering, how could he tell? Hasn't he perhaps really found the locket and thrown it out of the window? In anger he's capable of it, you know. He's thrown it out and now he's sad about it himself and sorry he threw it out. I've been already with Matryona to look under the window—I found nothing. Every trace has vanished. I've been crying all night. It's the first night I haven't made the sign of the cross over her. Och, it's a bad sign, Ivan Petrovitch, it's a bad sign, it's an omen of evil; for two days I've been crying without stopping. I've been expecting you, my dear, as an angel of God, if only to relieve my heart . . ." and the poor lady wept bitterly.

"Oh yes, I forgot to tell you," she began suddenly, pleased at remembering. "Have you heard anything from him about an orphan girl ? "

" Yes, Anna Andreyevna. He told me you had both thought of it, and agreed to take a poor girl, an orphan, to bring up. Is that true ? "

" I've never thought of it, my dear boy, I've never thought of it ; I don't want any orphan girl. She'll remind me of our bitter lot, our misfortune ! I want no one but Natasha. She was my only child, and she shall remain the only one. But what does it mean that he should have thought of an orphan ? What do you think, Ivan Petrovitch ? Is it to comfort me, do you suppose, looking at my tears, or to drive his own daughter out of his mind altogether, and attach himself to another child. What did he say about me as you came along ? How did he seem to you—morose, angry ? Tss ! Here he is ! Afterwards, my dear, tell me afterwards. . . . Don't forget to come to-morrow."

CHAPTER XIII

THE old man came in. He looked at us with curiosity and as though ashamed of something, frowned, and went up to the table.

"Where's the samovar ? " he asked. " Do you mean to say she couldn't bring it till now ? "

" It's coming, my dear, it's coming. Here, she's brought it ! " said Anna Andreyevna fussily.

Matryona appeared with the samovar as soon as she saw Nikolay Sergeyitch, as though she had been waiting to bring it till he came in. She was an old, tried and devoted servant, but the most self-willed and grumbling creature in the world, with an obstinate and stubborn character. She was afraid of

Nikolay Sergeyitch and always curbed her tongue in his presence. But she made up for it with Anna Andreyevna, was rude to her at every turn, and openly attempted to govern her mistress, though at the same time she had a warm and genuine affection for her and for Natasha. I had known Matryona in the old days at Ichmenyevka.

"Hm! . . . It's not pleasant when one's wet through and they *won't* even get one tea," the old man muttered.

Anna Andreyevna at once made a sign to me. He could not endure these mysterious signals; and though at the minute he tried not to look at us, one could see from his face that Anna Andreyevna had just signalled to me about him, and that he was fully aware of it.

"I have been to see about my case, Vanya," he began suddenly. "It's such a wretched business. Did I tell you? It's going against me altogether. It appears I've no proofs; none of the papers I ought to have. My facts cannot be authenticated it seems. Hm! . . ."

He was speaking of his lawsuit with the prince, which was still dragging on, but had taken a very bad turn for Nikolay Sergeyitch. I was silent, not knowing what to answer. He looked suspiciously at me.

"Well!" he brought out suddenly, as though irritated by our silence, "the quicker the better! They won't make a scoundrel of me, even if they do decide I must pay I have my conscience, so let them decide. Anyway, the case will be over; it will be settled. I shall be ruined. . . . I'll give up everything and go to Siberia."

"Good heavens! What a place to go to. And why so far?" Anna Andreyevna could not resist saying.

"And here what are we near?" he asked gruffly, as though glad of the objection.

"Why, near people . . . anyway," began Anna Andreyevna, and she glanced at me in distress.

"What sort of people?" he cried, turning his feverish eyes from me to her and back again. "What people? Robbers, slanderers, traitors? There are plenty such everywhere; don't be uneasy, we shall find them in Siberia too. If you don't want to come with me you can stay here. I won't take you against your will."

"Nikolay Sergeyitch, my dear! With whom should I stay without you? Why, I've no one but you in the whole . . ."

She faltered, broke off, and turned to me with a look of alarm.

E

as though begging for help and support. The old man was irritated, and was ready to take offence at anything; it was impossible to contradict him.

"Come now, Anna Andreyevna," said I. "It's not half as bad in Siberia as you think. If the worst comes to the worst and you have to sell Ichmenyevka, Nikolay Sergeyitch's plan is very good in fact. In Siberia you might get a good private job, and then . . ."

"Well, you're talking sense, Ivan, anyway. That's just what I thought. I'll give up everything and go away."

"Well, that I never did expect," cried Anna Andreyevna, flinging up her hands. "And you, too, Vanya! I didn't expect it of you! . . . Why, you've never known anything but kindness from us, and now . . ."

"Ha, ha, ha! What else did you expect? Why, what are we to live upon, consider that! Our money's spent, we've come to our last farthing. Perhaps you'd like me to go to Prince Pyotr Alexandrovitch and beg his pardon, eh?"

Hearing the prince's name, Anna Andreyevna trembled with alarm. The teaspoon in her hand tinkled against the saucer.

"Yes, speaking seriously," the old man went on, working himself up with malicious, obstinate pleasure, "what do you think, Vanya? Shouldn't I really go to him? Why go to Siberia? I'd much better comb my hair, put on my best clothes, and brush myself to-morrow; Anna Andreyevna will get me a new shirt-front (one can't go to see a person like that without!), buy me gloves, to be the correct thing; and then I'll go to his excellency: 'Your excellency, little father, benefactor! Forgive me and have pity on me! Give me a crust of bread! I've a wife and little children! . . .' Is that right, Anna Andreyevna? Is that what you want?"

"My dear; I want nothing! I spoke without thinking. Forgive me if I vexed you, only don't shout," she brought out, trembling more and more violently in her terror.

I am convinced that everything was topsy-turvy and aching in his heart at that moment, as he looked at his poor wife's tears and alarm. I am sure that he was suffering far more than she was, but he could not control himself. So it is sometimes with the most good-natured people of weak nerves, who in spite of their kindliness are carried away till they find enjoyment in their own grief and anger, and try to express themselves at any cost, even that of wounding some other innocent creature, always by preference the one nearest and dearest. A woman sometimes has a craving to feel unhappy and aggrieved, though she has no misfortune or grievance. There are many men like women in this respect, and men, indeed, by no means feeble, and who have very little that is feminine about them. The old man had a compelling impulse to quarrel, though he was made miserable by it himself.

I remember that the thought dawned on me at the time: Hadn't he perhaps really before this gone out on some project such as Anna Andreyevna suspected? What if God had softened his heart, and he had really been going to Natasha, and had changed his mind on the way, or something had gone wrong, and made him give up his intentions, as was sure to happen; and so he had returned home angry and humiliated, ashamed of his recent feelings and wishes, looking out for some one on whom to vent his anger for his weakness, and pitching on the very ones whom he suspected of sharing the same feelings and wishes. Perhaps when he wanted to forgive his daughter, he pictured the joy and rapture of his poor Anna Andreyevna, and when it came to nothing she was of course the first to suffer for it.

But her look of hopelessness, as she trembled with fear before him, touched him. He seemed ashamed of his wrath, and for a minute controlled himself. We were all silent. I was trying not to look at him. But the good moment did not last long. At all costs he must express himself by some outburst, or a curse if need be.

"You see, Vanya," he said suddenly, "I'm sorry. I didn't want to speak, but the time has come when I must speak out openly without evasion, as every straightforward man ought . . . do you understand, Vanya? I'm glad you have come, and so I want to say aloud in your presence so that *others* may hear that I am sick of all this nonsense, all these tears, and sighs, and misery. What I have torn out of my heart, which bleeds and aches perhaps, will never be back in my heart again. Yes! I've said so and I'll act on it. I'm speaking of what happened six months ago—you understand, Vanya? And I speak of this so openly, so directly, that you may make no mistake about my words," he added, looking at me with blazing eyes and obviously avoiding his wife's frightened glances. "I repeat: this is nonsense; I won't have it! . . . It simply maddens me that every one looks upon me as capable of having such a low, weak feeling, as though I were a fool, as though I were the most abject scoundrel . . . they imagine I am going mad with grief. . . . Nonsense! I have cast away, I have forgotten my old feelings! I have no memory of it! No! no! no! and no! . . ."

He jumped up from his chair; and struck the table so that the cups tinkled.

"Nikolay Sergeyitch! Have you no feeling for Anna Andreyevna! Look what you are doing to her!" I said, unable to restrain myself and looking at him almost with indignation. But it was only pouring oil on the flames.

"No, I haven't!" he shouted, trembling and turning white. "I haven't, for no one feels for me! For in my own house they're all plotting against me in my dishonour and on the side of my depraved daughter, who deserves my curse, and any punishment! . . ."

"Nikolay Sergeyitch, don't curse her! . . . Anything you like only don't curse our daughter!" screamed Anna Andreyevna.

"I will curse her!" shouted the old man, twice as loud as before; "because, insulted and dishonoured as I am, I am expected to go to the accursed girl and ask her forgiveness. Yes, yes, that's it! I'm tormented in this way in my own house day and night, day and night, with tears and sighs and stupid hints! They try to soften me. . . . Look, Vanya, look," he added, with trembling hands hastily taking papers out of his side-pocket, "here are the notes of our case. It's made out that I'm a thief, that I'm a cheat, that I have robbed my benefactor! . . . I am discredited, disgraced, because of her! There, there, look, look! . . ."

And he began pulling out of the side-pocket of his coat various papers, and throwing them on the table one after another, hunting impatiently amongst them for the one he wanted to show me; but, as luck would have it, the one he sought was not forthcoming. Impatiently he pulled out of his pocket all he had clutched in his hand, and suddenly something fell heavily on the table with a clink. Anna Andreyevna uttered a shriek. It was the lost locket.

I could scarcely believe my eyes. The blood rushed to the old man's head and flooded his cheeks; he started. Anna Andreyevna stood with clasped hands looking at him imploringly. Her face beamed with joyful hope. The old man's flush, his shame before us. . . . Yes, she was not mistaken, she knew now how her locket had been lost!

She saw that he had picked it up, had been delighted at his find, and, perhaps, quivering with joy, had jealously hidden it from all eyes; that in solitude, unseen by all, he had gazed at the face of his adored child with infinite love, had gazed and could not gaze enough; that perhaps like the poor mother he had shut himself away from every one to talk to his precious Natasha, imagining her replies and answering them himself; and at night with agonizing grief, with suppressed sobs he had caressed and kissed the dear image, and instead of curses invoked forgiveness and blessings on her whom he would not see and cursed before others.

"My dear, so you love her still!" cried Anna Andreyevna, unable to restrain herself further in the presence of the stern father who had just cursed her Natasha.

But no sooner had he heard her exclamation than an insane fury flashed in his eyes. He snatched up the locket, threw it violently on the ground, and began furiously stamping on it.

"I curse you, I curse you, for ever and ever!" he shouted hoarsely, gasping for breath. "For ever! For ever!"

"Good God!" cried the mother. "Her! My Natasha! Her little face! ... trampling on it! Trampling on it! Tyrant! cruel, unfeeling, proud man!"

Hearing his wife's wail the frantic old man stopped short, horrified at what he was doing. All at once he snatched up the locket from the floor and rushed towards the door, but he had not taken two steps when he fell on his knees, and dropping his arms on the sofa before him, let his head fall helplessly.

He sobbed like a child, like a woman. Sobs wrung his breast as though they would rend it. The threatening old man became all in a minute weaker than a child. Oh, now he could not have cursed her; now, he felt no shame before either of us, and in a sudden rush of love covered with kisses the portrait he had just been trampling underfoot. It seemed as though all his tenderness, all his love for his daughter so long restrained, burst out now with irresistible force, and shattered his whole being.

"Forgive, forgive her!" Anna Andreyevna exclaimed, sobbing, bending over him and embracing him. "Bring her back to her home, my dear, and at the dread day of judgment God will reward you for your mercy and humility! . . ."

"No, no! Not for anything! Never!" he exclaimed in a husky, choking voice, "never! never!"

CHAPTER XIV

It was late, ten o'clock, when I got to Natasha's. She was living at that time in Fontanka, near the Semyonov bridge, on the fourth floor, in the dirty block of buildings belonging to the merchant Kolotushkin. When first she left home she had lived for a time with Alyosha in a very nice flat, small, but pretty and convenient, on the third storey of a house in Liteyny. But the young prince's resources were soon exhausted. He did not become a music teacher, but borrowed money and was soon very heavily in debt. He spent his money on decorating the flat and on making presents to Natasha, who tried to check his extravagance, scolded him, and sometimes even cried about it. Alyosha, with his emotional and impressionable nature, revelled sometimes for a whole week in dreams of how he would make her a present and how she would receive it, making of this a real treat for himself, and rapturously telling me beforehand of his dreams and anticipations. Then he was so downcast at her tears and reproofs that one felt sorry for him, and as time went on these presents became the occasion of reproaches, bitterness, and quarrels. Moreover, Alyosha spent a great deal of money without telling Natasha, was led away by his companions, and was unfaithful to her. He visited all sorts of Josephines and Minnas; though at the same time he loved her dearly. His love for her was a torment to him. He often came to see me depressed and melancholy, declaring that he was not worth Natasha's little finger, that he was coarse and wicked, incapable of understanding her and unworthy of her love. He was to some extent right. There was no sort of equality between them; he felt like a child compared with her, and she always looked upon him as a child. He repented with tears of his relations with Josephine, while he besought me not to speak of them to Natasha. And when, timid and trembling after these open confessions, he went back to her with me (insisting on my coming, declaring that he was afraid to look at her after what he had done, and that I was the one person who could help him through), Natasha knew from the first glance at him what was the matter. She was terribly jealous, and I don't know how it was she always forgave him all his lapses. This was how it usually happened: Alyosha would go in with me, timidly address her, and look with timid tenderness into her eyes. She guessed at once that he had been doing wrong, but showed no sign of it, was never the first to begin on the subject, on the contrary, always redoubled her caresses and became tenderer and more lively—and this was not acting or premeditated strategy on her part. No; for her fine nature there was a sort of infinite bliss in forgiving and being merciful; as though in the very process of forgiving Alyosha she found a peculiar, subtle charm. It is true that so far it was only the question of Josephines. Seeing her kind and forgiving, Alyosha could not restrain himself and at once confessed the whole story without being asked any questions—to relieve his heart and "to be the same as before," as he said. When he had received her forgiveness he grew ecstatic at once, sometimes even cried with joy and emotion, kissed and embraced her. Then at once his spirits rose, and he would begin with childlike openness, giving her a full account of his adventures with Josephine; he smiled and laughed, blessed Natasha, and praised her to the skies, and the evening ended happily and merrily. When all his money was spent he began selling things. As Natasha insisted upon it, a cheap little flat in Fontanka was found for her. Their things went on being sold; Natasha now even sold her clothes and began looking for work. When Alyosha heard of it his despair knew no bounds; he cursed himself, cried out that he despised himself, but meantime did nothing to improve the position. By now this last resource was exhausted; nothing was left for Natasha but work, and that was very poorly paid!

At first when they lived together, there had been a violent quarrel between Alyosha and his father. Prince Valkovsky's designs at the time to marry his son to Katerina Fyodorovna Filimonov, the countess's stepdaughter, were so far only a project. But the project was a cherished one. He took Alyosha to see the young lady, coaxed him to try and please her, and attempted to persuade him by arguments and severity. But the plan fell through owing to the countess. Then Alyosha's father began to shut his eyes to his son's affair with Natasha, leaving it to time. Knowing Alyosha's fickleness and frivolity he hoped that the love affair would soon be over. As for the possibility of his marrying Natasha the prince had till lately ceased to trouble his mind about it. As for the lovers, they put off the question till a formal reconciliation with his father was possible, or vaguely till some change of circumstances. And Natasha was evidently unwilling to discuss the subject. Alyosha told me in secret that his father was in a way rather pleased at the whole business. He was pleased at the humiliation of Ichmenyev. For form's sake he kept up a show of displeasure with his son, decreased his by no means liberal allowance (he was exceedingly stingy with him), and threatened to stop even that. But he soon went away to Poland in pursuit of the countess, who had business there. He was still as actively set on his project of the match. For though Alyosha was, it is true, rather young to be married, the girl was very wealthy, and it was too good a chance to let slip. The prince at last attained his object. The rumour reached us that the match was at last agreed upon. At the time I am describing, the prince had only just returned to Petersburg. He met his son affectionately, but the persistence of Alyosha's connexion with Natasha was an unpleasant surprise to him. He began to have doubts, to feel nervous. He sternly and emphatically insisted on his son's breaking it off, but soon hit upon a much more effectual mode of attack, and carried off Alyosha to the countess. Her stepdaughter, though she was scarcely more than a child, was almost a beauty, gay, clever, and sweet, with a heart of rare goodness and a candid, uncorrupted soul. The prince calculated that the lapse of six months must have had some effect, that Natasha could no longer have the charm of novelty, and that his son would not now look at his proposed fiancée with the same eyes as he had six months before. He was only partly right in his reckoning . . . Alyosha certainly was attracted. I must add that the father became all at once extraordinarily affectionate to him (though he still refused to give him money). Alyosha felt that his father's greater warmth covered an unchanged, inflexible determination, and he was unhappy—but not so unhappy as he would have been if he had not seen Katerina Fyodorovna every day. I knew that he had not shown himself to Natasha for five days. On my way to her from the Ichmenyevs I guessed uneasily what she wanted to discuss with me. I could see a light in her window a long way off. It had long been arranged between us that she should put a candle in the window if she were in great and urgent need of me, so that if I happened to pass by (and this did happen nearly every evening) I might guess from the light in the window that I was expected and she needed me. Of late she had often put the candle in the window. . . .

CHAPTER XV

I FOUND Natasha alone. She was slowly walking up and down the room, with her hands clasped on her bosom, lost in thought. A samovar stood on the table almost burnt out. It had been got ready for me long before. With a smile she held out her hand to me without speaking. Her face was pale and had an expression of suffering. There was a look of martyrdom, tenderness, patience, in her smile. Her clear blue eyes seemed to have grown bigger, her hair looked thicker from the wanness and thinness of her face.

"I began to think you weren't coming," she said, giving me her hand. "I was meaning to send Mavra to inquire; I was afraid you might be ill again."

"No, I'm not ill. I was detained. I'll tell you directly. But what's the matter, Natasha, what's happened?"

"Nothing's happened," she answered, surprised. "Why?"

"Why, you wrote . . . you wrote yesterday for me to come, and fixed the hour that I might not come before or after; and that's not what you usually do."

"Oh yes! I was expecting *him* yesterday."

"Why, hasn't he been here yet?"

"No. I thought if he didn't come I must talk things over with you," she added, after a pause.

"And this evening, did you expect him?"

"No, this evening he's *there*."

"What do you think, Natasha, won't he come back at all?"

"Of course he'll come," she answered, looking at me with peculiar earnestness. She did not like the abruptness of my question. We lapsed into silence, walking up and down the room.

"I've been expecting you all this time, Vanya," she began again with a smile. "And do you know what I was doing? I've been walking up and down, reciting poetry. Do you remember the bells, the winter road, 'My samovar boils on the table of oak' . . . ? We read it together:

> "The snowstorm is spent; there's a glimmer of light
> From the millions of dim watching eyes of the night.

"And then:

> "There's the ring of a passionate voice in my ears
> In the song of the bell taking part;
> Oh, when will my loved-one return from afar
> To rest on my suppliant heart?
> My life is no life! Rosy beams of the dawn
> Are at play on the pane's icy screen;
> My samovar boils on my table of oak,
> With the bright crackling fire the dark corner awoke,
> And my bed with chintz curtains is seen.

"How fine that is. How tormenting those verses are, Vanya. And what a vivid, fantastic picture! It's just a canvas with a mere pattern chalked on it. You can embroider what you like! Two sensations: the earliest, and the latest. That samovar, that chintz curtain—how homelike it all is. It's like some little cottage in our little town at home; I feel as though I could see that cottage : a new one made of logs not yet weather-boarded. . . . And then another picture.

> "Of a sudden I hear the same voice ringing out
> With the bell; its sad accents I trace:
> Oh, where's my old friend ? And I fear he'll come in
> With eager caress and embrace.
> What a life I endure ! But my tears are in vain.
> Oh, how dreary my room ! Through the chinks the wind blows
> And outside the house but one cherry-tree grows,
> Perhaps that has perished by now though—who knows ?
> It's hid by the frost on the pane.
> The flowers on the curtain have lost their gay tone,
> And I wander sick; all my kinsfolk I shun,
> There's no one to scold me or love me, not one,
> The old woman grumbles alone. . . .

"'I wander sick.' That sick is so well put in. 'There's no one to scold me.' What tenderness, what softness in that line; and what agonies of memory, agonies one has caused oneself, and one broods over them. Heavens, how fine it is! How true it is ! . . ."

She ceased speaking, as though struggling with a rising spasm in her throat.

"Dear Vanya!" she said a minute later, and she paused again, as though she had forgotten what she meant to say, or had spoken without thinking, from a sudden feeling.

Meanwhile we still walked up and down the room. A lamp burned before the ikon. Of late Natasha had become more and more devout, and did not like one to speak of it to her.

"Is to-morrow a holiday ?" I asked. "Your lamp is lighted."

"No, it's not a holiday . . . but, Vanya, sit down. You must be tired. Will you have tea ? I suppose you've not had it yet ?"

"Let's sit down, Natasha. I've had tea already."

"Where have you come from ?"

"From *them*."

That's how we always referred to her old home.

"From them ? How did you get time ? Did you go of your own accord ? Or did they ask you ?"

She besieged me with questions. Her face grew still paler with emotion. I told her in detail of my meeting with her father, my conversation with her mother, and the scene with the locket. I told her in detail, describing every shade of feeling. I never concealed anything from her. She listened eagerly, catching every word I uttered. The tears glittered in her eyes. The scene with the locket affected her deeply.

"Stay, stay, Vanya," she said, often interrupting my story.

"Tell me more exactly everything, everything as exactly as possible; you don't tell me exactly enough. . . ."

I repeated it again and again, replying every moment to her continual questions about the details.

"And you really think he was coming to see me?"

"I don't know, Natasha, and in fact I can't make up my mind; that he grieves for you and loves you is clear; but that he was coming to you is . . . is . . ."

"And he kissed the locket?" she interrupted. "What did he say when he kissed it?"

"It was incoherent. Nothing but exclamations; he called you by the tenderest names; he called for you."

"Called for me?"

"Yes."

She wept quietly.

"Poor things!" she said. "And if he knows everything," she added after a brief silence, "it's no wonder. He hears a great deal about Alyosha's father, too."

"Natasha," I said timidly, "let us go to them."

"When?" she asked, turning pale and almost getting up from her chair.

She thought I was urging her to go at once.

"No, Vanya," she added, putting her two hands on my shoulders, and smiling sadly; "no, dear, that's what you're always saying, but . . . we'd better not talk about it."

"Will this horrible estrangement never be ended?" I cried mournfully. "Can you be so proud that you won't take the first step? It's for you to do it; you must make the first advance. Perhaps your father's only waiting for that to forgive you. . . . He's your father; he has been injured by you! Respect his pride; it's justifiable, it's natural! You ought to do it. Only try, and he will forgive you unconditionally."

"Unconditionally! That's impossible. And don't reproach me, Vanya, for nothing. I'm thinking of it day and night, and I think of it now. There's not been a day perhaps since I left them that I haven't thought of it. And how often we have talked about it! You know yourself it's impossible."

"Try!"

"No, my dear, it's impossible. If I were to try I should only make him more bitter against me. There's no bringing back what's beyond recall. And you know what it is one can never bring back? One can never bring back those happy, childish days I spent with them. If my father forgave me he would hardly know me now. He loved me as a little girl ; a grown-up child. He admired my childish simplicity. He used to pat me on the head just as when I was a child of seven and used to sit upon his knee and sing him my little childish songs. From my earliest childhood up to the last day he used to come to my bed and bless me for the night. A month before our troubles he bought me some ear-rings as a secret (but I knew all about it), and was as pleased as a child, imagining how delighted I should be with the present, and was awfully angry with every one, and with me especially, when he found out that I had known all about his buying the ear-rings for a long time. Three days before I went away he noticed that I was depressed, and he became so depressed himself that it made him ill, and—would you believe it—to divert my mind he proposed taking tickets for the theatre ! . . . Yes, indeed, he thought that would set me right. I tell you he knew and loved me as a little girl, and refused even to think that I should one day be a woman. . . . It's never entered his head. If I were to go home now he would not know me. Even if he did forgive me he'd meet quite a different person now. I'm not the same ; I'm not a child now. I have gone through a great deal. Even if he were satisfied with me he still would sigh for his past happiness, and grieve that I am not the same as I used to be when he loved me as a child. The past always seems best ! It's remembered with anguish ! Oh, how good the past was, Vanya ! " she cried, carried away by her own words, and interrupting herself with this exclamation which broke painfully from her heart.

"That's all true that you say, Natasha," I said. "So he will have to learn to know and love you afresh. To know you, especially. He will love you, of course. Surely you can't think that he's incapable of knowing and understanding you, he, with his heart ? "

"Oh, Vanya, don't be unfair ! What is there to understand in me ? I didn't mean that. You see, there's something else : a father's love is jealous, too, he's hurt that all began and was settled with Alyosha without his knowledge, that he didn't know it and failed to see it. He knows that he did not foresee it, and he puts down the unhappy consequences of our love and my flight to my 'ungrateful' secretiveness. I did not come to him at the beginning. I did not afterwards confess every impulse of my heart to him ; on the contrary I hid it in myself. I concealed it from him and I assure you, Vanya, this is secretly a worse injury, a worse insult to him than the facts themselves—that I left them and have abandoned myself to my lover. Supposing he did meet me now like a father, warmly and affectionately, yet the seed of discord would remain. The next day, or the day after, there would be disappointments, misunderstandings, reproaches. What's more, he won't forgive without conditions, even if I say—and say it truly from the bottom of my heart—that I understand how I have wounded him, and how badly I've behaved to him. And though it will hurt me if he won't understand how much all this happiness with Alyosha has cost me myself, what miseries I have been through, I will stifle my feelings, I will put up with anything—but that won't be enough for him. He will insist on an impossible atonement; he will insist on my cursing my past, cursing Alyosha and repenting of my love for him. He wants what's impossible, to bring back the past, and to erase the last six months from our life. But I won't curse anyone, and I can't repent. It's no one's doing; it just happened so. . . . No, Vanya, it can't be now. The time has not come."

"When will the time come?"

"I don't know. . . . We shall have to work out our future happiness by suffering; pay for it somehow by fresh miseries. Everything is purified by suffering. . . . Oh, Vanya, how much pain there is in the world!"

I was silent and looked at her thoughtfully.

"Why do you look at me like that, Alyosha—I mean Vanya!" she said, smiling at her own mistake.

"I am looking at your smile, Natasha. Where did you get it? You used not to smile like that."

"Why, what is there in my smile?"

"The old childish simplicity is still there, it's true. . . . But when you smile it seems as though your heart were aching dreadfully. You've grown thinner, Natasha, and your hair seems thicker. . . . What dress have you got on? You used to wear that at home, didn't you?"

"How you love me, Vanya," she said, looking at me affectionately. "And what about you? What are you doing? How are things going with you?"

"Just the same. I'm still writing my novel. But it's difficult. I can't get on. The inspiration's dried up. I dare say I could knock it off somehow, and it might turn out interesting. But it's a pity to spoil a good idea. It's a favourite idea of mine. But it must be ready in time for the magazine. I've even thought of throwing up the novel, and knocking off a short story, something light and graceful, and without a trace of pessimism. Quite without a trace. . . . Every one ought to be cheerful and happy."

"You're such a hard worker, you poor boy! And how about Smith?"

"But Smith's dead."

"And he hasn't haunted you? I tell you seriously, Vanya, you're ill and your nerves are out of order; you're always lost in such dreams. When you told me about taking that room I noticed it in you. So the room's damp, not nice?"

"Yes, I had an adventure there this evening. . . . But I'll tell you about it afterwards."

She had left off listening and was sitting plunged in deep thought.

"I don't know how I could have left *them* then. I was in a fever," she added at last, looking at me with an expression that did not seem to expect an answer.

If I had spoken to her at that moment she would not have heard me.

"Vanya," she said in a voice hardly audible, "I asked you to come for a reason."

"What is it?"

"I am parting from him."

"You have parted, or you're going to part?"

"I must put an end to this life. I asked you to come that I might tell you everything, all, all that has been accumulating, and that I've hidden from you till now."

This was always how she began, confiding to me her secret intentions, and it almost always turned out that I had learnt the whole secret from her long before.

"Ach, Natasha, I've heard that from you a thousand times. Of course it's impossible for you to go on living together. Your relation is such a strange one. You have nothing in common. But will you have the strength?"

"It's only been an idea before, Vanya, but now I have quite made up my mind. I love him beyond everything, and yet it seems I am his worst enemy. I shall ruin his future. I must set him free. He can't marry me; he hasn't the strength to go against his father. I don't want to bind him either. And so I'm really glad he has fallen in love with the girl they are betrothing him to. It will make the parting easier for him.

I ought to do it! It's my duty. . . . If I love him I ought to sacrifice everything for him. I ought to prove my love for him; it's my duty! Isn't it?"

"But you won't persuade him, you know."

"I'm not going to persuade him. I shall be just the same with him if he comes in this minute. But I must find some means to make it easier for him to leave me without a conscience-prick. That's what worries me, Vanya. Help me. Can't you advise something?"

"There is only one way," I said, "to leave off loving him altogether and fall in love with some one else. But I doubt whether even that will do it; surely you know his character. Here he's not been to see you for five days. Suppose he had left you altogether. You've only to write that you are leaving him, and he'd run to you at once."

"Why do you dislike him, Vanya?"

"I?"

"Yes, you, you! You're his enemy, secret, and open. You can't speak of him without vindictiveness. I've noticed a thousand times that it's your greatest pleasure to humiliate him and blacken him! Yes, blacken him, it's the truth!"

"And you've told me so a thousand times already. Enough, Natasha, let's drop this conversation."

"I've been wanting to move into another lodging," she began again after a silence. "Don't be angry, Vanya."

"Why, he'd come to another lodging, and I assure you I'm not angry."

"Love, a new, strong love might hold him back. If he came back to me it would only be for a moment, don't you think?"

"I don't know, Natasha. Everything with him is so inconsistent. He wants to marry that girl, and to love you, too. He's somehow able to do all that at once."

"If I knew for certain that he loved her I would make up my mind . . . Vanya! Don't hide anything from me! Do you know something you don't want to tell me?"

She looked at me with an uneasy, searching gaze.

"I know nothing, my dear. I give you my word of honour; I've always been open with you. But I'll tell you what I do think: very likely he's not nearly so much in love with the countess's stepdaughter as we suppose. It's nothing but attraction. . . ."

"You think so, Vanya? My God, if I were sure of that! Oh, how I should like to see him at this moment, simply to look at him! I should find out everything from his face! But he doesn't come! He doesn't come!"

"Surely you don't expect him, Natasha?"

"No, he's *with her;* I know. I sent to find out. How I should like to have a look at her, too. . . . Listen, Vanya, I'm talking nonsense, but is it really impossible for me to see her, is it impossible to meet her anywhere? What do you think?"

She waited anxiously to hear what I should say.

"You might see her. But simply to see her wouldn't amount to much."

"It would be enough for me only to see her; I should be able to tell then, for myself. Listen, I have become so stupid, you know. I walk up and down, up and down here, always alone, always alone, always thinking, thoughts come rushing like a whirlwind! It's so horrible! One thing I've thought of, Vanya; couldn't you get to know her? You know the countess admired your novel (you said so yourself at the time). You sometimes go to Prince R——'s evenings; she's sometimes there. Manage to be presented to her. Or perhaps Alyosha could introduce you. Then you could tell me all about her."

"Natasha, dear, we'll talk of that later. Tell me, do you seriously think you have the strength to face a separation? Look at yourself now; you're not calm."

"I . . . shall . . . have!" she answered, hardly audibly, "Anything for him. My whole life for his sake. But you know, Vanya, I can't bear his being with her now, and having forgotten me; he is sitting by her, talking, laughing, as he used to sit here, do you remember? He's looking into her eyes; he always does look at people like that—and it never occurs to him that I am here . . . with you."

She broke off without finishing and looked at me in despair.

"Why, Natasha, only just now you were saying . . ."

"Let's separate both at once, of our own accord," she interrupted with flashing eyes. "I will give him my blessing for that . . . but it's hard, Vanya, that he should forget me first! Ah, Vanya, what agony it is! I don't understand myself. One thinks one thing, but it's different when it comes to doing it. What will become of me!"

"Hush, hush, Natasha, calm yourself!"

"And now it's five days. Every hour, every minute. . . . If I sleep I dream of nothing but him, nothing but him! I tell you what, Vanya, let's go there. You take me!"

"Hush, Natasha!"

"Yes, we will go! I've only been waiting for you! I've been thinking about it for the last three days. That was what I meant in my letter to you. . . . You must take me; you mustn't refuse me this . . . I've been expecting you . . . for three days. . . . There's a party there this evening. . . . He's there . . . let us go!"

She seemed almost delirious. There was a noise in the passage; Mavra seemed to be wrangling with some one.

"Stay, Natasha, who's that?" I asked. "Listen."

She listened with an incredulous smile, and suddenly turned fearfully white.

"My God! Who's there?" she said, almost inaudibly.

She tried to detain me, but I went into the passage to Mavra. Yes! It actually was Alyosha. He was questioning Mavra about something. She refused at first to admit him.

"Where have you turned up from?" she asked, with an air of authority. "Well, what have you been up to? All right, then, go in, go in! You won't come it over me with your butter! Go in! I wonder what you've to say for yourself!"

"I'm not afraid of anyone! I'm going in!" said Alyosha somewhat disconcerted, however.

"Well, go in then! You're a sauce-box!"

"Well, I'm going in! Ah! you're here, too!" he said, catching sight of me. "How nice it is that you're here! Well, here I am, you see. . . . What had I better do?"

"Simply go in," I answered. "What are you afraid of?"

"I'm not afraid of anything, I assure you, for upon my word I'm not to blame. You think I'm to blame? You'll see; I'll explain it directly. Natasha, can I come in?" he cried with a sort of assumed boldness, standing before the closed door. No one answered.

"What's the matter?" he asked uneasily.

"Nothing; she was in there just now," I answered. "Can anything . . ."

Alyosha opened the door cautiously and looked timidly about the room. There was no one to be seen.

Suddenly he caught sight of her in the corner, between the cupboard and the window. She stood as though in hiding, more dead than alive. As I recall it now I can't help smiling. Alyosha went up to her slowly and warily.

F

"Natasha, what is it? How are you, Natasha?" he brought out timidly, looking at her with a sort of dismay.

"Oh, it's all right!" she answered in terrible confusion, as though she were in fault. "You . . . will you have some tea?"

"Natasha, listen," Alyosha began, utterly overwhelmed. "You're convinced perhaps that I'm to blame. But I'm not, not a bit. You'll see; I'll tell you directly."

"What for?" Natasha whispered. "No, no, you needn't. . . . Come, give me your hand and . . . it's over . . . the same as before. . . ."

And she came out of the corner. A flush began to come into her cheeks. She looked down as though she were afraid to glance at Alyosha.

"Good God!" he cried ecstatically. "If I really were to blame I shouldn't dare look at her after that. Look, look!" he exclaimed, turning to me, "she thinks I am to blame; everything's against me; all appearances are against me! I haven't been here for five days! There are rumours that I'm with my betrothed—and what? She has forgiven me already! Already she says, 'Give me your hand and it's over'! Natasha, my darling, my angel! It's not my fault, and you must know that! Not the least little bit! Quite the contrary! Quite the contrary!"

"But . . . but you were to be *there* now. . . . You were invited *there* now. . . . How is it you're here? Wh-what time is it?"

"Half-past ten! I have been there . . . but I said I wasn't well and came away—and—and it's the first time, the first time I've been free these five days. It's the first time I've been able to tear myself away and come to you, Natasha. That is, I could have come before, but I didn't on purpose. And why? You shall know directly. I ll explain; that's just what I've come for, to explain. Only this time I'm really not a bit to blame, not a bit, not a bit!"

Natasha raised her head and looked at him. . . . But the eyes that met her were so truthful; his face was so full of joy, sincerity and good-humour that it was impossible to disbelieve him. I expected that they would cry out and rush into each other's arms, as had often happened before at such reconciliations. But Natasha seemed overcome by her happiness; she let her head sink on her breast and . . . began crying softly. . . . Then Alyosha couldn't restrain himself. He threw himself at her feet. He kissed her hands, her feet. He seemed frantic. I pushed an easy-chair towards her. She sank into it. Her legs were giving way beneath her.

PART II

CHAPTER I

A MINUTE later we were all laughing as though we were crazy.

"Let me explain; let me explain!" cried Alyosha, his ringing voice rising above our laughter. "They think it's just as usual . . that I've come with some nonsense. . . . I say, I've something most interesting to tell you. But will you ever be quiet?"

He was extremely anxious to tell his story. One could see from his face that he had important news. But the dignified air he assumed in his naïve pride at the possession of such news tickled Natasha at once. I could not help laughing, too. And the angrier he was with us the more we laughed. Alyosha's vexation and then childish despair reduced us at last to the condition of Gogol's midshipman who roared with laughter if one held up one's finger. Mavra, coming out of the kitchen, stood in the doorway and looked at us with grave indignation, vexed that Alyosha had not come in for a good " wigging " from Natasha, as she had been eagerly anticipating for the last five days, and that we were all so merry instead.

At last Natasha, seeing that our laughter was hurting Alyosha's feelings, left off laughing.

"What do you want to tell us?" she asked.

"Well, am I to set the samovar?" asked Mavra, interrupting Alyosha without the slightest ceremony.

"Be off, Mavra, be off!" he cried, waving his hands at her, in a hurry to get rid of her. "I'm going to tell you everything that has happened, is happening, and is going to happen, because I know all about it. I see, my friends, you want to know where I've been for the last five days—that's what I want to tell you, but you won't let me. To begin with I've been deceiving you all this time, Natasha, I've been deceiving you for ever so long, and that's the chief thing."

"Deceiving me?"

"Yes, deceiving you for the last month; I had begun it before my father came back. Now the time has come for complete openness. A month ago, before father came back, I got an immense letter from him, and I said nothing to either of you about it. In his letter he told me, plainly and simply—and, I assure you, in such a serious tone that I was really alarmed—that my engagement was a settled thing, that my fiancée was simply perfection; that of course I wasn't good enough for her, but that I must marry her all the same; and so I must be prepared to put all this nonsense out of my head, and so on, and so on—we know of course what he means by nonsense. Well, that letter I concealed from you."

"You didn't!" Natasha interposed. "See how he flatters himself! As a matter of fact he told us all about it at once. I remember how obedient and tender you were all at once, and wouldn't leave my side, as though you were feeling guilty about something, and you told us the whole letter in fragments."

"Impossible, the chief point I'm sure I didn't tell you. Perhaps you both guessed something, but that's your affair. I didn't tell you. I kept it secret and was fearfully unhappy about it."

"I remember, Alyosha, you were continually asking my advice and told me all about it, a bit at a time, of course, as though it were an imaginary case," I added, looking at Natasha.

"You told us everything! Don't brag, please," she chimed in. "As though you could keep anything secret! Deception is not your strong point. Even Mavra knew all about it. Didn't you, Mavra?"

"How could I help it?" retorted Mavra, popping her head in at the door. "You'd told us all about it before three days were over. You couldn't deceive a child."

"Foo! How annoying it is to talk to you! You're doing all this for spite, Natasha! And you're mistaken too, Mavra. I remember, I was like a madman then. Do you remember, Mavra?"

"To be sure I do, you're like a madman now."

"No, no, I don't mean that. Do you remember, we'd no money then, and you went to pawn my silver cigar-case. And what's more, Mavra, let me tell you you're forgetting yourself and being horribly rude to me. It's Natasha has let you get into such ways. Well, suppose I did tell you all about it at the time, bit by bit (I do remember it now), but you don't know the tone of the letter, the tone of it. And the tone was what mattered most in the letter, let me tell you. That's what I'm talking about."

"Why, what was the tone ?" asked Natasha.

"Listen, Natasha, you keep asking questions as though you were in fun. *Don't joke* about it. I assure you that it's very important. It was in such a tone that I was in despair. My father had never spoken to me like that. It was as though he would sooner expect an earthquake of Lisbon than that he should fail to get his own way ; that was the tone of it."

"Well, well, tell us. Why did you want to conceal it from me ?"

"Ach, my goodness ! Why, for fear of frightening you ! I hoped to arrange it all myself. Well, after that letter, as soon as my father came my troubles began. I prepared myself to answer him firmly, distinctly and earnestly, but somehow it never came off. He never asked me about it, he's cunning ! On the contrary he behaved as though the whole thing were settled and as though any difference or misunderstanding between us were impossible. Do you hear, *impossible*, such confidence ! And he was so affectionate, so sweet to me. I was simply amazed. How clever he is, Ivan Petrovitch, if only you knew ! He has read everything ; he knows everything ; you've only to look at him once and he knows all your thoughts as though they were his own. That's no doubt why he has been called a Jesuit. Natasha doesn't like me to praise him. Don't be cross, Natasha. Well, so that's how it is . . . oh, by the way ! At first he wouldn't give me any money, but now he has. He gave me some yesterday. Natasha, my angel ! Our poverty is over now ! Here, look ! All he took off my allowance these last six months to punish me, he paid yesterday. See how much there is ; I haven't counted it yet. Mavra, look what a lot of money, now we needn't pawn our spoons and studs ! "

He brought out of his pocket rather a thick bundle of notes, fifteen hundred roubles, and laid it on the table. Mavra looked at Alyosha with surprise and approval. Natasha eagerly urged him on.

"Well, so I wondered what I was to do," Alyosha went on. "How was I to oppose him ? If he'd been nasty to me I assure you I wouldn't have thought twice about it. I'd have told him plainly I wouldn't, that I was grown up now, and a man, and that that was the end of it. And believe me, I'd have stuck to it. But as it is, what could I say to him? But don't blame me. I see you seem displeased, Natasha. Why do you look at one another? No doubt you're thinking: here they've caught him at once and he hasn't a grain of will. I have will, I have more than you think. And the proof of it is that in spite of my position I told myself at once, 'it is my duty; I must tell my father everything, everything,' and I began speaking and told him everything, and he listened."

"But what? What did you tell him exactly?" Natasha asked anxiously.

"Why, that I don't want any other fiancée, and that I have one already—you. That is, I didn't tell him that straight out, but I prepared him for it, and I shall tell him to-morrow. I've made up my mind. To begin with I said that to marry for money was shameful and ignoble, and that for us to consider ourselves aristocrats was simply stupid (I talk perfectly openly to him as though he were my brother). Then I explained to him that I belonged to the *tiers état*, and that the *tiers état c'est l'essentiel*, that I am proud of being just like everybody else, and that I don't want to be distinguished in any way; in fact, I laid all those sound ideas before him. . . . I talked warmly, convincingly. I was surprised at myself. I proved it to him even from his own point of view. . . . I said to him straight out—how can we call ourselves princes? It's simply a matter of birth; for what is there princely about us? We're not particularly wealthy, and wealth's the chief point. The greatest prince nowadays is Rothschild. And secondly, it's a long time since anything has been heard of us in real society. The last was Uncle Semyon Valkovsky, and he was only known in Moscow, and he was only famous for squandering his last three hundred serfs, and if father hadn't made money for himself, his grandsons might have been ploughing the land themselves. There are princes like that. We've nothing to be stuck-up over. In short, I told him everything that I was brimming over with—everything, warmly and openly, in fact I said something more. He did not even answer me, but simply began blaming me for having given up going to Count Nainsky's, and then told me I must try and keep in the good graces of Princess K., my godmother, and that if Princess K. welcomes me then I shall be received everywhere, and my career is assured, and he went on and on about that! It was all hinting at my having given up every one since I've been with you, Natasha, and that's being all your influence. But he hasn't spoken about you directly so far. In fact he evidently avoids it. We're both fencing, waiting, catching one another, and you may be sure that our side will come off best."

"Well, that's all right. But how did it end, what has he decided. That's what matters. And what a chatterbox you are, Alyosha!"

"Goodness only knows. There's no telling what he's decided. But I'm not a chatterbox at all; I'm talking sense. He didn't settle anything, but only smiled at all my arguments; and such a smile, as though he were sorry for me. I know it's humiliating, but I'm not ashamed of it. 'I quite agree with you,' he said, 'but let's go to Count Nainsky's, and mind you don't say anything there. I understand you, but they won't.' I believe he's not very well received everywhere himself; people are angry with him about something. He seems to be disliked in society now. The count at first received me very majestically, quite superciliously, as though he had quite forgotten I grew up in his house; he began trying to remember, he did, really. He's simply angry with me for ingratitude, though really there was no sort of ingratitude on my part. It was horribly dull in his house, so I simply gave up going. He gave my father a very casual reception too; so casual, that I can't understand why he goes there. It all revolted me. Poor father almost has to eat humble pie before him. I understand that it's all for my sake, but I don't want anything. I wanted to tell my father what I felt about it, afterwards, but I restrained myself. And indeed, what would be the good? I shan't change his convictions, I shall only make him angry, and he is having a bad time as it is. Well, I thought, I'll take to cunning and I'll outdo them all—I'll make the count respect me—and what do you think? I at once gained my object, everything was changed in a single day. Count Nainsky can't make enough of me now, and that was all my doing, only mine, it was all through my cunning, so that my father was quite astonished!"

"Listen, Alyosha, you'd better keep to the point!" Natasha cried impatiently. "I thought you would tell me something about us, and you only want to tell us how you distinguished yourself at Count Nainsky's. Your count is no concern of mine!"

"No concern! Do you hear, Ivan Petrovitch, she says it's no concern of hers! Why, it's the greatest concern! You'll see it is yourself, it will all be explained in the end. Only let me tell you about it. And in fact (why not be open about it ?) I'll tell you what, Natasha, and you too, Ivan Petrovitch, perhaps I really am sometimes very, very injudicious, granted even I'm sometimes stupid (for I know it is so at times). But in this case, I assure you, I showed a great deal of cunning . . . in fact . . . of cleverness, so that I thought you'd be quite pleased that I'm not always so . . . stupid."

"What are you saying, Alyosha ? Nonsense, dear ! "

Natasha couldn't bear Alyosha to be considered stupid. How often she pouted at me, though she said nothing when I proved to Alyosha without ceremony that he had done something stupid ; it was a sore spot in her heart. She could not bear to see Alyosha humiliated, and probably felt it the more the more she recognized his limitations. But she didn't give him a hint of her opinion for fear of wounding his vanity. He was particularly sensitive on this point, and always knew exactly what she was secretly thinking. Natasha saw this and was very sorry, and she at once tried to flatter and soothe him. That is why his words now raised painful echoes in her heart.

"Nonsense, Alyosha, you're only thoughtless. You're not at all like that," she added. "Why do you run yourself down ? "

"Well, that's all right. So let me prove it to you. Father was quite angry with me after the reception at the count's. I thought, ' wait a bit.' We were driving then to the princess's. I heard long ago that she was so old that she was almost doting, and deaf besides, and awfully fond of little dogs. She has a perfect pack of them, and adores them. In spite of all that she has an immense influence in society, so that even Count Nainsky, *le superbe*, does *l'antichambre* to her. So I hatched a complete plan of future action on the way. And what do you think I built it all on ? Why, on the fact that dogs always like me, yes, really. I have noticed it. Either there's some magnetism in me, or else it's because I'm fond of all animals, I don't know. Dogs do like me, anyway. And, by the way, talking of magnetism, I haven't told you, Natasha, we called up spirits the other day, I was at a spiritualist's. It's awfully curious, Ivan Petrovitch ; it really impressed me. I called up Julius Cæsar."

"My goodness ! What did you want with Julius Cæsar ? " cried Natasha, going off into a peal of laughter. "That's the last straw ! "

"Why not . . . as though I were such a . . . why shouldn't

I call up Julius Cæsar ? What does it matter to him ? Now she's laughing ! "

" Of course it wouldn't matter to him at all . . . oh, you dear ! Well, what did Julius Cæsar say to you ? "

" Oh, he didn't say anything. I simply held the pencil, and the pencil moved over the paper and wrote of itself. They said it was Julius Cæsar writing. I don't believe in it."

" But what did he write, then ? "

" Why, he wrote something like the ' dip it in ' in Gogol. Do leave off laughing ! "

" Oh, tell us about the princess, then."

" Well, you keep interrupting me. We arrived at the princess's and I began by making love to Mimi. Mimi is a most disgusting, horrid old dog, obstinate, too, and fond of biting. The princess dotes on her, she simply worships her ; 1 believe they are the same age. I began by feeding Mimi with sweetmeats, and in about ten minutes I had taught her to shake hands, which they had never been able to teach her before. The princess was in a perfect ecstasy, she almost cried with joy.

" ' Mimi ! Mimi ! Mimi is shaking hands ! '

" Some one came in.

" ' Mimi shakes hands, my godson here has taught her.'

" Count Nainsky arrived.

" ' Mimi shakes hands ! '

" She looked at me almost with tears of tenderness. She's an awfully nice old lady ; I feel quite sorry for her. I was on the spot then, I flattered her again. On her snuff-box she has her own portrait, painted when she was a bride, sixty years ago. Well, she dropped her snuff-box. I picked up the snuff-box and exclaimed :

" ' Quelle charmante peinture ! ' just as if I didn't know. ' It's an ideal beauty ! '

" Well, that melted her completely. She talked to me of this and that ; asked me where I had been studying, and whom I visit, and what splendid hair 1 had, and all that sort of thing. I made her laugh too. I told her a shocking story. She likes that sort of thing. She shook her finger at me, but she laughed a great deal. When she let me go, she kissed me and blessed me, and insisted I should go in every day to amuse her. The count pressed my hand ; his eyes began to look oily. And as for father, though he's the kindest, and sincerest, and most honourable man in the world, if you'll believe me, he almost cried with joy on the way home. He hugged me, and became confidential, mysteriously confidential about a career, connexions, marriages, money; I couldn't understand a lot of it. It was then he gave me the money. That was all yesterday. To-morrow I'm to go to the princess's again. But still, my father's a very honourable man—don't you imagine anything—and although he keeps me away from you, Natasha, it's simply because he's dazzled by Katya's millions, and wants to get hold of them, and you haven't any; and he wants them simply for my sake, and it's merely through ignorance he is unjust to you. And what father doesn't want his son's happiness? It's not his fault that he has been accustomed to think that happiness is to be found in millions. They're all like that. One must look at him from that standpoint, you know, and no other, and then one can see at once that he's right. I've hurried to come to you, Natasha, to assure you of that, for I know you're prejudiced against him, and of course that's not your fault. I don't blame you for it. . . ."

"Then all that's happened is that you've made yourself a position at the princess's. Is that all your cunning amounts to?" asked Natasha.

"Not at all. What do you mean? That's only the beginning. . . . I only told you about the princess because, you understand, through her I shall get a hold over my father, but my story hasn't begun yet."

"Well, tell it then!"

"I've had another adventure this morning, and a very strange one too. I haven't got over it yet," Alyosha went on. "You must observe that, although it's all settled about our engagement between my father and the countess, there's been no formal announcement so far, so we can break it off at any moment without a scandal. Count Nainsky's the only person who knows it, but he's looked upon as a relation and a benefactor. What's more, though I've got to know Katya very well this last fortnight, till this very evening I've never said a word to her about the future, that is about marriage or . . . love. Besides, it's been settled to begin by asking the consent of Princess K., from whom is expected all sorts of patronage and showers of gold. The world will say what she says. She has such connexions. . . . And what they want more than anything is to push me forward in society. But it's the countess, Katya's stepmother, who insists most strongly on this arrangement. The point is that perhaps the princess so far won't receive her because of her doings abroad, and if the princess won't receive her, most likely nobody else will. So my engagement to Katya is a good chance for her. So the countess, who used to be against the engagement, was highly delighted at my success with the princess; but that's beside the point. What matters is this. I saw something of Katerina Fyodorovna last year, but I was a boy then, and I didn't understand things, and so I saw nothing in her then . . ."

"Simply you loved me more then," Natasha broke in, "that's why you saw nothing in her; and now . . ."

"Not a word, Natasha!" cried Alyosha, hotly. "You are quite mistaken, and insulting me. . . . I won't even answer you; listen, and you'll see. . . . Ah, if only you knew Katya! If only you knew what a tender, clear, dove-like soul she is! But you will know. Only let me finish. A fortnight ago, when my father took me to see Katya as soon as they had arrived, I began to watch her intently. I noticed she watched me too. That roused my curiosity, to say nothing of my having a special intention of getting to know her, an intention I had had ever since I got that letter from my father, that impressed me so much. I'm not going to say anything about her. I'm not going to praise her. I'll only say one thing. She's a striking contrast to all her circle. She has such an original nature, such a strong and truthful soul, so strong in its purity and truthfulness, that I'm simply a boy beside her, like a younger brother, though she is only seventeen. Another thing I noticed, there's a great deal of sadness about her, as though she had some secret; she is not talkative; at home she's almost always silent as though afraid to speak. . . . She seems to be brooding over something. She seems to be afraid of my father. She doesn't like her stepmother—I could see that; it's the countess spreads the story that her stepdaughter is so fond of her, for some object of her own. That's all false. Katya simply obeys her without question, and it seems as though there's some agreement between them about it. Four days ago, after all my observations, I made up my mind to carry out my intention, and this evening I did. My plan was to tell Katya everything, to confess everything, get her on our side, and so put a stop to it all. . . ."

"What! Tell her what, confess what?" Natasha asked uneasily.

"Everything, absolutely everything," answered Alyosha, "and thank God for inspiring me with the thought, but listen, listen! Four days ago I made up my mind to keep away from you both and stop it all myself. If I had been with you I should have been hesitating all the time. I should have been listening to you, and unable to decide on anything. By remaining alone, and putting myself in the position in which I was bound to repeat to myself every minute that I ought to stop it, that I *must* stop it, I screwed up my courage and—have stopped it! I meant to come back to you with the matter settled, and I've come with it settled!"

"What then? What? What has happened? Tell me quickly."

"It's very simple! I went straight to her, boldly and honestly. But I must first tell you one thing that happened just before, and struck me very much. Just before we set off father received a letter. I was just going into his study and was standing in the doorway. He did not see us. He was so much overcome by the letter that he talked to himself, uttered some exclamations, walked about the room quite beside himself, and suddenly burst out laughing, holding the letter in his hand. I was quite afraid to go in, and waited for a minute. Father was so delighted about something, so delighted; he spoke to me rather queerly; then suddenly broke off and told me to get ready at once, though it was not time for us to go. They had no one there to-day, only us two, and you were mistaken, Natasha, in thinking it was a party. You were told wrong."

"Oh, do keep to the point, Alyosha, please; tell me, how you told Katya."

"Luckily I was left for two hours alone with her. I simply told her that though they wanted to make a match between us, our marriage was impossible, that I had a great affection for her in my heart, and that she alone could save me. Then I told her everything. Only fancy, she knew nothing at all about our story, about you and me, Natasha. If only you could have seen how touched she was; at first she was quite scared. She turned quite white. I told her our whole story; how for my sake you'd abandoned your home; how we'd been living together, how harassed we were now, how afraid of everything, and that now we were appealing to her (I spoke in your name too, Natasha), that she would take our side, and tell her step-mother straight out that she wouldn't marry me; that that would be our one salvation, and that we had nothing to hope for from anyone else. She listened with such interest, such sympathy. What eyes she had at that moment! Her whole soul was in them. Her eyes are perfectly blue. She thanked me for not doubting her, and promised to do all she could to help us. Then she began asking about you ; said she wanted very much to know you, asked me to tell you that she loved you already like a sister, and that she hoped you would love her like a sister. And as soon as she heard I had not seen you for five days she began at once urging me to go to you."

Natasha was touched.

"And you could tell us first of your triumphs with some deaf princess ! Ach, Alyosha ! Alyosha ! " she exclaimed, looking at him reproachfully. "Well, tell me about Katya, was she happy, cheerful, when she said good-bye to you ? "

"Yes, she was glad that she was able to do something generous, but she was crying. For she loves me too, Natasha ! She confessed that she had begun to love me; that she sees hardly anyone, and that she was attracted by me long ago. She noticed me particularly because she sees cunning and deception all round her, and I seemed to her a sincere and honest person. She stood up and said : 'Well, God be with you, Alexey Petrovitch. And I was expecting . . .' She burst out crying and went away without saying what. We decided that to-morrow she should tell her stepmother that she won't have me, and that tomorrow I should tell my father everything and speak out boldly and firmly. She reproached me for not having told him before, saying that an honourable man ought not to be afraid of anything. She is such a noble-hearted girl. She doesn't like my father either. She says he's cunning and mercenary. I defended him ; she didn't believe me. If I don't succeed to-morrow with my father (and she feels convinced I shan't) then she advises me to get Princess K. to support me. Then no one would dare to oppose it. We promised to be like brother and sister to each other. Oh, if only you knew her story too, how unhappy she is, with what aversion she looks on her life with her stepmother, all her surroundings. She didn't tell me directly, as though she were afraid even of me, but I guessed it from some words, Natasha, darling ! How delighted she would be with you if she could see you ! And what a kind heart she has ! One is so at home with her ! You are created to be sisters and to love one another. I've been thinking so all along. And really I should like to bring you two together, and stand by admiring you. Don't imagine anything, Natasha, little one, and let me talk about her. I want to talk to you about her and to her about you. You know I love you more than anyone, more than her. ... You're everything to me!"

Natasha looked at him caressingly, and as it were mournfully, and did not speak. His words seemed like a caress, and yet a torment to her.

"And I saw how fine Katya was a long time ago, at least a fortnight," he went on. "I've been going to them every evening you see. As I went home I kept thinking of you both, kept comparing you."

"Which of us came off best?" asked Natasha, smiling.

"Sometimes you and sometimes she. But you were always the best in the long run. When I talk to her I always feel I become somehow better, cleverer, and somehow finer. But tomorrow, to-morrow will settle everything!"

"And aren't you sorry for her? She loves you, you know. You say you've noticed it yourself."

"Yes, I am, Natasha! But we'll all three love one another, and then..."

"And then 'good-bye'!" Natasha brought out quietly, as though to herself.

Alyosha looked at her in amazement.

But our conversation was suddenly interrupted in the most unexpected way. In the kitchen, which was at the same time the entry, we heard a slight noise as though some one had come in. A minute later Mavra opened the door and began nodding to Alyosha on the sly, beckoning to him. We all turned to her.

"Some one's asking for you. Come along," she said in a mysterious voice.

"Who can be asking for me now?" said Alyosha, looking at us in bewilderment. "I'm coming!"

In the kitchen stood his father's servant in livery. It appeared that the prince had stopped his carriage at Natasha's lodging on his way home, and had sent to inquire whether Alyosha were there. Explaining this the footman went away at once.

"Strange! This has never happened before," said Alyosha, looking at us in confusion. "What does it mean?"

Natasha looked at him uneasily. Suddenly Mavra opened the door again.

"Here's the prince himself!" she said in a hurried whisper, and at once withdrew.

Natasha turned pale and got up from her seat. Suddenly her eyes kindled. She stood leaning a little on the table, and looked in agitation towards the door, by which the uninvited visitor would enter.

"Natasha, don't be afraid! You're with me. I won't let you be insulted," whispered Alyosha, disconcerted but not overwhelmed. The door opened, and Prince Valkovsky in his own person appeared on the threshold.

CHAPTER II

HE took us all in in a rapid attentive glance. It was impossible to guess from this glance whether he had come as a friend or as an enemy. But I will describe his appearance minutely. He struck me particularly that evening.

I had seen him before. He was a man of forty-five, not more, with regular and strikingly handsome features, the expression of which varied according to circumstances; but it changed abruptly, completely, with extraordinary rapidity, passing from the most agreeable to the most surly or displeased expression, as though some spring were suddenly touched. The regular oval of his rather swarthy face, his superb teeth, his small, rather thin, beautifully chiselled lips, his rather long straight nose, his high forehead, on which no wrinkle could be discerned, his rather large grey eyes, made him handsome, and yet his face did not make a pleasant impression. The face repelled because its expression was not spontaneous, but always, as it were, artificial, deliberate, borrowed, and a blind conviction grew upon one that one would never read his real expression. Looking more carefully one began to suspect behind the invariable mask something spiteful, cunning, and intensely egoistic. One's attention was particularly caught by his fine eyes, which were grey and frank-looking. They were not completely under the control of his will, like his other features. He might want to look mild and friendly, but the light in his eyes was as it were twofold, and together with the mild friendly radiance there were flashes that were cruel, mistrustful, searching and spiteful. . . . He was rather tall, elegantly, rather slimly built, and looked strikingly young for his age. His soft dark brown hair had scarcely yet begun to turn grey. His ears, his hands, his feet were remarkably fine. It was preeminently the beauty of race. He was dressed with refined elegance and freshness but with some affectation of youth, which suited him, however. He looked like Alyosha's elder brother.

At any rate no one would have taken him for the father of so grown-up a son.

He went straight up to Natasha and said, looking at her firmly:

"My calling upon you at such an hour, and unannounced, is strange, and against all accepted rules. But I trust that you will believe I can at least recognize the eccentricity of my behaviour. I know, too, with whom I have to deal; I know that you are penetrating and magnanimous. Only give me ten minutes, and I trust that you will understand me and justify it."

He said all this courteously but with force, and, as it were, emphasis.

"Sit down," said Natasha, still unable to shake off her confusion and some alarm.

He made a slight bow and sat down.

"First of all allow me to say a couple of words to him," he said, indicating his son. "As soon as you had gone away, Alyosha, without waiting for me or even taking leave of us, the countess was informed that Katerina Fyodorovna was ill. She was hastening to her, but Katerina Fyodorovna herself suddenly came in distressed and violently agitated. She told us, forthwith, that she could not marry you. She said, too, that she was going into a nunnery, that you had asked for her help, and had told her that you loved Natalya Nikolaevna. This extraordinary declaration on the part of Katerina Fyodorovna, especially at such a moment, was of course provoked by the extreme strangeness of your explanation with her. She was almost beside herself, you can understand how shocked and alarmed I was. As I drove past just now I noticed a light in your window," he went on, addressing Natasha, "then an idea which had been haunting me for a long time gained such possession of me that I could not resist my first impulse, and came in to see you. With what object? I will tell you directly, but I beg you beforehand not to be surprised at a certain abruptness in my explanation. It is all so sudden . . ."

"I hope I shall understand and appreciate what you are going to say as I ought," answered Natasha, faltering.

The prince scrutinized her intently as though he were in a hurry to understand her through and through in one minute. "I am relying on your penetration too," he went on, "and I have ventured to come to you now just because I knew with whom I should have to deal. I have known you for a long time now, although I was at one time so unfair to you and did you injustice. Listen. You know that between me and your father there are disagreements of long standing. I don't justify myself; perhaps I have been more to blame in my treatment of him than I had supposed till now. But if so I was myself deceived. I am suspicious, and I recognize it. I am disposed to suspect evil rather than good: an unhappy trait, characteristic of a cold heart. But it is not my habit to conceal my failings. I believed in the past all that was said against you, and when you left your parents I was terror-stricken for Alyosha. But then I did not know you. The information I have gathered little by little has completely reassured me. I have watched you, studied you, and am at last convinced that my suspicions were groundless. I have learnt that you are cut off from your family. I know, too, that your father is utterly opposed to your marriage with my son, and the mere fact that, having such an influence, such power, one may say, over Alyosha, you have not hitherto taken advantage of that power to force him to marry you—that alone says much for you. And yet I confess it openly, I was firmly resolved at that time to hinder any possibility of your marriage with my son. I know I am expressing myself too straightforwardly, but at this moment straightforwardness on my part is what is most needed. You will admit that yourself when you have heard me to the end. Soon after you left your home I went away from Petersburg, but by then I had no further fears for Alyosha. I relied on your generous pride. I knew that you did not yourself want a marriage before the family dissensions were over, that you were unwilling to destroy the good understanding between Alyosha and me—for I should never have forgiven his marriage with you—that you were unwilling, too, to have it said of you that you were trying to catch a prince for a husband, and to be connected with our family. On the contrary, you showed a positive neglect of us, and were perhaps waiting for the moment when I should come to beg you to do us the honour to give my son your hand. Yet I obstinately remained your ill-wisher. I am not going to justify myself, but I will not conceal my reasons. Here they are. You have neither wealth nor position. Though I have property, we need more; our family is going downhill. We need money and connexions. Though Countess Zinaida Fyodorovna's stepdaughter has no connexions, she is very wealthy. If we delayed, suitors would turn up and carry her off. And such a chance was not to be lost. So, though

Alyosha is still so young, I decided to make a match for him. You see I am concealing nothing. You may look with scorn on a father who admits himself that from prejudice and mercenary motives he urged his son to an evil action: for to desert a generous-hearted girl who has sacrificed every one to him, and whom he has treated so badly, is an evil action. But I do not defend myself. My second reason for my son's proposed marriage was that the girl is highly deserving of love and respect. She is handsome, well-educated, has a charming disposition, and is very intelligent, though in many ways still a child. Alyosha has no character, he is thoughtless, extremely injudicious, and at two-and-twenty is a perfect child. He has at most one virtue, a good heart, positively a dangerous possession with his other failings. I have noticed for a long time that my influence over him was beginning to grow less; the impulsiveness and enthusiasm of youth are getting the upper hand, and even get the upper hand of some positive duties. I perhaps love him too fondly; but I am convinced that I am not a sufficient guide for him. And yet he must always be under some good influence. He has a submissive nature, weak and loving, liking better to love and to obey than to command. So he will be all his life. You can imagine how delighted I was at finding in Katerina Fyodorovna the ideal girl I should have desired for my son's wife. But my joy came too late. He was already under the sway of another influence that nothing could shake—yours. I have kept a sharp watch on him since I returned to Petersburg a month ago, and I notice with surprise a distinct change for the better in him. His irresponsibility and childishness are scarcely altered; but certain [generous feelings are stronger in him. He begins to be interested not only in playthings, but in what is lofty, noble, and more genuine. His ideas are queer, unstable, sometimes absurd; but the desire, the impulse, the feeling is finer, and that is the foundation of everything; and all this improvement in him is undoubtedly your work. You have remodelled him. I will confess the idea did occur to me, then, that you rather than anyone might secure his happiness. But I dismissed that idea, I did not wish to entertain it. I wanted to draw him away from you at any cost. I began to act, and thought I had gained my object. Only an hour ago I thought that the victory was mine. But what has just happened at the countess's has upset all my calculations at once, and what struck me most of all was something unexpected: the earnestness and constancy of Alyosha's devotion to you, the persistence and vitality of that devotion—which seemed strange in him. I repeat, you have remodelled him completely. I saw all at once that the change in him had gone further than I had supposed. He displayed to-day before my eyes a sudden proof of an intelligence of which I had not the slightest suspicion, and at the same time an extraordinary insight and subtlety of feeling. He chose the surest way of extricating himself from what he felt to be a difficult position. He touched and stirred the noblest chords in the human heart—the power of forgiving and repaying good for evil. He surrendered himself into the hands of the being he was injuring, and appealed to her for sympathy and help. He roused all the pride of the woman who already loved him by openly telling her she had a rival, and aroused at the same time her sympathy for her rival, and forgiveness and the promise of disinterested, sisterly affection for himself. To go into such explanations without rousing resentment and mortification—to do that is sometimes beyond the capacity of the subtlest and cleverest ; only pure young hearts under good guidance can do this. I am sure, Natalya Nikolaevna, that you took no part by word or suggestion in what he did to-day. You have perhaps only just heard of it from him. I am not mistaken. Am I ? "

" You are not mistaken," Natasha assented. Her face was glowing, and her eyes shone with a strange light as though of inspiration. Prince Valkovsky's eloquence was beginning to produce its effect. " I haven't seen Alyosha for five days," she added. " He thought of all this himself and carried it all out himself."

" Exactly so," said Prince Valkovsky, " but, in spite of that, all this surprising insight, all this decision and recognition of duty, this creditable manliness, in fact, is all the result of your influence on him. I had thought all this out and was reflecting on it on my way home, and suddenly felt able to reach a decision. The proposed match with the countess's stepdaughter is broken off, and cannot be renewed ; but if it were possible it could never come to pass. What if I have come to believe that you are the only woman that can make him happy, that you are his true guide, that you have already laid the foundations of his future happiness ! I have concealed nothing from you and I am concealing nothing now ; I think a great deal of a career, of money, of position, and even of rank in the service. With my intellect I recognize that a great deal of this is conventional, but I like these conventions, and am absolutely disinclined to run counter to them. But there are circumstances when other considerations have to come in, when everything cannot be judged by the same standard. . . . Besides, I love my son dearly. In short, I have come to the conclusion that Alyosha must not be parted from you, because without you he will be lost. And must I confess it ? I have perhaps been coming to this conclusion for the last month, and only now realize that the conclusion is a right one. Of course, I might have called on you to-morrow to tell you all this, instead of disturbing you at midnight. But my haste will show you, perhaps, how warmly, and still more how sincerely, I feel in the matter I am not a boy, and I could not at my age make up my mind to any step without thinking it over. Everything had been thought over and decided before I came here. But I feel that I may have to wait some time before you will be convinced of my sincerity. . . . But to come to the point ! Shall I explain now why I came here ? I came to do my duty to you, and solemnly, with the deepest respect, I beg you to make my son happy and to give him your hand. Oh, do not imagine that I have come like an angry father, who has been brought at last to forgive his children and graciously to consent to their happiness. No ! No ! You do me an injustice if you suppose I have any such idea. Do not imagine either that I reckon on your consent, relying on the sacrifices you have made for my son ; no again ! I am the first to declare aloud that he does not deserve you, and (he is candid and good) he will say the same himself. But that is not enough. It is not only this that has brought me here at such an hour . . . I have come here" (and he rose from his seat respectfully and with a certain solemnity), " I have come here to become your friend ! I know I have no right whatever to this, quite the contrary ! But—allow me to earn the right ! Let me hope . . . ! "

Making a respectful bow to Natasha he awaited her reply. I was watching him intently all the time he was speaking. He noticed it.

He made his speech coldly, with some display of eloquence, and in parts with a certain nonchalance. The tone of the whole speech was incongruous indeed with the impulse that had brought him to us at an hour so inappropriate for a first visit, especially under such circumstances. Some of his expressions were evidently premeditated, and in some arts of his long speech—which was strange from its very length—he seemed to be artificially assuming the air of an eccentric man struggling to conceal an overwhelming feeling under a show of humour, carelessness and jest. But I only made all these reflections afterwards; at the time the effect was different. He uttered the last words so sincerely, with so much feeling, with such an air of genuine respect for Natasha, that it conquered us all. There was actually the glimmer of a tear on his eyelashes. Natasha's generous heart was completely won. She, too, got up, and, deeply moved, held out her hand to him without a word. He took it and kissed it with tenderness and emotion. Alyosha was beside himself with rapture.

"What did I tell you, Natasha?" he cried. "You wouldn't believe me. You wouldn't believe in his being the noblest man in the world! You see, you see for yourself! . . ."

He rushed to his father, and hugged him warmly. The latter responded as warmly, but hastened to cut short the touching scene, as though ashamed to show his emotion.

"Enough," he said, and took his hat. "I must go. I asked you to give me ten minutes and I have been here a whole hour," he added, laughing. "But I leave you with impatient eagerness to see you again as soon as possible. Will you allow me to visit you as often as I can?"

"Yes, yes," answered Natasha, "as often as you can . . . I want to make haste . . . to be fond of you . . ." she added in embarrassment.

"How sincere you are, how truthful," said Prince Valkovsky, smiling at her words. "You won't be insincere even to be polite. But your sincerity is more precious than all artificial politeness. Yes! I recognize that it will take me a long, long time to deserve your love."

"Hush, don't praise me. . . . Enough," Natasha whispered in confusion. How delightful she was at that moment!

"So be it," Prince Valkovsky concluded. "I'll say only a couple of words of something practical. You cannot imagine how unhappy I am! Do you know I can't be with you to-morrow—neither to-morrow nor the day after. I received a letter this evening of such importance to me (requiring my presence on business at once) that I cannot possibly neglect it. I am leaving Petersburg to-morrow morning. Please do not imagine that I came to you to-night because I should have no time to-morrow or the day after. Of course you don't think so, but that is just an instance of my suspicious nature. Why should I fancy that you must think so ? Yes, my suspicious nature has often been a drawback to me in my life, and my whole misunderstanding with your family has perhaps been due to my unfortunate character ! . . . To-day is Tuesday. Wednesday, Thursday, and Friday I shall not be in Petersburg. I hope to return on Saturday for certain ; and I will be with you the same day. Tell me, may I come to you for the whole evening ? "

"Of course, of course !" cried Natasha. "On Saturday evening I shall expect you ! I shall expect you impatiently !"

"Ah, how happy I am ! I shall get to know you better and better ! But . . . I must go ! I cannot go without shaking hands with you though," he added, turning to me. "I beg your pardon ! We are all talking so disconnectedly. I have several times had the pleasure of meeting you, and once, indeed, we were introduced. I cannot take my leave without telling you how glad I should be to renew our acquaintance. . . ."

"We have met, it's true," I answered, taking his hand. "But I don't remember that we became acquainted."

"At Prince M.'s, last year."

"I beg your pardon, I've forgotten. But I assure you this time I shall not forget. This evening will always remain in my memory."

"Yes, you are right. I feel the same. I have long known that you have been a good and true friend to Natalya Nikolaevna and my son. I hope you three will admit me as a fourth. May I ?" he added, addressing Natasha.

"Yes, he is a true friend to us, and we must all hold together," Natasha answered with deep feeling.

Poor girl ! She was positively beaming with delight that the prince had not overlooked me. How she loved me !

"I have met many worshippers of your talent," Prince Valkovsky went on. "And I know two of your most sincere admirers—the countess, my dearest friend, and her stepdaughter, Katerina Fyodorovna Filimonov. They would so like to know you personally. Allow me to hope that you will let me have the pleasure of presenting you to those ladies."

"You are very flattering, though now I see so few people . . ."

"But give me your address ! Where do you live ? I shall do myself the pleasure . . ."

"I do not receive visitors, prince. At least not at present."

"But, though I have not deserved to be an exception . . . I . . ."

"Certainly, since you insist I shall be delighted. I live at —— Street, in Klugen's Buildings."

"Klugen's Buildings!" he cried, as though surprised at something. "What! Have you . . . lived there long?"

"No, not long," I answered, instinctively watching him. "I live at No. 44."

"Forty-four? You are living . . . alone?"

"Quite alone."

"O-oh! I ask you because I think I know the house. So much the better. . . . I will certainly come and see you, certainly! I shall have much to talk over with you and I look for great things from you. You can oblige me in many ways. You see I am beginning straight off by asking you a favour. But good-bye! Shake hands again!"

He shook my hand and Alyosha's, kissed Natasha's hand again and went out without suggesting that Alyosha should follow him.

We three remained overwhelmed. It had all happened so unexpectedly, so casually. We all felt that in one instant everything had changed, and that something new and unknown was beginning. Alyosha without a word sat down beside Natasha and softly kissed her hand. From time to time he peeped into her face as though to see what she would say.

"Alyosha, darling, go and see Katerina Fyodorovna to-morrow," she brought out at last.

"I was thinking of that myself," he said, "I shall certainly go."

"But perhaps it will be painful for her to see you. What's to be done?"

"I don't know, dear. I thought of that too. I'll look round. I shall see . . . then I'll decide. Well, Natasha, everything is changed for us now," Alyosha said, unable to contain himself.

She smiled and gave him a long, tender look.

"And what delicacy he has. He saw how poor your lodging is and not a word . . ."

"Of what?"

"Why . . . of your moving . . . or anything," he added reddening.

"Nonsense, Alyosha, why ever should he?"

"That's just what I say. He has such delicacy. And how

he praised you! I told you so ... I told you. Yes, he's capable of understanding and feeling anything! But he talked of me as though I were a baby; they all treat me like that. But I suppose I really am."

"You're a child, but you see further than any of us. You're good, Alyosha!"

"He said that my good heart would do me harm. How's that? I don't understand. But I say, Natasha, oughtn't I to make haste and go to him? I'll be with you as soon as it's light to-morrow."

"Yes, go, darling, go. You were right to think of it. And be sure to show yourself to him, do you hear? And come to-morrow as early as you can. You won't run away from me for five days now?" she added slyly, with a caressing glance.

We were all in a state of quiet, unruffled joy.

"Are you coming with me, Vanya?" cried Alyosha as he went off.

"No, he'll stay a little. I've something more to say to you, Vanya. Mind, quite early to-morrow."

"Quite early. Good-night, Mavra."

Mavra was in great excitement. She had listened to all the prince said, she had overheard it all, but there was much she had not understood. She was longing to ask questions, and make surmises. But meantime she looked serious, and even proud. She, too, realized that much was changed.

We remained alone. Natasha took my hand, and for some time was silent, as though seeking for something to say.

"I'm tired," she said at last in a weak voice. "Listen, are you going to *them* to-morrow?"

"Of course."

"Tell mamma, but don't speak to *him*."

"I never speak of you to him, anyway."

"Of course; he'll find out without that. But notice what he says. How he takes it. Good heavens, Vanya, will he really curse me for this marriage? No, impossible."

"The prince will have to make everything right," I put in hurriedly. "They must be reconciled and then everything will go smoothly."

"My God! If that could only be! If that could only be!" she cried imploringly.

"Don't worry yourself, Natasha, everything will come right. Everything points to it."

She looked at me intently.

"Vanya, what do you think of the prince?"

"If he was sincere in what he said, then to my thinking he's a really generous man."

"Sincere in what he said? What does that mean? Surely he couldn't have been speaking insincerely?"

"I agree with you," I answered. "Then some idea did occur to her" I thought. "That's strange!"

"You kept looking at him . . . so intently. . . ."

"Yes, I thought him rather strange."

"I thought so too. He kept on talking so . . . my dear, I'm tired. You know, you'd better be going home. And come to me to-morrow as early as you can after seeing them. And one other thing: it wasn't rude of me to say that I wanted to get fond of him, was it?"

"No, why rude?"

"And not . . . stupid? You see it was as much as to say that so far I didn't like him."

"On the contrary, it was very good, simple, spontaneous. You looked so beautiful at that moment! He's stupid if he doesn't understand that with his aristocratic breeding!"

"You seem as though you were angry with him, Vanya. But how horrid I am, how suspicious, and vain! Don't laugh at me; I hide nothing from you, you know. Ah, Vanya, my dear! If I am unhappy again, if more trouble comes you'll be here beside me, I know; perhaps you'll be the only one! How can I repay you for everything! Don't curse me ever, Vanya!"

Returning home, I undressed at once and went to bed. My room was as dark and damp as a cellar. Many strange thoughts and sensations were hovering in my mind, and it was long before I could get to sleep.

But how one man must have been laughing at us that moment as he fell asleep in his comfortable bed—that is, if he thought us worth laughing at! Probably he didn't!

CHAPTER III

At ten o'clock next morning as I was coming out of my lodgings, hurrying off to the Ichmenyevs in Vassilyevsky Island, and meaning to go from them to Natasha, I suddenly came upon my yesterday's visitor, Smith's grandchild, at the door. She was coming to see me. I don't know why, but I remember I was awfully pleased to see her. I had hardly had time to get a good look at her the day before, and by daylight she surprised me more than ever. And, indeed, it would have been difficult to have found a stranger or more original creature—in appearance, anyway. With her flashing black eyes, which looked somehow foreign, her thick, dishevelled, black hair, and her mute, fixed, enigmatic gaze, the little creature might well have attracted the notice of anyone who passed her in the street. The expression in her eyes was particularly striking. There was the light of intelligence in them, and at the same time an inquisitorial mistrust, even suspicion. Her dirty old frock looked even more hopelessly tattered by daylight. She seemed to me to be suffering from some wasting, chronic disease that was gradually and relentlessly destroying her. Her pale, thin face had an unnatural sallow, bilious tinge. But in spite of all the ugliness of poverty and illness, she was positively pretty. Her eyebrows were strongly marked, delicate and beautiful. Her broad, rather low brow was particularly beautiful, and her lips were exquisitely formed with a peculiar proud bold line, but they were pale and colourless.

"Ah, you again!" I cried. "Well, I thought you'd come. Come in!"

She came in, stepping through the doorway slowly just as before, and looking about her mistrustfully. She looked carefully round the room where her grandfather had lived, as though noting how far it had been changed by another inmate.

"Well, the grandchild is just such another as the grandfather," I thought. "Is she mad, perhaps?"

She still remained mute; I waited.

"For the books!" she whispered at last, dropping her eyes.

"Oh yes, your books; here they are, take then! I've been keeping them on purpose for you."

She looked at me inquisitively, and her mouth worked strangely as though she would venture on a mistrustful smile. But the effort at a smile passed and was replaced by the same severe and enigmatic expression.

"Grandfather didn't speak to you of me, did he?" she asked, scanning me ironically from head to foot.

"No, he didn't speak of you, but . . ."

"Then how did you know I should come? Who told you?" she asked, quickly interrupting me.

"I thought your grandfather couldn't live alone, abandoned by every one. He was so old and feeble; I thought some one must be looking after him. . . . Here are your books, take them. Are they your lesson-books?"

"No."

"What do you want with them, then?"

"Grandfather taught me when I used to see him. . . ."

"Why did you leave off coming then?"

"Afterwards . . . I didn't come. I was ill," she added, as though defending herself.

"Tell me, have you a home, a father and mother?"

She frowned suddenly and looked at me, seeming almost scared. Then she looked down, turned in silence and walked softly out of the room without deigning to reply, just as she had done the day before. I looked after her in amazement. But she stood still in the doorway.

"What did he die of?" she asked me abruptly, turning slightly towards me with exactly the same movement and gesture as the day before, when she had asked after Azorka, stopping on her way out with her face to the door.

I went up to her and began rapidly telling her. She listened mutely and with curiosity, her head bowed and her back turned to me. I told her, too, how the old man had mentioned Sixth Street as he was dying.

"I imagined," I added, "that some one dear to him lived there, and that's why I expected some one would come to inquire after him. He must have loved you, since he thought of you at the last moment.

"No," she whispered, almost unconsciously it seemed; "he didn't love me."

She was strangely moved. As I told my story I bent down and looked into her face. I noticed that she was making a great effort to suppress her emotion, as though too proud to let me see it. She turned paler and paler and bit her lower lip. But what struck me especially was the strange thumping of her heart. It throbbed louder and louder, so that one could hear it two or three paces off, as in cases of aneurism. I thought she would suddenly burst into tears as she had done the day before; but she controlled herself.

"And where is the fence?"

"What fence?"

"That he died under."

"I will show you . . . when we go out. But, tell me, what do they call you?"

"No need to . . ."

"No need to—what?"

"Never mind . . . it doesn't matter. . . . They don't call me anything," she brought out jerkily, seeming annoyed, and she moved to go away. I stopped her.

"Wait a minute, you queer little girl! Why, I only want to help you. I felt so sorry for you when I saw you crying in the corner yesterday. I can't bear to think of it. Besides, your grandfather died in my arms, and no doubt he was thinking of you when he mentioned Sixth Street, so it's almost as if he left you in my care. I dream of him. . . . Here, I've kept those books for you, but you're such a wild little thing, as though you were afraid of me. You must be very poor and an orphan, perhaps living among strangers; isn't that so?"

I did my utmost to conciliate her, and I don't know how it was she attracted me so much. There was something besides pity in my feeling for her. Whether it was the mysteriousness of the whole position, the impression made on me by Smith, or my own fantastic mood—I can't say; but something drew me irresistibly to her. My words seemed to touch her. She bent on me a strange look, not severe now, but soft and deliberate, then looked down again as though pondering.

"Elena," she brought out unexpectedly, and in an extremely low voice.

"That's your name, Elena?"

"Yes. . . ."

"Well, will you come and see me?"

"I can't. . . . I don't know. . . . I will," she whispered, as though pondering and struggling with herself.

At that moment a clock somewhere struck.

She started, and with an indescribable look of heartsick anguish she whispered:

"What time was that?"

"It must have been half-past ten."

She gave a cry of alarm.

"Oh, dear!" she cried, and was making away. But again I stopped her in the passage.

"I won't let you go like that," I said. "What are you afraid of? Are you late?"

"Yes, yes. I came out secretly. Let me go! She'll beat

me," she cried out, evidently saying more than she meant to, and breaking away from me.

"Listen, and don't rush away; you're going to Vassilyevsky Island, so am I, to Thirteenth Street. I'm late, too. I'm going to take a cab. Will you come with me? I'll take you. You'll get there quicker than on foot. . . ."

"You can't come back with me, you can't," she cried, even more panic-stricken. Her features positively worked with terror at the thought that I might come to the house where she was living.

"But I tell you I'm going to Thirteenth Street on business of my own. I'm not coming to your home! I won't follow you. We shall get there sooner with a cab. Come along!"

We hurried downstairs. I hailed the first driver I met with a miserable droshky. It was evident Elena was in great haste, since she consented to get in with me. What was most baffling was that I positively did not dare to question her. She flung up her arms and almost leapt off the droshky when I asked her who it was at home she was so afraid of. "What is the mystery?" I thought.

It was very awkward for her to sit on the droshky. At every jolt to keep her balance she clutched at my coat with her left hand, a dirty, chapped little hand. In the other hand she held her books tightly. One could see that those books were very precious to her. As she recovered her balance she happened to show her leg, and to my immense astonishment I saw that she had no stockings, nothing but torn shoes. Though I had made up my mind not to question her, I could not restrain myself again.

"Have you really no stockings?" I asked. "How can you go about barefoot in such wet weather and when it's so cold?"

"No," she answered abruptly.

"Good heavens! But you must be living with some one! You ought to ask some one to lend you stockings when you go out."

"I like it best. . . ."

"But you'll get ill. You'll die!"

"Let me die."

She evidently did not want to answer and was angry at my question.

"Look! this was where he died," I said, pointing out the house where the old man had died.

She looked intently, and suddenly turning with an imploring look, said to me :

"For God's sake don't follow me. But I'll come, I'll come again ! As soon as I've a chance I'll come."

"Very well. I've told you already I won't follow you. But what are you afraid of ? You must be unhappy in some way It makes me sad to look at you."

"I'm not afraid of anyone," she replied, with a note of irritation in her voice.

"But you said just now ' she'll beat me ! ' "

"Let her beat me ! " she answered, and her eyes flashed. "Let her, let her ! " she repeated bitterly, and her upper lip quivered and was lifted disdainfully.

At last we reached Vassilyevsky Island. She stopped the droshky at the beginning of Sixth Street, and jumped off, looking anxiously round.

"Drive away ! I'll come, I'll come," she repeated, terribly uneasy, imploring me not to follow her. "Go on, make haste, make haste ! "

I drove on. But after driving a few yards further along the embankment I dismissed the cab, and going back to Sixth Street ran quickly across the road. I caught sight of her; she had not got far away yet, though she was walking quickly, and continually looking about her. She even stopped once or twice to look more carefully whether I were following her or not. But I hid in a handy gateway, and she did not see me. She walked on. I followed her, keeping on the other side of the street.

My curiosity was roused to the utmost. Though I did not intend to follow her in, I felt I must find which house she lived in, to be ready in case of emergency. I was overcome by a strange, oppressive sensation, not unlike the impression her grandfather had made on me when Azorka died in the restaurant.

CHAPTER IV

WE walked a long way, as far as Little Avenue. She was almost running. At last she went into a little shop. I stood still and waited   " Surely she doesn't live at the shop," I thought.

She did in fact come out a minute later, but without the books. Instead of the books she had an earthenware cup in her hand.

Going on a little further she went in at the gateway of an unattractive-looking house. It was an old stone house of two storeys, painted a dirty-yellow colour, and not large. In one of the three windows on the ground floor there was a miniature red coffin—as a sign that a working coffin-maker lived there. The windows of the upper storey were extremely small and perfectly square with dingy-green broken panes, through which I caught a glimpse of pink cotton curtains. I crossed the road, went up to the house, and read on an iron plate over the gate, " Mme. Bubnov."

But I had hardly deciphered the inscription when suddenly I heard a piercing, female scream, followed by shouts of abuse in Mme. Bubnov's yard. I peeped through the gate. On the wooden steps of the house stood a stout woman, dressed like a working woman with a kerchief on her head, and a green shawl. Her face was of a revolting purplish colour. Her little, puffy, bloodshot eyes were gleaming with spite. It was evident that she was not sober, though it was so early in the day. She was shrieking at poor Elena, who stood petrified before her with the cup in her hand. A dishevelled female, painted and rouged, peeped from the stairs behind the purple-faced woman.

A little later a door opened on the area steps leading to the basement, and a poorly dressed, middle-aged woman of modest and decent appearance came out on the steps, probably attracted by the shouting. The other inhabitants of the basement, a decrepit-looking old man and a girl, looked out from the half-opened door. A big, hulking peasant, probably the porter, stood still in the middle of the yard with the broom in his hand, looking lazily at the scene.

" Ah, you damned slut, you bloodsucker, you louse ! " squealed the woman, letting off at one breath all her store of abuse, for the most part without commas or stops, but with a sort of gasp. " So this is how you repay me for my care of you, you ragged wench ! She was just sent for some cucumbers and off she slipped ! My heart told me she'd slip off when I sent her out ! My heart ached it did ! Only last night I all but pulled her hair out for it, and here she runs off again to-day. And where have you to go, you trollop ? Where have you to go ! Who do you go to, you damned mummy, you staring viper, you poisonous vermin, who, who is it ? Speak, you rotten scum, or I'll choke you where you stand ! "

And the infuriated woman flew at the poor girl, but seeing the woman looking at her from the basement steps, she suddenly checked herself, and addressing her, squealed more shrilly than ever, waving her arms as though calling her to witness the monstrous crimes of her luckless victim.

"Her mother's hopped the twig! You all know, good neighbours, she's left alone in the world. I saw she was on your hands, poor folks as you are, though you'd nothing to eat for yourselves. There, thought I, for St. Nikolay's sake I'll put myself out and take the orphan. So I took her; and would you believe it, here I've been keeping her these two months, and upon my word she's been sucking my blood and wearing me to a shadow, the leech, the rattlesnake, the obstinate limb of Satan. You may beat her, or you may let her alone, she won't speak. She might have a mouth full of water, the way she holds her tongue! She breaks my heart holding her tongue! What do you take yourself for, you saucy slut, you green monkey? If it hadn't been for me you'd have died of hunger in the street. You ought to be ready to wash my feet and drink the water, you monster, you black French poker! You'd have been done for but for me!"

"But why are you upsetting yourself so, Anna Trifonovna? How's she vexed you again?" respectfully inquired the woman who had been addressed by the raving fury.

"You needn't ask, my good soul, that you needn't. I don't like people going against me! I am one for having things my own way, right or wrong—I'm that sort! She's almost sent me to my grave this morning! I sent her to the shop to get some cucumbers, and it was three hours before she was back. I'd a feeling in my heart when I sent her—it ached it did, didn't it ache! Where's she been? Where did she go? What protectors has she found for herself? As though I'd not been a good friend to her. Why, I forgave her slut of a mother a debt of fourteen roubles, buried her at my own expense, and took the little devil to bring up, you know that, my dear soul, you know it yourself! Why, have I no rights over her, after that? She should feel it, but instead of feeling it she goes against me! I wished for her good. I wanted to put her in a muslin frock, the dirty slut! I bought her boots at the Gostiny Dvor, and decked her out like a peacock, a sight for a holiday! And would you believe it, good friends! two days later she'd torn up the dress, torn it into rags, and that's how she goes about, that's how she goes about! And what do you think, she tore it on purpose—I wouldn't tell a lie, I saw it myself; as much as to say she would go in rags, she wouldn't wear muslin! Well, I paid her out! I did give her a drubbing! Then I called in the doctor afterwards and had to pay him, too. If I throttled you, you vermin, I should be quit with not touching milk for a week; that would be penance enough for strangling you. I made her scrub the floor for a punishment; and what do you think, she scrubbed and scrubbed, the jade! It vexed me to see her scrubbing. Well, thought I, she'll run away from me now. And I'd scarcely thought it when I looked round and off she'd gone, yesterday. You heard how I beat her for it yesterday, good friends. I made my arms ache, I took away her shoes and stockings—she won't go off barefoot, thought I; yet she gave me the slip to-day, too! Where have you been? Speak! Who have you been complaining of me to, you nettle-seed? Who have you been telling tales to? Speak, you gipsy, you foreign mask! Speak!"

And in her frenzy she rushed at the little girl, who stood petrified with horror, clutched her by the hair, and flung her on the ground. The cup with the cucumbers in it was dashed aside and broken. This only increased the drunken fury's rage. She beat her victim about the face and the head; but Elena remained obstinately mute; not a sound, not a cry, not a complaint escaped her, even under the blows.

I rushed into the yard, almost beside myself with indignation, and went straight to the drunken woman.

"What are you about? How dare you treat a poor orphan like that?" I cried, seizing the fury by her arm.

"What's this? Why, who are you?" she screamed, leaving Elena, and putting her arms akimbo. "What do you want in my house?"

"To tell you you're a heartless woman," I cried. "How dare you bully a poor child like that? She's not yours. I've just heard that she's only adopted, a poor orphan."

"Lord Jesus!" cried the fury. "But who are you, poking your nose in. Did you come with her, eh? I'll go straight to the police-captain! Andrey Timofeyitch himself treats me like a lady. Why, is it to see you she goes, eh? Who is it? He's come to make an upset in another person's house. Police!"

And she flew at me, brandishing her fists But at that instant we heard a piercing, inhuman shriek. I looked. Elena, who had been standing as though unconscious, uttering a strange, unnatural scream, fell with a thud on the ground, writhing in awful convulsions. Her face was working. She was in an epileptic fit. The dishevelled female and the woman from the basement ran, lifted her up, and hurriedly carried her up the steps.

"She may choke for me, the damned slut!" the woman shrieked after her. "That's the third fit this month! . . . Get off, you pickpocket"; and she rushed at me again. "Why are you standing there, porter? What do you get your wages for?"

"Get along, get along! Do you want a smack on the head?" the porter boomed out lazily, apparently only as a matter of form. "Two's company and three's none. Make your bow and take your hook!"

There was no help for it. I went out at the gate, feeling that my interference had been useless. But I was boiling with indignation. I stood on the pavement facing the gateway, and looked through the gate. As soon as I had gone out the woman rushed up the steps, and the porter having done his duty vanished. Soon after, the woman who had helped to carry up Elena hurried down the steps on the way to the basement. Seeing me she stood still and looked at me with curiosity. Her quiet, good-natured face encouraged me. I went back into the yard and straight up to her.

"Allow me to ask," I said, "who is that girl and what is that horrible woman doing with her? Please don't imagine that I ask simply from curiosity. I've met the girl, and owing to special circumstances I am much interested in her."

"If you're interested in her you'd better take her home or find some place for her than let her come to ruin here," said the woman with apparent reluctance, making a movement to get away from me.

"But if you don't tell me, what can I do? I tell you I know nothing about her. I suppose that's Mme. Bubnov herself, the woman of the house?"

"Yes."

"Then how did the girl fall into her hands? Did her mother die here?"

"Oh, I can't say. It's not our business."

And again she would have moved away.

"But please do me a kindness. I tell you it's very interesting to me. Perhaps I may be able to do something. Who is the girl? What was her mother? Do you know?"

"She looked like a foreigner of some sort; she lived down below with us; but she was ill; she died of consumption."

"Then she must have been very poor if she shared a room in the basement?"

"Ough! she was poor! My heart was always aching for her. We simply live from hand to mouth, yet she owed us six roubles in the five months she lived with us. We buried her, too. My husband made the coffin."

"How was it then that woman said she'd buried her?"

"As though she'd buried her!"

"And what was her surname?"

"I can't pronounce it, sir. It's difficult. It must have been German."

"Smith?"

"No, not quite that. Well, Anna Trifonovna took charge of the orphan, to bring her up, she says. But it's not the right thing at all. . . ."

"I suppose she took her for some object?"

"She's a woman who's up to no good," answered the woman, seeming to ponder and hesitate whether to speak or not. "What is it to us? We're outsiders."

"You'd better keep a check on your tongue," I heard a man's voice say behind us.

It was a middle-aged man in a dressing-gown with a full-coat over the dressing-gown, who looked like an artisan, the woman's husband.

"She's no call to be talking to you, sir; it's not our business," he said, looking askance at me. "And you go in. Good-bye, sir; we're coffin-makers. If you ever need anything in our way we shall be pleased . . . but apart from that we've nothing to say. . . ."

I went out, musing, and greatly excited. I could do nothing, but I felt that it was hard for me to leave it like this. Some words dropped by the coffin-maker's wife revolted me particularly. There was something wrong here; I felt that.

I was walking away, looking down and meditating, when suddenly a sharp voice called me by my surname. I looked up. Before me stood a man who had been drinking and was almost staggering, dressed fairly neatly, though he had a shabby overcoat and a greasy cap. His face was very familiar. I looked more closely at it. He winked at me and smiled ironically.

"Don't you know me?"

CHAPTER V

"AH, why it's you, Masloboev!" I cried, suddenly recognizing him as an old schoolfellow who had been at my provincial gymnasium. "Well, this is a meeting!"

"Yes, a meeting indeed! We've not met for six years. Or rather, we have met, but your excellency hasn't deigned to look at me. To be sure, you're a general, a literary one that is, eh! ..."

He smiled ironically as he said it.

"Come, Masloboev, old boy, you're talking nonsense!" I interrupted. "Generals look very different from me even if they are literary ones, and besides, let me tell you, I certainly do remember having met you twice in the street. But you obviously avoided me. And why should I go up to a man if I see he's trying to avoid me? And do you know what I believe? If you weren't drunk you wouldn't have called to me even now. That's true, isn't it? Well, how are you? I'm very, very glad to have met you, my boy."

"Really? And I'm not compromising you by my ... 'unconventional' appearance? But there's no need to ask that. It's not a great matter; I always remember what a jolly chap you were, old Vanya. Do you remember you took a thrashing for me? You held your tongue and didn't give me away, and, instead of being grateful, I jeered at you for a week afterwards. You're a blessed innocent! Glad to see you, my dear soul!" (We kissed each other.) "How many years I've been pining in solitude—'From morn till night, from dark till light'; but I've not forgotten old times. They're not easy to forget. But what have you been doing, what have you been doing?"

"I? Why, I'm pining in solitude, too."

He gave me a long look, full of the deep feeling of a man slightly inebriated; though he was a very good-natured fellow at any time.

"No, Vanya, your case is not like mine," he brought out at last in a tragic tone. "I've read it, Vanya, you know, I've read it, I've read it! . . . But I say, let us have a good talk! Are you in a hurry?"

"I am in a hurry, and I must confess I'm very much upset about something. I'll tell you what's better. Where do you live?"

"I'll tell you. But that's not better; shall I tell you what is better?"

"Why, what?"

"Why, this, do you see?" and he pointed out to me a sign a few yards from where we were standing. "You see, confectioner's and restaurant; that is simply an eating-house, but it's a good place. I tell you it's a decent place, and the vodka—there's no word for it! It's come all the way from Kieff on foot. I've tasted it, many a time I've tasted it, I know; and they wouldn't dare offer me poor stuff here. They know Filip Filippitch. I'm Filip Filippitch, you know. Eh? You make a face? No, let me have my say. Now it's a quarter past eleven; I've just looked. Well, at twenty-five to twelve exactly I'll let you go. And in the meantime we'll drain the flowing bowl. Twenty minutes for an old friend. Is that right?"

"If it will really be twenty minutes, all right; because, my dear chap, I really am busy. . . ."

"Well, that's a bargain. But I tell you what. Two words to begin with: you don't look cheerful . . . as though you were put out about something, is that so?"

"Yes."

"I guessed it. I am going in for the study of physiognomy, you know; it's an occupation, too. So, come along, we'll have a talk. In twenty minutes I shall have time in the first place to sip the cup that cheers and to toss off a glass of birch wine, and another of orange bitters, then a *parfait amour*, and anything else I can think of. I drink, old man! I'm good for nothing except on a holiday before service. But don't you drink. I want you just as you are. Though if you did drink you'd betray a peculiar nobility of soul. Come along! We'll have a little chat and then part for another ten years. I'm not fit company for you, friend Vanya!"

"Don't chatter so much, but come along. You shall have twenty minutes and then let me go."

To get to the eating-house we had to go up a wooden staircase of two flights, leading from the street to the second storey.

But on the stairs we suddenly came upon two gentlemen, very drunk. Seeing us they moved aside, staggering.

One of them was a very young and youthful-looking lad, with an exaggeratedly stupid expression of face, with only a faint trace of moustache, and no beard. He was dressed like a dandy, but looked ridiculous, as though he were dressed up in some one else's clothes. He had expensive-looking rings on his fingers, an expensive pin in his tie, and his hair was combed up into a crest which looked particularly absurd. He kept smiling and sniggering. His companion, a thick-set, corpulent, bald-headed man of fifty, with a puffy, drunken, pock-marked face, and a nose like a button, was dressed rather carelessly, though he, too, had a big pin in his tie and wore spectacles. The expression of his face was malicious and sensual. His nasty, spiteful and suspicious-looking little eyes were lost in fat and seemed to be peeping through chinks. Evidently they both knew Masloboev, but the fat man made a momentary grimace of vexation on seeing us, while the young man subsided into a grin of obsequious sweetness. He even took off his cap. He was wearing a cap.

"Excuse us, Filip Filippitch," he muttered, gazing tenderly at him.

"What's up?"

"I beg your pardon—I'm. . . ." (He flicked at his collar.) "Mitroshka's in there. So it seems he's a scoundrel, Filip Filippitch."

"Well, what's the matter?"

"Why, it seems so. . . . Why, last week he" (here he nodded towards his companion) "got his mug smeared with sour cream in a shocking place, all through that chap Mitroshka . . khe-e."

His companion, looking annoyed, poked him with his elbow.

"You should come with us, Filip Filippitch. We'd empty a half-dozen. May we hope for your company?"

"No, my dear man, I can't now," answered Masloboev, "I've business."

"Khe-e! And I've a little business, too . . . concerning you. . . ."

Again his companion nudged him with his elbow.

"Afterwards! Afterwards!"

Masloboev was unmistakably trying not to look at them. But no sooner had we entered the outer room, along the whole length of which ran a fairly clean counter, covered with eatables, pies, tarts, and decanters of different coloured liqueurs, when Masloboev drew me into a corner and said :

"The young fellow's Sizobryuhov, the son of the celebrated corn-dealer ; he came in for half a million when his father died, and now he's having a good time. He went to Paris, and there he got through no end of money. He'd have spent all there, perhaps, but he came in for another fortune when his uncle died, and he came back from Paris. So he's getting through the rest of it here. In another year he'll be sending the hat round. He's as stupid as a goose. He goes about in the best restaurants and in cellars and taverns, and with actresses, and he's trying to get into the hussars—he's just applied for a commission. The other, the old fellow, Arhipov, is something in the way of a merchant, too, or an agent ; he had something to do with government contracts, too. He's a beast, a rogue, and now he's a pal of Sizobryuhov's. He's a Judas and a Falstaff, both at once ; he's twice been made bankrupt, and he's a disgusting, sensual brute, up to all sorts of tricks. I know one criminal affair in that line that he was mixed up in ; but he managed to get off. For one thing, I'm very glad I met him here ; I was on the lookout for him. . . . He's plucking Sizobryuhov now, of course. He knows all sorts of queer places, which is what makes him of use to young fellows like that. I've had a grudge against him for ever so long. Mitroshka's got a bone to pick with him, too —that dashing-looking fellow with the gipsy face in the smart tunic, standing by the window. He deals in horses ; he's known to all the hussars about here. I tell you, he's such a clever rogue that he'll make a false bank-note before your very eyes, and pass it off upon you though you've seen it. He wears a tunic, though it's a velvet one, and looks like a Slavophile (though I think it suits him) ; but put him into a fine dress-coat, or something like it, and take him to the English club and call him the great landowner, Count Barabanov ; he'll pass for a count for two hours, play whist, and talk like a count, and they'll never guess ; he'll take them in. He'll come to a bad end. Well, Mitroshka's got a great grudge against the fat man, for Mitroshka's hard up just now. Sizobryuhov used to be very thick with him, but the fat man's carried him off before Mitroshka had time to fleece him. If they met in the eating-house just now there must be something up. I know something about it, too, and can guess what it is, for Mitroshka and no one else told me that they'd be here, and be hanging about these parts after some mischief. I want to take advantage of Mitroshka's hatred for Arhipov, for I have my own reasons, and indeed I came here chiefly on that account. I don't want to let Mitroshka see, and don't you keep looking at him, but when we go out he's sure to come up of himself and tell me what I want to know. . . . Now come along, Vanya, into the other room, do you see ? Now, Stepan," he said, addressing the waiter, " you understand what I want."

" Yes, sir."

" And you'll bring it."

" Yes, sir."

" Mind you do. Sit down, Vanya. Why do you keep looking at me like that ? I see you're looking at me. Are you surprised ? Don't be surprised. Anything may happen to a man, even what he's never dreamed of . . . especially in the days when . . . well, in the days when we used to cram Cornelius Nepos together. And, Vanya, be sure of one thing : though Masloboev may have strayed from the true path his heart is still unchanged, it's only circumstances that have altered. Though I may be in the soot I'm no dirtier than the rest. I set up for being a doctor, and I trained as a teacher of Russian literature, and I wrote an article on Gogol, and thought of going to the gold-diggings, and meant to get married. A living soul longs for something sweet in life, and *she* consented, though I was so poor I had nothing to tempt a cat with. I was on the point of borrowing a pair of good boots for the marriage ceremony, for mine had been in holes for eighteen months. . . . But I didn't get married. She married a teacher, and I went as a counting-house clerk, not a commercial counting-house, but just a counting-house. But then the tune changed. Years have rolled by, and though I'm not in the service I make enough to jog along : I take bribes without ruth and yet stand firm for the truth. I hunt with the hounds and I run with the hare. I have principles. I know, for instance, that one can't fight single-handed, and I mind my own business. My business is chiefly in the confidential line, you understand."

" You're not some sort of detective, are you ? "

" No, not exactly a detective, but I do take up jobs, partly professionally, and partly on my own account. It's this way, Vanya : I drink vodka. But as I haven't drunk my wits away, I know what lies before me. My time is past ; there's no washing a black nag white. One thing I will say : if the man in me were not echoing still I should not have come up to you to-day, Vanya. You're right, I'd met you and seen you before, and many a time I longed to speak, but still I didn't dare, and put it off. I'm not worthy of you. And you were right, Vanya, when you said that I spoke this time only because I was drunk; and though this is all awful rot we'll finish with me now. We'd better talk of you. Well, my dear soul, I've read it! I've read it through. I'm talking of your first-born. When I read it, I almost became a respectable man, my friend. I was almost becoming one, but I thought better of it, and preferred to remain a disreputable man. So there it is. . . ."

And he said much more. He got more and more drunk, and became very maudlin, almost lachrymose. Masloboev had always been a capital fellow, but cunning, and as it were precocious; he had been a shrewd, crafty, artful dodger from his school-days upwards, but he really had a good heart; he was a lost man. Among Russians there are many such. They often have great abilities, but everything seems topsy-turvy in them, and what's more they are quite capable of acting against their conscience in certain cases through weakness, and not only come to ruin, but know beforehand that they are on the road to ruin. Masloboev, for instance, was drowning in vodka.

"One more word now, friend," he went on. "I heard what a noise your fame made at first; I read several criticisms on you afterwards. (I really did; you imagine I never read anything.) I met you afterwards in shabby boots, in the mud without goloshes, with a battered hat, and I drew my own conclusions. You're going in for being a journalist now, eh?"

"Yes, Masloboev."

"Joined the literary hacks, I suppose?"

"That's about it."

"Well, I tell you what then, my boy: drinking's better. Here I drink; I lie on the sofa (and I have a capital sofa with springs), and I imagine myself Homer, or Dante, or some Frederick Barbarossa—one can fancy what one likes, you know, but you can't fancy yourself a Dante, or a Frederick Barbarossa, in the first place because you want to be yourself, and secondly, because all wishing is forbidden you; for you're a literary hack. I have fancy, but you have reality. Listen, tell me openly, straightforwardly, speaking as a brother (if you won't you'll offend and humiliate me for ten years), don't you want money? I've plenty. Oh, don't make faces. Take some of it, pay off the entrepreneurs, throw off the yoke, then, when you're secure of a year's living, settle down to your cherished idea, write a great book! Eh? What do you say?"

"Listen, Masloboev! I appreciate your brotherly offer, but I can't make any answer at present, and the reason why is a long story. There are circumstances. But I promise that I'll tell you everything afterwards, like a brother. I thank you for your offer. I promise that I'll come to you, and I'll come often. But this is what I want to tell you. You have been open with me, and so I've made up my mind to ask your advice, especially as I believe you're first-rate in such affairs."

I told him the whole story of Smith and his granddaughter, beginning with the scene in the restaurant. Strange to say, as I told my tale it seemed to me from his eyes that he knew something about the story. I asked him.

"No, not exactly," he answered, "though I had heard something about Smith, a story of some old man dying in a restaurant. But I really do know something about Mme. Bubnov. Only two months ago I got some money out of that lady. *Je prends mon bien où je le trouve*, and that's the only respect in which I am like Molière. Though I squeezed a hundred roubles out of her, I vowed at the time I'd wring another five hundred out of her before I'd done. She's a nasty woman! She's in an unmentionable line of business. That wouldn't matter, but sometimes it goes too far. Don't imagine I'm a Don Quixote, please. The point is that I may make a very good thing of it, and when I met Sizobryuhov half an hour ago I was awfully pleased. Sizobryuhov was evidently brought here, and the fat man brought him, and as I know what the fat man's special trade is, I conclude . . . oh, well, I'll show him up! I'm very glad I heard from you about that girl; it's another clue for me. I undertake all sorts of private jobs, you know, and I know some queer people! I investigated a little affair for a prince not long ago, an affair, I tell you, one wouldn't have expected from that prince. Or would you care to hear another story about a married woman? You come and see me, old man, and I shall have subjects ready for you that people will never believe in if you write about them. . . ."

"And what was the name of that prince?" I asked, with a foreboding of something.

"What do you want to know for? All right, it's Valkovsky."

"Pyotr?"

"Yes. Do you know him?"

"Yes, but not very well. Well, Masloboev, I shall come to you to inquire about that gentleman more than once again," I said, getting up. "You've interested me greatly."

"Well, old boy, you can come as often as you like. I can tell you fine tales, though only within certain limits, do you understand? Or else one loses one's credit and honour, in business that is, and all the rest of it."

"All right, as far as honour permits."

I was really agitated. He noticed it.

"Well, what do you say about the story I told you? Have you thought of something?"

"Your story? Well, wait a couple of minutes. I will pay."

He went up to the buffet, and there, as though by chance, stood close by the young man in the tunic, who was so unceremoniously called Mitroshka. It seemed to me that Masloboev knew him a good deal better than he had admitted to me. Anyway, it was evident that they were not meeting for the first time.

Mitroshka was a rather original-looking fellow. In his sleeveless tunic and red silk shirt, with his sharp but handsome features, with his young-looking, swarthy face, and his bold, sparkling eyes, he made a curious and not unattractive impression. There was an assumption of jauntiness in his gestures, and yet at the moment he was evidently restraining himself, aiming rather at an air of businesslike gravity and sedateness.

"Look here, Vanya," said Masloboev, when he rejoined me, "look me up this evening at seven o'clock, and I may have something to tell you. By myself, you see, I'm no use; in old days I was, but now I'm only a drunkard and have got out of the way of things. But I've still kept my old connexions; I may find out something. I sniff about among all sorts of sharp people; that's how I get on. In my free time, that is when I'm sober, I do something myself, it's true, through friends, too . . . mostly in the investigation line. . . . But that's neither here nor there. Enough. Here's my address, in Shestilavotchny Street. But now, my boy, I'm really too far gone. I'll swallow another—and home. I'll lie down a bit. If you come I'll introduce you to Alexandra Semyonovna, and if there's time we'll discuss poetry."

"Well, and that too?"

"All right; that, too, perhaps."

"Perhaps I'll come. I'll certainly come. . . ."

CHAPTER VI

ANNA ANDREYEVNA had long been expecting me. What I had told her the day before, about Natasha's note, had greatly excited her curiosity; and she had expected me much earlier in the morning, by ten o'clock at the latest. By the time I turned up at two o'clock in the afternoon the poor woman's agonies of suspense had reached an extreme pitch. She was longing, too, to talk to me of the new hopes aroused in her the day before, and of Nikolay Sergeyitch, who had been ailing since then, who was gloomy, and at the same time seemed specially tender to her. When I made my appearance she received me with an expression of coldness and displeasure in her face, hardly opened her mouth, and showed no sign of interest, almost as though she would ask why I had come, and what possessed me to drop in every day. She was angry at my coming so late. But I was in a hurry, and without further delay I described to her the whole scene at Natasha's the evening before. As soon as she heard of the elder prince's visit and his solemn proposal, her assumed indifference vanished instantly. I cannot find words to describe how delighted she was; she seemed quite beside herself, crossed herself, shed tears, bowed down before the ikons, embraced me, and was on the point of running to Nikolay Sergeyitch to tell him of her joy.

"Bless me, my dear, why, it's all the insults and humiliations he's been through that are making him ill, and as soon as he knows that full reparation will be made to Natasha, he'll forget it all in a twinkling."

I had much ado to dissuade her. Though the good lady had lived twenty-five years with her husband she did not understand him. She was desperately anxious, too, to set off with me immediately to Natasha's. I put it to her not only that Nikolay Sergeyitch would disapprove of her action, but that we might even ruin the whole business by going. With difficulty she was brought to think better of it, but she detained me another half-hour unnecessarily, talking herself the whole time.

"With whom shall I be left here?" she said, "sitting alone within four walls with such joy in my heart?"

At last I persuaded her to let me go, reminding her that Natasha must be sick of waiting for me. She made the sign of the cross several times to bless me on my way, sent a special blessing to Natasha, and almost shed tears when I absolutely refused to come back again that evening, unless anything special had happened at Natasha's. I did not see Nikolay Sergeyitch on this occasion; he had been awake all night, complained of a headache, a chill, and was now asleep in his study.

Natasha, too, had been expecting me all the morning. When I went in she was, as usual, walking up and down the room, with her hands clasped, meditating. Even now when I think of her I always see her alone in a poor room, dreamy, deserted. waiting with folded hands, and downcast eyes, walking aimlessly up and down.

Still walking up and down she asked me in a low voice why I was so late. I gave her a brief account of all my adventures, but she scarcely listened. One could see she was in great anxiety about something.

"Anything fresh?" I asked her.

"Nothing fresh," she answered. But I guessed at once from her face that there was something fresh, and that she was expecting me on purpose to tell me, and she would tell me, not at once but just as I was going, as she always did.

That was always our habit. I was used to her and I waited.

We began, of course, talking of the previous evening. I was particularly struck by the fact that we were quite agreed in our impression of Prince Valkovsky; and she positively disliked him, disliked him much more than she had at the time. And when we analysed the visit, point by point, Natasha suddenly said:

"Listen, Vanya, you know it's always like that, if one doesn't like a man at first, it's almost a sure sign that one will like him afterwards. That's how it's always been with me, anyway."

"Let us hope so, Natasha. And this is my opinion, and it's a final one. I went over it all, and what I deduced was that though the prince was perhaps jesuitical, he is giving his consent to your marriage genuinely and in earnest."

Natasha stood still in the middle of the room and looked at me sternly. Her whole face was transformed; her lips twitched a little.

"But how could he in a case like *this* begin deceiving and . . . lying?"

"Of course not, of course not!" I assented hurriedly.

"Of course he wasn't lying. It seems to me there's no need to think of that. There's no excuse to be found for such deception. And, indeed, am I so abject in his eyes that he could jeer at me like that? Could any man be capable of such an insult?"

"Of course not, of course not," I agreed, thinking to myself, "you're thinking of nothing else as you pace up and down, my poor girl, and very likely you're more doubtful about it than I am."

"Ah, how I could wish he were coming back sooner!" she said. "He wanted to spend the whole evening with me, and then. . . . It must have been important business, since he's given it all up and gone away. You don't know what it was, Vanya? You haven't heard anything?"

"The Lord only knows. You know he's always making money. I've heard he's taking up a share in some contract in Petersburg. We know nothing about business, Natasha."

"Of course we don't. Alyosha talked of some letter yesterday."

"News of some sort. Has Alyosha been here?"

"Yes."

"Early?"

"At twelve o'clock; he sleeps late, you know. He stayed a little while. I sent him off to Katerina Fyodorovna. Shouldn't I have, Vanya?"

"Why, didn't he mean to go himself?"

"Yes, he did."

She was about to say more, but checked herself. I looked at her and waited. Her face was sad. I would have questioned her, but she sometimes particularly disliked questions.

"He's a strange boy," she said at last, with a slight twist of her mouth, trying not to look at me.

"Why? I suppose something's happened?"

"No, nothing; I just thought so. . . . He was sweet though. . . . But already . . ."

"All his cares and anxieties are over now," said I.

Natasha looked intently and searchingly at me. She felt inclined perhaps to answer, "he hadn't many cares or anxieties before," but she fancied that my words covered the same thought. She pouted.

But she became friendly and cordial again at once. This time she was extraordinarily gentle. I spent more than an hour with her. She was very uneasy. The prince had frightened her. I noticed from some of her questions that she was very anxious to know what sort of impression she had made on him. Had she behaved properly? Hadn't she betrayed her joy too openly? Had she been too ready to take offence? Or on the contrary too conciliatory? He mustn't imagine anything. He mustn't laugh at her! He mustn't feel contempt for her! . . . Her cheeks glowed like fire at the thought!

"How can you be so upset simply at a bad man's imagining something? Let him imagine anything!" said I.

"Why is he bad?" she asked.

Natasha was suspicious but pure-hearted and straightforward. Her doubts came from no impure source. She was proud and with a fine pride, and would not endure what she looked upon as higher than anything to be turned into a laughing-stock before her. She would, of course, have met with contempt the contempt of a base man, but at the same time her heart would have ached at mockery of what she thought sacred, whoever had been the mocker. This was not due to any lack of firmness. It arose partly from too limited a knowledge of the world, from being unaccustomed to people, from having been shut up in her own little groove. She had spent all her life in her own little corner and had hardly left it. And finally that characteristic of good-natured people, inherited perhaps from her father—the habit of thinking highly of people, of persistently thinking them better than they really are, warmly exaggerating everything good in them—was highly developed in her. It is hard for such people to be disillusioned afterwards; and it is hardest of all when one feels one is oneself to blame. Why did one expect more than could be given? And such a disappointment is always in store for such people. It is best for them to stay quietly in their corners and not to go out into the world; I have noticed, in fact, that they really love their corners so much that they grow shy and unsociable in them. Natasha, however, had suffered many misfortunes, many mortifications. She was already a wounded creature, and she cannot be blamed, if indeed there be any blame in what I have said.

But I was in a hurry and got up to go. She was surprised and almost cried at my going, though she had shown no particular affection for me all the while I was with her; on the contrary, she seemed rather colder to me than usual. She kissed me warmly and looked for a long time into my face.

"Listen," she said. "Alyosha was very absurd this morning and quite surprised me He was very sweet, very happy apparently, but flew in, such a butterfly, such a dandy, and kept prinking before the looking-glass. He's a little too unceremonious now. . . . Yes, and he didn't stay long. Fancy, he brought me some sweets."

"Sweets? Why, that's very charming and simple-hearted. Ah, what a pair you are. Now you've begun watching and spying on one another, studying each other's faces, and reading hidden thoughts in them (and understanding nothing about it). He's not different. He's merry and schoolboyish as he always was. But you, you!"

And whenever Natasha changed her tone and came to me with some complaint against Alyosha, or to ask for a solution of same ticklish question, or to tell me some secret, expecting me to understand her at half a word, she always, I remember, looked at me with a smile, as it were imploring me to answer somehow so that she should feel happy at heart at once. And I remember, too, I always in such cases assumed a severe and harsh tone as though scolding some one, and this happened quite unconsciously with me, but it was always *successful*. My severity and gravity were what was wanted; they seemed more authoritative, and people sometimes feel an irresistible craving to be scolded. Natasha was sometimes left quite consoled.

"No, Vanya, you see," she went on, keeping one of her little hands on my shoulder, while her other pressed my hand and her eyes looked into mine, "I fancied that he was somehow too little affected . . . he seemed already such a *mari*—you know, as though he'd been married ten years but was still polite to his wife. Isn't that very premature? . . . He laughed, and prinked, but just as though all that didn't matter, as though it only partly concerned me, not as it used to be . . . he was in a great hurry to see Katerina Fyodorovna. . . . If I spoke to him he didn't listen to me, or began talking of something else, you know, that horrid, aristocratic habit we've both been getting him out of. In fact, he was too . . . even indifferent it seemed . . . but what am I saying! Here I'm doing it, here I've begun! Ah, what exacting, capricious despots we all are, Vanya! Only now I see it! We can't forgive a man for a trifling change in his face, and God knows what has made his face change! You were right, Vanya, in reproaching me just now! It's all my fault! We make our own troubles and then we complain of them. . . . Thanks, Vanya, you have quite comforted me. Ah, if he would only come to-day! But there! perhaps he'll be angry for what happened this morning."

"Surely you haven't quarrelled already!" I cried with surprise.

"I made no sign! But I was a little sad, and though he came in so cheerful he suddenly became thoughtful, and I fancied he said good-bye coldly. Yes, I'll send for him. . . . You come, too, to-day, Vanya."

"Yes, I'll be sure to, unless I'm detained by one thing."

"Why, what thing is it?"

"I've brought it on myself! But I think I'm sure to come all the same."

CHAPTER VII

At seven o'clock precisely I was at Masloboev's. He lived in a lodge, a little house, in Shestilavotchny Street. He had three rather grubby but not badly furnished rooms. There was even the appearance of some prosperity, at the same time an extreme slovenliness. The door was opened by a very pretty girl of nineteen, plainly but charmingly dressed, clean, and with very good-natured, merry eyes. I guessed at once that this was the Alexandra Semyonovna to whom he had made passing allusion that morning, holding out an introduction to her as an allurement to me. She asked who I was, and hearing my name said that Masloboev was expecting me, but that he was asleep now in his room, to which she took me. Masloboev was asleep on a very good soft sofa with his dirty great-coat over him, and a shabby leather pillow under his head. He was sleeping very lightly. As soon as we went in he called me by my name.

"Ah, that was you? I was expecting you. I was just dreaming you'd come in and wake me. So it's time. Come along."

"Where are we going?"

"To see a lady."

"What lady? Why?"

"Mme. Bubnov, to pay her out. Isn't she a beauty?" he drawled, turning to Alexandra Semyonovna, and he positively kissed his finger-tips at the thought of Mme. Bubnov.

"Get along, you're making it up!" said Alexandra Semyonovna, feeling it incumbent on her to make a show of anger.

"Don't you know her? Let me introduce you, old man. Here, Alexandra Semyonovna, let me present to you a literary general; it's only once a year he's on view for nothing, at other times you have to pay."

"Here he is up to his nonsense again! Don't you listen to him; he's always laughing at me. How can this gentleman be a general!"

"That's just what I tell you, he's a special sort. But don't you imagine, your excellency, that we're silly; we are much cleverer than we seem at first sight."

"Don't listen to him! He's always putting me to confusion before honest folk, the shameless fellow. He'd much better take me to the theatre sometimes."

"Alexandra Semyonovna, love your household. . . . Haven't you forgotten what you must love? Haven't you forgotten the word? the one I taught you!"

"Of course I haven't! It means some nonsense."

"Well, what was the word then?"

"As if I were going to disgrace myself before a visitor! Most likely it means something shameful. Strike me dumb if I'll say it!"

"Well, you have forgotten then."

"Well, I haven't then, penates! . . . love your penates, that's what he invents! Perhaps there never were any penates. And why should one love them. He's always talking nonsense!"

"But at Mme. Bubnov's . . ."

"Foo! You and your Bubnov!"

And Alexandra Semyonovna ran out of the room in great indignation.

"It's time to go. Good-bye, Alexandra Semyonovna."

We went out.

"Look here, Vanya, first let's get into this cab. That's right. And secondly, I found out something after I had said good-bye to you yesterday, and not by guesswork, but for a certainty. I spent a whole hour in Vassilyevsky Island. That fat man's an awful scoundrel, a nasty, filthy brute, up to all sorts of tricks, and with vile tastes of all kinds. This Bubnov has long been notorious for some shifty doings in the same line. She was almost caught over a little girl of respectable family the other day. The muslin dress she dressed that orphan up in (as you described this morning) won't let me rest, because I've heard something of the sort already. I learnt something else this morning, quite by chance, but I think I can rely on it. How old is she?"

"From her face I should say thirteen."

"But small for her age. Well, this is how she'll do then. When need be she'll say she's eleven, and another time that she's fifteen. And as the poor child has no one to protect her she's . . ."

"Is it possible!"

"What do you suppose? Mme. Bubnov wouldn't have adopted an orphan simply out of compassion. And if the fat man's hanging round, you may be sure it's that. He saw her yesterday. And that blockhead Sizobryuhov's been promised a beauty to-day, a married woman, an officer's wife, a woman of rank. These profligate merchants' sons are always keen on that; they're always on the look-out for rank. It's like, that rule in the Latin grammar, do you remember: the significance takes precedence of the ending. But I believe I'm still drunk from this morning. But Bubnov had better not dare meddle in such doings. She wants to dupe the police, too; but that's rot! And so I'll give her a scare, for she knows that for the sake of old scores . . . and all the rest of it, do you understand?"

I was terribly shocked. All these revelations alarmed me. I kept being afraid we were too late and urged on the cabman.

"Don't be uneasy. Measures have been taken," said Masloboev. "Mitroshka's there. Sizobryuhov will pay for it with money; but the fat scoundrel with his skin. That was settled this morning. Well, and Bubnov comes to my share . . . for don't let her dare . . ."

We drew up at the eating-house; but the man called Mitroshka was not there. Telling the cabman to wait for us at the eating-house steps, we walked to Mme. Bubnov's. Mitroshka was waiting for us at the gate. There was a bright light in the windows, and we heard Sizobryuhov's drunken, giggling laugh.

"They're all here, have been a quarter of an hour," Mitroshka announced; "now's the very time."

"But how shall we get in?" I asked.

"As visitors," replied Masloboev. "She knows me, and she knows Mitroshka, too. It's true it's all locked up, but not for us."

He tapped softly at the gate, and it was immediately opened. The porter opened it and exchanged a signal with Mitroshka. We went in quietly; we were not heard from the house. The porter led us up the steps and knocked. His name was called from within. He answered that a gentleman said he wanted to speak to her.

The door was opened and we all went in together. The porter vanished.

"Aie, who's this?" screamed Mme. Bubnov, standing drunken and dishevelled in the tiny entry with the candle in her hand.

"Who?" answered Masloboev quickly. "How can you ask, Anna Trifonovna. Don't you know your honoured guests? Who, if not me? Filip Filippitch."

"Ah, Filip Filippitch! It's you . . . very welcome. . . . But how is it you. . . . I don't know . . . please walk in."

She was completely taken aback.

"Where? Here? But there's a partition here! No, you must give us a better reception. We'll have a drop of champagne. But aren't there any little mam'zelles?"

The woman regained her confidence at once.

"Why, for such honoured guests I'd get them if I had to dig for them underground. I'd send for them from the kingdom of China."

"Two words, Anna Trifonovna, darling; is Sizobryuhov here?"

"Yes."

"He's just the man I want. How dare he go off on the spree without me, the rascal?"

"I expect he has not forgotten you. He seems expecting some one; it must be you."

Masloboev pushed the door, and we found ourselves in a small room with two windows with geraniums in them, with wickerwork chairs, and a wretched-looking piano; all as one would expect. But even before we went in, while we were still talking in the passage, Mitroshka had disappeared. I learned afterwards that he had not come in, but had been waiting behind the door. He had some one to open it to him afterwards. The dishevelled and painted woman I had seen peeping over Mme. Bubnov's shoulder that morning was a pal of his.

Sizobryuhov was sitting on a skimpy little sofa of imitation mahogany, before a round table with a cloth on it. On the table were two bottles of tepid champagne, and a bottle of horrible rum; and there were plates of sweets from the confectioner's, biscuits and nuts of three sorts. At the table facing Sizobryuhov sat a repulsive-looking, pock-marked female of forty wearing a black taffeta dress and a bronze brooch and bracelets. This was the "officer's wife," unmistakably a sham. Sizobryuhov was drunk and perfectly satisfied. His fat friend was not with him.

"That's how people behave!" Masloboev bawled at the top of his voice. "After inviting one to Dussot's, too!"

"Filip Filippitch, doing us the pleasure?" muttered Sizobryuhov, getting up to meet us with a blissful air.

"Are you drinking?"

"Excuse me."

"Don't apologize, but invite your guests to join you. We've come to keep it up with you. Here, I've brought a friend to join us."

Masloboev pointed to me.

"Delighted, that is, you do me pleasure. . . . K-k-k-he!"

"Ugh, do you call this champagne? It's more like kvas."

"You insult me."

"So you don't dare show yourself at Dussot's! And after inviting one!"

"He's just been telling me he's been in Paris," put in the officer's wife. "He must be fibbing."

"Fedosya Titishna, don't insult me. I have been there. I've travelled."

"A peasant like him in Paris!"

"We have been! We could! Me and Karp Vassilitch—we cut a dash there. Do you know Karp Vassilitch?"

"What do I want with your Karp Vassilitch?"

"Why, it's only just . . . it might be worth your while. Why, it was there, in Paris, at Mme. Joubert's, we broke an English pier-glass."

"What did you break?"

"A pier-glass. There was a looking-glass over the whole wall; and Karp Vassilitch was that drunk that he began jabbering Russian to Mme. Joubert. He stood by that pier-glass and leaned his elbow against it. And Joubert screamed at him in her own way, that the pier-glass cost seven hundred francs (that is four hundred roubles), and that he'd break it! He grinned and looked at me. And I was sitting on a sofa opposite, and a beauty beside me, not a mug like this one here, but a stunner, that's the only word for it. He cries out, 'Stepan Terentyitch, hi, Stepan Terentyitch! We'll go halves, shall we?' And I said 'done!' And then he banged his fist on the looking-glass, crash! The glass was all in splinters. Joubert squealed and went for him straight in the face: 'What are you about, you ruffian?' (In her own lingo, that is.) 'Mme. Joubert,' says he, 'here's the price of it and don't disperse my character.' And on the spot he forked out six hundred and fifty francs. They haggled over the other fifty."

At that moment a terrible, piercing shriek was heard two or three rooms away from the one in which we were. I shuddered, and I, too, cried out. I recognized that shriek: it was the voice of Elena. Immediately after that pitiful shriek we heard other outcries, oaths, a scuffle, and finally the loud, resonant, distinct sound of a slap in the face. It was probably Mitroshka inflicting retribution in his own fashion. Suddenly the door was violently flung open and Elena rushed into the room with a white face and dazed eyes in a white muslin dress, crumpled and torn, and her hair, which had been carefully arranged, dishevelled as though by a struggle. I stood facing the door, and she rushed straight to me and flung her arms round me. Every one jumped up. Everybody was alarmed. There were shouts and exclamations when she appeared. Then Mitroshka appeared in the doorway, dragging after him by the hair his fat enemy, who was in a hopelessly dishevelled condition. He dragged him up to the door and flung him into the room.

"Here he is! Take him!" Mitroshka brought out with an air of complete satisfaction.

"I say," said Masloboev, coming quietly up to me and tapping me on the shoulder, "take our cab, take the child with you and drive home; there's nothing more for you to do here. We'll arrange the rest to-morrow."

I did not need telling twice. I seized Elena by the arm and took her out of that den. I don't know how things ended there. No one stopped us. Mme. Bubnov was panic-stricken. Everything had passed so quickly that she did not know how to interfere. The cab was waiting for us, and in twenty minutes we were at my lodgings.

Elena seemed half-dead. I unfastened the hooks of her dress, sprinkled her with water, and laid her on the sofa. She began to be feverish and delirious. I looked at her white little face, at her colourless lips, at her black hair, which had been done up carefully and pomaded, though it had come down on one side, at her whole get-up, at the pink bows which still remained here and there on her dress—and I had no doubt at all about the revolting facts. Poor little thing! She grew worse and worse.

I did not leave her, and I made up my mind not to go to Natasha's that evening. From time to time Elena raised her long, arrow-like eyelashes to look at me, and gazed long and intently as though she recognized me. It was late, past midnight when at last she fell asleep. I slept on the floor not far from her.

CHAPTER VIII

I GOT up very early. I had waked up almost every half hour through the night, and gone up to look intently at my poor little visitor. She was in a fever and slightly delirious. But towards morning she fell into a sound sleep. A good sign, I thought, but when I waked in the morning I decided to run for the doctor while the poor little thing was still asleep. I knew a doctor, a very good-natured old bachelor, who with his German housekeeper had lived in Vladimirsky Street from times immemorial. I set off to him. He promised to be with me at ten o'clock. It was eight when I reached him. I felt much inclined to call in at Masloboev's on the way, but I thought better of it. He was sure not to be awake yet after yesterday, besides, Elena might wake up and be frightened at finding herself alone in my room. In her feverish state she might well forget how and when she had come there.

She waked up at the moment when I went into the room. I went up to her and cautiously asked her how she felt. She did not answer, but bent a long, long, intent look upon me with her expressive black eyes. I thought from the look in her eyes that she was fully conscious and understood what had happened. Her not answering me perhaps was just her invariable habit. Both on the previous day, and on the day before that when she had come to see me she had not uttered a word in answer to some of my questions, but had only looked into my face with her slow, persistent stare, in which there was a strange pride as well as wonder and wild curiosity. Now I noticed a severity, even a sort of mistrustfulness in her eyes. I was putting my hand on her forehead to feel whether she were still feverish, but quietly, without a word, she put back my hand with her little one and turned away from me to the wall. I walked away that I might not worry her.

I had a big copper kettle. I had long used it instead of a samovar, for boiling water. I had wood, the porter had brought me up enough to last for five days. I lighted the stove, fetched some water and put the tea-pot on. I laid the tea-things on the table. Elena turned towards me and watched it all with curiosity. I asked her whether she would not have something? But again she turned away from me and made no answer.

"Why is she angry with me?" I wondered. "Queer little girl!"

My old doctor came at ten o'clock as he had promised.

He examined the patient with German thoroughness, and greatly cheered me by saying that though she was feverish there was no special danger. He added that she probably had another chronic disease, some irregularity in the action of the heart, "but that point would want special watching, for now she's out of danger." More from habit than necessity he prescribed her a mixture and some powders, and at once proceeded to ask me how she came to be with me. At the same time he looked about my room wonderingly. The old man was an awful chatterbox.

He was struck with Elena. She pulled her hand away when he tried to feel her pulse, and would not show him her tongue; to all his questions she did not answer one word. All the while she stared intently at the enormous Stanislav order that hung upon his neck.

"Most likely her head is aching badly," said the old man, "but how she does stare!"

I did not think it necessary to tell him all about Elena, so I put him off, saying it was a long story.

"Let me know if there's any need," said he as he went away. "But at present there's no danger."

I made up my mind to stay all day with Elena, and to leave her alone as rarely as possible till she was quite well. But knowing that Natasha and Anna Andreyevna would be worried if they expected me in vain, I decided to let Natasha know by post that I could not be with her that day. I could not write to Anna Andreyevna. She had asked me herself once for all not to send her letters, after I had once sent her news when Natasha was ill. "My old man scowls when he sees a letter from you," she said. "He wants to know, poor dear, what's in the letter, and he can't ask, he can't bring himself to. And so he's upset for the whole day. And besides, my dear, you only tantalize me with letters. What's the use of a dozen lines. One wants to ask the details and you're not there." And so I wrote only to Natasha, and when I took the prescription to the chemist's I posted the letter.

Meanwhile Elena fell asleep again. She moaned faintly and started in her sleep. The doctor had guessed right, she had a bad headache. From time to time she cried out and woke up. She looked at me with positive vexation, as though my attention was particularly irksome. I must confess this wounded me.

At eleven o'clock Masloboev turned up. He was preoccupied and seemed absent-minded; he only came in for a minute, and was in a great hurry to get away.

"Well, brother, I didn't expect that you lived in great style," he observed, looking round, "but I didn't think I should find you in such a box. This is a box, not a lodging. But that's nothing, though what does matter is that all these outside worries take you off your work. I thought of that yesterday when we were driving to Bubnov's. By natural temperament, brother, and by social position I'm one of those people who can do nothing sensible themselves, but can read sermons to other people. Now, listen; I'll look in, perhaps, to-morrow or next day, and you be sure to come and see me on Sunday morning. I hope by then the problem of this child will be completely settled; then we'll talk things over seriously, for you need looking after in earnest. You can't go on living like this. I only dropped a hint yesterday, but now I'll put it before you logically. And tell me, in short, do you look on it as a dishonour to take money from me for a time?"

"Come, don't quarrel," I interrupted. "You'd better tell me how things ended there yesterday."

"Well, they ended most satisfactorily. My object was attained, you understand. I've no time now. I only looked in for a minute to tell you I'm busy and have no time for you, and to find out by the way whether you're going to place her somewhere, or whether you mean to keep her yourself. Because it wants thinking over and settling."

"That I don't know for certain yet, and I must own I was waiting to ask your advice. How could I keep her?"

"Why, as a servant. . . ."

"Please don't speak so loud. Though she's ill she's quite conscious, and I noticed she started when she saw you. No doubt she remembered yesterday."

Then I told him about her behaviour and all the peculiarities I had noticed in her. Masloboev was interested in what I told him. I added that perhaps I could place her in a household, and told him briefly about my old friends. To my astonishment he knew something of Natasha's story, and when I asked him how he had heard of it:

"Oh," he said, "I heard something about it long ago in connexion with some business. I've told you already that I know Prince Valkovsky. That's a good idea of yours to send her to those old people. She'd only be in your way. And another thing, she wants some sort of a passport. Don't you worry about that. I'll undertake it. Good-bye. Come and see me often. Is she asleep now?"

"I think so," I answered.

But as soon as he had gone Elena called to me.

"Who's that?" she asked. Her voice shook, but she looked at me with the same intent and haughty expression. I can find no other word for it.

I told her Masloboev's name, and said that it was by his help I got her away from Mme. Bubnov's, and that Mme. Bubnov was very much afraid of him. Her cheeks suddenly flushed fiery red probably at the recollection of the past.

"And she will never come here?" asked Elena, with a searching look at me.

I made haste to reassure her. She remained silent, and was taking my hand in her burning fingers, but she dropped it again at once as though recollecting herself.

"It cannot be that she really feels such an aversion for me," I thought. "It's her manner or else . . . or else the poor little thing has had so much trouble that she mistrusts every one."

At the hour fixed I went out to fetch the medicine, and at the same time went into a restaurant where they knew me and gave me credit. I took a pot with me, and brought back some chicken broth for Elena. But she would not eat, and the soup remained for the time on the stove.

I gave her her medicine and sat down to my work. I thought she was asleep, but chancing to look round at her I saw that she had raised her head, and was intently watching me write. I pretended not to notice her.

At last she really did fall asleep, and to my great delight she slept quietly without delirium or moaning. I fell into a reverie. Natasha, not knowing what was the matter, might well be angry with me for not coming to-day, would be sure, indeed, I reflected, to be hurt at my neglect, just when, perhaps, she needed me most. She might at this moment have special worries, perhaps some service to ask of me, and I was staying away as though expressly.

As for Anna Andreyevna, I was completely at a loss as to how I should excuse myself to her next day. I thought it over and suddenly made up my mind to run round to both of them. I should only be absent about two hours. Elena was asleep and would not hear me go out. I jumped up, took my coat and cap, but just as I was going out Elena called me. I was surprised. Could she have been pretending to be asleep?

I may remark in parenthesis that, though Elena made a show of not wanting to speak to me, these rather frequent appeals, this desire to apply to me in every difficulty, showed a contrary feeling, and I confess it really pleased me.

"Where do you mean to send me?" she asked when I went up to her.

She generally asked her questions all of a sudden, when I did not expect them. This time I did not take in her meaning at first.

"You were telling your friend just now that you meant to place me in some household. I don't want to go."

I bent down to her; she was hot all over, another attack of fever had come on. I began trying to soothe and pacify her, assuring her that if she cared to remain with me I would not send her away anywhere. Saying this I took off my coat and cap. I could not bring myself to leave her alone in such a condition.

"No, go," she said, realizing at once that I was meaning to stay. "I'm sleepy; I shall go to sleep directly."

"But how will you get on alone?" I said, uncertainly. "Though I'd be sure to be back in two hours' time. . . ."

"Well, go then. Suppose I'm ill for a whole year, you can't stay at home all the time."

And she tried to smile, and looked strangely at me as though struggling with some kindly feeling stirring in her heart. Poor little thing! Her gentle, tender heart showed itself in glimpses in spite of her aloofness and evident mistrust.

First I ran round to Anna Andreyevna. She was waiting for me with feverish impatience and she greeted me with reproaches; she was in terrible anxiety. Nikolay Sergeyitch had gone out immediately after dinner, and she did not know where. I had a presentiment that she had not been able to resist telling him everything, in hints, of course, as she always did. She practically admitted it herself, telling me that she could not resist sharing such joyful tidings with him, but that Nikolay Sergeyitch had become, to use her expression, "blacker than night, that he had said nothing. He wouldn't speak, wouldn't even answer my questions, and suddenly after dinner had got ready and gone out." When she told me this Anna Andreyevna was almost trembling with dismay, and besought me to stay with her until Nikolay Sergeyitch came back. I excused myself and told her almost flatly that perhaps I should not come next day either, and that I had really hurried to her now to tell her so, this time we almost quarrelled. She shed tears, reproached me harshly and bitterly, and only when I was just going out at the door she suddenly threw herself on my neck, held me tight in both arms and told me not to be angry with a lonely creature like her, and not to resent her words.

Contrary to my expectations, I found Natasha again alone. And, strange to say, it seemed to me that she was by no means so pleased to see me as she had been the day before and on other occasions, as though I were in the way or somehow annoying her. When I asked whether Alyosha had been there that day she answered:

"Of course he has, but he didn't stay long. He promised to look in this evening," she went on, hesitating.

"And yesterday evening, was he here?"

"N-no. He was detained," she added quickly. "Well, Vanya, how are things going with you?"

I saw that she wanted to stave off our conversation and begin a fresh subject. I looked at her more intently. She was evidently upset. But noticing that I was glancing at her and watching her closely, she looked at me rapidly and, as it were, wrathfully and with such intensity that her eyes seemed to blaze at me. "She is miserable again," I thought, "but she doesn't want to speak to me about it."

In answer to her question about my work I told her the whole story of Elena in full detail. She was extremely interested and even impressed by my story.

"Good heavens! And you could leave her alone, and ill!" she cried.

I told her that I had meant not to come at all that day, but that I was afraid she would be angry with me and that she might be in need of me.

"Need," she said to herself as though pondering. "Perhaps I do need you, Vanya, but that had better be another time. Have you been to my people?"

I told her.

"Yes, God only knows how my father will take the news. Though what is there to take after all? . . ."

"What is there to take?" I repeated. "A transformation like this!"

"I don't know about that. . . . Where can he have gone again? That time before, you thought he was coming to me. Do you know, Vanya, come to me to-morrow if you can. I shall tell you something perhaps. . . . Only I'm ashamed to trouble you. But now you'd better be going home to your visitor. I expect it's two hours since you came out."

"Yes, it is. Good-bye, Natasha. Well, and how was Alyosha with you to-day?"

"Oh, Alyosha. All right. . . . I wonder at your curiosity."

"Good-bye for now, my friend."

"Good-bye."

She gave me her hand carelessly and turned away from my last, farewell look. I went out somewhat surprised. 'She has plenty to think about, though," I thought. "It's no jesting matter. To-morrow she'll be the first to tell me all about it."

I went home sorrowful, and was dreadfully shocked as soon as I opened the door. By now it was dark. I could make out Elena sitting on the sofa, her head sunk on her breast as though plunged in deep thought. She didn't even glance at me. She seemed lost to everything. I went up to her. She was muttering something to herself. "Isn't she delirious?" I thought.

"Elena, my dear, what's the matter?" I asked, sitting beside her and putting my arm round her.

"I want to go away. . . . I'd better go to her," she said, not raising her head to look at me.

"Where? To whom?" I asked in surprise.

"To her. To Bubnov. She's always saying I owe her a lot of money; that she buried mother at her expense. I don't want her to say nasty things about mother. I want to work there, and pay her back. . . . Then I'll go away of myself. But now I'm going back to her."

"Be quiet, Elena, you can't go back to her," I said. "She'll torment you. She'll ruin you. . . ."

"Let her ruin me, let her torment me." Elena caught up

the words feverishly. "I'm not the first. Others better than I are tormented. A beggar woman in the street told me that. I'm poor and I want to be poor. I'll be poor all my life. My mother told me so when she was dying. I'll work. . . . I don't want to wear this dress. . . ."

"I'll buy you another one to-morrow. And I'll get you your books. You shall stay with me. I won't send you away to anyone unless you want to go. Don't worry yourself. . . ."

"I'll be a work-girl!"

"Very well, very well. Only be quiet. Lie down. Go to sleep."

But the poor child burst into tears. By degrees her tears passed into sobs. I didn't know what to do with her. I offered her water and moistened her temples and her head. At last she sank on the sofa completely exhausted, and she was overcome by feverish shivering. I wrapped her up in what I could find and she fell into an uneasy sleep, starting and waking up continually. Though I had not walked far that day, I was awfully tired, and I decided to go to bed as early as possible. Tormenting doubts swarmed in my brain. I foresaw that I should have a lot of trouble with this child. But my chief anxiety was about Natasha and her troubles. Altogether as I remember now I have rarely been in a mood of such deep dejection as when I fell asleep that unhappy night.

CHAPTER IX

I WAKED up late, at ten o'clock in the morning, feeling ill. I felt giddy and my head was aching; I glanced towards Elena's bed. The bed was empty. At the same moment from my little room on the right sounds reached me as though some one were sweeping with a broom. I went to look. Elena had a broom in her hand, and holding up her smart dress which she had kept on ever since that evening, she was sweeping the floor. The wood for the stove was piled up in the corner. The table had been scrubbed, the kettle had been cleaned. In a word, Elena was doing the housework.

"Listen, Elena," I cried. "Who wants you to sweep the floor? I don't wish it, you're ill. Have you come here to be a drudge for me?"

"Who is going to sweep the floor here?" she answered,

drawing herself up, and looking straight at me. "I'm not ill now."

"But I didn't take you to make you work, Elena. You seem to be afraid I shall scold you like Mme. Bubnov for living with me for nothing. And where did you get that horrid broom ? I had no broom," I added, looking at her in wonder.

"It's my broom. I brought it here myself, I used to sweep the floor here for grandfather too. And the broom's been lying here ever since under the stove."

I went back to the other room musing. Perhaps I may have been in error, but it seemed to me that she felt oppressed by my hospitality and that she wanted in every possible way to show me that she was doing something for her living.

"What an embittered character, if so," I thought. Two minutes later she came in and without a word sat down on the sofa in the same place as yesterday, looking inquisitively at me. Meanwhile I boiled the kettle, made the tea, poured out a cup for her and handed it her with a slice of white bread. She took it in silence and without opposition. She had had nothing for twenty-four hours.

"See, you've dirtied your pretty dress with that broom," I said, noticing a streak of dirt on her skirt.

She looked down and suddenly, to my intense astonishment, she put down her cup, and apparently calm and composed, she picked up a breadth of the muslin skirt in both hands and with one rip tore it from top to bottom. When she had done this she raised her stubborn, flashing eyes to me in silence. Her face was pale.

"What are you about, Elena ?" I cried, feeling sure the child was mad.

"It's a horrid dress," she cried, almost gasping with excitement. "Why do you say it's a nice dress ? I don't want to wear it !" she cried suddenly, jumping up from her place. "I'll tear it up. I didn't ask her to dress me up. She did it herself, by force. I've torn one dress already. I'll tear that one ! I'll tear it, I'll tear it, I'll tear it ! . . ."

And she fell upon her luckless dress with fury. In one moment she had torn it almost into rags. When she had finished she was so pale she could hardly stand. I looked with surprise at such rage. She looked at me with a defiant air as though I too had somehow offended her. But I knew now what to do.

I made up my mind to buy her a new dress that morning.

This wild, embittered little creature must be tamed by kindness. She looked as though she had never met anyone kind. If once already in spite of severe punishment she had torn another similar dress to rags, with what fury she must look on this one now, when it recalled to her those awful moments.

In Tolkutchy Market one could buy a good, plain dress very cheaply. Unfortunately at that moment I had scarcely any money. But as I went to bed the night before I had made up my mind to go that morning to a place where I had hopes of getting some. It was fortunately not far from the market. I took my hat. Elena watched me intently as though expecting something.

"Are you going to lock me in again?" she asked when I took up the key to lock the door behind me, as I had done the day before and the day before that.

"My dear," I said, going up to her. "Don't be angry at that. I lock the door because some one might come. You are ill, and you'd perhaps be frightened. And there's no knowing who might not come. Perhaps Bubnov might take it into her head to...."

I said this on purpose. I locked her in because I didn't trust her. I was afraid that she might suddenly take it into her head to leave me. I determined to be cautious for a time. Elena said nothing and I locked her in again.

I knew a publisher who had been for the last twelve years bringing out a compilation in many volumes. I often used to get work from him when I was obliged to make money somehow. He payed regularly. I applied to him, and he gave me twenty-five roubles in advance, engaging me to compile an article by the end of the week. But I hoped to pick up time on my novel. I often did this when it came to the last necessity. Having got the money I set off to the market. There I soon found an old woman I knew who sold old clothes of all sorts. I gave her Elena's size approximately, and she instantly picked me out a light coloured cotton dress priced extremely cheaply, though it was quite strong and had not been washed more than once. While I was about it I took a neckerchief too. As I paid for them I reflected that Elena would need a coat, mantle, or something of that kind. It was cold weather and she had absolutely nothing. But I put off that purchase for another time. Elena was so proud and ready to take offence. Goodness knows, I thought, how she'll take this dress even though I purposely picked out the most ordinary garment as plain and unattractive as possible. I did, however, buy her two pairs of thread stockings and one pair of woollen. Those I could give her on the ground that she was ill and that it was cold in the room. She would need underclothes too. But all that I left till I should get to know her better. Then I bought some old curtains for the bed. They were necessary and might be a great satisfaction to Elena.

With all these things I returned home at one o'clock in the afternoon. My key turned almost noiselessly in the lock, so that Elena did not at once hear me come in. I noticed that she was standing at the table turning over my books and papers. Hearing me she hurriedly closed the book she was reading, and moved away from the table, flushing all over. I glanced at the book. It was my first novel which had been republished in book form and had my name on the title-page.

"Some one knocked here while you were away!" she said in a tone which seemed to taunt me for having locked her in.

"Wasn't it the doctor?" I said. "Didn't you call to him, Elena?"

"No!"

I made no answer, but took my parcel, untied it, and took out the dress I had bought.

"Here, Elena, my dear!" I said going up to her. "You can't go about in such rags as you've got on now. So I've bought you a dress, an everyday one, very cheap. So there's no need for you to worry about it It only cost one rouble twenty kopecks. Wear it with my best wishes."

I put the dress down beside her. She flushed crimson and looked at me for some time with open eyes.

She was extremely surprised and at the same time it seemed to me that she was horribly ashamed for some reason. But there was a light of something soft and tender in her eyes. Seeing that she said nothing I turned away to the table. What I had done had evidently impressed her, but she controlled herself with an effort, and sat with her eyes cast down.

My head was going round and aching more and more. The fresh air had done me no good. Meanwhile I had to go to Natasha's. My anxiety about her was no less than yesterday. On the contrary it kept growing more and more. Suddenly I fancied that Elena called me. I turned to her.

"Don't lock me in when you go out," she said, looking away

and picking at the border of the sofa, as though she were entirely absorbed in doing so. "I will not go away from you."

"Very well, Elena, I agree. But what if some stranger comes? There's no knowing who may!"

"Then leave me the key and I'll lock myself in and if they knock I shall say, 'not at home.'"

And she looked slyly at me as much as to say, "see how simply that's done!"

"Who washes your clothes?" she asked suddenly, before I had had time to answer her.

"There's a woman here, in this house."

"I know how to wash clothes. And where did you get the food yesterday?"

"At a restaurant."

"I know how to cook, too. I will do your cooking."

"That will do, Elena. What can you know about cooking? You're talking nonsense. . . ."

Elena looked down and was silent. She was evidently wounded at my remark. Ten minutes at least passed. We were both silent.

"Soup!" she said suddenly, without raising her head.

"What about soup? What soup?" I asked, surprised.

"I can make soup. I used to make it for mother when she was ill. I used to go to market too."

"See, Elena, just see how proud you are," I said, going up to her and sitting down beside her on the sofa. "I treat you as my heart prompts me. You are all alone, without relations, and unhappy. I want to help you. You'd help me in the same way if I were in trouble. But you won't look at it like that, and it's disagreeable to you to take the smallest present from me. You want to repay it at once, to pay for it by work as though I were Mme. Bubnov, and would taunt you with it. If that is so, it's a shame, Elena."

She made no answer. Her lips quivered. I believe she wanted to say something; but she controlled herself and was silent. I got up to go to Natasha. That time I left Elena the key, begging her if anybody should come and knock, to call out and ask who was there. I felt perfectly sure that something dreadful was happening to Natasha, and that she was keeping it dark from me for the time, as she had done more than once before. I resolved in any case to look in only for one moment for fear of irritating her by my persistence.

And it turned out I was right. She met me again with a look of harsh displeasure. I ought to have left her at once but my legs were giving way under me.

"I've only come for a minute, Natasha," I began, "to ask your advice what I'm to do with my visitor."

And I began briefly telling her all about Elena. Natasha listened to me in silence.

"I don't know what to advise you, Vanya," she said. "Everything shows that she's a very strange little creature. Perhaps she has been dreadfully ill-treated and frightened. Give her time to get well, anyway. You think of my people for her?"

"She keeps saying that she won't go anywhere away from me. And goodness knows how they'll take her, so I don't know what to do. Well, tell me, dear, how you are. You didn't seem quite well yesterday," I said timidly.

"Yes . . . my head aches rather to-day, too," she answered absent-mindedly. "Haven't you seen any of our people?"

"No. I shall go to-morrow. To-morrow's Saturday, you know. . . ."

"Well, what of it?"

"The prince is coming in the evening."

"Well? I've not forgotten."

"No, I only. . . ."

She stood still, exactly opposite me, and looked for a long time intently into my face. There was a look of determination, of obstinacy in her eyes, something feverish and wrathful.

"Look here, Vanya," she said, "be kind, go away, you worry me."

I got up from my chair and looked at her, unutterably astonished.

"Natasha, dear, what's the matter? What has happened?" I cried in alarm.

"Nothing's happened. You'll know all about it to-morrow, but now I want to be alone. Do you hear, Vanya? Go away at once. I can't bear, I can't bear to look at you!"

"But tell me at least. . . ."

"You'll know all about it to-morrow! Oh, my God! Are you going?"

I went out. I was so overcome that I hardly knew what I was doing. Mavra started out into the passage to meet me.

"What, is she angry?" she asked me. "I'm afraid to go near her."

"But what's the matter with her?"

"Why, our young gentleman hasn't shown his nose here for the last three days!"

"Three days!" I repeated in amazement. "Why, she told me yesterday that he had been here in the morning and was coming again in the evening. . . ."

"She did? He never came near us in the morning! I tell you we haven't set eyes on him for three days. You don't say she told you yesterday that he'd been in the morning?"

"Yes, she said so."

"Well," said Mavra, musing, "it must have cut her to the quick if she won't own it even to you. Well, he's a pretty one!"

"But what does it mean?" I cried.

"It means I don't know what to do with her," said Mavra, throwing up her hands. "She was sending me to him yesterday, but twice she turned me back as I was starting. And to-day she won't even speak to me. If only you could see him. I daren't leave her now."

I rushed down the staircase, beside myself.

"Will you be here this evening?" Mavra called after me.

"We'll see then," I called up to her. "I may just run in to you to ask how she is. If only I'm alive myself."

I really felt as though something had struck me to the very heart.

CHAPTER X

I WENT straight to Alyosha's. He lived with his father in Little Morskaya. Prince Valkovsky had a rather large flat, though he lived alone. Alyosha had two splendid rooms in the flat. I had very rarely been to see him, only once before, I believe, in fact. He had come to see me much oftener, especially at first, during the early period of his connexion with Natasha.

He was not at home. I went straight to his rooms and wrote him the following note:

"Alyosha, you seem to have gone out of your mind. As on Tuesday evening your father himself asked Natasha to do you the honour of becoming your wife, and you were delighted at his doing so as I saw myself you must admit that your behaviour is somewhat strange. Do you know what you are doing to Natasha ? In any case this note will remind you that your behaviour towards your future wife is unworthy and frivolous in the extreme. I am very well aware that I have no right to lecture you, but I don't care about that in the least.

"P.S.—She knows nothing about this letter, and in fact it was not she who told me about you."

I sealed up the letter and left it on his table. In answer to my question the servant said that Alexey Petrovitch was hardly ever at home, and that he would not be back now till the small hours of the morning.

I could hardly get home I was overcome with giddiness, and my legs were weak and trembling. My door was open. Nikolay Sergeyitch Ichmenyev was sitting waiting for me. He was sitting at the table watching Elena in silent wonder, and she, too, was watching him with no less wonder, though she was obstinately silent. "To be sure," I thought, "he must think her queer."

"Well, my boy, I've been waiting for you for a good hour, and I must confess I had never expected to find things . . . like this," he went on, looking round the room, with a scarcely perceptible sign towards Elena.

His face expressed his astonishment. But looking at him more closely I noticed in him signs of agitation and distress. His face was paler than usual.

"Sit down, sit down," he said with a preoccupied and anxious air. "I've come round to you in a hurry. I've something to say to you. But what's the matter ? You don't look yourself."

"I'm not well. I've been giddy all day."

"Well, mind, you musn't neglect that. Have you caught cold or what ?"

"No, it's simply a nervous attack. I sometimes have them. But aren't you unwell ?"

"No, no ! It's nothing ; it's excitement. I've something to say. Sit down."

I moved a chair over and sat down at the table, facing him. The old man bent forward to me, and said in a half whisper :

"Mind, don't look at her, but seem as though we were speaking of something else. What sort of visitor is this you've got here ?"

"I'll explain to you afterwards, Nikolay Sergeyitch. This

poor girl is absolutely alone in the world. She's the grandchild of that old Smith who used to live here and died at the confectioner's."

"Ah, so he had a grandchild! Well, my boy, she's a queer little thing! How she stares, how she stares! I tell you plainly if you hadn't come in I couldn't have stood it another five minutes. She would hardly open the door, and all this time not a word! It's quite uncanny; she's not like a human being. But how did she come here? I suppose she came to see her grandfather, not knowing he was dead?"

"Yes, she has been very unfortunate. The old man thought of her when he was dying."

"Hm! She seems to take after her grandfather. You'll tell me all about that later. Perhaps one could help her somehow, in some way, if she's so unfortunate. But now, my boy, can't you tell her to go away, for I want to talk to you of something serious."

"But she's nowhere to go. She's living here."

I explained in a few words as far as I could, adding that he could speak before her, that she was only a child.

"To be sure . . . she's a child. But you have surprised me, my boy. She's staying with you! Good heavens!"

And the old man looked at her again in amazement.

Elena, feeling that we were talking about her, sat silent, with her head bent, picking at the edge of the sofa with her fingers. She had already had time to put on her new dress, which fitted her perfectly. Her hair had been brushed more carefully than usual, perhaps in honour of the new dress. Altogether, if it had not been for the strange wildness of her expression, she would have been a very pretty child.

"Short and clear, that's what I have to tell you," the old man began again. "It's a long business, an important business."

He sat looking down, with a grave and meditative air, and in spite of his haste and his "short and clear," he could find no words to begin. "What's coming?" I wondered.

"Do you know, Vanya, I've come to you to ask a very great favour. But first . . . as I realize now myself, I must explain to you certain circumstances . . . very delicate circumstances."

He cleared his throat and stole a look at me; looked and flushed red; flushed and was angry with himself for his awkwardness; he was angry and pressed on.

"Well, what is there to explain! You understand yourself!

The long and short of it is, I am challenging Prince Valkovsky to a duel, and I beg you to make the arrangements and be my second."

I fell back in my chair and gazed at him, beside myself with astonishment.

"Well, what are you staring at? I've not gone out of my mind."

"But, excuse me, Nikolay Sergeyitch! On what pretext? With what object? And, in fact, how is it possible?"

"Pretext! Object!" cried the old man. "That's good!"

"Very well, very well. I know what you'll say; but what good will you do by your action? What will be gained by the duel? I must own I don't understand it."

"I thought you wouldn't understand. Listen, our lawsuit is over (that is, it will be over in a few days. There are only a few formalities to come). I have lost the case. I've to pay ten thousand; that's the decree of the court. Ichmenyevka is the security for it. So now this base man is secure of his money, and giving up Ichmenyevka I have paid him the damages and become a free man. Now I can hold up my head and say, 'You've been insulting me one way and another, honoured prince, for the last two years; you have sullied my name and the honour of my family, and I have been obliged to bear all this! I could not then challenge you to a duel. You'd have said openly then, "You cunning fellow, you want to kill me in order not to pay me the money which you foresee you'll be sentenced to pay sooner or later. No, first let's see how the case ends and then you can challenge me." Now, honoured prince, the case is settled, you are secure, so now there are no difficulties, and so now will you be pleased to meet me at the barrier?' That's what I have to say to you. What, to your thinking haven't I the right to avenge myself, for everything, for everything?"

His eyes glittered. I looked at him for a long time without speaking. I wanted to penetrate to his secret thought.

"Listen, Nikolay Sergeyitch," I said at last, making up my mind to speak out on the real point without which we could not understand each other. "Can you be perfectly open with me?"

"I can," he answered firmly.

"Tell me plainly. Is it only the feeling of revenge that prompts you to challenge him, or have you other objects in view?"

"Vanya," he answered, "you know that I allow no one to

touch on certain points with me, but I'll make an exception in the present case. For you, with your clear insight, have seen at once that we can't avoid the point. Yes, I have another aim. That aim is to save my lost daughter and to rescue her from the path of ruin to which recent events are driving her now."

"But how will you save her by this duel ? That's the question."

"By hindering all that is being plotted among them now. Listen ; don't imagine that I am actuated by fatherly tenderness or any weakness of that sort. All that's nonsense ! I don't display my inmost heart to anyone. Even you don't know it. My daughter has abandoned me, has left my house with a lover, and I have cast her out of my heart—I cast her out once for all that very evening—you remember ? If you have seen me sobbing over her portrait, it doesn't follow that I want to forgive her. I did not forgive her then. I wept for my lost happiness, for my vain dreams, but not for *her* as she is now. I often weep perhaps. I'm not ashamed to own it, just as I'm not ashamed to own that I once loved my child more than anything on earth. All this seems to belie my conduct now. You may say to me 'if it's so, if you are indifferent to the fate of her whom you no longer look on as a daughter, why do you interfere in what they are plotting there ?' I answer : in the first place that I don't want to let that base and crafty man triumph, and secondly, from a common feeling of humanity. If she's no longer my daughter she's a weak creature, defenceless and deceived, who is being still more deceived, that she may be utterly ruined. I can't meddle directly, but indirectly, by a duel, I can. If I am killed or my blood is shed, surely she won't step over our barrier, perhaps over my corpse, and stand at the altar beside the son of my murderer, like the daughter of that king (do you remember in the book you learnt to read out of ?) who rode in her chariot over her father's body ? And, besides, if it comes to a duel, our princes won't care for the marriage themselves. In short, I don't want that marriage, and I'll do everything I can to prevent it. Do you understand me now ? "

"No. If you wish Natasha well, how can you make up your mind to hinder her marriage, that is, the one thing that can establish her good name ? She has all her life before her ; she will have need of her good name."

"She ought to spit on the opinion of the world. That's how she ought to look at it. She ought to realize that the greatest disgrace of all for her lies in that marriage, in being connected with those vile people, with that paltry society. A noble pride—that should be her answer to the world. Then perhaps I might consent to hold out a hand to her, and then we would see who dared cry shame on my child!"

Such desperate idealism amazed me. But I saw at once that he was not himself and was speaking in anger.

"That's too idealistic," I answered, "and therefore cruel. You're demanding of her a strength which perhaps you did not give her at her birth. Do you suppose that she is consenting to this marriage because she wants to be a princess? Why, she's in love; it's passion; it's fate. You expect of her a contempt for public opinion while you bow down before it yourself! The prince has insulted you, has publicly accused you of a base scheme to ally yourself with his princely house, and now you are reasoning that if she refuses them now after a formal offer of marriage from their side it will, of course, be the fullest and plainest refutation of the old calumny. That's what you will gain by it. You are deferring to the opinion of the prince himself, and you're struggling to make him recognize his mistake. You're longing to turn him into derision, to revenge yourself on him, and for that you will sacrifice your daughter's happiness. Isn't that egoism?"

The old man sat gloomy and frowning, and for a long time he answered not a word.

"You're unjust to me, Vanya," he said at last, and a tear glistened on his eyelashes. "I swear you are unjust. But let us leave that! I can't turn my heart inside out before you," he went on, getting up and taking his hat. "One thing I will say—you spoke just now of my daughter's happiness. I have absolutely and literally no faith in that happiness. Besides which, the marriage will never come off, apart from my interference."

"How so? What makes you think so? Perhaps you know something?" I cried with curiosity.

"No. I know nothing special. But that cursed fox can never have brought himself to such a thing. It's all nonsense, all a trap. I'm convinced of that, and, mark my words, it will turn out so. And secondly, even if this marriage did take place, which could only happen if that scoundrel has some special, mysterious interests to be served by it—interests which no one knows anything about, and I'm utterly at a loss to understand—

tell me, ask your own heart, will she be happy in that marriage ? Taunts, humiliations, with the partner of her life a wretched boy who is weary of her love already, and who will begin to neglect her, insult her, and humiliate her as soon as he is married. At the same time her own passion growing stronger as his grows cooler ; jealousy, tortures, hell, divorce, perhaps crime itself. . . . No, Vanya ! If you're all working for that end, and you have a hand in it, you'll have to answer to God for it. I warn you, though it will be too late then ! Good-bye."

I stopped him.

"Listen, Nikolay Sergeyitch. Let us decide to wait a bit. Let me assure you that more than one pair of eyes is watching over this affair. And perhaps it will be settled of itself in the best possible way without violence and artificial interference, such as a duel, for instance. Time is the very best arbiter. And, finally, let me tell you, your whole plan is utterly impossible. Could you for a moment suppose that Prince Valkovsky would accept your challenge ? "

" Not accept it ? What do you mean by that ? "

" I swear he wouldn't ; and believe me, he'd find a perfectly satisfactory way out of it ; he would do it all with pedantic dignity and meanwhile you would be an object of derision. . . ."

" Upon my word, my boy, upon my word ! You simply overwhelm me ! How could he refuse to accept it ? No, Vanya, you're simply a romancer, a regular romancer ! Why, do you suppose there is anything unbecoming in his fighting me ? I'm just as good as he is. I'm an old man, an insulted father. You're a Russian author, and therefore also a respectable person. You can be a second and . . . and . . . I can't make out what more you want. . . ."

" Well, you'll see. He'll bring forward such excuses that you'll be the first to see that it will be utterly impossible for you to fight him."

" Hm ! . . . very well, my friend. Have it your own way ! I'll wait, for a certain time, that is. We'll see what time will do. But one thing, my dear, give me your word of honour that you'll not speak of this conversation *there*, nor to Anna Andreyevna."

" I promise."

" Do me another favour, Vanya, never begin upon the subject again."

" Very well. I promise."

"And one more request: I know, my dear, that it's dull for you perhaps, but come and see us as often as ever you can. My poor Anna Andreyevna is so fond of you, and ... and ... she's so wretched without you. ... You understand, Vanya."

And he pressed my hand warmly. I promised him with all my heart.

"And now, Vanya, the last delicate question. Have you any money?"

"Money?" I repeated with surprise.

"Yes." (And the old man flushed and looked down.) "I look at you, my boy, at your lodgings ... at your circumstances ... and when I think that you may have other, outside expenses (and that you may have them just now) then ... Here, my boy, a hundred and fifty roubles as a first instalment...."

"A hundred and fifty! *As a first instalment.* And you've just lost your case!"

"Vanya, I see you didn't understand me at all! You may have *exceptional* calls on you, understand that. In some cases money may help to an independent position, an independent decision. Perhaps you don't need it now, but won't you need it for something in the future? In any case I shall leave it with you It's all I've been able to get together. If you don't spend it you can give it back. And now good-bye. My God, how pale you are! Why, you're quite ill ..."

I took the money without protest. It was quite clear why he left it with me.

"I can scarcely stand up," I answered.

"You must take care of yourself, Vanya, darling! Don't go out to-day. I shall tell Anna Andreyevna what a state you're in. Oughtn't you to have a doctor? I'll see how you are to-morrow; I'll try my best to come, anyway, if only I can drag my legs along myself. Now you'd better lie down. ... Well, good-bye. Good-bye, little girl; she's turned her back! Listen, my dear, here are another five roubles. That's for the child, but don't tell her I gave it her. Simply spend it for her. Get her some shoes or underclothes. She must need all sorts of things. Good-bye, my dear. ..."

I went down to the gate with him. I had to ask the porter to go out to get some food for me. Elena had had no dinner.

CHAPTER XI

But as soon as I came in again I felt my head going round and fell down in the middle of the room. I remember nothing but Elena's shriek. She clasped her hands and flew to support me. That is the last moment that remains in my memory. . . .

When I regained consciousness I found myself in bed. Elena told me later on, that with the help of the porter who came in with some eatables, she had carried me to the sofa.

I waked up several times, and always saw Elena's compassionate and anxious little face leaning over me. But I remember all that as in a dream, as through a mist, and the sweet face of the poor child came to me in glimpses, through my stupor, like a vision, like a picture. She brought me something to drink, arranged my bedclothes, or sat looking at me with a distressed and frightened face, and smoothing my hair with her fingers. Once I remember her gentle kiss on my face. Another time suddenly waking up in the night, by the light of the smouldering candle that had been set on a little table by my bedside, I saw Elena lying with her face on my pillow with her warm cheek resting on her hand, and her pale lips half parted in an uneasy sleep. But it was only early next morning that I fully regained consciousness. The candle had completely burnt out. The vivid rosy beams of early sunrise were already playing on the wall. Elena was sitting at the table, asleep, with her tired little head pillowed on her left arm, and I remember I gazed a long time at her childish face, full, even in sleep, of an unchildlike sadness and a sort of strange, sickly beauty. It was pale with long arrowy eyelashes lying on the thin cheeks, and pitch-black hair that fell thick and heavy in a careless knot on one side. Her other arm lay on my pillow. Very softly I kissed that thin little arm. But the poor child did not wake, though there was a faint glimmer of a smile on her pale lips. I went on gazing at her, and so quietly fell into a sound healing sleep. This time I slept almost till midday. When I woke up I felt almost well again. A feeling of weakness and heaviness in my limbs was the only trace left of my illness. I had had such sudden nervous attacks before ; I knew them very well. The attack generally passed off within twenty-four hours, though the symptoms were acute and violent for that time.

THE INSULTED AND INJURED 157

It was nearly midday. The first thing I saw was the curtain I had bought the day before, which was hanging on a string across the corner. Elena had arranged it, screening off the corner as a separate room for herself. She was sitting before the stove boiling the kettle. Noticing that I was awake she smiled cheerfully and at once came up to me.

"My dear," I said, taking her hand, "you've been looking after me all night. I didn't know you were so kind."

"And how do you know I've been looking after you? Perhaps I've been asleep all night," she said, looking at me with shy and good-humoured slyness, and at the same time flushing shamefacedly at her own words.

"I waked up and saw you. You only fell asleep at daybreak."

"Would you like some tea?" she interrupted, as though feeling it difficult to continue the conversation, as all delicately modest and sternly truthful people are apt to when they are praised.

"I should," I answered, "but did you have any dinner yesterday?"

"I had no dinner but I had some supper. The porter brought it. But don't you talk. Lie still. You're not quite well yet," she added, bringing me some tea and sitting down on my bed.

"Lie still, indeed! I will lie still, though, till it gets dark, and then I'm going out. I really must, Lenotchka."

"Oh, you must, must you! Who is it you're going to see? Not the gentleman who was here yesterday?"

"No, I'm not going to him."

"Well, I'm glad you're not. It was he upset you yesterday. To his daughter then?"

"What do you know about his daughter?"

"I heard all you said yesterday," she answered, looking down. Her face clouded over. She frowned.

"He's a horrid old man," she added.

"You know nothing about him. On the contrary, he's a very kind man."

"No, no, he's wicked. I heard," she said with conviction.

"Why, what did you hear?"

"He won't forgive his daughter. . . ."

"But he loves her. She has behaved badly to him; and he is anxious and worried about her."

"Why doesn't he forgive her? If he does forgive her now she shouldn't go back to him."

"How so ? Why not ? "

"Because he doesn't deserve that she should love him," she answered hotly. "Let her leave him for ever and let her go begging, and let him see his daughter begging, and be miserable."

Her eyes flashed and her cheeks glowed. "There must be something behind her words," I thought.

"Was it to his home you meant to send me ? " she added after a pause.

"Yes, Elena."

"No, I'd better get a place as a servant."

"Ah, how wrong is all that you're saying, Lenotchka ! And what nonsense ! Who would take you as a servant ? "

"Any peasant," she answered impatiently, looking more and more downcast.

She was evidently hot-tempered.

"A peasant doesn't want a girl like you to work for him," I said, laughing.

"Well, a gentleman's family, then."

"You live in a gentleman's family with your temper ? "

"Yes."

The more irritated she became, the more abrupt were her answers.

"But you'd never stand it."

"Yes I would. They'd scold me, but I'd say nothing on purpose. They'd beat me, but I wouldn't speak, I wouldn't speak. Let them beat me—I wouldn't cry for anything. That would annoy them even more if I didn't cry."

"Really, Elena ! What bitterness, and how proud you are ! You must have seen a lot of trouble. . . ."

I got up and went to my big table. Elena remained on the sofa, looking dreamily at the floor, and picking at the edge of the sofa. She did not speak. I wondered whether she were angry at what I had said.

Standing by the table I mechanically opened the books I had brought the day before, for the compilation, and by degrees I became absorbed in them. It often happens to me that I go and open a book to look up something, and go on reading so that I forget everything.

"What are you always writing ? " Elena asked with a timid smile, coming quietly to the table.

"All sorts of things, Lenotchka. They give me money for it."

"Petitions ? "

"No, not petitions."

And I explained to her as far as I could that I wrote all sorts of stories about different people, and that out of them were made books that are called novels. She listened with great curiosity.

"Is it all true what you write?"

"No, I make it up."

"Why do you write what isn't true?"

"Why, here, read it. You see this book; you've looked at it already. You can read, can't you?"

"Yes."

"Well, you'll see then. I wrote this book."

"You? I'll read it. . . ."

She was evidently longing to say something, but found it difficult, and was in great excitement. Something lay hidden under her questions.

"And are you paid much for this?" she asked at last.

"It's as it happens. Sometimes a lot, sometimes nothing, because the work doesn't come off. It's difficult work, Lenotchka."

"Then you're not rich?"

"No, not rich."

"Then I shall work and help you."

She glanced at me quickly, flushed, dropped her eyes, and taking two steps towards me suddenly threw her arms round me and pressed her face tightly against my breast; I looked at her with amazement.

"I love you . . . I'm not proud," she said. "You said I was proud yesterday. No, no, I'm not like that. I love you. You are the only person who cares for me. . . ."

But her tears choked her. A minute later they burst out with as much violence as the day before. She fell on her knees before me, kissed my hands, my feet. . . .

"You care for me!" she repeated. "You're the only one, the only one."

She embraced my knees convulsively. All the feeling which she had repressed for so long broke out at once, in an uncontrollable outburst, and I understood the strange stubbornness of a heart that for a while shrinkingly masked its feeling, the more harshly, the more stubbornly, as the need for expression and utterance grew stronger till the inevitable outburst came, when the whole being forgot itself and gave itself up to the craving for love, to gratitude, to affection and to tears. She sobbed till she became hysterical. With an effort I loosened her arms, lifted her up and carried her to the sofa. For a long time she went on sobbing, hiding her face in the pillow as though ashamed to look at me. But she held my hand tight, and kept it pressed to her heart.

By degrees she grew calmer, but still did not raise her face to me. Twice her eyes flitted over my face, and there was a great softness, and a sort of timorous and shrinking emotion in them.

At last she flushed and smiled.

"Are you better?" I asked, "my sensitive little Lenotchka, my sick little child!"

"Not Lenotchka, no . . ." she whispered, still hiding her face from me.

"Not Lenotchka? What then?"

"Nellie."

"Nellie? Why must it be Nellie? If you like; it's a very pretty name. I'll call you so if that's what you wish."

"That's what mother called me. And no one else ever called me that, no one but she. . . . And I would not have anyone call me so but mother. But you call me so. I want you to. I will always love you, always."

"A loving and proud little heart," I thought. "And how long it has taken me to win the right to call you Nellie!"

But now I knew her heart was gained for ever.

"Nellie, listen," I said, as soon as she was calmer. "You say that no one has ever loved you but your mother. Is it true your grandfather didn't love you?"

"No, he didn't."

"Yet you cried for him; do you remember, here, on the stairs?"

For a minute she did not speak.

"No, he didn't love me. . . . He was wicked."

A look of pain came into her face.

"But we mustn't judge him too harshly, Nellie, I think he had grown quite childish with age. He seemed out of his mind when he died. I told you how he died."

"Yes. But he had only begun to be quite forgetful in the last month. He would sit here all day long, and if I didn't come to him he would sit on for two or three days without eating or drinking. He used to be much better before."

"What do you mean by ' before ' ? "

" Before mother died."

" Then it was you brought him food and drink, Nellie ? "

" Yes, I used to."

" Where did you get it ? From Mme. Bubnov ? "

" No, I never took anything from Bubnov," she said emphatically, with a shaking voice.

" Where did you get it ? You had nothing, had you ? "

Nellie turned fearfully pale and said nothing ; she bent a long, long look upon me.

" I used to beg in the streets. . . . When I had five kopecks I used to buy him bread and snuff. . . ."

" And he let you ! Nellie ! Nellie ! "

" At first I did it without telling him. But when he found out he used to send me out himself I used to stand on the bridge and beg of passers-by, and he used to walk up and down near the bridge, and when he saw me given anything he used to rush at me and take the money, as though I wanted to hide it from him, and were not getting it for him."

As she said this she smiled a sarcastic, bitter smile.

" That was all when mother was dead," she added. " Then he seemed to have gone quite out of his mind."

" So he must have loved your mother very much. How was it he didn't live with her ? "

" No, he didn't love her. . . . He was wicked and didn't forgive her . . . like that wicked old man yesterday," she said quietly, almost in a whisper, and grew paler and paler.

I started. The plot of a whole drama seemed to flash before my eyes. That poor woman dying in a cellar at the coffin-maker's, her orphan child who visited from time to time the old grandfather who had cursed her mother, the queer crazy old fellow who had been dying in the confectioner's shop after his dog's death.

" And Azorka used to be mother's dog," said Nellie suddenly, smiling at some reminiscence. " Grandfather used to be very fond of mother once, and when mother went away from him she left Azorka behind. And that's why he was so fond of Azorka. He didn't forgive mother, but when the dog died he died too," Nellie added harshly, and the smile vanished from her face.

" What was he in old days, Nellie ? " I asked her after a brief pause.

"He used to be rich. . . . I don't know what he was," she answered. "He had some sort of factory. So mother told me. At first she used to think I was too little and didn't tell me everything. She used to kiss me and say, 'You'll know everything, the time will come when you'll know everything, poor, unhappy child!' She was always calling me poor and unhappy. And sometimes at night when she thought I was asleep (though I was only pretending to be asleep on purpose) she used to be always crying over me, she would kiss me and say 'poor, unhappy child'!"

"What did your mother die of?"

"Of consumption; it's six weeks ago."

"And you do remember the time when your grandfather was rich?"

"But I wasn't born then. Mother went away from grandfather before I was born."

"With whom did she go?"

"I don't know," said Nellie softly, as though hesitating. "She went abroad and I was born there."

"Abroad? Where?"

"In Switzerland. I've been everywhere. I've been in Italy and in Paris too."

I was surprised.

"And do you remember it all, Nellie?"

"I remember a great deal."

"How is it you know Russian so well, Nellie?"

"Mother used to teach me Russian even then. She was Russian because her mother was Russian. But grandfather was English, but he was just like a Russian too. And when we came to Russia a year and a half ago I learnt it thoroughly. Mother was ill even then. Then we got poorer and poorer. Mother was always crying. At first she was a long time looking for grandfather here in Petersburg, and always crying and saying that she had behaved badly to him. How she used to cry! And when she knew grandfather was poor she cried more than ever. She often wrote letters to him, and he never answered."

"Why did your mother come back here? Was it only to see her father?"

"I don't know. But there we were so happy." And Nellie's eyes sparkled. "Mother used to live alone, with me. She had one friend, a kind man like you. He used to know her before she went away. But he died out there and mother came back . . ."

"So it was with him that your mother went away from your grandfather?"

"No, not with him. Mother went away with some one else, and he left her . . ."

"Who was he, Nellie?"

Nellie glanced at me and said nothing. She evidently knew the name of the man with whom her mother had gone away and who was probably her father. It was painful to her to speak that name even to me.

I did not want to worry her with questions. Hers was a strange character, nervous and fiery, though she suppressed her impulses, lovable, though she entrenched herself behind a barrier of pride and reserve. Although she loved me with her whole heart, with the most candid and ingenuous love, almost as she had loved the dead mother of whom she could not speak without pain, yet all the while I knew her she was rarely open with me, and except on that day she rarely felt moved to speak to me of her past; on the contrary, she was, as it were, austerely reserved with me, but on that day through convulsive sobs of misery that interrupted her story, she told me in the course of several hours all that most distressed and tortured her in her memories, and I shall never forget that terrible story, but the greater part of it will be told later. . . .

It was a fearful story. It was the story of a woman abandoned and living on after the wreck of her happiness, sick, worn out and forsaken by every one, rejected by the last creature to whom she could look—her father, once wronged by her and crazed by intolerable sufferings and humiliations. It was the story of a woman driven to despair, wandering through the cold, filthy streets of Petersburg, begging alms with the little girl whom she regarded as a baby; of a woman who lay dying for months in a damp cellar, while her father, refusing to forgive her to the last moment of her life, and only at the last moment relenting, hastened to forgive her only to find a cold corpse instead of the woman he loved above everything on earth.

It was a strange story of the mysterious, hardly comprehensible relations of the crazy old man with the little grandchild who already understood him, who already, child as she was, understood many things that some men do not attain to in long years of their smooth and carefully guarded lives. It was a gloomy story, one of those gloomy and distressing dramas which are so often played out unseen, almost mysterious, under the heavy sky of Petersburg, in the dark secret corners of the vast town, in the midst of the giddy ferment of life, of dull egoism, of clashing interests, of gloomy vice and secret crimes, in that lowest hell of senseless and abnormal life. . . .

But that story will be told later. . . .

PART III

CHAPTER I

TWILIGHT had fallen, the evening had come on before I roused myself from the gloomy nightmare and came back to the present.

"Nellie," I said, "you're ill and upset, and I must leave you alone, in tears and distress. My dear! Forgive me, and let me tell you that there's some one else who has been loved and not forgiven, who is unhappy, insulted, and forsaken. She is expecting me. And I feel drawn to her now after your story, so that I can't bear not to see her at once, this very minute."

I don't know whether she understood all that I said. I was upset both by her story and by my illness; but I rushed to Natasha's. It was late, nine o'clock, when I arrived.

In the street I noticed a carriage at the gate of the house where Natasha lodged, and I fancied that it was the prince's carriage. The entry was across the courtyard. As soon as I began to mount the stairs I heard, a flight above me, some one carefully feeling his way, evidently unfamiliar with the place. I imagined this must be the prince, but I soon began to doubt it. The stranger kept grumbling and cursing the stairs as he climbed up, his language growing stronger and more violent as he proceeded. Of course the staircase was narrow, filthy, steep, and never lighted; but the language I heard on the third floor was such that I could not believe it to be the prince: the ascending gentleman was swearing like a cabman. But there was a glimmer of light on the third floor; a little lamp was burning at Natasha's door. I overtook the stranger at the door, and what was my astonishment when I recognized him as Prince Valkovsky! I fancied he was extremely annoyed at running up against me so unexpectedly. At the first moment he did not recognize me, but suddenly his whole face changed. His first glance of anger and hatred relaxed into an affable, good-humoured expression, and he held out both hands to me with extraordinary delight.

"Ach, that's you! And I was just about to kneel down to thank God my life was safe! Did you hear me swearing?"

And he laughed in the most good-natured way. But suddenly his face assumed an earnest and anxious expression.

"How could Alyosha let Natalya Nikolaevna live in such a place!" he said, shaking his head. "It's just these so-called trifles that show what a man's made of. I'm anxious about him. He is good-natured, he has a generous heart, but here you have an example: he's frantically in love, yet he puts the girl he loves in a hole like this. I've even heard she has sometimes been short of food," he added in a whisper, feeling for the bell-handle. "My head aches when I think about his future and still more of the future of *Anna* Nikolaevna when she is his wife. . . ."

He used the wrong name, and did not notice it in his evident vexation at not finding the bell-handle. But there was no bell.

I tugged at the door-handle and Mavra at once opened the door to us, and met us fussily. In the kitchen, which was divided off from the tiny entry by a wooden screen, through an open door some preparations could be seen; everything seemed somehow different from usual, cleaned and polished; there was a fire in the stove, and some new crockery on the table. It was evident that we were expected. Mavra flew to help us off with our coats.

"Is Alyosha here?" I asked her.

"He has not been," she whispered mysteriously. We went in to Natasha. There was no sign of special preparation in her room. Everything was as usual. But everything in her room was always so neat and charming that there was no need to arrange it. Natasha met us, facing the door. I was struck by the wasted look in her face, and its extreme pallor, though there was a flush of colour for a moment on her wan cheeks. Her eyes were feverish. Hastily she held out her hand to the prince without speaking, visibly confused and agitated. She did not even glance at me. I stood and waited in silence.

"Here I am!" said the prince with friendly gaiety. "I've only been back a few hours. You've never been out of my mind all these days" (he kissed her hand tenderly) "and how much, how much I have thought about you. How much I have thought of to say to you. . . . Well, we can talk to our hearts' content! In the first place my feather-headed youngster who is not here yet . . ."

"Excuse me, prince," Natasha interrupted, flushing and embarrrassed, "I have to say a word to Ivan Petrovitch. Vanya, come along . . . two words . . ."

She seized my hand and drew me behind the screen.

"Vanya," she said in a whisper, leading me to the furthest corner, " will you forgive me ? "

"Hush, Natasha, what do you mean ? "

"No, no, Vanya, you have forgiven me too much, and too often. But there's an end to all patience. You will never leave off caring for me, I know. But you'll call me ungrateful. And I was ungrateful to you yesterday and the day before yesterday, selfish, cruel . . ."

She suddenly burst into tears and pressed her face on my shoulder.

"Hush, Natasha," I hastened to reassure her. "I've been very ill all night, and I can hardly stand now, that's why I didn't come yesterday or to-day, and you've been thinking I was angry. Dearest, do you suppose I don't understand what's going on in your heart now ? "

"Well, that's right then . . . then you've forgiven me as you always do," she said, smiling through her tears, and squeezing my hand till it hurt. "The rest later. I've a lot I must say to you, Vanya. But now come back to him. . . ."

"Make haste, Natasha, we left him so suddenly. . . ."

"You'll see, you'll see what's coming directly," she whispered to me. "Now I understand it all, I see through it all. It's all *his* doing. A great deal will be decided this evening. Come along ! "

I didn't understand, but there was no time to ask. Natasha came up to the prince with a serene expression. He was still standing with his hat in his hand. She apologized good-humouredly, took his hat from him, moved up a chair for him and we three sat down round her little table.

"I was beginning about my feather-headed boy," the prince went on. "I've only seen him for a moment and that was in the street when he was getting into his carriage to drive to the Countess Zinaida Fyodorovna. He was in a terrible hurry, and would you believe it, wouldn't even stop to come to my room, after four days of absence, and I believe it's my fault, Natalya Nikolaevna, that he's not here and that we've arrived before him. I seized the chance. As I couldn't be at the countess's myself to-day, I gave him a message to her. But he will be here in a minute or two."

"I supposed he promised you to come to-day?" asked Natasha, looking at the prince with a look of perfect simplicity.

"Good heavens, as though he wouldn't have come anyway! How can you ask!" he exclaimed, looking at her in wonder. "I understand though, you are angry with him. Indeed, it does seem wrong of him to be the last to come. But I repeat that it's my fault. Don't be angry with him. He's shallow, frivolous. I don't defend him, but certain special circumstances make it necessary that he should not give up the countess and some other connexions, but, on the contrary, should go to see them as often as possible. And as now he never leaves your side, I expect, and has forgotten everything else on earth, please do not be angry if I sometimes take him off for an hour or two, not more, to do things for me. I dare say he has not been to see Princess A. once since that evening, and I'm vexed that I have not had time to question him yet! . . ."

I glanced towards Natasha. She was listening to Prince Valkovsky with a slight, half-mocking smile. But he spoke so frankly, so naturally. It seemed impossible to suspect him.

"And did you really not know that he has not been near me all these days?" asked Natasha in a quiet and gentle voice, as though she were talking of the most ordinary matter.

"What? not been here once? Good heavens, what are you saying!" said the prince, apparently in extreme astonishment.

"You were with me late on Tuesday evening. Next morning he came in to see me for half an hour, and I've not seen him once since then."

"But that's incredible!" (He was more and more astonished.) "I expected that he would never leave your side. Excuse me, this is so strange . . . it's simply beyond belief."

"But it's true, though, and I'm so sorry. I was looking forward to seeing you. I was expecting to learn from you where he has been."

"Upon my soul! But he'll be here directly. But what you tell me is such a surprise to me that . . . I confess I was prepared for anything from him, but this, this!"

"How it surprises you! While I thought that, so far from being surprised, you knew beforehand that it would be so."

"Knew! I? But I assure you, Natalya Nikolaevna, that I've only seen him for one moment to-day, and I've questioned no one about him. And it strikes me as odd that you don't seem to believe me," he went on, scanning us both.

"God forbid!" Natasha exclaimed. "I'm quite convinced that what you say is true."

And she laughed again, right in Prince Valkovsky's face, so that he almost winced.

"Explain yourself!" he said in confusion.

"Why, there's nothing to explain. I speak very simply. You know how heedless and forgetful he is. And now that he has been given complete liberty he is carried away."

"But to be carried away like that is impossible. There's something behind it, and as soon as he comes in I'll make him explain what it is. But what surprises me most of all is that you seem to think me somehow to blame, when I've not even been here. But I see, Natalya Nikolaevna, that you are very angry with him—and I can quite understand. You've every right to be so, and of course I'm the first person to blame if only that I'm the first to turn up. That's how it is, isn't it?" he went on, turning to me, with angry derision.

Natasha flushed red.

"Certainly, Natalya Nikolaevna," he continued with dignity, "I'll admit I am to blame, but only for going away the day after I made your acquaintance; so with the suspiciousness of character I observe in you, you have already changed your opinion of me—circumstances, of course, have given some grounds for this. Had I not gone away, you would have known me better, and Alyosha would not have been so heedless with me to look after him. You shall hear yourself what I say to him this evening."

"That is, you'll manage to make him begin to feel me a burden. Surely, with your cleverness, you can't imagine that that would be any help to me."

"Do you mean to hint that I would intentionally try to make him feel you a burden? You insult me, Natalya Nikolaevna."

"I try to speak without hints when I can, whoever the person may be I am speaking to," answered Natasha. "I always try, on the contrary, to be as open as I can, and you will perhaps be convinced of that this evening. I don't wish to insult you, and there's no reason I should; if only because you won't be insulted by my words, whatever I may say. Of that I am quite certain, for I quite realize the relation in which we stand to one another. You can't take it seriously, can you? But if I really have been rude to you, I am ready to ask your pardon that I may not be lacking in any of the obligations of . . . hospitality."

In spite of the light and even jesting tone with which she uttered these words, and the smile on her lips, I had never seen Natasha so intensely irritated. It was only now that I realized what her heartache must have been during those three days. Her enigmatic saying that she knew everything now and that she guessed it all frightened me; it referred directly to Prince Valkovsky. She had changed her opinion of him and looked upon him as her enemy; that was evident. She apparently attributed her discomfiture with Alyosha to his influence and had perhaps some grounds for this belief. I was afraid there might be a scene between them at any moment. Her mocking tone was too manifest, too undisguised. Her last words to the prince that he could not take their relations seriously, the phrase about the obligations of hospitality, her promise, that looked like a threat, to show him that she knew how to be open—all this was so biting, so unmistakable, that it was impossible that the prince should not understand it. I saw his face change, but he was well able to control himself. He at once pretended not to have noticed these words, not to have seen their significance, and took refuge of course in raillery.

"God forbid I should ask for apologies!" he cried, laughing. "That's not at all what I wanted, and indeed it's against my rules to ask apologies from a woman. At our first interview I warned you what I was like, so you're not likely to be angry with me for one observation, especially as it applies to all women. You probably agree with this remark," he went on, politely turning to me. "I have noticed as a trait in the female character that if a woman is in fault in any way, she will sooner smoothe over her offence with a thousand caresses later on than admit her fault and ask forgiveness at the moment when she is confronted with it. And so, supposing even that I have been insulted by you, I am not anxious for an apology. It will be all the better for me later on when you own your mistake and want to make it up to me . . . with a thousand caresses. And you are so sweet, so pure, so fresh, so open, that the moment of your penitence will, I foresee, be enchanting. You had better, instead of apologizing, tell me now whether I cannot do something this evening to show you that I am behaving much more sincerely and straightforwardly than you suppose."

Natasha flushed. I, too, fancied that there was somewhat too flippant, even too casual a tone, in Prince Valkovsky's answer, a rather unseemly jocosity.

"You want to prove that you are simple and straightforward with me?" asked Natasha, looking at him with a challenging air.

"Yes."

"If so, do what I ask."

"I promise beforehand."

"And that is, not by one word, one hint, to worry Alyosha about me, either to-day or to-morrow. No reproof for having forgotten me; no remonstrance. I want to meet him as though nothing had happened, so that he may notice nothing. That's what I want. Will you make me such a promise?"

"With the greatest pleasure," answered Prince Valkovsky, "and allow me to add with all my heart that I have rarely met a more sensible and clear-sighted attitude in such circumstances.... But I believe this is Alyosha."

A sound was in fact heard in the passage. Natasha started and seemed to prepare herself for something. Prince Valkovsky sat with a serious face waiting to see what would happen. He was watching Natasha intently. But the door opened and Alyosha flew in.

CHAPTER II

He literally flew in with a beaming face, gay and joyous. It was evident that he had spent those four days gaily and happily. One could see from his face that he had something he was longing to tell us.

"Here I am!" he cried out, addressing us all, "I, who ought to have been here before anyone. But I'll tell you everything directly, everything, everything! I hadn't time to say two words to you this morning, daddy, and I had so much to say to you. It's only in his sweet moments he lets me speak to him like that," he interrupted himself, addressing me. "I assure you at other times he forbids it! And I'll tell you what he does. He begins to use my full name. But from this day I want him always to have good minutes, and I shall manage it! I've become quite a different person in these last four days, utterly, utterly different, and I'll tell you all about it. But that will be presently. The great thing now is that she's here. Here she is! Again! Natasha, darling, how are you, my angel!" he said, sitting down beside her and greedily kissing her hand. "How I've been missing you all this time ! But there it is ! I couldn't help it ! I wasn't able to manage it, my darling ! You look a little thinner, you've grown so pale . . ."

He rapturously covered her hands with kisses, and looked eagerly at her with his beautiful eyes, as though he could never look enough. I glanced at Natasha, and from her face I guessed that our thoughts were the same : he was absolutely innocent. And indeed when and how could this *innocent* be to blame ? A bright flush suddenly overspread Natasha's pale cheeks, as though all the blood had suddenly rushed from her heart to her head. Her eyes flashed and she looked proudly at Prince Valkovsky.

"But where . . . have you been so many days ? " she said in a suppressed and breaking voice. She was breathing in hard uneven gasps. My God, how she loved him !

"To be sure I must have seemed to blame, and it's not only *seeming*, indeed ! Of course I've been to blame, and I know it myself, and I've come, knowing it. Katya told me yesterday and to-day that no woman could forgive such negligence (she knows all that happened here on Tuesday ; I told her next day); I argued with her, I maintained that there is such a woman and her name is Natasha, and that perhaps there was only one other woman equal to her in the world and that was Katya ; and I came here of course knowing I'd won the day. Could an angel like you refuse to forgive ? 'He's not come, so something must have kept him. It's not that he doesn't love me ! '—that's what my Natasha will think ! As though one could leave off loving you ! As though it were possible ! My whole heart has been aching for you. I'm to blame all the same. But when you know all about it you'll be the first to stand up for me. I'll tell you all about it directly ; I want to open my heart to you all ; that's what I've come for. I wanted to fly to you to-day (I was free for half a minute) to give you a flying kiss, but I didn't succeed even in that. Katya sent for me on important business. That was before you saw me in the carriage, father. That was the second time I was driving to Katya after a second note. Messengers are running all day long with notes between the two houses. Ivan Petrovitch, I only had time to read your note last night and you are quite right in all you say in it. But what could I do ? It was a physical impossibility ! And so I thought 'to-morrow evening I'll set it all straight,' for it was impossible for me not to come to you this evening, Natasha."

"What note ? " asked Natasha.

"He went to my rooms and didn't find me. Of course he pitched into me roundly in the letter he left for me for not having been to see you. And he's quite right. It was yesterday."

Natasha glanced at me.

"But if you had time to be with Katerina Fyodorovna from morning till night . . ." Prince Valkovsky began.

"I know, I know what you'll say," Alyosha interrupted. "If I could be at Katya's I ought to have had twice as much reason to be here. I quite agree with you and will add for myself not twice as much reason but a million times as much. But, to begin with, there are strange unexpected events in life which upset everything and turn it topsy-turvy, and it's just things of that sort that have been happening to me. I tell you I've become an utterly different person during the last days. New all over to the tips of my fingers. So they must have been important events!"

"Oh, dear me, but what has happened to you? Don't keep us in suspense, please!" cried Natasha, smiling at Alyosha's heat.

He really was rather absurd, he talked very fast, his words rushed out pell-mell in a quick, continual patter. He was longing to tell us everything, to speak, to talk. But as he talked he still held Natasha's hand and continually raised it to his lips as though he could never kiss it enough.

"That's the whole point—what has happened to me," Alyosha went on. "Ah, my friends, the things I've been seeing and doing, the people I've got to know! To begin with Katya! Such a perfect creature! I didn't know her a bit, not a bit till now. Even the other day, that Tuesday when I talked about her, do you remember, Natasha, with such enthusiasm, even then I hardly knew her a bit. She hasn't shown her real self to me till now. But now we've got to know each other thoroughly. We call each other Katya and Alyosha. But I'll begin at the beginning. To begin with, Natasha, if only you could hear all that she said to me when I spoke to her about you the other day, Wednesday it was, and told her all that had happened here. . . . And by the way, I remember how stupid I was when I came to see you on Wednesday! You greeted me with enthusiasm, you were full of our new position; you wanted to talk to me about it all; you were sad, and at the same time you were full of mischief and playing with me; while I was trying to be dignified. Oh, fool, fool that I was! Would you believe it, I was longing to show off, to boast that I was soon to be a husband, a dignified person, and to think of my showing off to you. Ah, how you must have laughed at me and how I deserved your ridicule!"

Prince Valkovsky sat in silence, looking with a sort of triumphantly ironical smile at Alyosha. He seemed to be glad that his son was showing himself so flighty and even ridiculous. I watched him carefully all that evening, and came to the conclusion that he was not at all fond of his son, though he was always talking of his warm fatherly devotion to him.

"From you I went to Katya," Alyosha rattled on. "I've told you already that it was only that morning we got to know each other thoroughly, and it's queer how it happened . . . I don't remember how it was . . . some warm words, some feelings, thoughts frankly uttered and we—were friends for ever. You must know her, you must, Natasha. How she talked to me, how she interpreted you to me. How she explained to me what a treasure you are. By degrees she made me understand all her ideas, all her views of life; she's such an earnest, such an enthusiastic girl! She talked of duty, of our mission in life, of how we all ought to serve humanity and, as we thoroughly agreed, after five or six hours of conversation, we ended by swearing eternal friendship, and that we would work together all our lives!"

"Work at what?" asked his father in astonishment.

"I'm so changed, father, that all this must surprise you. I know all your objections beforehand," Alyosha responded triumphantly. "You are all practical people, you have so many grave, severe principles that are out of date. You look with mistrust, with hostility, with derision at everything new, everything young and fresh. But I'm not the same now as you knew me a few days ago. I'm a different man! I look everything and every one in the world boldly in the face. If I know that my conviction is right I will follow it up to its utmost limit; and if I'm not turned aside from my path I'm an honest man. That's enough for me. You can say what you like after that. I believe in myself."

"Oh-ho!" said the prince jeeringly.

Natasha looked round at us uneasily. She was afraid for Alyosha. It often happened that he showed to great disadvantage in conversation, and she knew it. She did not want Alyosha to make himself ridiculous before us, and especially before his father.

"What are you saying, Alyosha? I suppose it's some sort of philosophy," she said. "Some one's been lecturing you. . . . You'd much better tell us what you've been doing."

"But I am telling you!" cried Alyosha. "You see, Katya has two distant relations, cousins of some sort, called Levinka and Borinka. One's a student, the other's simply a young man. She's on friendly terms with them, and they're simply extraordinary men. They hardly ever go to the countess's, on principle. When Katya and I talked of the destiny of man, of our mission in life and all that, she mentioned them to me, and gave me a note to them at once; I flew immediately to make their acquaintance. We became close friends that very evening. There were about twelve fellows of different sorts there. Students, officers, artists. There was one author. They all know you, Ivan Petrovitch. That is, they've read your books and expect great things of you in the future. They told me so themselves. I told them I knew you and promised to introduce them to you. They all received me with open arms like a brother. I told them straight off that I should soon be a married man, so they received me as a married man. They live on the fifth storey right under the roof. They meet as often as they can, chiefly on Wednesdays at Levinka's and Borinka's. They're all fresh young people filled with ardent love for all humanity. We all talked of our present, of our future, of science and literature, and talked so well, so frankly and simply. . . . There's a high-school boy who comes too. You should see how they behave to one another, how generous they are! I've never seen men like them before! Where have I been all this time? What have I seen? What ideas have I grown up in? You're the only one, Natasha, who has ever told me anything of this sort. Ah, Natasha, you simply must get to know them; Katya knows them already. They speak of her almost with reverence. And Katya's told Levinka and Borinka already that when she comes into her property she'll subscribe a million to the common cause at once."

"And I suppose Levinka and Borinka and all their crew will be the trustees for that million?" Prince Valkovsky asked.

"That's false, that's false! It's a shame to talk like that, father!" Alyosha cried with heat. "I suspect what you're thinking! We certainly have talked about that million, and spent a long time discussing how to use it We decided at last on public enlightenment before everything else. . . ."

"Yes, I see that I did not quite know Katerina Fyodorovna, certainly," Prince Valkovsky observed as it were to himself, still with the same mocking smile. "I was prepared for many things from her, but this . . ."

"Why this?" Alyosha broke in. "Why do you think it so odd? Because it goes somewhat beyond your established routine? because no one has subscribed a million before, and she subscribes it? What of it! What if she doesn't want to live at the expense of others, for living on those millions means living at the expense of others (I've only just found that out). She wants to be of service to her country and all, and to give her mite to the common cause. We used to read of that mite in our copy-books, and when that mite means a million you think there's something wrong about it! And what does it all rest on, this common sense that's so much praised and that I believed in so? Why do you look at me like that, father? As though you were looking at a buffoon, a fool! What does it matter my being a fool? Natasha, you should have heard what Katya said about that. 'It's not the brains that matter most, but that which guides them—the character, the heart, generous qualities, progressive ideas.' But better still, Bezmygin has a saying about that that's full of genius. Bezmygin is a friend of Levinka's and Borinka's, and between ourselves he is a man of brains and a real leader of genius. Only yesterday he said in conversation, 'the fool who recognizes that he is a fool is no longer a fool.' How true that is! One hears utterances like that from him every minute. He positively scatters truths."

"A sign of genius, certainly," observed Prince Valkovsky.

"You do nothing but laugh. But I've never heard anything like that from you, and I've never heard anything like it from any of your friends either. On the contrary, in your circle you seem to be hiding all this, to be grovelling on the ground, so that all figures, all noses may follow precisely certain measurements, certain rules—as though that were possible; as though that were not a thousand times more impossible than what we talk about and what we think. And yet they call us Utopian! You should have heard what they said to me yesterday . . ."

"Well, but what is it you talk and think about? Tell us, Alyosha. I can't quite understand yet," said Natasha.

"Of everything in general that leads up to progress, to humanity, to love, it's all in relation to contemporary questions. We talk about the need of a free press, of the reforms that are beginning, of the love of humanity, of the leaders of to-day; we criticize them and read them. But above all we've promised to be perfectly open with one another and to tell everything about ourselves, plainly, openly, without hesitation. Nothing but openness and straightforwardness can attain our object. That's what Bezmygin is striving most for. I told Katya about that and she is in complete sympathy with Bezmygin. And so all of us, under Bezmygin's leadership, have promised to act honestly and straightforwardly all our lives, and not to be disconcerted in any way, not to be ashamed of our enthusiasm, our fervour, our mistakes, and to go straight forward whatever may be said of us and however we may be judged. If you want to be respected by others, the great thing is to respect yourself. Only by that, only by self-respect will you compel others to respect you. That's what Bezmygin says, and Katya agrees with him entirely. We're agreeing now upon our convictions in general, and have resolved to pursue the study of ourselves severally, and when we meet to explain ourselves to each other."

"What a string of nonsense!" cried Prince Valkovsky uneasily. "And who is this Bezmygin? No, it can't be left like this. . . ."

"What can't be left?" cried Alyosha. "Listen, father, why I say all this before you. It's because I want and hope to bring you, too, into our circle. I've pledged myself in your name already. You laugh; well, I knew you'd laugh! But hear me out. You are kind and generous, you'll understand. You don't know, you've never seen these people, you haven't heard them. Supposing you have heard of all this, and have studied it all, you are horribly learned, yet you haven't seen them themselves, have not been in their house, and so how can you judge of them correctly? You only imagine that you know them. You be with them, listen to them, and then—then I'll give you my word you'll be one of us. Above all I want to use every means I can to rescue you from ruin in the circle to which you have so attached yourself, and so save you from your convictions."

Prince Valkovsky listened to this sally in silence, with a malignant sneer; there was malice in his face. Natasha was watching him with unconcealed repulsion. He saw it, but pretended not to notice it. But as soon as Alyosha had finished, his father broke into a peal of laughter. He fell back in his chair as though he could not control himself. But the laughter was certainly not genuine. He was quite unmistakably laughing simply to wound and to humiliate his son as deeply as possible. Alyosha was certainly mortified. His whole face betrayed intense sadness. But he waited patiently until his father's merriment was over.

"Father," he began mournfully, "why are you laughing at me?

M

I have come to you frankly and openly. If, in your opinion, what I say is silly, teach me better, and don't laugh at me. And what do you find to laugh at? At what is for me good and holy now? Why, suppose I am in error, suppose this is all wrong, mistaken, suppose I am a little fool as you've called me several times; if I am making a mistake I'm sincere and honest in it; I've done nothing ignoble. I am enthusiastic over lofty ideas. They may be mistaken, but what they rest upon is holy. I've told you that you and all your friends have never yet said anything to me that could guide me, or influence me. Refute them, tell me something better than they have said, and I will follow you, but do not laugh at me, for that grieves me very much."

Alyosha pronounced these words with extreme sincerity, and a sort of severe dignity. Natasha watched him sympathetically. The prince heard his son with genuine amazement, and instantly changed his tone.

"I did not mean to grieve you, my dear," he answered. "On the contrary I am sorry for you. You are preparing to take such a step in life that it is only seemly for you to leave off being such a feather-headed boy. That's what is in my mind. I could not help laughing, and had no wish to hurt your feelings."

"Why was it that I thought so?" said Alyosha, with bitter feeling. "Why has it seemed for a long time past that you look at me as though you were antagonistic to me, with cold mockery, not like a father. Why is it I feel that if I were in your place I should not laugh so offensively as you do at me. Listen, let us speak openly with one another, at once, and for ever, that there may be no further misunderstanding. And . . . I want to tell you the whole truth. I thought when I came here that there was some misunderstanding. It was not like this that I expected to meet you all together. Am I right? If I am, wouldn't it be better for each of us to say openly what he feels. How much evil may be averted by openness!"

"Speak, speak, Alyosha," said Prince Valkovsky. "What you propose is very sensible. Perhaps you ought to have begun with that," he added, glancing at Natasha.

"Don't be angry with my perfect frankness," began Alyosha. "You desire it and call for it yourself. Listen, you have agreed to my marriage with Natasha; you've made us happy by doing so, and for the sake of it you have overcome your own feelings. You have been magnanimous and we have all appreciated your generosity. But why is it now that with a sort of glee you keep hinting that I'm a ridiculous boy, and am not fit to be a husband. What's more, you seem to want to humiliate me and make me ridiculous, and even contemptible, in Natasha's eyes. You are always delighted when you can make me look absurd. I've noticed that before now, for a long time past. As though you were trying for some reason to show us that our marriage is absurd and foolish, and that we are not fitted for one another. It's really as though you didn't believe yourself in what you design for us; as though you look upon it all as a joke, as an absurd fancy, as a comic farce. I don't think so only from what you've said to-day. That very evening, that Tuesday when I came back to you from here, I heard some strange expressions from you which surprised and hurt me. And on Wednesday, too, as you were going away you made some allusions to our present position, and spoke of her, not slightingly, quite the contrary, but yet not as I would like to hear you speak, somehow too lightly, without affection, without the respect for her. . . . It's difficult to describe, but the tone was clear; one feels it in one's heart. Tell me that I'm mistaken. Reassure me, comfort me and . . . and her, for you've wounded her too. I guessed that from the first moment I came in. . . ."

Alyosha said this with warmth and resolution. Natasha listened to him with a certain triumph, and, her face glowing with excitement, she said, as though to herself, once or twice during his speech, "Yes, yes. That's true." Prince Valkovsky was taken aback.

"My dear boy," he answered, "of course I can't remember everything I've said to you; but it's very strange you should have taken my words in that way. I'm quite ready to reassure you in every way I can. If I laughed just now that was quite natural. I tell you that I tried to hide under a laugh my bitter feeling. When I imagine that you are about to be a husband it seems to me now so utterly incredible, so absurd, excuse my saying so, even ludicrous. You reproach me for that laugh, but I tell you that it is all your doing. I am to blame, too. Perhaps I haven't been looking after you enough of late, and so it's only this evening that I have found out of what you are capable. Now I tremble when I think of your future with Natalya Nikolaevna. I have been in too great a hurry; I see that there is a great disparity between you. Love always passes, but incompatibility remains for ever. I'm not speaking now of your fate, but if your intentions are honest, do consider; you will ruin Natalya

Nikolaevna as well as yourself, you certainly will! Here you've been talking for an hour of love for humanity, of the loftiness of your convictions, of the noble people you've made friends with. But ask Ivan Petrovitch what I said to him just now as we climbed up that nasty staircase to the fourth storey, and were standing at the door, thanking God that our lives and limbs were safe. Do you know the feeling that came into my mind in spite of myself? I was surprised that with your love for Natalya Nikolaevna you could bear to let her live in such a flat. How is it you haven't realized that, if you have no means, if you are not in a position to do your duty, you have no right to be a husband, you have no right to undertake any responsibilities. Love alone is a small matter; love shows itself in deeds, but your motto is 'live with me if you have to suffer with me' —that's not humane, you know, not honourable to talk of love for all humanity, to go into raptures over the problems of the universe, and at the same time to sin against love without noticing it—it's incomprehensible! Don't interrupt me, Natalya Nikolaevna, let me finish. I feel it too bitterly, I must speak out. You've been telling us, Alyosha, that during these last days you've been attracted by everything that's honourable, fine, and noble, and you have reproached me that among my friends there are no such attractions, nothing but cold common sense. Only imagine, to be attracted by everything lofty and fine, and, after what happened here on Tuesday, to neglect for four whole days the woman who, one would have thought, must be more precious to you than anything on earth. You positively confess that you argued with Katerina Fyodorovna that Natalya Nikolaevna is so generous and loves you so much that she will forgive you your behaviour. But what right have you to reckon on such forgiveness, and make bets about it? And is it possible you haven't once reflected what distress, what bitter feelings, what doubts, what suspicions you've been inflicting on Natalya Nikolaevna all this time? Do you think that because you've been fascinated there by new ideas, you had the right to neglect your first duty? Forgive me, Natalya Nikolaevna, for breaking my word. But the present position is more important than any promise, you will realize that yourself. . . . Do you know, Alyosha, that I found Natalya Nikolaevna in such agonies of distress that it was plain what a hell you had made of these four days for her, which should, one would have thought, have been the happiest in her life. Such conduct on one side and on the other—words, words, words . . . am I not right ? And you can blame me when it's entirely your own fault ? "

Prince Valkovsky finished. He was really carried away by his own eloquence and could not conceal his triumph from us. When Alyosha heard of Natasha's distress he looked at her with painful anxiety, but Natasha had already come to a decision.

"Never mind, Alyosha, don't be unhappy," she said. "Others are more to blame than you. Sit down and listen to what I have to say to your father. It's time to make an end of it ! "

"Explain yourself, Natalya Nikolaevna ! " cried the prince. "I beg you most earnestly ! For the last two hours I have been listening to these mysterious hints. It is becoming intolerable, and I must admit I didn't expect such a welcome here."

"Perhaps ; because you expected so to fascinate us with words that we should not notice your secret intentions. What is there to explain to you ? You know it all and understand it all yourself. Alyosha is right. Your first desire is to separate us. You knew beforehand, almost by heart, everything that would happen here, after last Tuesday, and you were reckoning on it all. I have told you already that you don't take me seriously, nor the marriage you have planned. You are making fun of us, you are playing, and you have your own objects. Your game is a safe one. Alyosha was right when he reproached you for looking on all this as a farce. You ought, on the contrary, to be delighted and not scold Alyosha, for without knowing anything about it he has done all that you expected of him, and perhaps even more."

I was petrified with astonishment. I had expected some catastrophe that evening. But I was utterly astounded at Natasha's ruthless plain speaking and her frankly contemptuous tone. Then she really must know something, I thought, and has irrevocably determined upon a rupture. Perhaps she had been impatiently expecting the prince in order to tell him everything to his face. Prince Valkovsky turned a little pale. Alyosha's face betrayed naive alarm and agonizing expectation.

"Think what you have just accused me of," cried the prince, "and consider your words a little . . . I can make nothing of it."

"Ah ! So you don't care to understand at a word," said Natasha. "Even he, even Alyosha, understood you as I did, and we are not in any agreement about it. We have not even seen each other ! He, too, fancied that you were playing an ignoble and insulting game with us, and he loves you and believes in you as though you were a god. You haven't thought it necessary to be cautious and hypocritical enough with him, you reckoned that he would not see through you. But he has a tender, sensitive, impressionable heart, and your words, your *tone*, as he says, have left a trace in his heart . . ."

"I don't understand a word of it, not a word of it," repeated Prince Valkovsky, turning to me with an air of the utmost perplexity, as though he were calling me to witness. He was hot and angry.

"You are suspicious, you are agitated," he went on, addressing her. "The fact is you are jealous of Katerina Fyodorovna, and so you're ready to find fault with every one, and me especially . . . and, allow me to say, you give one a strange idea of your character . . I am not accustomed to such scenes. I would not remain here another moment if it were not for my son's interests. I am still waiting. Will you condescend to explain?"

"So you still persist and will not understand though you know all this by heart. Do you really want me to speak out?"

"That is all I am anxious for."

"Very well then, listen," cried Natasha, her eyes flashing with anger. "I'll tell you everything, everything."

CHAPTER III

She got up and began to speak standing, unconscious of doing so in her excitement. After listening for a time, Prince Valkovsky too, stood up. The whole scene became quite solemn.

"Remember your own words on Tuesday," Natasha began. "You said you wanted money, to follow the beaten track, importance in the world—do you remember?"

"I remember."

"Well, to gain that money, to win all that success which was slipping out of your hands, you came here on Tuesday and made up this match, calculating that this practical joke would help you to capture what was eluding you."

"Natasha!" I cried. "Think what you're saying!"

"Joke! Calculating!" repeated the prince with an air of insulted dignity.

Alyosha sat crushed with grief and gazed scarcely comprehending.

"Yes, yes, don't stop me. I have sworn to speak out," Natasha went on, irritated. "Remember, Alyosha was not obeying you. For six whole months you had been doing your utmost to draw him away from me. He held out against you. And at last the time came when you could not afford to lose a moment. If you let it pass, the heiress, the money—above all the money, the three millions of dowry would slip through your fingers. Only one course was left you, to make Alyosha love the girl you destined for him; you thought that if he fell in love with her he would abandon me."

"Natasha! Natasha!" Alyosha cried in distress, "what are you saying?"

"And you have acted accordingly," she went on, not heeding Alyosha's exclamation, "but—it was the same old story again! Everything might have gone well, but I was in the way again. There was only one thing to give you hope. A man of your cunning and experience could not help seeing even then that Alyosha seemed at times weary of his old attachment. You could not fail to notice that he was beginning to neglect me, to be bored, to stay away for five days at a time. You thought he might get tired of it altogether and give me up, when suddenly on Tuesday Alyosha's decided action came as a shock to you. What were you to do!"

"Excuse me," cried Prince Valkovsky, "on the contrary, that fact . . ."

"I say," Natasha went on emphatically, "you asked yourself that evening what you were to do, and resolved to sanction his marrying me not in reality but only in *words*, simply to soothe him. The date of the wedding could be deferred, you thought, indefinitely, and meanwhile the new feeling was growing; you saw that. And on the growth of this new love you rested all your hopes."

"Novels, novels," the prince pronounced in an undertone, as though speaking to himself, "solitude, brooding, and novel-reading."

"Yes, on this new love you rested everything," Natasha repeated, without listening or attending to his words, more and more carried away in a fever of excitement. "And the chances in favour of this new love! It had begun before he knew all the girl's perfections. At the very moment when he disclosed to her that evening that he could not love her, that duty and another love forbade it—the girl suddenly displayed such nobility of character, such sympathy for him and for her rival, such spontaneous forgiveness, that though he had believed in her beauty, he only realized then how splendid she was. When he came to me he talked of nothing but her, she had made such an impression upon him. Yes, he was bound next day to feel an irresistible impulse to see this noble being again, if only from gratitude. And, indeed, why shouldn't he go to her? His old love was not in distress now, her future was secured, his whole life was to be given up to her, while the other would have only a minute. And how ungrateful Natasha would be if she were jealous even of that minute. And so without noticing it he robs his Natasha not of a minute, but of one day, two days, three. . . . And meantime, in those three days, the girl shows herself to him in a new and quite unexpected light. She is so noble, so enthusiastic, and at the same time such a naïve child, and in fact so like himself in character. They vow eternal friendship and brotherhood, they wish never to be parted. *In five or six hours of conversation* his soul is opened to new sensations and his whole heart is won. The time will come at last, you reckon, when he will compare his old feeling with his new, fresh sensations. There everything is familiar, and the same as usual; there it's all serious and exacting; there he finds jealousy and reproaches; there he finds tears. . . . Or if there is lightness and playfulness, he is treated like a child not an equal. . . But worst of all, it's all familiar, the same as ever. . . ."

Tears and a spasm of bitterness choked her, but Natasha controlled herself for a minute longer.

"And what besides? Why, time. The wedding with Natasha is not fixed yet, you think; there's plenty of time and all will change. . . . And then your words, hints, arguments, eloquence. . . . You may even be able to trump up something against that troublesome Natasha. You may succeed in putting her in an unfavourable light and . . . there's no telling how it will be done; but the victory is yours! Alyosha! Don't blame me, my dear! Don't say that I don't understand your love and don't appreciate it. I know you love me even now, and that perhaps at this moment you don't understand what I complain of. I know I've done very wrong to say all this. But what am I to do, understanding all this, and loving you more and more . . . simply madly!"

She hid her face in her hands, fell back in her chair, and sobbed like a child. Alyosha rushed to her with a loud exclamation. He could never see her cry without crying too.

Her sobs were, I think, of great service to the prince; Natasha's vehemence during this long explanation, the violence of her attack on him which he was bound, if only from decorum, to resent, all this might be set down to an outburst of insane jealousy, to wounded love, even to illness. It was positively appropriate to show sympathy.

"Calm yourself, don't distress yourself, Natalya Nikolaevna," Prince Valkovsky encouraged her. "This is frenzy, imagination, the fruits of solitude. You have been so exasperated by his thoughtless behaviour. It is only thoughtlessness on his part, you know. The most important fact on which you lay so much stress, what happened on Tuesday, ought rather to prove to you the depth of his love for you, while you have been imagining on the contrary . . ."

"Oh, don't speak to me, don't torture me even now!" cried Natasha, weeping bitterly. "My heart has told me everything, has told me long ago! Do you suppose I don't understand that our old love is over. . . . Here, in this room, alone . . . when he left me, forgot me. . . . I have been through everything, thought over everything. . . . What else have I to do? I don't blame you, Alyosha. . . . Why are you deceiving me? Do you suppose I haven't tried to deceive myself? Oh, how often, how often! Haven't I listened to every tone of his voice? Haven't I learnt to read his face, his eyes? It's all, all over. It's all buried. . . . Oh! how wretched I am!"

Alyosha was crying on his knees before her.

"Yes, yes, it's my fault! It's all my doing!" he repeated through his sobs.

"No, don't blame yourself, Alyosha. It's other people . . . our enemies. . . . It's their doing . . . theirs!"

"But excuse me," the prince began at last with some impatience, "what grounds have you for ascribing to me all these . . . crimes? These are all your conjectures. There's no proof of them. . . ."

"No proof!" cried Natasha, rising swiftly from her easy chair. "You want proof, treacherous man. You could have had no other motive, no other motive when you came here with your project! You had to soothe your son, to appease his conscience-pricks that he might give himself up to Katya with a freer and easier mind. Without that he would always have remembered me, he would have held out against you, and you have got tired of waiting. Isn't that true?"

"I confess," said the prince, with a sarcastic smile, "if I had wanted to deceive you that would certainly have been my calculation. You are very . . . quick-witted, but you ought to have proofs before you insult people with such reproaches."

"Proofs! But all your behaviour in the past when you were trying to get him away from me. A man who trains his son to disregard such obligations, and to play with them for the sake of worldly advantage, for the sake of money, is corrupting him! What was it you said just now about the staircase and the poorness of my lodging? Didn't you stop the allowance you used to give him to force us to part through poverty and hunger? This lodging and the staircase are your fault, and now you reproach him with it—double-faced man! And what was it roused in you that night such warmth, such new and uncharacteristic convictions? And why was I so necessary to you? I've been walking up and down here for these four days; I've thought over everything, I have weighed every word you uttered, every expression of your face, and I'm certain that it has all been a pretence, a sham, a mean, insulting and unworthy farce. . . . I know you, I've known you for a long time. Whenever Alyosha came from seeing you I could read from his face all that you had been saying to him, all that you had been impressing on him. No, you can't deceive me! Perhaps you have some other calculations now; perhaps I haven't said the worst yet; but no matter! You have deceived me—that's the chief thing. I had to tell you that straight to your face!"

"Is that all? Is that all the proof you have? But think, you frantic woman: by that farce as you call my proposal on Tuesday I bound myself too much, it would be too irresponsible on my part . . ."

"How, how did you bind youself? What does it mean for you to deceive me? And what does it signify to insult a girl in my position? A wretched runaway, cast off by her father, defenceless, who has *disgraced* herself, *immoral!* Is there any need to be squeamish with her if this *joke* can be of the very smallest use!"

"Only think what a position you are putting yourself into, Natalya Nikolaevna. You insist that you have been insulted by me. But such an insult is so great, so humiliating, that I can't understand how you can even imagine it, much less insist on it. What must you be accustomed to, to be able to suppose this so easily, if you will excuse my saying so. I have the right to reproach you, because you are setting my son against me. If he does not attack me now on your account his heart is against me."

"No, father, no!" cried Alyosha, "if I haven't attacked you it's because I don't believe you could be guilty of such an insult, and I can't believe that such an insult is possible!"

"Do you hear?" cried Prince Valkovsky.

"Natasha, it's all my fault! Don't blame him. It's wicked and horrible."

"Do you hear, Vanya? He is already against me!" cried Natasha.

"Enough!" said the prince. "We must put an end to this painful scene. This blind and savage outburst of unbridled jealousy shows your character in quite a new light. I am forewarned. We have been in too great a hurry. We certainly have been in too great a hurry. You have not even noticed how you have insulted me. That's nothing to you. We were in too great a hurry . . . too great a hurry . . . my word ought to be sacred of course, but . . . I am a father, and I desire the happiness of my son. . . ."

"You go back from your word!" cried Natasha, beside herself. "You are glad of the opportunity. But let me tell you that here, alone, I made up my mind two days ago to give him back his promise, and now I repeat it before every one. I give him up!"

"That is, perhaps, you want to reawaken his old anxieties again, his feeling of duty, all his worrying about his obligations (as you expressed it just now yourself), so as to bind him to you again. This is the explanation on your own theory. That is why I say so; but enough, time will decide. I will await a calmer moment for an explanation with you. I hope we may not break off all relations. I hope, too, that you may learn to appreciate me better. I meant to-day to tell you of my projects for your family, which would have shown you. . . . But enough! Ivan Petrovitch," he added, coming up to me, "I have always wanted to know you better, and now, more than ever, I should appreciate it. I hope you understand me. I shall come and see you in a day or two if you will allow me."

I bowed. It seemed to me, too, that now I could not avoid making his acquaintance. He pressed my hand, bowed to Natasha without a word, and went out with an air of affronted dignity.

CHAPTER IV

For some minutes we all said nothing. Natasha sat in thought, sorrowful and exhausted. All her energy had suddenly left her. She looked straight before her seeing nothing, holding Alyosha's hand in hers and seeming lost in oblivion. He was quietly giving vent to his grief in tears, looking at her from time to time with timorous curiosity.

At last he began timidly trying to comfort her, besought her not to be angry, blamed himself; it was evident that he was very anxious to defend his father, and that this was very much on his mind. He began on the subject several times, but did not dare to speak out, afraid of rousing Natasha's wrath again. He protested his eternal unchanging love, and hotly justified his devotion to Katya, continually repeating that he only loved Katya as a sister, a dear, kind sister, whom he could not abandon altogether; that that would be really coarse and cruel on his part, declaring that if Natasha knew Katya they would be friends at once, so much so that they would never part and never quarrel. This idea pleased him particularly. The poor fellow was perfectly truthful. He did not understand her apprehensions, and indeed had no clear understanding of what she had just said to his father. All he understood was that they had quarrelled, and that above all lay like a stone on his heart.

"You are blaming me on your father's account?" asked Natasha.

"How can I blame you?" he said with bitter feeling, "when I'm the cause, and it's all my fault? It's I who have driven you into such a fury, and in your anger you blamed him too, because you wanted to defend me. You always stand up for me, and I don't deserve it. You had to fix the blame on some one, so you fixed it on him. And he's really not to blame!" cried Alyosha, warming up. "And was it with that thought he came here? Was that what he expected?"

But seeing that Natasha was looking at him with distress and reproach, he was abashed at once.

"Forgive me, I won't, I won't," he said. "It's all my fault!"

"Yes, Alyosha," she went on with bitter feeling. "Now he

has come between us and spoilt all our peace, for all our lives. You always believed in me more than in anyone. Now he has poured distrust and suspicion of me into your heart; you blame me; he has already taken from me half your heart. The black cat has run between us."

"Don't speak like that, Natasha. Why do you talk of the 'black cat'?"

He was hurt by the expression.

"He's won you by his false kindness, his false generosity," Natasha continued. "And now he will set you more and more against me."

"I swear that it isn't so," said Alyosha with still greater heat. "He was irritated when he said he was 'in too great a hurry.' You will see to-morrow, in a day or two, he'll think better of it; and if he's so angry that he really won't have our marriage I swear I won't obey him. I shall have the strength, perhaps, for that. And do you know who will help us?" he cried, delighted with his idea. "Katya will help us! And you will see, you will see what a wonderful creature she is! You will see whether she wants to be your rival and part us. And how unfair you were just now when you said that I was one of those who might change the day after marriage! It was bitter to me to hear that! No, I'm not like that, and if I went often to see Katya . . ."

"Hush, Alyosha! Go and see her whenever you like. That wasn't what I meant just now. You didn't understand it all. Be happy with anyone you like. I can't ask more of your heart than it can give me. . . ."

Mavra came in.

"Am I to bring in the tea? It's no joke to keep the samovar boiling for two hours It's eleven o'clock."

She spoke rudely and crossly. She was evidently out of humour and angry with Natasha. The fact was that ever since Tuesday she had been in the greatest delight that her young lady (whom she was very fond of) was to be married, and had already had time to proclaim it all over the house and neighbourhood, in the shop, and to the porter. She had been boasting of it and relating triumphantly that a prince, a man of consequence, and a general, awfully rich, had come himself to beg her young lady's consent, and she, Mavra, had heard it with her own ears, and now, suddenly, it had all ended in smoke. The prince had gone away furious, and no tea had been offered to him, and of course it was all her young lady's fault. Mavra had heard her speaking disrespectfully to him.

"Oh . . . yes," answered Natasha.

"And the savouries?"

"Yes, bring them too."

Natasha was confused.

"We've been making such preparations, such preparations," Mavra went on. "I've been run off my feet ever since yesterday. I ran to the Nevsky for wine, and here . . ."

And she went out, slamming the door angrily.

Natasha reddened and looked at me rather strangely.

Meanwhile tea was served, and with it savouries. There was game, fish of some sort, two bottles of excellent wine from Eliseyev. What were all these preparations for, I wondered.

"You see what I am, Vanya," said Natasha, going up to the table, and she was ashamed even to face me. "I foresaw it would all end as it has ended, you know; and still I thought that perhaps it wouldn't end so. I thought Alyosha might come, and begin to make peace and we should be reconciled. All my suspicions would turn out to be unjust, I should be convinced . . . and I got a supper ready on the chance. I thought perhaps we should sit and talk till late."

Poor Natasha! She blushed so deeply as she said this. Alyosha was delighted.

"There, you see, Natasha!" he cried. "You didn't believe it yourself. Two hours ago you didn't believe in your suspicions yourself. Yes, it must all be set right. I'm to blame. It's all my fault and I'll make it all right. Natasha, let me go straight to my father. I must see him; he is hurt, he is offended; I must comfort him. I will tell him everything, speaking only for myself, only for myself! You shan't be mixed up in it. And I'll settle everything. Don't be angry with me for being so anxious to get to him and ready to leave you. It's not that at all. I am sorry for him; he will justify himself to you, you will see. To-morrow I'll be with you as soon as it's light, and I'll spend the whole day with you. I won't go to Katya's."

Natasha did not detain him; she even urged him to go. She was dreadfully afraid that Alyosha would now force himself to stay with her from morning till night, and would weary of her. She only begged him to say nothing in her name, and tried to smile at him more cheerfully at parting. He was just on the point of going, but he suddenly went up to her, took her by both hands and sat down beside her. He looked at her with indescribable tenderness.

"Natasha, my darling, my angel, don't be angry with me, and don't let us ever quarrel. And give me your word that you'll always believe me, and I will believe you. There, my angel, I'll tell you now. We quarrelled once; I don't remember what about; it was my fault. We wouldn't speak to one another. I didn't want to be the first to beg pardon and I was awfully miserable. I wandered all over the town, lounged about everywhere, went to see my friends, and my heart was so heavy, so heavy. . . . And then the thought came into my mind, what if you fell ill, for instance, and died? And when I imagined that, I suddenly felt such despair as though I had really lost you for ever. My thoughts grew more and more oppressive and terrible. And little by little I began to imagine going to your tomb, falling upon it in despair, embracing it, and swooning with anguish. I imagined how I would kiss that tomb, and call you out of it, if only for a moment, and pray God for a miracle that for one moment you might rise up before me; I imagined how I would rush to embrace you, press you to me, kiss you, and die, it seemed, with bliss at being able once more for one instant to hold you in my arms as before. And as I was imagining that, the thought suddenly came to me: why, I shall pray to God for one minute of you, and meanwhile you have been with me six months, and during those six months how many times we've quarrelled, how many days we wouldn't speak to one another. For whole days we've been on bad terms and despised our happiness, and here I'm praying you to come for one minute from the tomb, and I'm ready to give my whole life for that minute. . . . When I fancied all that I couldn't restrain myself, but rushed to you as fast as I could; I ran here, and you were expecting me, and when we embraced after that quarrel I remember I held you in my arms as tightly as though I were really losing you, Natasha. Don't let us ever quarrel! It always hurts me so. And, good heavens, how could you imagine that I could leave you!"

Natasha was crying. They embraced each other warmly, and Alyosha swore once more that he would never leave her. Then he flew off to his father. He was firmly convinced that he would settle everything, that he would make everything come right.

"It's all ended! It's all over!" said Natasha, pressing my

hand convulsively. "He loves me and he will never cease to love me. But he loves Katya, too, and in a little time he'll love her more than me. And that viper, the prince, will keep his eyes open, and then . . ."

"Natasha! I, too, believe that the prince is not acting straightforwardly, but . . ."

"You don't believe all I've said to him! I saw that from your face. But wait a little, you'll see for yourself whether I'm right. I was only speaking generally, but heaven knows what else he has in his mind! He's an awful man. I've been walking up and down this room for the last four days, and I see through it all. He had to set Alyosha free, to relieve his heart from the burden of sadness that's weighing on his life, from the duty of loving me. He thought of this project of marriage with the idea, too, of worming his way in between us and influencing us, and of captivating Alyosha by his generosity and magnanimity. That's the truth, that's the truth, Vanya! Alyosha's just that sort of character. His mind would be set at rest about me, his uneasiness on my account would be over. He would think, 'why, she's my wife now, and mine for life,' and would unconsciously pay more attention to Katya. The prince has evidently studied Katya, and realizes that she's suited to him, and that she may attract him more than I can. Ach, Vanya, you are my only hope now! He wants for some reason to approach you, to get to know you. Don't oppose this, and for goodness' sake, dear, try to find some way of going to the countess's soon, make friends with this Katya, study her thoroughly and tell me what she is like. I want to know what you think of her. No one knows me as you do, and you will understand what I want. Find out, too, how far their friendship goes, how much there is between them, what they talk about. It's Katya, Katya, you must observe chiefly. Show me this once more, dear, darling Vanya, show me this once more what a true friend you are to me! You are my hope, my only hope now."

. . . . .

It was nearly one o'clock by the time I got home. Nellie opened the door to me with a sleepy face. She smiled and looked at me brightly. The poor child was very much vexed with herself for having fallen asleep. She had been very anxious to sit up for me. She told me some one had been and inquired for me, had sat and waited for a time, and had left a note on the table for me. The note was from Masloboev. He asked me to go to him next day between twelve and one. I wanted to question Nellie, but I put it off till next morning, insisting that she should go to bed at once. The poor child was tired as it was with sitting up for me, and had only fallen asleep half an hour before I came in.

CHAPTER V

In the morning Nellie told me some rather strange details about the visit of the previous evening. Indeed, the very fact that Masloboev had taken it into his head to come that evening at all was strange. He knew for a fact that I should not be at home. I had warned him of it myself at our last meeting, and I remembered it distinctly. Nellie told me that at first she had been unwilling to open the door, because she was afraid—it was eight o'clock in the evening. But he persuaded her to do so through the door, assuring her that if he did not leave a note for me that evening it would be very bad for me next day. When she let him in he wrote the note at once, went up to her, and sat down beside her on the sofa.

"I got up, and didn't want to talk to him," said Nellie. "I was very much afraid of him; he began to talk of Mme. Bubnov, telling me how angry she was, that now she wouldn't dare to take me, and began praising you; said that he was a great friend of yours and had known you as a little boy. Then I began to talk to him. He brought out some sweets, and asked me to take some. I didn't want to; then he began to assure me he was a good-natured man, and that he could sing and dance. He jumped up and began dancing. It made me laugh. Then he said he'd stay a little longer—'I'll wait for Vanya, maybe he'll come in'; and he did his best to persuade me not to be afraid of him, but to sit down beside him. I sat down, but I didn't want to say anything to him. Then he told me he used to know mother and grandfather and . . . then I began to talk. And he stayed a long time. . . ."

"What did you talk about?"

"About mother . . . Mme. Bubnov . . . grandfather. He stayed two hours."

Nellie seemed unwilling to say what they had talked about. I did not question her, hoping to hear it all from Masloboev.

N

But it struck me that Masloboev had purposely come when I was out, in order to find Nellie alone. "What did he do that for?" I wondered.

She showed me three sweetmeats he had given her. They were fruit-drops done up in green and red paper, very nasty ones, probably bought at a greengrocer's shop. Nellie laughed as she showed me them.

"Why didn't you eat them?" I asked.

"I don't want to," she answered seriously, knitting her brows. "I didn't take them from him; he left them on the sofa himself. . . ."

I had to run about a great deal that day. I began saying good-bye to Nellie.

"Will you be dull all alone?" I asked her as I went away.

"Dull and not dull. I shall be dull because you won't be here for a long while."

And with what love she looked at me as she said this. She had been looking at me tenderly all that morning, and she seemed so gay, so affectionate, and at the same time there was something shamefaced, even timid in her manner, as though she were afraid of vexing me in some way, and losing my affection and . . . and of showing her feelings too strongly, as though she were ashamed of them.

"And why aren't you dull then? You said you were 'dull and not dull,'" I could not help asking, smiling to her—she had grown sweet and precious to me.

"I know why," she answered laughing and for some reason abashed again.

We were talking in the open doorway. Nellie was standing before me with her eyes cast down, with one hand on my shoulder, and with the other pinching my sleeve.

"What is it, a secret?" I asked.

"No . . . it's nothing. . . . I've . . . I've begun reading your book while you were away," she brought out in a low voice, and turning a tender penetrating look upon me she flushed crimson.

"Ah, that's it! Well, do you like it?"

I felt the embarrassment of an author praised to his face, but I don't know what I would have given to have kissed her at that moment. But it seemed somehow impossible to kiss her. Nellie was silent for a moment.

"Why, why did he die?" she asked with an expression of

the deepest sadness, stealing a glance at me and then dropping her eyes again.

"Who?"

"Why, that young man in consumption . . . in the book."

"It couldn't be helped. It had to be so, Nellie."

"It didn't have to at all," she answered, hardly above a whisper, but suddenly, abruptly, almost angrily, pouting and staring still more obstinately at the floor.

Another minute passed.

"And she . . . they . . . the girl and the old man," she whispered, still plucking at my sleeve, more hurriedly than before. "Will they live together? And will they leave off being poor?"

"No, Nellie, she'll go far away; she'll marry a country gentleman, and he'll be left alone," I answered with extreme regret, really sorry that I could not tell her something more comforting.

"Oh, dear! . . . How dreadful! Ach, what people! . . . I don't want to read it now!"

And she pushed away my arm angrily, turned her back on me quickly, walked away to the table and stood with her face to the corner, and her eyes on the ground. She was flushed all over, and breathed unsteadily, as though from some terrible disappointment.

"Come, Nellie, you're angry," I said, going up to her. "You know, it's not true what's written in it, it's all made up; what is there to be angry about! You're such a sensitive little girl!"

"I'm not angry," she said timidly, looking up at me with clear and loving eyes; then she suddenly snatched my hand, pressed her face to my breast, and for some reason began crying.

But at the same moment she laughed—laughed and cried together. I, too, felt it was funny, and somehow . . . sweet. But nothing would make her lift her head, and when I began pulling her little face away from my shoulder she pressed it more and more closely against me, and laughed more and more.

At last this sentimental scene was over. We parted. I was in a hurry. Nellie, flushed, and still seeming as it were shamefaced, with eyes that shone like stars, ran after me out on the stairs, and begged me to come back early. I promised to be sure to be back to dinner, and as early as possible.

To begin with I went to the Ichmenyevs. They were both ill. Anna Andreyevna was quite ill; Nikolay Sergeyitch was sitting in his study. He heard that I had come, but I knew that, as usual, he would not come out for a quarter of an hour, so as to give us time to talk. I did not want to upset Anna Andreyevna too much, and so I softened my account of the previous evening as far as I could, but I told the truth. To my surprise, though my old friend was disappointed, she was not astonished to hear the possibility of a rupture.

"Well, my dear boy, it's just as I thought," she said. "When you'd gone I pondered over it, and made up my mind that it wouldn't come to pass. We've not deserved such a blessing; besides he's such a mean man; one can't expect anything good to come from him. It shows what he is that he's taking ten thousand roubles from us for nothing. He knows it's for nothing, but he takes it all the same. He's robbing us of our last crust of bread; Ichmenyevka will be sold. And Natasha's right and sensible not to believe him. But do you know, my dear boy," she went on, dropping her voice, "my poor man! My poor man! He's absolutely against this marriage. He let it out. 'I won't have it,' said he. At first I thought it was only foolishness; no, he meant it. What will happen to her then, poor darling. Then he'll curse her utterly. And how about Alyosha? What does he say?"

And she went on questioning me for a long time, and as usual she sighed and moaned over every answer I gave her. Of late I noticed that she seemed to have quite lost her balance. Every piece of news upset her. Her anxiety over Natasha was ruining her health and her nerves.

The old man come in in his dressing-gown and slippers. He complained of being feverish, but looked fondly at his wife, and all the time that I was there he was looking after her like a nurse, peeping into her face, and seeming a little timid with her in fact. There was a great deal of tenderness in the way he looked at her. He was frightened at her illness; he felt he would be bereaved of everything on earth if he lost her.

I sat with them for an hour. When I took leave he came into the passage with me and began speaking of Nellie. He seriously thought of taking her into his house to fill the place of his daughter, Natasha. He began consulting me how to predispose Anna Andreyevna in favour of the plan. With special curiosity he questioned me about Nellie, asking whether I had found out anything fresh about her. I told him briefly. My story made an impression on him.

"We'll speak of it again," he said decisively. "And meanwhile . . . but I'll come to you myself, as soon as I'm a little better. Then we'll settle things."

At twelve o'clock precisely I reached Masloboev's. To my intense amazement the first person I met when I went in was Prince Valkovsky. He was putting on his overcoat in the entry, and Masloboev was officiously helping him and handing him his cane. He had already told me that he was acquainted with the prince, but yet this meeting astonished me extremely.

Prince Valkovsky seemed confused when he saw me.

"Ach, that's you!" he cried with somewhat exaggerated warmth. "What a meeting, only fancy! But I have just heard from Mr. Masloboev that he knew you. I'm glad, awfully glad to have met you. I was just wishing to see you, and hoping to call on you as soon as possible. You will allow me? I have a favour to ask of you. Help me, explain our present position. You understand, of course, that I am referring to what happened yesterday. . . . You are an intimate friend; you have followed the whole course of the affair; you have influence. . . . I'm awfully sorry that I can't stay now. . . . Business! But in a few days, and perhaps sooner, I shall have the pleasure of calling on you. But now . . ."

He shook my hand with exaggerated heartiness, exchanged a glance with Masloboev, and went away.

"Tell me for mercy's sake . . ." I began, as I went into the room.

"I won't tell you anything," Masloboev interrupted, hurriedly snatching up his cap and going towards the entry. "I've business. I must run, too, my boy. I'm late."

"Why, you wrote to me yourself to come at twelve o'clock."

"What if I did write twelve o'clock? I wrote to you yesterday, but to-day I've been written to myself, and such a piece of business that my head's in a whirl! They're waiting for me. Forgive me, Vanya, the only thing I can suggest to you by way of satisfaction is to punch my head for having troubled you for nothing. If you want satisfaction punch it; only, for Christ's sake, make haste! Don't keep me. I've business, I'm late. . . ."

"What should I punch your head for? Make haste then if you've business; things unforeseen may happen to any one. Only . . ."

"Yes, as for that *only*, let me tell you," he interrupted,

dashing out into the entry and putting on his coat (I followed his example). "I have business with you, too; very important business; that's why I asked you to come; it directly concerns you and your interests. And as it's impossible to tell you about it in one minute now, for goodness' sake promise me to come to me to-day at seven o'clock, neither before nor after. I'll be at home."

"To-day," I said uncertainly. "Well, old man, I did mean this evening to go . . ."

"Go at once, dear boy, where you meant to go this evening, and come this evening to me. For you can't imagine, Vanya, the things I have to tell you."

"But, I say, what is it? I confess you make me curious."

Meanwhile we had come out of the gate and were standing on the pavement.

"So you'll come?" he asked insistently.

"I've told you I will."

"No, give me your word of honour."

"Foo! what a fellow! Very well, my word of honour."

"Noble and excellent. Which way are you going?"

"This way," I answered, pointing to the right.

"Well, this is my way," said he, pointing to the left. "Good-bye, Vanya. Remember, seven o'clock."

"Strange," thought I, looking after him.

I had meant to be at Natasha's in the evening. But as now I had given my word to Masloboev, I decided to call on Natasha at once. I felt sure I should find Alyosha there. And, as a fact, he was there and was greatly delighted when I came in.

He was very charming, extremely tender with Natasha, and seemed positively to brighten up at my arrival. Though Natasha tried to be cheerful it was obviously an effort. Her face looked pale and ill, and she had slept badly. To Alyosha she showed an exaggerated tenderness.

Though Alyosha said a great deal and told her all sorts of things, evidently trying to cheer her up and to bring a smile to her lips which seemed set in unsmiling gravity, he obviously avoided speaking of Katya or of his father. Evidently his efforts at reconciliation had not succeeded.

"Do you know what? He wants dreadfully to get away from me," Natasha whispered to me hurriedly when he went out for a minute to give some order to Mavra. "But he's afraid. And I'm afraid to tell him to go myself, for then perhaps he'll stay on purpose; but what I'm most afraid of is his being bored with me, and getting altogether cold to me through that! What am I to do?"

"Good heavens, what a position you've put yourselves in! And how suspicious, how watchful you are of one another. Simply explain to him and have done with it. Why, he may well be weary of such a position."

"What's to be done?" she cried, panic-stricken.

"Wait a minute. I'll arrange it all for you."

And I went into the kitchen on the pretext of asking Mavra to clean one of my overshoes which was covered with mud.

"Be careful, Vanya," she cried after me.

As soon as I went out to Mavra, Alyosha flew up to me as though he had been waiting for me.

"Ivan Petrovitch, my dear fellow, what am I to do? Do advise me. I promised yesterday to be at Katya's just at this time to-day. I can't avoid going. I love Natasha beyond expression; I would go through the fire for her, but you'll admit that I can't throw up everything over there. . . ."

"Well, go then."

"But what about Natasha? I shall grieve her, you know. Ivan Petrovitch, do get me out of it somehow. . . ."

"I think you'd much better go. You know how she loves you; she will be thinking all the while that you are bored with her and staying with her against your will. It's better to be more unconstrained. Come along, though. I'll help you."

"Dear Ivan Petrovitch, how kind you are!"

We went back; a minute later I said to him:

"I saw your father just now."

"Where?" he cried, frightened.

"In the street, by chance. He stopped to speak to me a minute, and asked again to become better acquainted with me. He was asking about you, whether I knew where you were now. He was very anxious to see you, to tell you something."

"Ach, Alyosha, you'd better go and show yourself," Natasha put in, understanding what I was leading up to.

"But where shall I meet him now? Is he at home?"

"No, I remember he said he was going to the countess's."

"What shall I do then? . . ." Alyosha asked naïvely, looking mournfully at Natasha.

"Why, Alyosha, what's wrong?" she said. "Do you really mean to give up that acquaintance to set my mind at rest?

Why, that's childish. To begin with, it's impossible, and secondly, it would be ungrateful to Katya. You are friends—it's impossible to break off relations so rudely. You'll offend me at last if you think I'm so jealous. Go at once, go, I beg you, and satisfy your father."

"Natasha, you're an angel, and I'm not worth your little finger," cried Alyosha rapturously and remorsefully. "You are so kind while I . . . I . . . well, let me tell you, I've just been asking Ivan Petrovitch out there in the kitchen to help me to get away. And this was his plan. But don't be hard on me, Natasha, my angel! I'm not altogether to blame, for I love you a thousand times more than anything on earth, and so I've made a new plan—to tell Katya everything and describe to her our present position and all that happened here yesterday. She'll think of something to save us; she's devoted to us, heart and soul. . . ."

"Well, go along," said Natasha, smiling. "And I tell you what, I am very anxious to make Katya's acquaintance myself. How can we arrange it?"

Alyosha's enthusiasm was beyond all bounds. He began at once making plans for bringing about a meeting. To his mind it was very simple; Katya would find a way. He enlarged on his idea, warmly, excitedly. He promised to bring an answer that day, within a couple of hours, and to spend the evening with Natasha.

"Will you really come?" asked Natasha, as she let him out.

"Can you doubt it? Good-bye, Natasha, good-bye my darling, my beloved for ever. Good-bye, Vanya. Ach, I called you Vanya by mistake. Listen, Ivan Petrovitch, I love you. Let me call you Vanya. Let's drop formality."

"Yes, let us."

"Thank goodness! It's been in my mind a hundred times, but I've never somehow dared to speak of it. Ivan Petrovitch—there I've done it again. You know, it's so difficult to say Vanya all at once. I think that's been described somewhere by Tolstoy: two people promise to call each other by their pet names, but they can't do it and keep avoiding using any name at all. Ach, Natasha, do let's read over 'Childhood and Boyhood' together. It is so fine."

"Come, be off, be off!" Natasha drove him away, laughing. "He's babbling with delight. . . ."

"Good-bye. In two hours' time I shall be with you."

He kissed her hand and hastened away.

"You see, you see, Vanya," said she, and melted into tears.

I stayed with her for about two hours, tried to comfort her and succeeded in reassuring her. Of course she was right about everything, in all her apprehensions. My heart was wrung with anguish when I thought of her present position. I was afraid; but what could I do?

Alyosha seemed strange to me, too. He loved her no less than before; perhaps, indeed, his feeling was stronger, more poignant than ever, from remorse and gratitude. But at the same time his new passion was taking a stronghold on his heart. It was impossible to see how it would end. I felt very inquisitive to see Katya. I promised Natasha again that I would make her acquaintance.

Natasha seemed to be almost cheerful at last. Among other things I told her all about Nellie, about Masloboev, and Mme. Bubnov, about my meeting Prince Valkovsky that morning at Masloboev's, and the appointment I had made with the latter at seven o'clock. All this interested her extremely. I talked a little about her parents, but I said nothing for the present about her father's visit to me; his project of a duel with the prince might have frightened her. She, too, thought it very strange that the prince should have anything to do with Masloboev, and that he should display such a great desire to make friends with me, though this could be to some extent explained by the position of affairs. . . .

At three o'clock I returned home. Nellie met me with her bright little face.

CHAPTER VI

At seven o'clock punctually I was at Masloboev's. He greeted me with loud exclamations and open arms. He was, of course, half drunk. But what struck me most was the extraordinary preparation that had been made for my visit. It was evident that I was expected. A pretty brass samovar was boiling on a little round table covered with a handsome and expensive tablecloth. The tea-table glittered with crystal, silver and china. On another table, which was covered with a tablecloth of a different kind, but no less gorgeous, stood plates of excellent sweets, Kiev preserves both dried and liquid, fruit-paste, jelly,

French preserves, oranges, apples, and three or four sorts of nuts; in fact a regular fruit-shop. On a third table, covered with a snow-white cloth, there were savouries of different sorts—caviare, cheese, a pie, sausage, smoked ham, fish and a row of fine glass decanters containing spirits of many sorts, and of the most attractive colours—green, ruby, brown and gold. Finally on a little table on one side—also covered with a white cloth—there were two bottles of champagne. On a table before the sofa there were three bottles containing Sauterne, Lafitte, and Cognac, very expensive brands from Eliseyev's. Alexandra Semyonovna was sitting at the tea-table, and though her dress and general get-up was simple, they had evidently been the subject of thought and attention, and the result was indeed very successful. She knew what suited her, and evidently took pride in it. She got up to meet me with some ceremony. Her fresh little face beamed with pleasure and satisfaction. Masloboev was wearing gorgeous Chinese slippers, a sumptuous dressing-gown, and dainty clean linen. Fashionable studs and buttons were conspicuous on his shirt everywhere where they could possibly be attached. His hair had been pomaded, and combed with a fashionable side parting.

I was so much taken aback that I stopped short in the middle of the room, and gazed open-mouthed, first at Masloboev and then at Alexandra Semyonovna, who was in a state of blissful satisfaction.

"What's the meaning of this, Masloboev? Have you got a party this evening?" I cried with some uneasiness.

"No, only you!" he answered solemnly.

"But why is this?" I asked (pointing to the savouries). "Why, you've food enough for a regiment!"

"And drink enough! You've forgotten the chief thing—drink!" added Masloboev.

"And is this only on my account?"

"And Alexandra Semyonovna's. It was her pleasure to get it all up."

"Well, upon my word. I knew that's how it would be," exclaimed Alexandra Semyonovna, flushing, though she looked just as satisfied. "I can't receive a visitor decently, or I'm in fault at once."

"Ever since the morning, would you believe it, as soon as she knew you were coming for the evening, she's been bustling about; she's been in agonies. . . ."

"And that's a fib! It's not since early morning, it's since last night. When you came in last night you told me the gentleman was coming to spend the whole evening."

"You misunderstood me."

"Not a bit of it. That's what you said. I never tell lies. And why shouldn't I welcome a guest? We go on and on, and no one ever comes to see us, though we've plenty of everything. Let our friends see that we know how to live like other people."

"And above all see what a good hostess and housekeeper you are," added Masloboev. "Only fancy, my friend, I've come in for something too. She's crammed me into a linen shirt, stuck in studs—slippers, Chinese dressing-gown—she combed my hair herself and pomaded it with bergamot; she wanted to sprinkle me with scent—crême brulée, but I couldn't stand that. I rebelled and asserted my conjugal authority."

"It wasn't bergamot. It was the best French pomatum out of a painted china pot," retorted Alexandra Semyonovna, firing up. "You judge, Ivan Petrovitch; he never lets me go to a theatre, or a dance, he only gives me dresses, and what do I want with dresses? I put them on and walk about the room alone. The other day I persuaded him and we were all ready to go to the theatre. As soon as I turned to fasten my brooch he went to the cupboard, took one glass after another until he was tipsy. So we stayed at home. No one, no one, no one ever comes to see us. Only of a morning people of a sort come about business, and I'm sent away. Yet we've samovars, and a dinner service and good cups—we've everything, all presents. And they bring us things to eat too. We scarcely buy anything but the spirits; and the pomade and the savouries there, the pie, the ham and sweets we bought for you. If anyone could see how we live! I've been thinking for a whole year: if a visitor would come, a real visitor, we could show him all this and entertain him. And folks would praise things and we should be pleased. And as for my pomading him, the stupid, he doesn't deserve it. He'd always go about in dirty clothes. Look what a dressing-gown he's got on. It was a present. But does he deserve a dressing-gown like that? He'd rather be tippling than anything. You'll see. He'll ask you to take vodka before tea."

"Well! That's sense indeed! Let's have some of the silver seal and some of the gold, Vanya, and then with souls refreshed we'll fall upon the other beverages."

"There, I knew that's how it would be!"

"Don't be anxious, Sashenka. We'll drink a cup of tea, too, with brandy in it, to your health."

"Well, there it is!" she cried, clasping her hands. "It's caravan tea, six roubles the pound, a merchant made us a present of it the day before yesterday, and he wants to drink it with brandy. Don't listen to him, Ivan Petrovitch, I'll pour you out a cup directly. You'll see . . . you'll see for yourself what it's like!"

And she busied herself at the samovar.

I realized that they were reckoning on keeping me for the whole evening. Alexandra Semyonovna had been expecting visitors for a whole year, and was now prepared to work it all off on me. This did not suit me at all.

"Listen, Masloboev," I said, sitting down. "I've not come to pay you a visit. I've come on business; you invited me yourself to tell me something. . . ."

"Well, business is business, but there's a time for friendly conversation too."

"No, my friend, don't reckon upon me. At half-past eight I must say good-bye. I've an appointment. It's a promise."

"Not likely. Good gracious, what a way to treat me! What a way to treat Alexandra Semyonovna. Just look at her, she's overwhelmed. What has she been pomading me for: why I'm covered with bergamot. Just think!"

"You do nothing but make jokes, Masloboev. I swear to Alexandra Semyonovna that I'll dine with you next week, on Friday if you like. But now, my boy, I've given my word; or rather it's absolutely necessary for me to be at a certain place. You'd better explain what you meant to tell me."

"Then can you really only stay till half-past eight?" cried Alexandra Semyonovna in a timid and plaintive voice, almost weeping as she handed me a cup of excellent tea.

"Don't be uneasy, Sashenka; that's all nonsense!" Masloboev put in. "He'll stay. That's nonsense. But I'll tell you what, Vanya, you'd much better let me know where it is you always go. What is your business? May I know? You keep running off somewhere every day. You don't work. . . ."

"But why do you want to know? I'll tell you perhaps afterwards. You'd better explain why you came to see me yesterday when I told you myself I shouldn't be at home."

"I remembered afterwards. But I forgot at the time. I

really did want to speak to you about something. But before everything I had to comfort Alexandra Semyonovna. 'Here,' says she, 'is a person, a friend, who has turned up. Why not invite him?' And here she's been pestering me about you for the last four days. No doubt they'll let me off forty sins for the bergamot in the next world, but I thought why shouldn't he spend an evening with us in a friendly way? So I had recourse to strategy: I wrote to you that I had such business that if you didn't come it would quite upset our apple-cart."

I begged him not to do like this in the future, but to speak to me directly. But this explanation did not altogether satisfy me.

"Well, but why did you run away from me this morning?" I asked.

"This morning I really had business. I'm not telling the least little fib."

"Not with the prince?"

"Do you like our tea?" Alexandra Semyonovna asked, in honied accents. For the last five minutes she had been waiting for me to praise the tea, but it never occurred to me.

"It's splendid, Alexandra Semyonovna, superb. I have never drunk anything like it."

Alexandra Semyonovna positively glowed with satisfaction and flew to pour me out some more.

"The prince!" cried Masloboev, "the prince! That prince, my boy, is a rogue, a rascal such as . . . Well! I can tell you, my boy, though I'm a rogue myself, from a mere sense of decency I shouldn't care to be in his skin. But enough. Mum's the word! That's all I can tell you about him."

"But I've come, among other things, on purpose to ask you about him. But that will do later. Why did you give my Elena sweetmeats and dance for her when I was away yesterday? And what can you have been talking about for an hour and a half!"

"Elena is a little girl of twelve, or perhaps eleven, who is living for the time at Ivan Petrovitch's," Masloboev exclaimed, suddenly addressing Alexandra Semyonovna. "Look, Vanya, look," he went on, pointing at her, "how she flushed up when she heard I had taken sweets to an unknown girl. Didn't she give a start and turn red as though we'd fired a pistol at her? . . . I say, her eyes are flashing like coals of fire! It's no use, Alexandra Semyonovna, it's no use to try and hide it! She's jealous. If I hadn't explained that it was a child of eleven she'd have pulled my hair and the bergamot wouldn't have saved me!'"

"It won't save you as it is!"

And with these words Alexandra Semyonovna darted at one bound from behind the tea-table, and before Masloboev had time to protect his head she snatched at a tuft of his hair and gave it a good pull.

"So there! So there! Don't dare to say I'm jealous before a visitor! Don't you dare! Don't you dare! Don't you dare."

She was quite crimson, and though she laughed, Masloboev caught it pretty hotly.

"He talks of all sorts of shameful things," she added seriously, turning to me.

"Well, Vanya, you see the sort of life I lead! That's why I must have a drop of vodka," Masloboev concluded, setting his hair straight and going almost at a trot to the decanter. But Alexandra Semyonovna was beforehand with him. She skipped up to the table, poured some out herself, handed it to him, and even gave him a friendly pat on the cheek. Masloboev winked at me, triumphantly clicked with his tongue, and solemnly emptied his glass.

"As for the sweets, it's difficult to say," he began, sitting down on the sofa beside me. "I bought them at a greengrocer's shop the other day when I was drunk, I don't know why. Perhaps it was to support home industries and manufactures, I don't know for sure. I only remember that I was walking along the street drunk, fell in the mud; clutched at my hair and cried at being unfit for anything. I forgot about the sweets, of course, so they remained in my pocket till yesterday when I sat down on your sofa and sat on them. The dances, too, were a question of inebriety. Yesterday I was rather drunk, and when I am drunk, if I'm contented with my lot I sometimes dance. That's all. Except perhaps that that little orphan excited my pity; besides, she wouldn't talk to me, she seemed cross. And so I danced to cheer her up and gave her the fruit-drops."

"And you weren't bribing her to try and find something out from her? Own up, honestly, didn't you come then on purpose knowing I shouldn't be at home, to talk to her *tête-à-tête*, and to get something out of her? You see, I know you spent an hour and a half with her, declared that you had known her dead mother, and that you questioned her about something."

Masloboev screwed up his eyes and laughed roguishly.

"Well, it wouldn't have been a bad idea," he said. "No, Vanya, that was not so. Though indeed, why shouldn't I question her if I got a chance; but it wasn't that. Listen, old friend, though as usual I'm rather drunk now, yet you may be sure that with *evil intent*, Filip will never deceive you, with *evil intent, that is*."

"Yes, but without evil intent ? "

"Well . . . even without evil intent. But, damn it all, let's have a drink and then to business. It's not a matter of much consequence," he went on after a drink ; " that Bubnov woman had no sort of right to keep the girl. I've gone into it all. There was no adoption or anything of that sort. The mother owed her money, and so she got hold of the child. Though the Bubnov woman's a sly hag and a wicked wretch, she's a silly woman like all women. The dead woman had a good passport and so everything was all right. Elena can live with you, though it would be a very good thing if some benevolent people with a family would take her for good and bring her up. But meanwhile let her stay with you. That's all right. I'll arrange it all for you. The Bubnov woman won't dare to stir a finger. I've found out scarcely anything certain about Elena's mother. She was a woman of the name of Salzmann."

"Yes, so Nellie told me."

"Well, so there the matter ends. " Now, Vanya," he began with a certain solemnity, " I've one great favour to ask of you. Mind you grant it. Tell me as fully as you can what it is you're busy about, where you're going and where you spend whole days at a time. Though I have heard something, I want to know about it much more fully."

Such solemnity suprised me and even made me uneasy.

"But what is it ? Why do you want to know ? You ask so solemnly."

"Well, Vanya, without wasting words, I want to do you a service. You see, my dear boy, if I weren't straight with you I could get it all out of you without being so solemn. But you suspect me of not being straight—just now, those fruit-drops ; I understood. But since I'm speaking with such seriousness, you may be sure it's not my interest but yours I'm thinking of. So don't have any doubts, but speak out the whole truth."

"But what sort of service ? Listen, Masloboev, why won't you tell me anything about the prince ? That's what I want. That would be a service to me."

"About the prince ? Hm! Very well, I'll tell you straight out. I'm going to question you in regard to the prince now."

"How so ? "

"I'll tell you how. I've noticed, my boy, that he seems to be somehow mixed up in your affairs; for instance, he questioned me about you. How he found out that we knew each other is not your business. The only thing that matters is that you should be on your guard against that man. He's a treacherous Judas, and worse than that too. And so, when I saw that he was mixed up in your affairs I trembled for you. But of course I know nothing about it; that's why I asked you to tell me, that I may judge. . . . And that's why I asked you to come here to-day. That's what the important business is. I tell you straight out."

"You must tell me something, anyway, if only why I need to be afraid of the prince."

"Very good, so be it. I am sometimes employed, my boy, in certain affairs. But I'm trusted by certain persons just because I'm not a chatterbox. Judge for yourself whether I should talk to you. So you mustn't mind if I speak somewhat generally, very generally in fact, simply to show what a scoundrel he is. Well, to begin with, you tell your story."

I decided there was really no need to conceal anything in my affairs from Masloboev. Natasha's affairs were not a secret; moreover I might expect to get some help for her from Masloboev. Of course I passed over certain points as far as possible in my story. Masloboev listened particularly attentively to all that related to Prince Valkovsky; he stopped me in many places, asked me about several points over again, so that in the end I told him the story rather fully. The telling of it lasted half an hour.

"Hm! That girl's got a head," Masloboev commented. "If she hasn't guessed quite correctly about the prince, it's a good thing anyway that she recognized from the first the sort of man she had to deal with, and broke off all relations with him. Bravo, Natalya Nikolaevna! I drink to her health." (He took a drink.) "It's not only brains, it must have been her heart too, that saved her from being deceived. And her heart didn't mislead her. Of course her game is lost. The prince will get his way and Alyosha will give her up. I'm only sorry for Ichmenyev—to pay ten thousand to that scoundrel

Why, who took up his case, who acted for him ? Managed it himself, I bet ! E-ech ! Just like all these noble, exalted people ! They're no good for anything ! That's not the way to deal with the prince. I'd have found a nice little lawyer for Ichmenyev—e-ech ! "

And he thumped on the table with vexation.

"Well, now about Prince Valkovsky ? "

"Ah, you're still harping on the prince. But what am I to say about him ? I'm sorry I've offered to, I only wanted, Vanya, to warn you against that swindler, to protect you, so to say, from his influence. No one is safe who comes in contact with him. So keep your eyes open, that's all. And here you've been imagining I had some mysteries of Paris I wanted to reveal to you. One can see you're a novelist. Well, what am I to tell you about the villain ? The villain's a villain. . . . Well, for example, I'll tell you one little story, of course without mentioning places, towns, or persons, that is, without the exactitude of a calendar. You know that when he was very young and had to live on his official salary, he married a very rich merchant's daughter. Well, he didn't treat that lady very ceremoniously, and though we're not discussing her case now, I may mention in passing, friend Vanya, that he has all his life been particularly fond of turning such affairs to profit. Here's another example of it. He went abroad. There. . . ."

"Stop, Masloboev, what journey abroad are you speaking of ? In what year ? "

"Just ninety-nine years and three months ago. Well, there he seduced the daughter of a certain father, and carried her off with him to Paris. And this is what he did ! The father was some sort of a manufacturer, or was a partner in some enterprise of that sort. I don't know for sure. What I tell you is what I've gathered from my own conjectures, and what I've concluded from other facts. Well, the prince cheated him, worming himself into his business too. He swindled him out and out, and got hold of his money. The old man, of course, had some legal documents to prove that the prince had had the money from him. The prince didn't want to give it back; that is, in plain Russian, wanted to steal it. The old man had a daughter, and she was a beauty, and she had an ideal lover, one of the Schiller brotherhood, a poet, and at the same time a merchant, a young dreamer ; in short a regular German, one Pfefferkuchen."

"Do you mean to say Pfefferkuchen was his surname ? "

"Well, perhaps it wasn't Pfefferkuchen; hang the man, he doesn't matter. But the prince made up to the daughter, and so successfully that she fell madly in love with him. The prince wanted two things at that time, first to possess the daughter, and secondly the documents relating to the money he had had from the old man. All the old man's keys were in his daughter's keeping. The old man was passionately fond of his daughter, so much so that he didn't want her to be married. Yes, really. He was jealous of every suitor she had, he didn't contemplate parting with her, and he turned Pfefferkuchen out. He was a queer fish the father, an Englishman. . . ."

"An Englishman ? But where did it all happen ? "

"I only called him an Englishman, speaking figuratively, and you catch me up. It happened in the town of Santa-fé-da-Bogota, or perhaps it was Cracow, but more likely it was in the principality of Nassau, like the label on the seltzer-water bottles, certainly it was Nassau. Is that enough for you ? Well, so the prince seduced the girl and carried her off from her father, and managed to induce the girl to lay hands on the documents and take them with her. There are cases of love like that, you know, Vanya. Fugh ! God have mercy upon us ! She was an honest girl, you know, noble, exalted. It's true she very likely didn't know much about the documents. The only thing that troubled her was that her father might curse her. The prince was equal to the occasion this time too ; he gave her a formal, legal promise of marriage in writing. By so doing he persuaded her that they were only going abroad for a time, for a holiday tour, and that when the old father's anger had subsided they would return to him married, and would, the three of them, live happy ever after, and so on, to infinity. She ran away, the old father cursed her and went bankrupt. She was followed to Paris by Frauenmilch, who chucked up everything, chucked up his business even ; he was very much in love with her."

"Stop, who's Frauenmilch ? "

"Why, that fellow! Feuerbach, wasn't it ? Damn the fellow, Pfefferkuchen! Well, of course, the prince couldn't marry her : what would Countess Hlestov * have said ? What would Baron Slops have thought ? So he had to deceive her. And he did deceive her, too brutally. To begin with he almost beat her, and secondly, he purposely invited Pfefferkuchen to

* The Russian "Mrs. Grundy."—*Translator's note.*

visit them. Well, he used to go and see them and became her friend. They would spend whole evenings alone, whimpering together, weeping over their troubles, and he would comfort her. To be sure, dear, simple souls ! The prince brought things to this pass on purpose. Once, he found them late at night, and pretended that they had an intrigue, caught at some pretext ; said he'd seen it with his own eyes. Well, he turned them both out of the house, and took his departure to London for a time. She was just on the eve of her confinement ; when he turned her out she gave birth to a daughter, that is, not a daughter but a son, to be sure, a little son. He was christened Volodka. Pfefferkuchen stood godfather. Well, so she went off with Pfefferkuchen. He had a little money. She travelled in Switzerland and Italy, through all the poetical places to be sure, most appropriately. She cried all the time, and Pfefferkuchen whimpered, and many years passed like that, and the baby grew into a little girl. And everything went right for the prince, only one thing was wrong, he hadn't succeeded in getting back the promise of marriage. 'You're a base man,' she had said to him at parting. 'You have robbed me, you have dishonoured me and now you abandon me. Good-bye. But I won't give you back your promise. Not because I ever want to marry you, but because you're afraid of that document. So I shall always keep it in my hands.' She lost her temper in fact, but the prince felt quite easy. Such scoundrels always come off well in their dealings with so-called lofty souls. They're so noble that it's always easy to deceive them, and besides they invariably confine themselves to lofty and noble contempt instead of practically applying the law to the case if it can be applied. That young mother, for instance, she took refuge in haughty contempt, and though she kept the promise of marriage, the prince knew, of course, that she'd sooner hang herself than make use of it ; so he felt secure for the time. And though she spat in his nasty face, she had her Volodka left on her hands ; if she had died what would have become of him ? But she didn't think about that. Bruderschaft, too, encouraged her and didn't think about it. They read Schiller. At last Bruderschaft sickened of something and died. . . ."

" You mean Pfefferkuchen ? "

" To be sure—hang him ! And she . . ."

" Stay. How many years had they been travelling ? "

" Exactly two hundred. Well, she went back to Cracow.

Her father wouldn't receive her, cursed her. She died, and the prince crossed himself for joy. I was there too, drank goblets not a few, our ears full of mead, but our mouths full of need; they gave me a flip, and I gave them the slip. . . . Let's drink, brother Vanya."

"I suspect that you are helping him in that business, Masloboev."

"You will have it so, will you?"

"Only I can't understand what you can do in it."

"Why, you see, when she went back under another name to Madrid after being away for ten years, all this had to be verified, and about Bruderschaft too, and about the old man and about the kid, and whether she was dead, and whether she'd any papers, and so on, to infinity. And something else besides, too. He's a horrid man, be on your guard, Vanya, and remember one thing about Masloboev, don't let anything make you call him a scoundrel. Though he's a scoundrel (to my thinking there's no man who isn't) he's not a scoundrel in his dealings with you. I'm very drunk, but listen. If ever sooner or later, now or next year, it seems to you that Masloboev has hoodwinked you (and please don't forget that word *hoodwinked*), rest assured that it's with no evil intent. Masloboev is watching over you. And so don't believe your suspicions, but come to Masloboev and have it out with him like a friend. Well, now, will you have a drink?"

"No."

"Something to eat?"

"No, brother, excuse me. . . ."

"Well then, get along with you. It's a quarter to nine and you're in a hurry. It's time for you to go."

"Well, what next? He's been drinking till he's drunk and now he sends away a guest. He's always like that. Ach, you shameless fellow!" cried Alexandra Semyonovna, almost in tears.

"A man on foot's poor company for a man on horseback, Alexandra Semyonovna; we shall be left alone to adore one another. And this is a general! No, Vanya, I'm lying, you're not a general, but I'm a scoundrel! Only see what I look like now! What am I beside you? Forgive me, Vanya, don't judge me and let me pour out . . ."

He embraced me and burst into tears. I prepared to go away.

"Good heavens! And we've prepared supper for you!"

cried Alexandra Semyonovna in terrible distress. "And will you come to us on Friday ? "

"I will, Alexandra Semyonovna. Honour bright, I will."

"Perhaps you look down on him because he's so . . . tipsy. Don't look down upon him, Ivan Petrovitch! He's a good-hearted man, such a good-hearted man, and how he loves you. He talks to me about you day and night, nothing but you. He bought your books on purpose for me. I haven't read them yet. I'm going to begin to-morrow. And how glad I shall be when you come! I never see anyone. No one ever comes to sit with us. We've everything we can want, but we're always alone. Here I've been sitting listening all the while you've been talking, and how nice it's been. . . . So good-bye till Friday."

CHAPTER VII

I WENT out and hurried home. Masloboev's words had made a great impression on me. All sorts of ideas occurred to me. . . . As luck would have it, at home an incident awaited me which startled me like an electric shock.

Exactly opposite the gate of the house where I lodged stood a street-lamp. Just as I was in the gateway a strange figure rushed out from under the street-lamp, so strange that I uttered a cry. It was a living thing, terror-stricken, shaking, half-crazed, and it caught at my hand with a scream. I was overwhelmed with horror. It was Nellie.

"Nellie, what is it ? " I cried. "What's the matter ? "

"There, upstairs . . . he's in our . . . rooms."

"Who is it ? Come along, come with me."

"I won't, I won't. I'll wait till he's gone away . . . in the passage . . . I won't."

I went up to my room with a strange foreboding in my heart, opened the door and saw Prince Valkovsky. He was sitting at the table reading my novel. At least, the book was open.

"Ivan Petrovitch," he cried, delighted. "I'm so glad you've come back at last. I was on the very point of going away. I've been waiting over an hour for you. I promised the countess at her earnest and particular wish to take you to see her this evening. She begged me so specially, she's so anxious to make your acquaintance. So as you had already promised me I thought

I would come and see you earlier before you'd had time to go out anywhere, and invite you to come with me. Imagine my distress. When I arrived your servant told me you were not at home. What could I do? I had given my word of honour that I'd take you with me. And so I sat down to wait for you, making up my mind to wait a quarter of an hour for you. But it's been a long quarter of an hour! I opened your novel and forgot the time, reading it. Ivan Petrovitch! It's a masterpiece! They don't appreciate you enough! You've drawn tears from me, do you know? Yes, I've been crying, and I don't often cry."

"So you want me to come? I must confess that just now . . . not that I'm against it, but . . ."

"For God's sake let us go! What a way to treat me! Why, I have been waiting an hour and a half for you. . . . Besides, I do so want to talk to you. You know what about. You understand the whole affair better than I do. . . . Perhaps we shall decide on something, come to some conclusion. Only think of it! For God's sake, don't refuse."

I reflected that sooner or later I should have to go. Of course Natasha was alone now, and needed me, but she had herself charged me to get to know Katya as soon as possible. Besides, Alyosha might be there. I knew that Natasha would not be satisfied till I had brought her news of Katya, and I decided to go. But I was worried about Nellie.

"Wait a minute," I said to the prince, and I went out on the stairs. Nellie was standing there in a dark corner.

"Why won't you come in, Nellie? What did he do? What did he say to you?"

"Nothing. . . . I don't want to, I won't . . ." she repeated. "I'm afraid."

I tried hard to persuade her, but nothing was any use. I agreed with her that as soon as I had gone out with the prince she should return and lock herself in.

"And don't let anyone in, Nellie, however much they try and persuade you."

"But are you going with him?"

"Yes."

She shuddered and clutched at my arm, as though to beg me not to go, but she didn't utter one word. I made up my mind to question her more minutely next day.

Apologizing to the prince, I began to dress. He began assuring me that I had no need to dress, no need to get myself up to go to the countess.

"Perhaps something a little more spruce," he added, eyeing me inquisitively from head to foot. "You know . . . these conventional prejudices . . . it's impossible to be rid of them altogether. It'll be a long time before we get to that ideal state in our society," he concluded, seeing with satisfaction that I had a dress-coat.

We went out. But I left him on the stairs, went back into the room into which Nellie had already slipped, and said good-bye to her again. She was terribly agitated. Her face looked livid. I was worried about her; I disliked having to leave her.

"That's a queer servant of yours," the prince said as we went downstairs. "I suppose that little girl is your servant?"

"No . . . she . . . is staying with me for the time."

"Queer little girl. I'm sure she's mad. Only fancy, at first she answered me civilly, but afterwards when she'd looked at me she rushed at me, screaming and trembling, clung to me . . . tried to say something, but couldn't. I must own I was scared. I wanted to escape from her, but thank God she ran away herself. I was astounded. How do you manage to get on with her?"

' She has epileptic fits," I answered.

"Ah, so that's it! Well, it's no wonder then . . . if she has fits."

The idea suddenly struck me that Masloboev's visit of the previous day when he knew I was not at home, my visit to Masloboev that morning, the story that Masloboev had just told me, when he was drunk and against his will, his pressing invitation for me to come at seven o'clock that evening, his urging me not to believe in his hoodwinking me and, finally, the prince's waiting for an hour and a half for me while perhaps he knew I was at Masloboev's, and while Nellie had rushed away from him into the street, that all these facts were somehow connected. I had plenty to think about.

Prince Valkovsky's carriage was waiting at the gate. We got in and drove off.

CHAPTER VIII

WE had not far to go, to the Torgovoy Bridge. For the first minute we were silent. I kept wondering how he would begin.

I fancied that he would try me, sound me, probe me. But he spoke without any beating about the bush, and went straight to the point.

"I am very uneasy about one circumstance, Ivan Petrovitch," he began, "about which I want to speak to you first of all, and to ask your advice. I made up my mind some time ago to forgo what I have won from my lawsuit and to give up the disputed ten thousand to Ichmenyev. How am I to do this?"

"It cannot be that you really don't know how to act," was the thought that flashed through my mind. "Aren't you making fun of me?"

"I don't know, prince," I answered as simply as I could; "in something else, that is, anything concerning Natalya Nikolaevna, I am ready to give you any information likely to be of use to you or to us, but in this matter you must know better than I do."

"No, no, I don't know so well, of course not. You know them, and perhaps Natalya Nikolaevna may have given you her views on the subject more than once, and they would be my guiding principle. You can be a great help to me. It's an extremely difficult matter. I am prepared to make a concession. I'm even determined to make a concession, however other matters may end. You understand? But how, and in what form, to make that concession? That's the question. The old man's proud and obstinate. Very likely he'll insult me for my good-nature, and throw the money in my face."

"But excuse me. How do you look upon that money? As your own or as his?"

"I won the lawsuit, so the money's mine."

"But in your conscience?"

"Of course I regard it as mine," he answered, somewhat piqued at my unceremoniousness. "But I believe you don't know all the facts of the case. I don't accuse the old man of intentional duplicity, and I will confess I've never accused him. It was his own choice to take it as an insult. He was to blame for carelessness, for not looking more sharply after business entrusted to him. And by our agreement he was bound to be responsible for some of his mistakes. But, do you know, even that's not really the point. What was really at the bottom of it was our quarrelling, our mutual recriminations at the time, in fact, wounded vanity on both sides. I might not have taken any notice of that paltry ten thousand, but you know, of course, how the whole case began and what it arose from. I'm ready to admit that I was suspicious and perhaps unjust (that is, unjust at the time), but I wasn't aware of it, and in my vexation and resentment of his rudeness I was unwilling to let the chance slip, and began the lawsuit. You may perhaps think all that not very generous on my part. I don't defend myself; only, I may observe, that anger, or still more, wounded pride, is not the same as lack of generosity, but is a natural human thing, and I confess, I repeat again, that I did not know Ichmenyev at all, and quite believed in those rumours about Alyosha and his daughter, and so was able to believe that the money had been intentionally stolen. . . . But putting that aside, the real question is, what am I to do now? I might refuse the money, but if at the same time I say that I still consider my claim was a just one, it comes to my giving him the money, and, add to that the delicate position in regard to Natalya Nikolaevna, he'll certainly fling the money in my face. . . ."

"There, you see, you say yourself he'll fling it in your face; so you do consider him an honest man, and that's why you can be perfectly certain that he did not steal your money. And if so, why shouldn't you go to him and tell him straight out that you consider your claim as unjustified. That would be honourable, and Ichmenyev would not perhaps find it difficult then to accept *his* money."

"Hm! *His* money . . . that's just the question; what sort of position do you put me into? Go to him and tell him I consider my claim illegal. 'Why did you make it then, if you considered it illegal?' that's what every one would say to my face. And I've not deserved it, for my claim was legal. I have never said and never written that he stole the money, but I am still convinced of his carelessness, his negligence, and incapacity in managing business. That money is undoubtedly mine, and therefore it would be mortifying to make a false charge against myself, and finally, I repeat, the old man brought the ignominy of it upon himself, and you want to force me to beg his pardon for that ignominy—that's hard."

"It seems to me that if two men want to be reconciled, then . . ."

"You think it's easy?"

"Yes."

"No, sometimes it's very far from easy, especially . . ."

"Especially if there are other circumstances connected with it. Yes, there I agree with you, prince. The position of

Natalya Nikolaevna and of your son ought to be settled by you in all those points that depend upon you, and settled so as to be fully satisfactory to the Ichmenyevs. Only then can you be quite sincere with Ichmenyev about the lawsuit too. Now, while nothing has been settled, you have only one course open to you : to acknowledge the injustice of your claim, and to acknowledge it openly, and if necessary even publicly, that's my opinion. I tell you so frankly because you asked me my opinion yourself. And probably you do not wish me to be insincere with you. And this gives me the courage to ask you why you are troubling your head about returning this money to Ichmenyev ? If you consider that you were just in your claim, why return it ? Forgive my being so inquisitive, but this has such an intimate bearing upon other circumstances."

"And what do you think ? " he asked suddenly, as though he had not heard my question. "Are you so sure that old Ichmenyev would refuse the ten thousand if it were handed to him without any of these evasions, and . . . and . . . and blandishments ? "

"Of course he would refuse it."

I flushed crimson and positively trembled with indignation. This impudently sceptical question affected me as though he had spat into my face. My resentment was increased by something else : the coarse, aristocratic manner in which, without answering my question, and apparently without noticing it, he interrupted it with another, probably to give me to understand that I had gone too far and had been too familiar in venturing to ask him such a question. I detested, I loathed that aristocratic manœuvre and had done my utmost in the past to get Alyosha out of it.

"Hm ! You are too impulsive, and things are not done in real life as you imagine," the prince observed calmly, at my exclamation. "But I think that Natalya Nikolaevna might do something to decide the question ; you tell her that she might give some advice."

"Not a bit of it," I answered roughly. "You did not deign to listen to what I was saying to you just now, but interrupted me. Natalya Nikolaevna will understand that if you return the money without frankness and without all those blandishments, as you call them, it amounts to your paying the father for the loss of his daughter, and her for the loss of Alyosha—in other words your giving them money compensation . . ."

"Hm ! . . . so that's how you understand me, my excellent Ivan Petrovitch," the prince laughed. Why did he laugh ?

"And meanwhile," he went on, "there are so many, many things we have to talk over together. But now there's no time. I only beg you to understand *one thing*: Natalya Nikolaevna and her whole future are involved in the matter, and all this depends to some extent on what we decide. You are indispensable, you'll see for yourself. So if you are still devoted to Natalya Nikolaevna, you can't refuse to go frankly into things with me, however little sympathy you may feel for me. But here we are. . . . *à bientôt.*"

CHAPTER IX

THE countess lived in good style. The rooms were furnished comfortably and with taste, though not at all luxuriously. Everything, however, had the special character of a temporary residence, not the permanent established habitation of a wealthy family with all the style of the aristocracy, and all the whims that they take for necessities. There was a rumour that the countess was going in the summer to her ruined and mortgaged property in the province of Simbirsk, and that the prince would accompany her. I had heard this already, and wondered uneasily how Alyosha would behave when Katya went away with the countess. I had not yet spoken of this to Natasha. I was afraid to. But from some signs I had noticed, I fancied that she, too, knew of the rumour. But she was silent and suffered in secret.

The countess gave me an excellent reception, held out her hand to me cordially, and repeated that she had long wished to make my acquaintance. She made tea herself from a handsome silver samovar, round which we all sat, the prince, and I and another gentleman, elderly and extremely aristocratic, wearing a star on his breast, somewhat starchy and diplomatic in his manners. This visitor seemed an object of great respect. The countess had not, since her return from abroad, had time that winter to make a large circle of acquaintances in Petersburg and to establish her position as she had hoped and reckoned upon doing. There was no one besides this gentleman, and no one else came in all the evening. I looked about for Katerina Fyodorovna; she was in the next room with Alyosha, but hearing that we had arrived she came in at once. The prince kissed her hand politely, and the countess motioned her towards me. The prince at once introduced us. I looked at her with impatient attention. She was a short, soft little blonde dressed in a white frock, with a mild and serene expression of face, with eyes of a perfect blue, as Alyosha had said; she had the beauty of youth, that was all. I had expected to meet the perfection of beauty, but it was not a case of beauty. The regular, softly outlined oval of the face, the fairly correct features, the thick and really splendid hair, the simple and homely style in which it was arranged, the gentle, attentive expression—all this I should have passed by without paying special attention to it if I had met her elsewhere. But this was only the first impression, and I succeeded in getting a fuller insight into her in the course of that evening. The very way in which she shook hands with me, standing looking into my face with a sort of naïvely exaggerated intentness, without saying a word, impressed me by its strangeness, and I could not help smiling at her. It was evident, I felt at once, that I had before me a creature of the purest heart. The countess watched her intently. After shaking hands Katya walked away from me somewhat hurriedly, and sat down at the other end of the room with Alyosha. As he greeted me Alyosha whispered: "I'm only here for a minute. I'm just going *there*."

The "diplomat," I don't know his name and call him a diplomat simply to call him something, talked calmly and majestically, developing some idea. The countess listened to him attentively. The prince gave him an encouraging and flattering smile. The orator often addressed himself to him, apparently appreciating him as a listener worthy of his attention. They gave me some tea and left me in peace, for which I was very thankful. Meanwhile I was looking at the countess. At first sight she attracted me in spite of myself. Perhaps she was no longer young, but she seemed to me not more than twenty-eight. Her face was still fresh, and in her first youth she must have been very beautiful. Her dark brown hair was still fairly thick; her expression was extremely kindly, but frivolous, and mischievously mocking. But just now she was evidently keeping herself in check. There was a look of great intelligence, too, in her eyes, but even more of good-nature and gaiety. It seemed to me that her predominant characteristic was a certain levity, an eagerness for enjoyment, and a sort of good-natured egoism; a great deal of egoism, perhaps. She was absolutely guided by the prince, who had an extraordinary influence on her. I knew that they had a liaison; I had heard, too, that he had been anything but a jealous lover while they had been abroad; but I kept fancying, and I think so still, that apart from their former relations there was something else, some rather mysterious tie binding them together, something like a mutual obligation resting upon motives of self-interest . . . in fact there certainly was something of the sort. I knew, too, that by now the prince was tired of her, and yet their relations had not been broken off. Perhaps what kept them together especially was their design for Katya, which must have owed its initiative to the prince. By persuading her to help him bring about Alyosha's marriage with her stepdaughter, the prince had good reasons for getting out of marriage with the countess, which she really had urged upon him. So, at least, I concluded from facts dropped in all simplicity by Alyosha; even he could not help noticing something. I kept fancying, too, partly from Alyosha's talk, that although the countess was completely under the prince's control he had some reason for being afraid of her. Even Alyosha had noticed this. I learnt afterwards that the prince was very anxious to get the countess married to some one else, and that it was partly with that object he was sending her off to Simbirsk, hoping to pick up a suitable husband for her in the province.

I sat still and listened, not knowing how I could quickly secure a *tête-à-tête* interview with Katerina Fyodorovna. The dipomat was answering some questions of the countess's about the present political position, about the reforms that were being instituted, and whether they were to be dreaded or not. He said a great deal at great length, calmly, like one having authority. He developed his idea subtly and cleverly, but the idea was a repulsive one. He kept insisting that the whole spirit of reform and improvement would only too soon bring forth certain results, that seeing those results "they would come to their senses," and that not only in society (that is, of course in a certain part of it) would this spirit of reform pass away, but they would learn their mistake from experience, and then with redoubled energy would return to the old traditions, that the experience, though distressing, would be of great benefit, because it would teach them to maintain that salutary tradition, would give fresh grounds for doing so, and that consequently it was to be hoped that the extreme limit of recklessness would be reached as soon as possible. "They cannot get on without *us*," he concluded, "no society has ever stood its ground without us. We shall lose nothing. On the contrary we stand to win. We shall rise to the surface, and our motto at the moment should be ' *pire ça va, mieux ça est!*' " Prince Valkovsky smiled to him with revolting sympathy. The orator was completely satisfied with himself. I was so stupid as to want to protest; my heart was boiling. But what checked me was the malignant expression of the prince; he stole a glance in my direction, and it seemed to me that he was just expecting some strange and youthful outburst from me. Perhaps he even wanted this in order to enjoy my compromising myself. Meanwhile I felt convinced that the diplomat would not notice my protest, nor perhaps me either. It was revolting for me to sit with them; but Alyosha rescued me.

He came up to me quietly, touched me on the shoulder, and asked to have a few words with me. I guessed he came with a message from Katya. And so it was. A minute later I was sitting beside her. At first she kept watching me intently as though saying to herself: "so that's what you're like," and for the first minute neither of us could find words to begin our conversation. I felt sure though that when once she began she would be ready to go on without stopping till next morning. The "five or six hours' talk" of which Alyosha had spoken came back to my mind. Alyosha sat by us, waiting impatiently for us to begin.

"Why don't you say anything?" he began, looking at us with a smile. "They come together and sit silent."

"Ach, Alyosha, how can you . . . we'll begin directly," answered Katya. "We have so much to talk over together, Ivan Petrovitch, that I don't know where to begin. We've been late in getting to know one another; we ought to have met long ago, though I've known you for ages. And I was very anxious to see you! I was even thinking of writing you a letter . . ."

"What about?" I asked, smiling involuntarily.

"Ever so many things," she answered earnestly. "Why, if only to know whether it's true what Alyosha says, that Natalya Nikolaevna is not hurt at his leaving her alone at such a time. Can anyone behave as he does? Why are you here now, tell me that, please?"

"Why, good heavens, I'm just going! I just said that I should only be here for a minute, simply to look at you two and see how you talk to one another, and then I'll be off to Natasha."

"Well, here we are together, we're sitting here, do you see? He's always like that," she added, flushing a little and pointing her finger at him. "One minute," he always says, "just one minute; and, mind, he'll stay on till midnight and then it's too late to go there. 'She won't be angry,' he says, 'she's kind.' That's how he looks at it. Is that right? Is that generous?"

"Well, I'll go if you like," Alyosha responded plaintively, "but I do want dreadfully to stay with you two. . . ."

"What do you want with us? On the contrary we must talk of lots of things alone. Listen, don't be cross. It's necessary—take that in thoroughly."

"If it's necessary I'll be off at once—what is there to be cross at? I'll just look in for a minute on Levinka, and then go on to her at once. I say, Ivan Petrovitch," he added, taking up his hat to go, "do you know that my father wants to refuse to take the money he won by his lawsuit with Ichmenyev?"

"I know. He told me."

"How generous he is in doing that. Katya won't believe that he's acting generously. Talk to her about that. Goodbye, Katya, and please don't doubt that I love Natasha. And why do you both always tie me down like this, scold me, and look after me—as though you had to watch over me. She knows how I love her, and is sure of me, and I'm sure that she's sure of me. I love her, apart from anything, apart from any obligations. I don't know how I love her, I simply love her. And so there's no need to question me as though I were to blame. You can ask Ivan Petrovitch, he's here now and he will confirm what I say, that Natasha's jealous, and though she loves me so much there's a great deal of egoism in her love, for she will never sacrifice anything for me."

"What's that?" I asked in amazement, hardly able to believe my ears.

"What are you saying, Alyosha?" Katya almost screamed, clasping her hands.

"Why, what is there so surprising in that? Ivan Petrovitch knows it. She's always insisting that I should stay with her. Not that she insists, exactly, but one can see that's what she wants."

"Aren't you ashamed? Aren't you ashamed?" said Katya, turning crimson with anger.

"What is there to be ashamed of? What a person you are, really, Katya! I love her more than she thinks, and if she really loves me as I love her, she certainly would sacrifice her pleasure to me. It's true she lets me go herself, but I see from her face that she hates doing it, so that it comes to the same thing as if she didn't let me."

"Oh, there's something behind that," cried Katya, turning to me again with flashing, angry eyes. "Own up, Alyosha, own up at once, it's your father who has put all that into your head. He's been talking to you to-day, hasn't he ? And please don't try and deceive me : I shall find out directly ! Is it so or not ?"

"Yes, he has been talking," Alyosha answered in confusion, " what of it ? He talked in such a kind and friendly way to-day, and kept praising her to me. I was quite surprised, in fact, that he should praise her like that after she had insulted him so."

"And you, you believed it ?" said I. "You, for whom she has given up everything she could give up ! And even now, this very day, all her anxiety was on your account, that you might not be bored, that you might not be deprived of the possibility of seeing Katerina Fyodorovna. She said that to me to-day herself. And you believe those false insinuations at once. Aren't you ashamed ?"

"Ungrateful boy ! But that's just it. He's never ashamed of anything," said Katya, dismissing him with a wave of her hand, as though he were lost beyond all hope.

"But really, how you talk !" Alyosha continued in a plaintive voice. "And you're always like that, Katya ! You're always suspecting me of something bad. . . . I don't count, Ivan Petrovitch ! You think I don't love Natasha. I didn't mean that when I said she was an egoist. I only meant that she loves me too much, so that it's all out of proportion, and I suffer for it, and she too. And my father never does influence me, though he's tried to. I don't let him. He didn't say she was an egoist in any bad sense ; I understood him. He said exactly what I said just now : that she loves me so much too much, so intensely, that it amounts to simple egoism and that that makes me suffer and her too, and that I shall suffer even more hereafter. He told the truth, and spoke from love of me, and it doesn't at all follow that he meant anything offensive to Natasha ; on the contrary, he saw the strength of her love, her immense, almost incredible love . . ."

But Katya interrupted him and would not let him finish. She began hotly upbraiding him, and maintaining that the prince had only praised Natasha to deceive him by a show of kindness, all in order to destroy their attachment, with the idea of invisibly and imperceptibly turning Alyosha against her. Warmly and cleverly she argued that Natasha loved him, that no love could forgive the way he was treating her, and that he himself, Alyosha, was the real egoist. Little by little Katya reduced him to utter misery and complete penitence. He sat beside us, utterly crushed, staring at the floor with a look of suffering on his face and gave up attempting to answer. But Katya was relentless. I kept looking at her with the greatest interest. I was eager to get to know this strange girl. She was quite a child, but a strange child, a child of *convictions*, with steadfast principles, and with a passionate, innate love of goodness and justice. If one really might call her a child she belonged to that class of *thinking* children, who are fairly numerous in our Russian families. It was evident that she had pondered on many subjects. It would have been interesting to peep into that little pondering head and to see the mixture there of quite childish images and fancies, with serious ideas and notions gained from experience of life (for Katya really had lived), and at the same time with ideas of which she had no real knowledge or experience, abstract theories she had got out of books, though she probably mistook them for generalizations gained by her own experience. These abstract ideas must have been very numerous. In the course of that evening and subsequently I studied her, I believe, pretty thoroughly; her heart was ardent and receptive. In some cases she, as it were, disdained self-control, putting genuineness before everything, and looking upon every restraint on life as a conventional prejudice. And she seemed to pride herself on that conviction, which is often the case indeed with persons of ardent temperament even in those who are not very young. But it was just that that gave her a peculiar charm. She was very fond of thinking and getting at the truth of things, but was so far from being pedantic, so full of youthful ways, that from the first moment one began to love all these originalities in her, and to accept them. I thought of Levinka and Borinka, and it seemed to me that that was all in the natural order of things. And strange to say her face, in which I had seen nothing particularly handsome at first sight, seemed that evening to grow finer and more attractive every minute. This naïve combination in her of the child and the thinking woman, this childlike and absolutely genuine thirst for truth and justice, and absolute faith in her impulses—all this lighted up her face with a fine glow of sincerity, giving it a lofty, spiritual beauty, and one began to understand that it was not so easy to gauge the full significance of that beauty which was not all at once apparent to every ordinary unsympathetic eye. And I realized that Alyosha was bound to be passionately attached to her. If he was himself incapable of thought and reasoning he was especially attracted by those who could do his thinking, and even wishing, for him, and Katya had already taken him under her wing. His heart was generous, and it instantly surrendered without a struggle to everything that was fine and honourable. And Katya had spoken openly of many things before him already with sympathy and all the sincerity of a child. He was absolutely without a will of his own. She had a very great deal of strong, insistent, and fervidly concentrated will; and Alyosha would only attach himself to one who could dominate and even command him. It was partly through this that Natasha had attracted him at the beginning of their relations, but Katya had a great advantage over Natasha in the fact that she was still a child herself and seemed likely to remain so for a long time. This childishness, her bright intelligence, and at the same time a certain lack of judgment, all this made her more akin to Alyosha. He felt this, and so Katya attracted him more and more. I am certain that when they talked alone together in the midst of Katya's earnest discussion of "propaganda," they sometimes relapsed into childish trivialities. And though Katya probably often lectured Alyosha and already had him under her thumb, he was evidently more at home with her than with Natasha. They were more equals, and that meant a great deal.

"Stop, Katya, stop. That's enough; you always have the best of it, and I'm always wrong. That's because your heart is purer than mine," said Alyosha, getting up and giving her his hand at parting. "I'm going straight to her and I won't look in on Levinka. . . ."

"There's nothing for you to do at Levinka's. But you're very sweet to obey and go now."

"And you're a thousand times sweeter than anybody," answered Alyosha sadly. "Ivan Petrovitch, I've a word or two I want to say to you."

We moved a couple of paces away.

"I've behaved shamefully to-day," he whispered to me.

"I've behaved vilely, I've sinned against every one in the world, and these two more than all. After dinner to-day father introduced me to Mlle. Alexandrine (a French girl)—a fascinating creature. I . . . was carried away and . . . but what's the good of talking. . . . I'm unworthy to be with them. . . . Good-bye, Ivan Petrovitch!"

"He's a kind, noble-hearted boy," Katya began hurriedly, when I had sat down beside her again, "but we'll talk a great deal about him later; first of all we must come to an understanding; what is your opinion of the prince?"

"He's a very horrid man."

"I think so too. So we're agreed about that, and so we shall be able to decide better. Now, of Natalya Nikolaevna . . . Do you know, Ivan Petrovitch, I am still, as it were, in the dark, I've been looking forward to you to bring me light. You must make it all clear to me, for about many of the chief points I can judge only by guesswork from what Alyosha tells me. There is no one else from whom I can learn anything. Tell me, in the first place (this is the chief point) what do you think: will Alyosha and Natasha be happy together or not? That's what I must know before everything, that I may make up my mind once for all how I must act."

"How can one tell that with any certainty?"

"No, of course, not with certainty," she interrupted, "but what do you think, for you are a very clever man?"

"I think that they can't be happy."

"Why?"

"They're not suited."

"That's just what I thought!"

And she clasped her hands as though deeply distressed.

"Tell me more fully. Listen, I'm awfully anxious to see Natasha, for there's a great deal I must talk over with her, and it seems to me that she and I can settle everything together. I keep picturing her to myself now. She must be very clever, serious, truthful, and beautiful. Isn't she?"

"Yes."

"I was sure of it. Well, if she is like that how could she love a baby like Alyosha? Explain that. I often wonder about it."

"That can't be explained, Katerina Fyodorovna. It's difficult to imagine how people can fall in love and what makes them. Yes, he's a child. But you know how one may love a child." (My heart melted looking at her and at her eyes fastened upon me intently with profound, earnest and impatient attention.) "And the less Natasha herself is like a child, the more serious she is, the more readily she might fall in love with him. He's truthful, sincere, awfully naïve, and sometimes charmingly naïve! Perhaps she fell in love with him—how shall I express it?—as it were from a sort of compassion. A generous heart may love from compassion. I feel though that I can't give any explanation, but I'll ask you instead: do you love him?"

I boldly asked her this question and felt that I could not disturb the infinite childlike purity of her candid soul by the abruptness of such a question.

"I really don't know yet," she answered me quietly, looking me serenely in the face, "but I think I love him very much...."

"There, you see. And can you explain why you love him?"

"There's no falsehood in him," she answered after thinking a moment, "and I like it when he looks into my eyes and says something. Tell me, Ivan Petrovitch, here I'm talking about this to you, I'm a girl and you're a man, am I doing right in this, or not?"

"Why, what is there in it?"

"Nothing. Of course there's nothing in it. But they," she glanced at the group sitting round the samovar, "they would certainly say it was wrong. Are they right or not?"

"No. Why, you don't feel in your heart you've done wrong, so..."

"That's how I always do," she broke in, evidently in haste to get in as much talk with me as she could. "When I'm confused about anything I always look into my own heart, and when it's at ease then I'm at ease. That's how I must always behave. And I speak as frankly to you as I would speak to myself because for one thing you are a splendid man and I know about your past, with Natasha, before Alyosha's time, and I cried when I heard about it."

"Why, who told you?"

"Alyosha, of course, and he had tears in his eyes himself when he told me. That was very nice of him, and I liked him for it. I think he likes you better than you like him, Ivan Petrovitch. It's in things like that I like him. And another reason why I am so open with you is that you're a very clever man, and you can give me advice and teach me about a great many things."

"How do you know that I'm clever enough to teach you?"

"Oh, well, you needn't ask!"

She grew thoughtful.

"I didn't mean to talk about that really. Let's talk of what matters most. Tell me, Ivan Petrovitch; here I feel now that I'm Natasha's rival, I know I am, how am I to act? That's why I asked you: would they be happy. I think about it day and night. Natasha's position is awful, awful! He has quite left off loving her, you know, and he loves me more and more. That is so, isn't it?"

"It seems so."

"Yet he is not deceiving her. He doesn't know that he is ceasing to love her, but no doubt she knows it. How miserable she must be!"

"What do you want to do, Katerina Fyodorovna?"

"I have a great many plans," she answered seriously, "and meanwhile I'm all in a muddle. That's why I've been so impatient to see you for you to make it all clear to me. You know all that so much better than I do. You're a sort of divinity to me now, you know. Listen, this is what I thought at first: if they love one another they must be happy, and so I ought to sacrifice myself and help them—oughtn't I?"

"I know you did sacrifice yourself."

"Yes, I did. But afterwards when he began coming to me and caring more and more for me, I began hesitating, and I'm still hesitating whether I ought to sacrifice myself or not. That's very wrong, isn't it?"

"That's natural," I answered, "that's bound to be so . . . and it's not your fault."

"I think it is. You say that because you are very kind. I think it is because my heart is not quite pure. If I had a pure heart I should know how to behave. But let us leave that. Afterwards I heard more about their attitude to one another, from the prince, from *maman*, from Alyosha himself, and guessed they were not suited, and now you've confirmed it. I hesitated more than ever, and now I'm uncertain what to do. If they're going to be unhappy, you know, why, they had better part. And so I made up my mind to ask you more fully about it, and to go myself to Natasha, and to settle it all with her."

"But settle it how? That's the question."

"I shall say to her, 'you love him more than anything, don't you, and so you must care more for his happiness than your own, and therefore you must part from him.'"

"Yes, but how will she receive that? And even if she agrees with you will she be strong enough to act on it?"

"That's what I think about day and night, and . . . and . . ."

And she suddenly burst into tears.

"You don't know how sorry I am for Natasha," she whispered, her lips quivering with tears.

There was nothing more to be said. I was silent, and I too felt inclined to cry as I watched her, for no particular reason, from a vague feeling like tenderness. What a charming child she was! I no longer felt it necessary to ask her why she thought she could make Alyosha happy.

"Are you fond of music?" she asked, growing a little calmer, though she was still subdued by her recent tears.

"Yes," I answered, with some surprise.

"If there were time I'd play you Beethoven's third concerto. That's what I'm playing now. All those feelings are in it . . . just as I feel them now. So it seems to me. But that must be another time, now we must talk."

We began discussing how she could meet Natasha, and how it was all to be arranged. She told me that they kept a watch on her, and though her stepmother was kind and fond of her, she would never allow her to make friends with Natalya Nikolaevna, and so she had decided to have recourse to deception. She sometimes went a drive in the morning, but almost always with the countess. Sometimes the countess didn't go with her but sent her out alone with a French lady, who was ill just now. Sometimes the countess had headaches, and so she would have to wait until she had one. And meanwhile she would over-persuade her Frenchwoman (an old lady who was some sort of companion), for the latter was very good-natured. The upshot of it was that it was impossible to fix beforehand what day she would be able to visit Natasha.

"You won't regret making Natasha's acquaintance," I said. "She is very anxious to know you too, and she must, if only to know to whom she is giving up Alyosha. Don't worry too much about it all. Time will settle it all, without your troubling. You are going into the country, aren't you?"

"Quite soon. In another month perhaps," she answered. "And I know the prince is insisting on it."

"What do you think—will Alyosha go with you?"

"I've thought about that," she said, looking intently at me. "He will go, won't he?"

"Yes, he will."

"Good heavens, how it will all end I don't know. I tell you what, Ivan Petrovitch, I'll write to you about everything, I'll write to you often, fully. Now I'm going to worry you, too. Will you often come and see us?"

"I don't know, Katerina Fyodorovna. That depends upon circumstances. Perhaps I may not come at all."

"Why not?"

"It will depend on several considerations, and chiefly what terms I am on with the prince."

"He's a dishonest man," said Katya with decision. "I tell you what, Ivan Petrovitch, how if I should come to see you? Will that be a good thing, or not?"

"What do you think yourself?"

"I think it would be a good thing. In that way I could bring you news," she added with a smile. "And I say this because I like you very much as well as respect you. And I could learn a great deal from you. And I like you. . . . And it's not disgraceful my speaking of it, is it?"

"Why should it be? You're as dear to me already as one of my own family."

"Then you want to be my friend?"

"Oh yes, yes!" I answered.

"And they would certainly say it was disgraceful and that a young girl ought not to behave like this," she observed, again indicating the group in conversation at the tea-table.

I may mention here that the prince seemed purposely to leave us alone that we might talk to our heart's content.

"I know very well," she added, "that the prince wants my money. They think I'm a perfect baby, and in fact they tell me so, openly. But I don't think so. I'm not a child now. They're strange people: they're like children themselves. What are they in such a fuss about?"

"Katerina Fyodorovna, I forgot to ask you, who are these Levinka and Borinka whom Alyosha goes to see so often?"

"They're distant relations. They're very clever and very honest, but they do a dreadful lot of talking. . . . I know them . . ."

And she smiled.

"Is it true that you mean to give them a million later on?"

"Oh, well, you see, what if I do? They chatter so much about that million that it's growing quite unbearable. Of course I shall be delighted to contribute to everything useful; what's the good of such an immense fortune? But what though I am going to give it some day, they're already dividing it, discussing it, shouting, disputing what's the best use to make of it, they even quarrel about it, so that it's quite queer. They're in too great a hurry. But they're honest all the same and clever. They are studying. That's better than going on as other people do. Isn't it?"

And we talked a great deal more. She told me almost her whole life, and listened eagerly to what I told her. She kept insisting that I should tell her more about Natasha and Alyosha. It was twelve o'clock when Prince Valkovsky came and let me know it was time to take leave. I said good-bye. Katya pressed my hand warmly and looked at me expressively. The countess asked me to come again; the prince and I went out.

I cannot refrain from one strange and perhaps quite inappropriate remark. From my three hours' conversation with Katya I carried away among other impressions the strange but positive conviction that she was still such a child that she had no idea of the inner significance of the relations of the sexes. This gave an extraordinarily comic flavour to some of her reflections, and in general to the serious tone in which she talked of many very important matters.

CHAPTER X

"I TELL you what," said Prince Valkovsky, as he seated himself beside me in the carriage, "what if we were to go to supper now, *hein*? What do you say to that?"

"I don't know, prince," I answered, hesitating. "I never eat supper."

"Well, of course, we'll have a *talk*, too, over supper," he added, looking intently and slyly into my face.

There was no misunderstanding! "He means to speak out," I thought; "and that's just what I want." I agreed.

"That's settled, then. To B.'s, in Great Morskaya."

"A restaurant?" I asked with some hesitation.

"Yes, why not? I don't often have supper at home. Surely you won't refuse to be my guest?"

"But I've told you already that I never take supper."

"But once in a way doesn't matter; especially as I'm inviting you. . . ."

Which meant he would pay for me. I am certain that he added that intentionally. I allowed myself to be taken, but made up my mind to pay for myself in the restaurant. We arrived. The prince engaged a private room, and with the taste of a connoisseur selected two or three dishes. They were expensive and so was the bottle of delicate wine which he ordered. All this was beyond my means. I looked at the bill of fare and ordered half a woodcock and a glass of Lafitte. The prince kicked at this.

"You won't sup with me! Why, this is positively ridiculous! Pardon, *mon ami*, but this is . . . revolting punctiliousness. It's the paltriest vanity. There's almost a suspicion of class feeling about this. I don't mind betting that's it. I assure you you're offending me."

But I stuck to my point.

"But, as you like," he added. "I won't insist. . . . Tell me, Ivan Petrovitch, may I speak to you as a friend?"

"I beg you to do so."

"Well, then, to my thinking such punctiliousness stands in your way. All you people stand in your own light in that way. You are a literary man; you ought to know the world, and you hold yourself aloof from everything. I'm not talking of your woodcock now, but you are ready to refuse to associate with our circle altogether, and that's against your interests. Apart from the fact that you lose a great deal, a career, in fact, if only that you ought to know what you're describing, and in novels we have counts and princes and boudoirs. . . . But what am I saying! Poverty is all the fashion with you now, lost coats,[*] inspectors, quarrelsome officers, clerks, old times, dissenters, I know, I know. . . ."

"But you are mistaken, prince. If I don't want to get into your so-called 'higher circle,' it's because in the first place it's boring, and in the second I've nothing to do there; though, after all, I do sometimes. . . ."

"I know; at Prince R.'s, once a year. I've met you there. But for the rest of the year you stagnate in your democratic pride, and languish in your garrets, though not all of you behave like that. Some of them are such adventurers that they sicken me. . . ."

[*] The reference is to Gogol's story "The Lost Coat."—*Translator's note.*

"I beg you, prince, to change the subject and not to return to our garrets."

"Dear me, now you're offended. But you know you gave me permission to speak to you as a friend. But it's my fault; I have done nothing to merit your friendship. The wine's very decent. Try it."

He poured me out half a glass from his bottle.

"You see, my dear Ivan Petrovitch, I quite understand that to force one's friendship upon anyone is bad manners. We're not all rude and insolent with you as you imagine. I quite understand that you are not sitting here from affection for me, but simply because I promised to *talk* to you. That's so, isn't it?"

He laughed.

"And as you're watching over the interests of a certain person you want to hear *what* I am going to say. That's it, isn't it?" he added with a malicious smile.

"You are not mistaken," I broke in impatiently. (I saw that he was one of those men who if anyone is ever so little in their power cannot resist making him feel it. I was in his power. I could not get away without hearing what he intended to say, and he knew that very well. His tone suddenly changed and became more and more insolently familiar and sneering.) "You're not mistaken, prince, that's just what I've come for, otherwise I should not be sitting here . . . so late."

I had wanted to say "I would not on any account have been supping with you," but I didn't say this, and finished my phrase differently, not from timidity, but from my cursed weakness and delicacy. And really, how can one be rude to a man to his face, even if he deserves it, and even though one may wish to be rude to him? I fancied the prince detected this from my eyes, and looked at me ironically as I finished my sentence, as though enjoying my faint-heartedness, and as it were challenging me with his eyes: "So you don't dare to be rude; that's it, my boy!" This must have been so, for as I finished he chuckled, and with patronizing friendliness slapped me on the knee.

"You're amusing, my boy!" was what I read in his eyes. "Wait a bit!" I thought to myself.

"I feel very lively to-night!" said he, "and I really don't know why. Yes, yes, my boy! It was just that young person I wanted to talk to you about. We must speak quite frankly; *talk* till we reach some conclusion, and I hope that this time you will thoroughly understand me. I talked to you just now about that money and that old fogey of a father, that babe of sixty summers. . . . Well! It's not worth mentioning it now. That was only talk, you know! Ha-ha-ha! You're a literary man, you ought to have guessed that."

I looked at him with amazement. I don't think he was drunk.

"As for that girl, I respect her, I assure you; I like her in fact. She's a little capricious but 'there's no rose without a thorn,' as they used to say fifty years ago, and it was well said too: thorns prick. But that's alluring and though my Alexey's a fool, I've forgiven him to some extent already for his good taste. In short, I like such young ladies, and I have" (and he compressed his lips with immense significance) "views of my own, in fact. . . . But of that later. . . ."

"Prince! Listen, prince!" I cried. "I don't understand your quick change of front but . . . change the subject, if you please."

"You're getting hot again! Very good. . . . I'll change it, I'll change it! But I'll tell you what I want to ask you, my good friend: have you a very great respect for her?"

"Of course," I answered, with gruff impatience.

"Ah, indeed. And do you love her?" he continued, grinning revoltingly and screwing up his eyes.

"You are forgetting yourself!" I cried.

"There, there, I won't! Don't put yourself out! I'm in wonderful spirits to-day. I haven't felt so gay for a long time. Shall we have some champagne? What do you say, my poet?"

"I won't have any. I don't want it."

"You don't say so! You really must keep me company to-day. I feel so jolly and as I'm soft-hearted to sentimentality, I can't bear to be happy alone. Who knows, we may come to drinking to our eternal friendship. Ha-ha-ha! No, my young friend, you don't know me yet! I'm certain you'll grow to love me. I want you this evening to share my grief and my joy, my tears and my laughter, though I hope that I at least may not shed any. Come, what do you say, Ivan Petrovitch? You see, you must consider that if I don't get what I want, all my inspiration may pass, be wasted and take wing and you'll hear nothing. And you know you're only sitting here in the hope of hearing something. Aren't you?" he added, winking at me insolently again. "So, make your choice."

The threat was a serious one. I consented. "Surely he doesn't want to make me drunk?" I thought. This is the place, by the way, to mention a rumour about the prince which had reached me long before. It was said that though he was so elegant and decorous in society he sometimes was fond of getting drunk at night, of drinking like a fish, of secret debauchery, of loathsome and mysterious vices. . . . I had heard awful rumours about him. It was said that Alyosha knew his father sometimes drank, and tried to conceal the fact from every one, especially from Natasha. Once he let something slip before me, but immediately changed the subject and would not answer my questions. I had not heard it from him, however, and I must admit I had not believed it. Now I waited to see what was coming.

The champagne was brought, the prince poured out a glass for himself and another for me.

"A sweet, sweet girl, though she did scold me," he went on, sipping his wine with relish, "but these sweet creatures are particularly sweet just at those moments. . . . And, you know, she thought no doubt she had covered me with shame, do you remember that evening when she crushed me to atoms? Ha-ha-ha! And how a blush suits her! Are you a connoisseur in women? Sometimes a sudden flush is wonderfully becoming to a pale cheek. Have you noticed that? Oh dear, I believe you're angry again!"

"Yes, I am angry!" I cried, unable to restrain myself. "And I won't have you speak of Natalya Nikolaevna . . . that is, speak in that tone . . . I . . . I won't allow you to do it!"

"Oho! Well, as you like, I'll humour you and change the conversation. I am as yielding and soft as dough. Let's talk of you. I like you, Ivan Petrovitch. If only you knew what a friendly, what a sincere interest I take in you."

"Prince, wouldn't it be better to keep to the point," I interrupted.

"You mean talk of *our affair*. I understand you with half a word, *mon ami*, but you don't know how closely we are touching on the point if we speak of you and you don't interrupt me of course. And so I'll go on. I wanted to tell you, my priceless Ivan Petrovitch, that to live as you're living is simply self-destruction. Allow me to touch on this delicate subject; I speak as a friend. You are poor, you ask your publisher for money in advance, you pay your trivial debts, with what's left you live for six months on tea, and shiver in your garret while you wait for your novel to be written for your publisher's magazine. That's so, isn't it?"

"If it is so, anyway it's . . ."

"More creditable than stealing, cringing, taking bribes, intriguing and so on, and so on. I know, I know what you want to say, all that's been printed long ago."

"And so there's no need for you to talk about my affairs. Surely, prince, I needn't give you a lesson in delicacy!"

"Well, certainly you needn't. But what's to be done if it's just that delicate chord we must touch upon? There's no avoiding it. But there, let's leave garrets alone. I'm by no means fond of them, except in certain cases," he added with a loathsome laugh. "But what surprises me is that you should be so set on playing a secondary part. Certainly one of you authors, I remember, said somewhere that the greatest achievement is for a man to know how to restrict himself to a secondary rôle in life. . . . I believe it's something of that sort. I've heard talk of that somewhere too, but you know Alyosha has carried off your fiancée. I know that and you, like some Schiller, are ready to go to the stake for them, you're waiting upon them, and almost at their beck and call. . . . You must excuse me, my dear fellow, but it's rather a sickening show of noble feeling. I should have thought you must be sick of it! It's really shameful! I believe I should die of vexation in your place and worst of all the shame of it, the shame of it!"

"Prince, you seem to have brought me here on purpose to insult me!" I cried, beside myself with anger.

"Oh no, my dear boy, not at all. At this moment I am simply a matter-of-fact person, and wish for nothing but your happiness. In fact I want to put everything right. But let's lay all that aside for a moment, you hear me to the end, try not to lose your temper if only for two minutes. Come, what do you think, how would it be for you to get married? You see, I'm talking of quite *extraneous* matters now. Why do you look at me in such astonishment?"

"I'm waiting for you to finish," I said, staring at him indeed with astonishment.

"But there's no need to enlarge. I simply wanted to know what you'd say if any one of your friends, anxious to secure your genuine permanent welfare, not a mere ephemeral happiness, were to offer you a girl, young and pretty, but . . . of some little experience ; I speak allegorically but you'll understand, after the style of Natalya Nikolaevna, say, of course with a suitable compensation (observe I am speaking of an irrelevant case, not of *our* affair) ; well, what would you say ? "

"I say you're . . . mad."

"Ha-ha-ha! Bah! Why, you're almost ready to beat me!"

I really was ready to fall upon him. I could not have restrained myself longer. He produced on me the impression of some sort of reptile, some huge spider which I felt an intense desire to crush. He was enjoying his taunts at me. He was playing with me like a cat with a mouse, supposing that I was altogether in his power. It seemed to me (and I understood it) that he took a certain pleasure, found a certain sensual gratification in the shamelessness, in the insolence, in the cynicism with which at last he threw off his mask before me. He wanted to enjoy my surprise, my horror. He had a genuine contempt for me and was laughing at me.

I had a foreboding from the very beginning that this was all premeditated, and that there was some motive behind it, but I was in such a position that whatever happened I was bound to listen to him. It was in Natasha's interests, and I was obliged to make up my mind to everything and endure it, for perhaps the whole affair was being settled at that moment. But how could I listen to his base, cynical jeers at her expense, how could I endure this coolly! And, to make things worse, he quite realized that I could not avoid listening to him, and that redoubled the offensiveness of it. Yet he is in need of me himself, I reflected, and I began answering him abruptly and rudely. He understood it.

"Look here, my young friend," he began, looking at me seriously, "we can't go on like this, you and I, and so we'd better come to an understanding. I have been intending, you see, to speak openly to you about something, and you are bound to be so obliging as to listen, whatever I may say. I want to speak as I choose and as I prefer ; yes, in the present case that's necessary. So how is to be, my young friend, will you be so obliging ? "

I controlled myself and was silent, although he was looking at me with such biting mockery, as though he were challenging me to the most outspoken protest. But he realized that I had already agreed not to go and he went on.

"Don't be angry with me, my friend! You are angry at something, aren't you? Merely at something external, isn't it? Why, you expected nothing else of me in substance, however I might have spoken to you, with perfumed courtesy, or as now; so the drift would have been the same in any case. You despise me, don't you? You see how much charming simplicity there is in me, what candour, what *bonhomie!* I confess everything to you, even my childish caprices. Yes, *mon cher*, yes, a little more *bonhomie* on your side too, and we should agree and get on famously, and understand one another perfectly in the end. Don't wonder at me. I am so sick of all this innocence, all these pastoral idyllics of Alyosha's, all this Schillerism, all the loftiness of this damnable intrigue with this Natasha (not that she's not a very taking little girl) that I am, so to speak, glad of an opportunity to have my fling at them. Well, the opportunity has come. Besides, I am longing to pour out my heart to you. Ha! ha! ha!"

"You surprise me, prince, and I hardly recognize you. You are sinking to the level of a Polichinello. These unexpected revelations. . . ."

"Ha! ha! ha! to be sure that's partly true! A charming comparison, ha-ha-ha! I'm out for a spree, my boy, I'm out for a spree! I'm enjoying myself! And you, my poet, must show me every possible indulgence. But we'd better drink," he concluded filling up his glass, perfectly satisfied with himself. "I tell you what, my boy, that stupid evening at Natasha's, do you remember, was enough to finish me off completely. It's true she was very charming in herself, but I came away feeling horribly angry, and I don't want to forget it. Neither to forget it nor to conceal it. Of course our time will come too, and it's coming quickly indeed, but we'll leave that for now. And among other things I wanted to explain to you that I have one peculiarity of which you don't know yet, that is my hatred for all these vulgar and worthless naïvetés and idyllic nonsense; and one of the enjoyments I relish most has always been putting on that style myself, falling in with that tone. making much of some ever-young Schiller, and egging him on, and then, suddenly, all at once crushing him at one blow, suddenly taking off my mask before him, and suddenly distorting my ecstatic countenance into a grimace, putting out my tongue at him when he is least of all expecting such a surprise. What? You don't understand that, you think it nasty, stupid, undignified perhaps, is that it?"

" Of course it is."

" You are candid. I dare say, but what am I to do if they plague me ? I'm stupidly candid too, but such is my character. But I want to tell you some characteristic incidents in my life. It will make you understand me better, and it will be very interesting. Yes, I really am, perhaps, like a Polichinello to-day, but a Polichinello is candid, isn't he ? "

" Listen, prince, it's late now, and really . . ."

" What ? Good heavens, what impatience ! Besides, what's the hurry ? You think I'm drunk. Never mind. So much the better. Ha-ha-ha ! These friendly interviews are always remembered so long afterwards, you know, one recalls them with such enjoyment. You're not a good-natured man, Ivan Petrovitch. There's no sentimentality, no feeling about you. What is a paltry hour or two to you for the sake of a friend like me ? Besides, it has a bearing on a certain affair. . . . Of course you must realize that, and you a literary man too ; yes, you ought to bless the chance. You might create a type from me, ha-ha-ha ! My word, how sweetly candid I am to-day ! "

He was evidently drunk. His face changed and began to assume a spiteful expression. He was obviously longing to wound, to sting. to bite, to jeer. " In a way it's better he's drunk," I thought, " men always let things out when they're drunk." But he knew what he was about.

" My young friend," he began, unmistakably enjoying himself, " I made you a confession just now, perhaps an inappropriate one, that I sometimes have an irresistible desire to put out my tongue at people in certain cases. For this naïve and simple-hearted frankness you compare me to Polichinello, which really amuses me. But if you wonder or reproach me for being rude to you now, and perhaps as unmannerly as a peasant, with having changed my tone to you in fact, in that case you are quite unjust. In the first place it happens to suit me, and secondly, I am not at home, but out with *you* . . . by which I mean we're out for a spree together like good friends, and thirdly, I'm awfully given to acting on my fancies. Do you know that once I had a fancy to become a metaphysician and a philanthropist, and came round almost to the same ideas as you ? But that was ages ago, in the golden days of my youth. I remember at that time going to my home in the country with humane intentions, and was, of course, bored to extinction. And you wouldn't believe what happened to me then. In my boredom I began to make the acquaintance of some pretty little girls . . . What, you're not making faces already ? Oh, my young friend ! Why, we're talking as friends now ! One must sometimes enjoy oneself, one must sometimes let oneself go ! I have the Russian temperament, you know, a genuine Russian temperament, I'm a patriot, I love to throw off everything; besides one must snatch the moment to enjoy life. We shall die—and what comes then ! Well, so I took to dangling after the girls. I remember one little shepherdess had a husband, a handsome lad he was. I gave him a sound thrashing and meant to send him for a soldier (past pranks, my poet), but I didn't send him for a soldier. He died in my hospital. I had a hospital in the village, with twelve beds, splendidly fitted up ; such cleanliness, parquet floors. I abolished it long ago though, but at that time I was proud of it: I was a philanthropist. Well, I nearly flogged the peasant to death on his wife's account. . . . Why are you making faces again ? It disgusts you to hear about it ? It revolts your noble feelings ? There, there, don't upset yourself ! All that's a thing of the past. I did that when I was in my romantic stage. I wanted to be a benefactor of humanity, to found a philanthropic society. . . . That was the groove I was in at that time. And then it was I went in for thrashing. Now I never do it ; now one has to grimace about it ; now we all grimace about it—such are the times. . . . But what amuses me most of all now, is that fool Ichmenyev. I'm convinced that he knew all about that episode with the peasant . . . and what do you think ? In the goodness of his heart, which is made, I do believe, of treacle, and because he was in love with me at that time, and was cracking me up to himself, he made up his mind not to believe a word of it, and he didn't believe a word of it ; that is, he refused to believe in the fact and for twelve years he stood firm as a rock for me, till he was touched himself. Ha-ha-ha ! But all that's nonsense ! Let us drink, my young friend. Listen : are you fond of women ? "

I made no answer. I only listened to him. He was already beginning the second bottle.

" Well, I'm fond of talking about them over supper. I could introduce you after supper to a Mlle. Philiberte I know. *Hein ?* What do you say ? But what's the matter ? You won't even look at me . . . hm ! "

He seemed to ponder. But he suddenly raised his head, glanced at me as it were significantly, and went on :

"I tell you what, my poet, I want to reveal to you a mystery of nature of which it seems to me you are not in the least aware. I'm certain that you're calling me at this moment a sinner, perhaps even a scoundrel, a monster of vice and corruption. But I can tell you this. If it were only possible (which, however, from the laws of human nature never can be possible), if it were possible for every one of us to describe all his secret thoughts, without hesitating to disclose what he is afraid to tell and would not on any account tell other people, what he is afraid to tell his best friends, what, indeed, he is even at times afraid to confess to himself, the world would be filled with such a stench that we should all be suffocated. That's why, I may observe in parenthesis, our social proprieties and conventions are so good. They have a profound value, I won't say for morality, but simply for self-preservation, for comfort, which, of course, is even more, since morality is really that same comfort, that is, it's invented simply for the sake of comfort. But we'll talk of the proprieties later; I'm wandering from the point, remind me later. I will conclude by saying: you charge me with vice, corruption, immorality, but perhaps I'm only to blame for being more open than other people, that's all; for not concealing what other people hide even from themselves, as I said before. . . . It's horrid of me but it's what I want to do just now. But don't be uneasy," he added with an ironical smile, "I said 'to blame' but I'm not asking forgiveness. Note this too: I'm not putting you to the blush. I'm not asking you whether you haven't yourself some such secrets, in order to justify myself. I am behaving quite nicely and honourably. I always behave like a gentleman. . . ."

"This is simply silly talk," I said, looking at him with contempt.

"Silly talk! Ha-ha-ha! But shall I tell you what you're thinking? You're wondering why I brought you here, and am suddenly, without rhyme or reason, beginning to be so open with you. Isn't that it?"

"Yes."

"Well, that you will find out later."

"The simplest explanation is that you've drunk two bottles and . . . are not sober."

"You mean I'm simply drunk. That may be, too. 'Not sober!' That's a milder way of putting it than drunk. Oh, youth, brimming over with delicacy! But . . . we seem to have begun abusing one another again, and we were talking of something so interesting. Yes, my poet, if there is anything sweet and pretty left in the world it's women."

"Do you know, prince, I still can't understand why you have selected me as a confidant of your secrets and your amorous . . . propensities."

"Hm! But I told you that you'd learn that later on. Don't excite yourself; but what if I've no reason; you're a poet, you'll understand me, but I've told you that already. There's a peculiar gratification in suddenly removing the mask, in the cynicism with which a man suddenly exposes himself before another without even deigning to consider decency in his presence. I'll tell you an anecdote. There was a crazy official in Paris, who was afterwards put into a madhouse when it was realized that he was mad. Well, when he went out of his mind this is what he thought of to amuse himself. He undressed at home, altogether, like Adam, only keeping on his shoes and socks, put on an ample cloak that came down to his heels, wrapped himself round in it, and with a grave and majestic air went out into the street. Well, if he's looked at sideways—he's a man like anyone else, going for a walk in a long cloak to please himself. But whenever he met anyone in a lonely place where there was no one else about, he walked up to him in silence, and with the most serious and profoundly thoughtful air suddenly stopped before him, threw open his cloak and displayed himself in all the . . . purity of his heart! That used to last for a minute, then he would wrap himself up again, and in silence, without moving a muscle of his face, he would stalk by the petrified spectator, as grave and majestic as the ghost in Hamlet. That was how he used to behave with every one, men, women, and children, and that was his only pleasure. Well, some degree of the same pleasure may be experienced when one flabbergasts some romantic Schiller, by putting out one's tongue at him when he least expects it. 'Flabbergast'—what a word! I met it somewhere in one of you modern writers!"

"Well, that was a madman, but you . . ."

"I'm in my right mind?"

"Yes."

Prince Valkovsky chuckled.

"You're right there, my boy!" he added, with a most insolent expression of face.

"Prince," I said, angered by his insolence, "you hate us

all, including me, and you're revenging yourself on me for every one and everything. It all comes from your petty vanity. You're spiteful, and petty in your spite. We have enraged you, and perhaps what you are most angry about is that evening. Of course, there's no way in which you could pay me out more effectually than by this absolute contempt. You throw off the most ordinary, universally obligatory civility which we all owe to one another. You want to show me clearly that you don't even deign to consider decency before me, so openly and unexpectedly throwing off your filthy mask before me, and exhibiting yourself in such moral cynicism. . . ."

"Why are you saying all this to me?" he asked, looking rudely and maliciously at me. "To show your insight?"

"To show that I understand you, and to put it plainly before you."

"*Quelle idée, mon cher*," he went on, changing his note and suddenly reverting to his former light-hearted, chatty and good-humoured tone. "You are simply turning me from my subject. *Buvons, mon ami*, allow me to fill your glass. I only wanted to tell you about a charming and most curious adventure. I will tell it you in outline. I used at one time to know a lady; she was not in her first youth, but about twenty-seven or twenty-eight. She was a beauty of the first rank. What a bust, what a figure, what a carriage! Her eyes were as keen as an eagle's, but always stern and forbidding; her manner was majestic and unapproachable. She was reputed to be as cold as the driven snow, and frightened every one by her immaculate, her menacing virtue. Menacing's the word. There was no one in the whole neighbourhood so harsh in judgment as she. She punished not only vice, but the faintest weakness in other women, and punished it inflexibly, relentlessly. She had great influence in her circle. The proudest and most terribly virtuous old women respected her and even made up to her. She looked upon every one with impartial severity, like the abbess of a mediæval convent. Young women trembled before her glances and her criticism. A single remark, a single hint from her was able to ruin a reputation, so great was her influence in society; even men were afraid of her. Finally she threw herself into a sort of contemplative mysticism of the same calm dignified character. . . . And, would you believe? You couldn't have found a sinner more profligate than she was, and I was so happy as to gain her complete confidence. I was, in fact, her secret and mysterious lover. Our meetings were contrived in such a clever, masterly fashion, that none even of her own household could have the slightest suspicion of them. Only her maid, a very charming French girl, was initiated into all her secrets, but one could rely on that girl absolutely. She had her share in the proceedings—in what way ?—I won't enter into that now. My lady's sensuality was such that even the Marquis de Sade might have taken lessons from her. But the intensest, the most poignant thrill in this sensuality was its secrecy, the audacity of the deception. This jeering at everything which in public the countess preached as being lofty, transcendent and inviolable, this diabolic inward chuckle in fact, and conscious trampling on everything held sacred, and all this unbridled and carried to the utmost pitch of licentiousness such as even the warmest imagination could scarcely conceive—in that, above all, lay the keenness of the gratification. Yes, she was the devil incarnate, but it was a devil supremely fascinating. I can't think of her now without ecstasy. In the very heat of voluptuousness she would suddenly laugh like one possessed, and I understood it thoroughly, I understood that laughter and laughed too. It makes me sigh now when I think of it, though it's long ago now. She threw me over in a year. If I had wanted to injure her I couldn't have. Who would have believed me ? A character like hers. What do you say, my young friend ? "

"Foo, how disgusting ! " I answered, listening to this avowal with repulsion.

"You wouldn't be my young friend, if your answer were different. I knew you'd say that. Ha-ha-ha ! Wait a bit, *mon ami*, live longer and you'll understand, but now, now you still need gilt on your gingerbread. No, you're not a poet if that's what you say. That woman understood life and knew how to make the most of it."

" But why descend to such beastliness ? "

" What beastliness ? "

" To which that woman descended, and you with her."

"Ah, you call that beastliness—a sign that you are still in bonds and leading strings. Of course, I recognize that independence may be shown in quite an opposite direction. Let's talk more straightforwardly, my friend . . . . you must admit yourself that all that's nonsense."

" What isn't nonsense ? "

" What isn't nonsense is personality—myself. All is for me,

the whole world is created for me. Listen, my friend, I still believe that it's possible to live happily on earth. And that's the best faith, for without it one can't even live unhappily: there's nothing left but to poison oneself. They say that this was what some fool did. He philosophized till he destroyed everything, everything, even the obligation of all normal and natural human duties, till at last he had nothing left. The sum total came to nil, and so he declared that the best thing in life was prussic acid. You say that's Hamlet. That's terrible despair in fact, something so grand that we could never dream of it. But you're a poet, and I'm a simple mortal, and so I say one must look at the thing from the simplest, most practical point of view. I, for instance, have long since freed myself from all shackles, and even obligations. I only recognize obligations when I see I have something to gain by them. You, of course, can't look at things like that, your legs are in fetters, and your taste is morbid. You talk of the ideal, of virtue. Well, my dear fellow, I am ready to admit anything you tell me to, but what am I to do if I know for a fact that at the root of all human virtues lies the completest egoism? And the more virtuous anything is, the more egoism there is in it. Love yourself, that's the one rule I recognize. Life is a commercial transaction, don't waste your money, but kindly pay for your entertainment, and you will be doing your whole duty to your neighbour. Those are my morals, if you really want to know them, though I confess that to my thinking it is better not to pay one's neighbour, but to succeed in making him do things for nothing. I have no ideals and I don't want to have them; I've never felt a yearning for them. One can live such a gay and charming life without ideals . . . and, en somme, I'm very glad that I can get on without prussic acid. If I were a little more virtuous I could not perhaps get on without it, like that fool philosopher (no doubt a German). No! There's still so much that's good left in life! I love consequence, rank, a mansion, a huge stake at cards (I'm awfully fond of cards). But best of all, best of all—woman . . . and woman in all her aspects: I'm even fond of secret, hidden vice, a bit more strange and original, even a little filthy for variety, ha-ha-ha! I'm looking at your face: with what contempt you are looking at me now!"

"You are right," I answered.

"Well, supposing you are right, anyway filth is better than prussic acid, isn't it?"

"No. Prussic acid is better."

"I asked you 'isn't it,' on purpose to enjoy your answer; I knew what you'd say. No, my young friend. If you're a genuine lover of humanity wish all sensible men the same taste as mine, even with a little filth, or sensible men will soon have nothing to do in the world and there'll be none but the fools left. It will be good luck for them. Though, indeed, there's a proverb even now that fools are lucky. And do you know there's nothing pleasanter than to live with fools and to back them up; it pays! You needn't wonder at my valuing convention, keeping up certain traditions, struggling for influence; I see, of course, that I'm living in a worthless world; but meanwhile it's snug there and I back it up, and show I stand firm for it. Though I'd be the first to leave it if occasion arose. I know all your modern ideas, though I've never worried about them, and had no reason to. I've never had any conscience-pricks about anything. I'll agree to anything so long as I'm all right, and there are legions like me, and we really are all right. Everything in the world may perish, but we shall not perish. We shall exist as long as the world exists. All the world may sink, but we shall float, we shall always float to the top. Consider, by the way, one thing: how full of life people like us are. We are pre-eminently, phenomenally tenacious of life; has that ever struck you? We live to be eighty, ninety. So nature itself protects us, he-he-he! I particularly want to live to be ninety. I'm not fond of death, and I'm afraid of it. The devil only knows what dying will be like. But why talk of it? It's that philosopher who poisoned himself that has put me on that track. Damn philosophy! *Buvons, mon cher.* We began talking about pretty girls. . . . Where are you off to?"

"I'm going home, and it's time for you to go."

"Nonsense, nonsense! I've, so to speak, opened my whole heart to you, and you don't seem to feel what a great proof of friendship it is. He-he-he! There's not much love in you, my poet. But wait a minute, I want another bottle. . . ."

"A third?"

"Yes. As for virtue, my young hopeful (you will allow me to call you by that sweet name), who knows, maybe, my precepts may come in useful one day. And so, my young hopeful, about virtue I have said already: the more virtuous virtue is, the more egoism there is in it. I should like to tell you a very pretty story apropos of that. I once loved a young girl, and loved her almost genuinely. She even sacrificed a great deal for me."

"Is that the one you robbed?" I asked rudely, unwilling to restrain myself longer.

Prince Valkovsky started, his face changed, and he fixed his blood-shot eyes on me. There was amazement and fury in them.

"Wait a minute, wait a minute," he said as though to himself, "let me consider, I really am drunk, and it's difficult for me to reflect."

He paused, and looked searchingly, with the same spitefulness at me, holding my hand in his as though afraid I should go away. I am convinced that at that moment he was going over things in his mind, trying to discover where I could have heard of this affair which scarcely anyone knew; and whether there were any danger in my knowing of it. This lasted for a minute; but suddenly his face changed quickly. The same mocking, drunken, good-humoured expression appeared in his eyes. He laughed.

"Ha-ha-ha! You're a Talleyrand, there's no other word for you. Why, I really stood before her dumbfoundered when she sprang it upon me that I had robbed her! How she shrieked then, how she scolded! She was a violent woman and with no self-control. But, judge for yourself: in the first place I hadn't robbed her as you expressed it just now. She gave me her money herself, and it was mine. Suppose you were to give me your best dress-coat" (as he said this he looked at my only and rather unshapely dress-coat which had been made for me three years ago by a tailor called Ivan Skornyagin), "that I thanked you and wore it and suddenly a year later you quarrel with me and ask for it back again when I've worn it out. . . . That would be ungentlemanly; why give it at all? And, secondly, though the money was mine I should certainly have returned it, but think; where could I have got hold of such a sum all at once? And, above all, I can't endure all this Schillerism and idyllic nonsense: I've told you so already—and that was at the back of it all. You can't imagine how she posed for my benefit, protesting that she would give me the money (which was mine already). I got angry at last and I suddenly succeeded in judging the position quite correctly, for I never lose my presence of mind; I reflected that by giving her back the money I should perhaps make her unhappy. I should have deprived her of the enjoyment of being miserable entirely owing to me, and of cursing me for it all her life. Believe me, my young friend, there is positively a lofty ecstasy in unhappiness of that kind, in feeling oneself magnanimous and absolutely in the right, and in having every right to call one's opponent a scoundrel. This ecstasy of spite is often to be met with in these Schilleresque people, of course; afterwards perhaps she may have had nothing to eat, but I am convinced that she was happy. I did not want to deprive her of that happiness and I did not send her back the money. And this fully justified my maxim that the louder and more conspicuous a person's magnanimity, the greater the amount of revolting egoism underlying it. . . . Surely that's clear to you. . . . But . . . you wanted to catch me, ha-ha-ha ! . . . Come, confess you were trying to catch me. . . . Oh, Talleyrand ! "

"Good-bye," I said, getting up.

"One minute! Two words in conclusion ! " he shouted, suddenly dropping his disgusting tone and speaking seriously. " Listen to my last words : from all I have said to you it follows clearly and unmistakably (I imagine you have observed it yourself) that I will never give up what's to my advantage for anyone. I'm fond of money and I need it. Katerina Fyodorovna has plenty. Her father held a contract for the vodka tax for ten years. She has three millions and those three millions would be very useful to me. Alyosha and Katya are a perfect match for one another ; they are both utter fools ; and that just suits me. And, therefore, I desire and intend their marriage to take place as soon as possible. In a fortnight or three weeks the countess and Katya are going to the country. Alyosha must escort them. Warn Natalya Nikolaevna that there had better be no idyllic nonsense, no Schillerism, that they had better not oppose me. I'm revengeful and malicious ; I shall stand up for myself. I'm not afraid of her. Everything will no doubt be as I wish it, and therefore if I warn her now it is really more for her sake. Mind there's no silliness, and that she behaves herself sensibly. Otherwise it will be a bad look-out for her, very. She ought to be grateful to me that I haven't treated her as I ought to have done, by law. Let me tell you, my poet, that the law protects the peace of the family, it guarantees a son's obedience to his father, and that those who seduce children from their most sacred duties to their parents are not encouraged by the laws. Remember, too, that I have connexions, that she has none, and . . . surely you must realize what I might do to her. . . . But

I have not done it, for so far she has behaved reasonably. Don't be uneasy. Every moment for the last six months, every action they have taken has been watched by sharp eyes. And I have known everything to the smallest trifle. And so I have waited quietly for Alyosha to drop her of himself, and that process is beginning; and meanwhile it has been a charming distraction for him: I have remained a humane father in his imagination, and 1 must have him think of me like that. Ha-ha-ha! When I remember that I was almost paying her compliments the other evening for having been so magnanimous and disinterested as not to marry him! I should like to know how she could have married him. As for my visit to her then, all that was simply because the time had come to put an end to the connexion. But I wanted to verify everything with my own eyes, my own experience. Well, is that enough for you? Or perhaps you want to know too, why I brought you here, why I have carried on like this before you, why I have been so simple and frank with you, when all this might have been said without any such frank avowals—yes?"

"Yes."

I controlled myself and listened eagerly. I had no need to answer more.

"Solely, my young friend, that I have noticed in you more common sense and clearsightedness about things than in either of our young fools. You might have known before the sort of man I am, have made surmises and conjectures about me, but I wanted to save you the trouble, and resolved to show you face to face, who it is you have to deal with. A first-hand impression is a great thing. Understand me, *mon ami:* you know whom you have to deal with, you love her, and so I hope now that you will use all your influence (and you have an influence over her) to save her from *certain* unpleasantness.* Otherwise there will be such unpleasantness and I assure you, I assure you it will be no joking matter. Finally, the third reason for my openness with you . . . (but of course you've guessed that, my dear boy) yes, I really did want to spit upon the whole business and to spit upon it before your eyes, too?"

"And you've attained your object, too," said I, quivering with excitement. "I agree that you could not have shown your

* Under the Russian system of regulation a girl in an irregular position may easily become the object of persecution and blackmail on the part of the *police de mœurs*, and this is what is suggested here.—*Translator's note.*

spite and your contempt for me and for all of us better than by your frankness to me. Far from being apprehensive that your frankness might compromise you in my eyes, you are not even ashamed to expose yourself before me. You have certainly been like that madman in the cloak. You have not considered me as a human being."

"You have guessed right, my young friend," he said, getting up, "you have seen through it all. You are not an author for nothing. I hope that we are parting as friends. Shan't we drink *brüderschaft* together ? "

"You are drunk, and that is the only reason that I don't answer you as you deserve. . . ."

"Again a figure of silence !—you haven't said all you might have said. Ha-ha-ha ! You won't allow me to pay for you ? "

"Don't trouble yourself. I'll pay for myself."

"Ah, no doubt of it. Aren't we going the same way ? "

"I am not coming with you."

"Farewell, my poet. I hope you've understood me. . . ."

He went out, stepping rather unsteadily and not turning to me again. The footman helped him into his carriage. I went my way. It was nearly three o'clock in the morning. It was raining. The night was dark. . . .

PART IV

CHAPTER I

I won't attempt to describe my exasperation. Though I might have expected anything, it was a blow; it was as though he had appeared before me quite suddenly in all his hideousness. But I remember my sensations were confused, as though I had been knocked down, crushed by something, and black misery gnawed more and more painfully at my heart. I was afraid for Natasha. I foresaw much suffering for her in the future, and I cast about in perplexity for some way by which to avoid it, to soften these last moments for her, before the final catastrophe. Of that catastrophe there could be no doubt. It was near at hand, and it was impossible not to see the form it would take.

I did not notice how I reached home, though I was getting wet with the rain all the way. It was three o'clock in the morning. I had hardly knocked at the door of my room when I heard a moan, and the door was hurriedly unlocked, as though Nellie had not gone to bed but had been watching for me all the time at the door. There was a candle alight. I glanced into Nellie's face and was dismayed; it was completely transformed; her eyes were burning as though in fever, and had a wild look as though she did not recognize me. She was in a high fever.

"Nellie, what's the matter, are you ill?" I asked, bending down and putting my arm round her.

She nestled up to me tremulously as though she were afraid of something, said something, rapidly and impetuously, as though she had only been waiting for me to come to tell me it. But her words were strange and incoherent; I could understand nothing. She was in delirium.

I led her quickly to bed. But she kept starting up and clinging to me as though in terror, as though begging me to protect her from some one, and even when she was lying in bed she kept seizing my hand and holding it tightly as though afraid that

I might go away again. I was so upset and my nerves were so shaken that I actually began to cry as I looked at her. I was ill myself. Seeing my tears she looked fixedly at me for some time with strained, concentrated attention, as though trying to grasp and understand something. It was evident that this cost her great effort. At last something like a thought was apparent in her face. After a violent epileptic fit she was usually for some time unable to collect her thoughts or to articulate distinctly. And so it was now. After making an immense effort to say something to me and realizing that I did not understand, she held out her little hand and began to wipe away my tears, then put her arm round my neck, drew me down to her and kissed me.

It was clear that she had had a fit in my absence, and it had taken place at the moment when she had been standing at the door. Probably on recovery she had been for a long time unable to come to herself. At such times reality is mixed up with delirium and she had certainly imagined something awful, some horror. At the same time she must have been dimly aware that I was to come back and should knock at the door, and so, lying right in the doorway on the floor, she had been on the alert for my coming and had stood up at my first tap.

"But why was she just at the door," I wondered, and suddenly I noticed with amazement that she was wearing her little wadded coat. (I had just got it for her from an old pedlar woman I knew who sometimes came to my room to offer me goods in repayment of money I had lent her.) So she must have been meaning to go out, and had probably been already unlocking the door when she was suddenly struck down by the fit. Where could she have been meaning to go? Was she already in delirium?

Meanwhile the fever did not leave her, and she soon sank into delirium and unconsciousness. She had twice already had a fit in my flat, but it had always passed off harmlessly; now, however, she seemed in a high fever. After sitting beside her for half an hour I pushed a chair up to the sofa and lay down, as I was, without undressing, close beside her that I might wake the more readily if she called me. I did not even put the candle out. I looked at her many times again before I fell asleep myself. She was pale; her lips were parched with fever and stained with blood, probably from the fall. Her face still retained the look of terror and a sort of poignant anguish which seemed to be still haunting her in her sleep. I made up my mind to go as early as possible next morning for the doctor, if she were worse. I was afraid that it might end in actual brain fever.

"It must have been the prince frightened her!" I thought, with a shudder, and I thought of his story of the woman who had thrown the money in his face.

CHAPTER II

A FORTNIGHT passed by. Nellie was recovering. She did not develop brain fever but she was seriously ill. She began to get up again on a bright sunny day at the end of April. It was Passion Week.

Poor little creature. I cannot go on with my story in the same consecutive way. Now that I am describing all this it is long past, but to this very minute I recall with an oppressive heart-rending anguish that pale, thin little face, the searching, intent gaze of her black eyes when we were sometimes left alone together, and she fixed upon me from her bed a prolonged gaze as though challenging me to guess what was in her mind, but seeing that I did not guess and was still puzzled she would smile gently, as it were, to herself, and would suddenly hold out to me her hot little hand, with its thin, wasted little fingers. Now it is all over, and everything is understood, but to this day I do not know the secrets of that sick, tortured and outraged little heart.

I feel that I am digressing, but at this moment I want to think only of Nellie. Strange to say, now that I am lying alone on a hospital bed, abandoned by all whom I loved so fondly and intensely, some trivial incident of that past, often unnoticed at the time and soon forgotten, comes back all at once to my mind and suddenly takes quite a new significance, completing and explaining to me what I had failed to understand till now.

For the first four days of her illness, we, the doctor and I, were in great alarm about her, but on the fifth day the doctor took me aside and told me that there was no reason for anxiety and she would certainly recover. This doctor was the one I had known so long, a good-natured and eccentric old bachelor whom I had called in in Nellie's first illness, and who had so impressed her by the huge Stanislav cross on his breast.

"So there's no reason for anxiety," I said, greatly relieved.

"No, she'll get well this time, but afterwards she will soon die."

"Die! But why?" I cried, overwhelmed at this death sentence.

"Yes, she is certain to die very soon. The patient has an organic defect of the heart, and at the slightest unfavourable circumstance she'll be laid up again. She will perhaps get better, but then she'll be ill again and at last she'll die."

"Do you mean nothing can be done to save her? Surely that's impossible."

"But it's inevitable. However, with the removal of unfavourable circumstances, with a quiet and easy life, with more pleasure in it, the patient might yet be kept from death and there even are cases . . . unexpected . . . strange and exceptional . . . in fact the patient may be saved by a concatenation of favourable conditions, but radically cured—never."

"But, good heavens, what's to be done now?"

"Follow my advice, lead a quiet life, and take the powders regularly. I have noticed this girl's capricious, of a nervous temperament, and fond of laughing. She much dislikes taking her powders regularly and she has just refused them absolutely."

"Yes, doctor. She certainly is strange, but I put it all down to her invalid state. Yesterday she was very obedient; to-day, when I gave her her medicine she pushed the spoon as though by accident and it was all spilt over. When I wanted to mix another powder she snatched the box away from me, threw it on the ground and then burst into tears. Only I don't think it was because I was making her take the powders," I added, after a moment's thought.

"Hm! Irritation! Her past great misfortunes." (I had told the doctor fully and frankly much of Nellie's history and my story had struck him very much.) "All that in conjunction, and from it this illness. For the time the only remedy is to take the powders and she must take the powders. I will go and try once more to impress on her the duty to obey medical instructions, and . . . that is speaking generally . . . take the powders."

We both came out of the kitchen (in which our interview had taken place) and the doctor went up to the sick child's bedside again. But I think Nellie must have overheard. Anyway she had raised her head from the pillow and turned her ear in our direction, listening keenly all the time. I noticed this through the crack of the half-opened door. When we went up to her the rogue ducked under the quilt, and peeped out at us with a mocking smile. The poor child had grown much thinner during the four days of her illness. Her eyes were sunken and she was still feverish, so that the mischievous expression and glittering, defiant glances so surprising to the doctor, who was one of the most good-natured Germans in Petersburg, looked all the more incongruous on her face.

Gravely, though trying to soften his voice as far as he could, he began in a kind and caressing voice to explain how essential and efficacious the powders were, and consequently how incumbent it was on every invalid to take them. Nellie was raising her head, but suddenly, with an apparently quite accidental movement of her arm, she jerked the spoon, and all the medicine was spilt on the floor again. No doubt she did it on purpose.

"That's very unpleasant carelessness," said the old man quietly, "and I suspect that you did it on purpose; that's very reprehensible. But . . . we can set that right and prepare another powder."

Nellie laughed straight in his face. The doctor shook his head methodically.

"That's very wrong," he said, opening another powder, "very, very reprehensible."

"Don't be angry with me," answered Nellie, and vainly tried not to laugh again. "I'll certainly take it. . . . But do you like me?"

"If you will behave yourself becomingly I shall like you very much."

"Very much?"

"Very much."

"But now, don't you like me?"

"Yes, I like you even now."

"And will you kiss me if I want to kiss you?"

"Yes, if you desire it."

At this Nellie could not control herself and laughed again.

"The patient has a merry disposition, but now—this is nerves and caprice," the doctor whispered to me with a most serious air.

"All right, I'll take the powder," Nellie cried suddenly, in her weak little voice. "But when I am big and grown up will you marry me?"

Apparently the invention of this new fancy greatly delighted her; her eyes positively shone and her lips twitched with laughter as she waited for a reply from the somewhat astonished doctor.

"Very well," he answered, smiling in spite of himself at this new whim, "very well, if you turn out a good, well-brought-up young lady, and will be obedient and will . . ."

"Take my powders?" put in Nellie.

"O-ho! To be sure, take your powders. A good girl," he whispered to me again; "there's a great deal, a great deal in her . . . that's good and clever but . . . to get married . . . what a strange caprice . . ."

And he took her the medicine again. But this time she made no pretence about it but simply jerked the spoon up from below with her hand and all the medicine was splashed on the poor doctor's shirt-front and in his face. Nellie laughed aloud, but not with the same merry, good-humoured laugh as before. There was a look of something cruel and malicious in her face. All this time she seemed to avoid my eyes, only looked at the doctor, and with mockery, through which some uneasiness was discernible, waited to see what the "funny" old man would do next.

"Oh! You've done it again! . . . What a misfortune! But . . . I can mix you another powder!" said the old man, wiping his face and his shirt-front with his handkerchief.

This made a tremendous impression on Nellie. She had been prepared for our anger, thought that we should begin to scold and reprove her, and perhaps she was unconsciously longing at that moment for some excuse to cry, to sob hysterically, to upset some more powders as she had just now and even to break something in her vexation, and with all this to relieve her capricious and aching little heart. Such capricious humours are to be found not only in the sick and not only in Nellie. How often I have walked up and down the room with the unconscious desire for some one to insult me or to utter some word that I could interpret as an insult in order to vent my anger upon some one. Women, venting their anger in that way, begin to cry, shedding the most genuine tears, and the more emotional of them even go into hysterics. It's a very simple and everyday experience, and happens most often when there is some other, often a secret, grief in the heart, to which one longs to give utterance but cannot.

But, struck by the angelic kindness of the old doctor and the patience with which he set to work to mix her another powder without uttering one word of reproach, Nellie suddenly subsided. The look of mockery vanished from her lips, the colour rushed to her face, her eyes grew moist. She stole a look at me and turned away at once. The doctor brought her the medicine.

She took it meekly and shyly, seized the old man's plump red hand, and looked slowly into his face.

"You . . . are angry that I'm horrid," she tried to say, but could not finish; she ducked under the quilt, hid her head and burst into loud, hysterical sobs.

"Oh, my child, don't weep! . . . It is nothing. . . . It's nerves, drink some water."

But Nellie did not hear.

"Be comforted . . . don't upset yourself," he went on, almost whimpering over her, for he was a very sensitive man. "I'll forgive you and be married to you if, like a good, well-brought-up girl, you'll . . ."

"Take my powders," came from under the quilt with a little nervous laugh that tinkled like a bell, and was broken by sobs— a laugh I knew very well.

"A good-hearted, grateful child!" said the doctor triumphantly, almost with tears in his eyes. "Poor girl!"

And a strange and wonderful affection sprang up from that day between him and Nellie. With me, on the contrary, Nellie became more and more sullen, nervous, and irritable. I didn't know what to ascribe this to, and wondered at her, especially as this change in her seemed to happen suddenly. During the first days of her illness she was particularly tender and caressing with me; it seemed as though she could not take her eyes off me; she would not let me leave her side, clutched my hand in her feverish little hand and made me sit beside her, and if she noticed that I was gloomy and anxious she tried to cheer me up, made jokes, played with me and smiled at me, evidently making an effort to overcome her own sufferings. She did not want me to work at night, or to sit up to look after her, and was grieved because I would not listen to her. Sometimes I noticed an anxious look in her face; she began to question me, and tried to find out why I was sad, what was in my mind. But strange to say, when Natasha's name was mentioned she immediately dropped the conversation or began to speak of something else. She seemed to avoid speaking of Natasha, and that struck me. When I came home she was delighted. When I took up my hat she looked at me dejectedly and rather strangely, following me with her eyes, as it were reproachfully.

On the fourth day of her illness I spent the whole evening with Natasha and stayed long after midnight. There was something we had to discuss. As I went out I said to my invalid that

I should be back very soon, as indeed I reckoned on being. Being detained almost unexpectedly at Natasha's, I felt quite easy in my mind about Nellie. Alexandra Semyonovna was sitting up with her, having heard from Masloboev, who came in to see me for a moment, that Nellie was ill and that I was in great difficulties and absolutely without help. Good heavens, what a fuss kind-hearted Alexandra Semyonovna was in!

"So of course he won't come to dinner with us now! . . . Ach, mercy on us! And he's all alone, poor fellow, all alone! Well, now we can show how kindly we feel to him. Here's the opportunity. We mustn't let it slip."

She immediately appeared at my flat, bringing with her in a cab a regular hamper. Declaring at the first word that she was going to stay and had come to help me in my trouble, she undid her parcels. In them there were syrups and preserves for the invalid, chickens, and a fowl in case the patient began to be convalescent, apples for baking, oranges, dry Kiev preserves (in case the doctor would allow them) and finally linen, sheets, dinner napkins, nightgowns, bandages, compresses—an outfit for a whole hospital.

"We've got everything," she said to me, articulating every word as though in haste, "and, you see, you live like a bachelor. You've not much of all this. So please allow me . . . and Filip Filippovitch told me to. Well, what now . . . make haste, make haste, what shall I do now? How is she? Conscious? Ah, how uncomfortably she is lying! I must put her pillow straight that she may lie with her head low, and, what do you think, wouldn't a leather pillow be better? The leather is cooler. Ah, what a fool I am! It never occurred to me to bring one. I'll go and get it. Oughtn't we to light a fire? I'll send my old woman to you. I know an old woman. You've no servant, have you? . . . Well, what shall I do now? What's that? Herbs . . . did the doctor prescribe them? For some herb tea, I suppose? I'll go at once and light the fire."

But I reassured her, and she was much surprised and even rather chagrined that there turned out to be not so very much to do. But this did not discourage her altogether. She made friends with Nellie at once and was a great help to me all through her illness. She visited us almost every day and she always used to come in looking as though something had been lost or had gone astray and she must hasten to catch it up. She always added that Filip Filippovitch had told her to come. Nellie liked her very much. They took to each other like two sisters, and I fancy that in many things Alexandra Semyonovna was as much of a baby as Nellie. She used to tell the child stories and amuse her, and Nellie often missed her when she had gone home. Her first appearance surprised my invalid, but she quickly guessed why the uninvited visitor had come, and as usual frowned and became silent and ungracious.

"Why did she come to see us?" asked Nellie with an air of displeasure after Alexandra Semyonovna had gone away.

"To help you, Nellie, and to look after you."

"Why? What for? I've never done anything like that for her."

"Kind people don't wait for that, Nellie. They like to help people who need it, without that. That's enough, Nellie; there are lots of kind people in the world. It's only your misfortune that you haven't met them and didn't meet them when you needed them."

Nellie did not speak. I walked away from her. But a quarter of an hour later she called me to her in a weak voice, asked for something to drink, and all at once warmly embraced me and for a long while would not let go of me. Next day, when Alexandra Semyonovna appeared, she welcomed her with a joyful smile, though she still seemed for some reason shamefaced with her.

CHAPTER III

It was on that day that I was the whole evening at Natasha's. I arrived home late. Nellie was asleep. Alexandra Semyonovna was sleepy too, but she was still sitting up with the invalid waiting for me to come in. At once in a hurried whisper she began to tell me that Nellie had at first been in very good spirits, even laughing a great deal, but afterwards she was depressed and, as I did not come back, grew silent and thoughtful. "Then she began complaining that her head ached, began to cry, and sobbed so that I really didn't know what to do with her," Alexandra Semyonovna added. "She began talking to me about Natalya Nikolaevna, but I could not tell her anything. She left off questioning me but went on crying afterwards, so that she fell asleep in tears. Well, good-bye, Ivan Petrovitch. She's better anyway, I can see that, and I must go home. Filip

Filippovitch told me to. I must confess that this time he only let me come for two hours but I stayed on of myself. But never mind, don't worry about me. He doesn't dare to be angry. . . . Only perhaps. . . . Ach, my goodness, Ivan Petrovitch, darling, what am I to do? He always comes home tipsy now! He's very busy over something, he doesn't talk to me, he's worried, he's got some important business in his mind; I can see that; but yet he is drunk every evening. . . . What I'm thinking is, if he has come home, who will put him to bed? Well, I'm going, I'm going, good-bye. Good-bye, Ivan Petrovitch. I've been looking at your books here. What a lot of books you've got, and they must all be clever. And I'm such a fool I've never read anything. . . . Well, till to-morrow . . ."

But next morning Nellie woke up depressed and sullen, and answered me unwillingly. She did not speak to me of her own accord, but seemed to be angry with me. Yet I noticed some looks bent upon me stealthily, as it were, on the sly; in those looks there was so much concealed and heart-felt pain, yet there was in them an unmistakable tenderness which was not apparent when she looked at me directly. It was on that day that the scene over the medicine took place with the doctor. I did not know what to think.

But Nellie was entirely changed to me. Her strange ways, her caprices, at times almost hatred for me, continued up to the day when she ceased to live with me, till the catastrophe which was the end of our romance. But of that later.

It happened, however, sometimes that she would be for an hour as affectionate to me as at first. Her tenderness was redoubled at such moments; most often at such times she wept bitterly. But these hours soon passed and she sank back into the same misery as before, and looked at me with hostility again or was as capricious as she had been with the doctor, or suddenly noticing that I did not like some new naughtiness on her part, she would begin laughing, and almost always end in tears.

She once quarrelled even with Alexandra Semyonovna, and told her that she wanted nothing from her. When I began to scold her in Alexandra Semyonovna's presence she grew angry, answered with an outburst of accumulated spite, but suddenly relapsed into silence and did not say another word to me for two days, would not take one of her medicines, was unwilling even to eat and drink and no one but the old doctor was able to bring her round and make her ashamed.

I have mentioned already that from the day of the scene over the medicine a surprising affection had sprung up between the doctor and her. Nellie was very fond of him and always greeted him with a good-humoured smile however sad she had been before he came. For his part the old man began coming to us every day and sometimes even twice a day even when Nellie had begun to get up and had quite recovered, and she seemed to have so bewitched him that he could not spend a day without hearing her laugh and make fun of him, sometimes very amusingly. He began bringing her picture-books, always of an edifying character. One of them he bought on purpose for her. Then he began bringing her dainties, sweetmeats in pretty boxes. On such occasions he would come in with an air of triumph, as though it were his birthday, and Nellie guessed at once that he had come with a present. But he did not display the presents, but only laughed slyly, seated himself beside Nellie, hinting that if a certain young lady knew how to behave herself and had been deserving of commendation in his absence the young lady in question would merit a handsome reward. And all the while he looked at her so simply and good-naturedly that though Nellie laughed at him in the frankest way, at the same time there was a glow of sincere and affectionate devotion in her beaming eyes at that moment. At last the old man solemnly got up from his chair, took out a box of sweets and as he handed it to Nellie invariably added: "to my future amiable spouse." At that moment he was certainly even happier than Nellie.

Then they began to talk, and every time he earnestly and persuasively exhorted her to take care of her health and gave her impressive medical advice.

"Above all one must preserve one's health," he declared dogmatically, "firstly and chiefly in order to remain alive, and secondly in order to be always healthy and so to attain happiness in life. If you have any sorrows, my dear child, forget them, and best of all try not to think of them. If you have no sorrows . . . well, then too, don't think about them, but try to think only of pleasant things . . . of something cheerful and amusing."

"And what shall I think of that's cheerful and amusing?" Nellie would ask.

The doctor was at once nonplussed.

"Well . . . of some innocent game appropriate to your age or, well . . . something of that . . ."

"I don't want to play games, I don't like games," said Nellie. "I like new dresses better."

"New dresses! Hm! Well, that's not so good. We should in all things be content with a modest lot in life. However . . . maybe . . . there's no harm in being fond of new dresses."

"And will you give me a lot of dresses when I'm married to you?"

"What an idea!" said the doctor and he could not help frowning. Nellie smiled slyly, and even forgetting herself for a minute, glanced at me.

"However, I'll give you a dress if you deserve it by your conduct," the doctor went on.

"And must I take my medicine every day when I'm married to you?"

"Well, then, perhaps you may not have to take medicine always."

And the doctor began to smile.

Nellie interrupted the conversation by laughing. The old man laughed with her, and watched her merriment affectionately.

"A playful sportive mind!" he observed turning to me. "But still one can see signs of caprice and a certain whimsicalness and irritability."

He was right. I could not make out what was happening to her. She seemed utterly unwilling to speak to me, as though I had treated her badly in some way. This was very bitter to me. I frowned myself, and once I did not speak to her for a whole day, but next day I felt ashamed. She was often crying and I hadn't a notion how to comfort her. On one occasion, however, she broke her silence with me.

One afternoon I returned home just before dusk and saw Nellie hurriedly hide a book under the pillow. It was my novel which she had taken from the table and was reading in my absence. What need had she to hide it from me? "Just as though she were ashamed," I thought, but I showed no sign of having noticed anything. A quarter of an hour later when I went out for a minute into the kitchen she quickly jumped out of bed and put the novel back where it had been before; when I came back I saw it lying on the table. A minute later she called me to her; there was a ring of some emotion in her voice. For the last four days she had hardly spoken to me.

"Are you . . . to-day . . . going to see Natasha?" she asked me in a breaking voice.

"Yes, Nellie. It's very necessary for me to see her to-day."

Nellie did not speak.

"You . . . are very . . . fond of her?" she asked again, in a faint voice.

"Yes, Nellie, I'm very fond of her."

"I love her too," she added softly.

A silence followed again.

"I want to go to her and to live with her," Nellie began again, looking at me timidly.

"That's impossible, Nellie," I answered, looking at her with some surprise. "Are you so badly off with me?"

"Why is it impossible?" And she flushed crimson. "Why, you were persuading me to go and live with her father; I don't want to go there. Has she a servant?"

"Yes."

"Well, let her send her servant away, and I'll be her servant. I'll do everything for her and not take any wages. I'll love her, and do her cooking. You tell her so to-day."

"But what for? What a notion, Nellie! And what an idea you must have of her; do you suppose she would take you as a cook? If she did take you she would take you as an equal, as her younger sister."

"No, I don't want to be an equal. I don't want it like that . . ."

"Why?"

Nellie was silent. Her lips were twitching. She was on the point of crying.

"The man she loves now is going away from her and leaving her alone now?" she asked at last.

I was surprised.

"Why, how do you know, Nellie?"

"You told me all about it yourself; and the day before yesterday when Alexandra Semyonovna's husband came in the morning I asked him; he told me everything."

"Why, did Masloboev come in the morning?"

"Yes," she answered, dropping her eyes.

"Why didn't you tell me he'd been here?"

"I don't know . . ."

I reflected for a moment. "Goodness only knows why Masloboev is turning up with his mysteriousness. What sort of terms has he got on to with her? I ought to see him," I thought.

"Well, what is it to you, Nellie, if he does desert her?"

"Why, you love her so much," said Nellie, not lifting her eyes to me. "And if you love her you'll marry her when he goes away."

"No, Nellie, she doesn't love me as I love her, and I . . . no, that won't happen, Nellie."

"And I would work for you both as your servant and you'd live and be happy," she said, almost in a whisper, not looking at me.

"What's the matter with her? What's the matter with her?" I thought, and I had a disturbing pang at my heart. Nellie was silent and she didn't say another word all the evening. When I went out she had been crying, and cried the whole evening, as Alexandra Semyonovna told me, and so fell asleep, crying. She even cried and kept saying something at night in her sleep.

But from that day she became even more sullen and silent, and didn't speak to me at all. It is true I caught two or three glances stolen at me on the sly, and there was such tenderness in those glances. But this passed, together with the moment that called forth that sudden tenderness, and as though in opposition to this impulse Nellie grew every hour more gloomy even with the doctor, who was amazed at the change in her character. Meanwhile she had almost completely recovered, and the doctor at last allowed her to go for a walk in the open air, but only for a very short time. It was settled weather, warm and bright. It was Passion Week, which fell that year very late; I went out in the morning; I was obliged to be at Natasha's and I intended to return earlier in order to take Nellie out for a walk. Meantime I left her alone at home.

I cannot describe what a blow was awaiting me at home. I hurried back. When I arrived I saw that the key was sticking in the outside of the lock. I went in. There was no one there. I was numb with horror. I looked, and on the table was a piece of paper, and written in pencil in a big, uneven handwriting:

"I have gone away, and I shall never come back to you. But I love you very much.   "Your faithful Nellie."

I uttered a cry of horror and rushed out of the flat.

CHAPTER IV

BEFORE I had time to run out into the street, before I had time to consider how to act, or what to do, I suddenly saw a droshky standing at the gate of our buildings, and Alexandra Semyonovna getting out of it leading Nellie by the arm. She was holding her tightly as though she were afraid she might run away again. I rushed up to them.

"Nellie, what's the matter!" I cried, "where have you been, why did you go?"

"Stop a minute, don't be in a hurry; let's make haste upstairs. There you shall hear all about it," twittered Alexandra Semyonovna. "The things I have to tell you, Ivan Petrovitch," she whispered hurriedly on the way. "One can only wonder.... Come along, you shall hear immediately."

Her face showed that she had extremely important news.

"Go along, Nellie, go along. Lie down a little," she said as soon as we got into the room, "you're tired, you know; it's no joke running about so far, and it's too much after an illness; lie down, darling, lie down. And we'll go out of the room for a little, we won't get in her way; let her have a sleep."

And she signed to me to go into the kitchen with her.

But Nellie didn't lie down, she sat down on the sofa and hid her face in her hands.

We went into the other room, and Alexandra Semyonovna told me briefly what had happened. Afterwards I heard about it more in detail. This is how it had been.

Going out of the flat a couple of hours before my return and leaving the note for me, Nellie had run first to the old doctor's. She had managed to find out his address beforehand. The doctor told me that he was absolutely petrified when he saw her, and "could not believe his eyes" all the while she was there. "I can't believe it even now," he added, as he finished his story, "and I never shall believe it." And yet Nellie actually had been at his house. He had been sitting quietly in the armchair in his study in his dressing-gown, drinking his coffee, when she ran in and threw herself on his neck before he had time to realize it. She was crying, she embraced and kissed him, kissed his hands, and earnestly though incoherently begged him to let her stay with him, declaring that she wouldn't and couldn't live with me any longer, and that's why she had left me; that she was unhappy; that she wouldn't laugh at him again or talk about new dresses, but would behave well and learn her lessons, that she would learn to "wash and get up his shirt-front" (probably she had thought over her whole speech on the way or perhaps even before), and that, in fact, she would be obedient and would take as many powders as he liked every day. And that as for her saying she wanted to marry him that had only been a joke, and she had no idea of the kind; the old German was so dumbfounded that he sat open-mouthed the whole time, forgetting the cigar he held in his hand till it went out.

"Mademoiselle," he brought out at last, recovering his powers of speech, "so far as I can understand you, you ask me to give you a situation in my household. But that's—impossible. As you see I'm very much cramped and have not a very considerable income . . . and, in fact, to act so rashly without reflection . . . is awful! And, in fact, you, so far as I can see, have run away from home. That is reprehensible and impossible. . . . And what's more, I only allowed you to take a short walk in charge of your benefactor, and you abandon your benefactor, and run off to me when you ought to be taking care of yourself and . . . and . . . taking your medicine. And, in fact . . . in fact . . . I can make nothing of it . . ."

Nellie did not let him finish. She began to cry and implored him again, but nothing was of use. The old man was more and more bewildered, and less and less able to understand. At last Nellie gave him up and crying "Oh, dear!" ran out of the room. "I was ill all that day," the old doctor said in conclusion, "and had taken a decoction in the evening . . ."

Nellie rushed off to the Masloboevs'. She had provided herself with their address too, and she succeeded in finding them, though not without trouble. Masloboev was at home. Alexandra Semyonovna clasped her hands in amazement when she heard Nellie beg them to take her in. When she asked her why she wanted it, what was wrong, whether she was unhappy with me, Nellie had made no answer, but flung herself sobbing on a chair. "She sobbed so violently, so violently," said Alexandra Semyonovna, "that I thought she would have died." Nellie begged to be taken if only as a housemaid or a cook, said she would sweep the floors and learn to do the washing (she seemed to rest her hopes especially on the washing and seemed for some reason to think this a great inducement for them to take her). Alexandra Semyonovna's idea was to keep her till the matter was cleared up, meanwhile letting me know. But Filip Filippovitch had absolutely forbidden it, and had told her to bring the runaway to me at once. On the way Alexandra Semyonovna had kissed and embraced her, which had made Nellie cry more than ever. Looking at her Alexandra Semyonovna, too, had shed tears. So both of them had been crying all the way in the cab.

THE INSULTED AND INJURED

"But why, Nellie, why don't you want to go on staying with him? What has he done. Is he unkind to you?" Alexandra Semyonovna asked, melting into tears.

"No."

"Well, why then?"

"Nothing . . . I don't want to stay with him . . . I'm always so nasty with him and he's so kind . . . but with you I won't be nasty, I'll work," she declared, sobbing as though she were in hysterics.

"Why are you so nasty to him, Nellie?"

"Nothing . . ."

"And that was all I could get out of her," said Alexandra Semyonovna, wiping her tears. "Why is she such an unhappy little thing? Is it her fits? What do you think, Ivan Petrovitch?"

We went in to Nellie. She lay with her face hidden in the pillow, crying. I knelt down beside her, took her hands, and began to kiss them. She snatched her hands from me and sobbed more violently than ever. I did not know what to say. At that moment old Ichmenyev walked in.

"I've come to see you on business, Ivan, how do you do?" he said, staring at us all, and observing with surprise that I was on my knees.

The old man had been ill of late. He was pale and thin, but as though in defiance of some one, he neglected his illness, refused to listen to Anna Andreyevna's exhortations, went about his daily affairs as usual, and would not take to his bed.

"Good-bye for the present," said Alexandra Semyonovna, staring at the old man. "Filip Filippovitch told me to be back as quickly as possible. We are busy. But in the evening at dusk I'll look in on you, and stay an hour or two."

"Who's that?" the old man whispered to me, evidently thinking of something else.

I explained.

"Hm! Well, I've come on business, Ivan."

I knew on what business he had come, and had been expecting his visit. He had come to talk to me and Nellie and to beg her to go to them. Anna Andreyevna had consented at last to adopt an orphan girl. This was a result of secret confabulations between us. I had persuaded the old lady, telling her that the sight of the child, whose mother, too, had been cursed by an unrelenting father, might turn our old friend's heart to other feelings. I explained my plan so clearly that now she began of herself to urge her husband to take the child. The old man readily fell in with it; in the first place he wanted to please his Anna Andreyevna, and he had besides motives of his own. . . . But all this I will explain later and more fully. I have mentioned already that Nellie had taken a dislike to the old man at his first visit. Afterwards I noticed that there was a gleam almost of hatred in her face when Ichmenyev's name was pronounced in her presence. My old friend began upon the subject at once, without beating about the bush. He went straight up to Nellie, who was still lying down, hiding her head in the pillow, and taking her by the hand asked her whether she would like to come and live with him and take the place of his daughter.

"I had a daughter. I loved her more than myself," the old man finished up, "but now she is not with me. She is dead. Would you like to take her place in my house and . . . in my heart?" And in his eyes that looked dry and inflamed from fever there gleamed a tear.

"No, I shouldn't," Nellie answered, without raising her head.

"Why not, my child? You have nobody belonging to you. Ivan cannot keep you with him for ever, and with me you'd be as in your own home."

"I won't, because you're wicked. Yes, wicked, wicked," she added, lifting up her head, and facing the old man. "I am wicked, we're all wicked, but you're more wicked than anyone."

As she said this Nellie turned pale, her eyes flashed; even her quivering lips turned pale, and were distorted by a rush of strong feeling. The old man looked at her in perplexity.

"Yes, more wicked than I am, because you won't forgive your daughter. You want to forget her altogether and take another child. How can you forget your own child? How can you love me? Whenever you look at me you'll remember I'm a stranger and that you had a daughter of your own whom you'd forgotten, for you're a cruel man. And I don't want to live with cruel people. I won't! I won't!"

Nellie gave a sob and glanced at me.

"The day after to-morrow is Easter; all the people will be kissing and embracing one another, they all make peace, they all forgive one another . . . I know. . . . But you . . . only you . . . ugh, cruel man! Go away!"

She melted into tears. She must have made up that speech beforehand and have learnt it by heart in case my old friend should ask her again.

My old friend was affected and he turned pale. His face betrayed the pain he was feeling.

"And why, why does everybody make such a fuss over me? I won't have it, I won't have it!" Nellie cried suddenly, in a sort of frenzy. "I'll go and beg in the street."

"Nellie, what's the matter? Nellie, darling," I cried involuntarily, but my exclamation only added fuel to the flames.

"Yes, I'd better go into the street and beg. I won't stay here!" she shrieked sobbing. "My mother begged in the street too, and when she was dying she said to me, 'Better be poor and beg in the street than . . .' 'It's not shameful to beg. I beg of all, and that's not the same as begging from one. To beg of one is shameful, but it's not shameful to beg of all'; that's what one beggar-girl said to me. I'm little, I've no means of earning money. I'll ask from all. I won't! I won't! I'm wicked, I'm wickeder than anyone. See how wicked I am!"

And suddenly Nellie quite unexpectedly seized a cup from the table and threw it on the floor.

"There, now it's broken," she added, looking at me with a sort of defiant triumph. "There are only two cups," she added, "I'll break the other . . . and then how will you drink your tea?"

She seemed as though possessed by fury, and seemed to get enjoyment from that fury, as though she were conscious that it was shameful and wrong, and at the same time were spurring herself on to further violence.

"She's ill, Vanya, that's what it is," said the old man, "or . . . or I don't understand the child. Good-bye!"

He took his cap and shook hands with me. He seemed crushed. Nellie had insulted him horribly. Everything was in a turmoil within me.

"You had no pity on him, Nellie!" I cried when we were left alone. "And aren't you ashamed? Aren't you ashamed? No, you're not a good girl! You really are wicked!"

And just as I was, without my hat, I ran after the old man. I wanted to escort him to the gate, and to say at least a few words to comfort him. As I ran down the staircase I was haunted by Nellie's face, which had turned terribly white at my reproaches.

I quickly overtook my old friend.

"The poor girl has been ill-treated, and has sorrow of her own, believe me, Ivan, and I began to tell her of mine," he said with a bitter smile. "I touched upon her sore place. They say that the well-fed cannot understand the hungry, but I would add that the hungry do not always understand the hungry. Well, good-bye!"

I would have spoken of something else; but the old man waved me off.

"Don't try to comfort me. You'd much better look out that your girl doesn't run away from you. She looks like it," he added with a sort of exasperation, and he walked away from me with rapid steps, brandishing his stick and tapping it on the pavement.

He had no idea of being a prophet.

What were my feelings when, on returning to my room, I found, to my horror, that Nellie had vanished again! I rushed into the passage, looked for her on the stairs, called her name, even knocked at the neighbours' doors and inquired about her. I could not, and would not, believe that she had run away again. And how could she have run away? There was only one gateway to the buildings; she must have slipped by us when I was talking to my old friend. But I soon reflected, to my great distress, that she might first have hidden somewhere on the stairs till I had gone back, and then have slipped off so that I should not meet her. In any case she could not have gone far.

In great anxiety I rushed off to search for her again, leaving my rooms unfastened in case she should return.

First of all I went to the Masloboevs'. I did not find either of them at home. Leaving a note for them in which I informed them of this fresh calamity, and begging them if Nellie came to let me know at once, I went to the doctor's. He was not at home either. The servant told me that there had been no visit since that of the day before. What was to be done? I set off for Mme. Bubnov's and learnt from my friend, the coffin-maker's wife, that her landlady had for some reason been detained at the police-station for the last two days; and Nellie had not been seen there since *that day*. Weary and exhausted I went back to the Masloboevs'. The same answer, no one had come, and they had not returned home themselves. My note lay on the table. What was I to do?

In deadly dejection I returned home late in the evening. I ought to have been at Natasha's that evening, she had asked me in the morning. But I had not even tasted food that day. The thought of Nellie set my whole soul in a turmoil.

"What does it mean?" I wondered. "Could it be some

strange consequence of her illness? Wasn't she mad, or going out of her mind? But, good God, where was she now? Where should I look for her?" I had hardly said this to myself when I caught sight of Nellie a few steps from me on the V——m Bridge. She was standing under a street lamp and she did not see me. I was on the point of running to her but I checked myself. "What can she be doing here now?" I wondered in perplexity, and convinced that now I should not lose her, I resolved to wait and watch her. Ten minutes passed. She was still standing, watching the passers-by. At last a well-dressed old gentleman passed and Nellie went up to him. Without stopping he took something out of his pocket and gave it to her. She curtsied to him. I cannot describe what I felt at that instant. It sent an agonizing pang to my heart, as if something precious, something I loved, had fondled and cherished was disgraced and spat upon at that minute before my very eyes. At the same time I felt tears dropping.

Yes, tears for poor Nellie, though at the same time I felt great indignation; she was not begging through need; she was not forsaken, not abandoned by some one to the caprice of destiny. She was not escaping from cruel oppressors, but from friends who loved and cherished her. It was as though she wanted to shock or alarm some one by her exploits, as though she were showing off before some one. But there was something secret maturing in her heart. . . . Yes, my old friend was right; she had been ill-treated; her hurt could not be healed, and she seemed purposely trying to aggravate her wound by this mysterious behaviour, this mistrustfulness of us all; as though she enjoyed her own pain by this *egoism of suffering* if I may so express it. This aggravation of suffering and this revelling in it I could understand; it is the enjoyment of many of the insulted and injured, oppressed by destiny, and smarting under the sense of its injustice. But of what injustice in us could Nellie complain? She seemed trying to astonish and alarm us by her exploits, her caprices and wild pranks, as though she really were asserting herself against us. . . . But no! Now she was alone. None of us could see that she was begging. Could she possibly have found enjoyment in it on her own account? Why did she want charity? What need had she of money? After receiving the gift she left the bridge and walked to the brightly lighted window of a shop. There she proceeded to count her gains. I was standing a dozen paces from her. She had a fair amount of money in her hand already,

She had evidently been begging since the morning. Closing her hand over it she crossed the road and went into a small fancy shop. I went up at once to the door of the shop which stood wide open, and looked to see what she was doing there.

I saw that she laid the money on the counter and was handed a cup, a plain tea-cup, very much like the one she had broken that morning, to show Ichmenyev and me how wicked she was. The cup was worth about fourpence, perhaps even less. The shopman wrapped it in paper, tied it up and gave it to Nellie, who walked hurriedly out of the shop, looking satisfied.

"Nellie!" I cried when she was close to me, "Nellie!"

She started, glanced at me, the cup slipped from her hands, fell on the pavement and was broken. Nellie was pale; but looking at me and realizing that I had seen and understood everything she suddenly blushed. In that blush could be detected an intolerable, agonizing shame. I took her hand and led her home. We had not far to go. We did not utter one word on the way. On reaching home I sat down. Nellie stood before me, brooding and confused, as pale as before, with her eyes fixed on the floor. She could not look at me.

"Nellie, you were begging?"

"Yes," she whispered and her head drooped lower than ever.

"You wanted to get money to buy a cup for the one broken this morning?"

"Yes . . ."

"But did I blame you, did I scold you, about that cup? Surely, Nellie, you must see what naughtiness there is in your behaviour? Is it right? Aren't you ashamed? Surely . . ."

"Yes," she whispered, in a voice hardly audible, and a tear trickled down her cheek.

"Yes . . ." I repeated after her. "Nellie, darling, if I've not been good to you, forgive me and let us make friends."

She looked at me, tears gushed from her eyes, and she flung herself on my breast.

At that instant Alexandra Semyonovna darted in.

"What? She's home? Again? Ach, Nellie, Nellie, what is the matter with you? Well, it's a good thing you're at home, anyway. Where did you find her, Ivan Petrovitch?"

I signed to Alexandra Semyonovna not to ask questions and she understood me. I parted tenderly from Nellie, who was still weeping bitterly, and asking kind-hearted Alexandra Semyonovna to stay with her till I returned home, I ran off to Natasha's. I was late and in a hurry.

That evening our fate was being decided. There was a great deal for Natasha and me to talk over. Yet I managed to slip in a word about Nellie and told her all that had happened in full detail. My story greatly interested Natasha and made a great impression on her in fact.

"Do you know what, Vanya," she said to me after a moment's thought, "I believe she's in love with you."

"What . . . how can that be ? " I asked, wondering.

"Yes, it's the beginning of love, real grown-up love."

"How can you, Natasha, nonsense ! Why, she's a child !"

"A child who will soon be fourteen. This exasperation is at your not understanding her love ; and probably she doesn't understand it herself. It's an exasperation in which there's a great deal that's childish, but it's in earnest, agonizing. Above all she's jealous of me. You love me so that probably even when you're at home you're always worrying, thinking and talking about me, and so don't take much notice of her. She has seen that and it has stung her. She wants perhaps to talk to you, longs to open her heart to you, doesn't know how to do it, is ashamed, and doesn't understand herself, she is waiting for an opportunity, and instead of giving her such an opportunity you keep away from her, run off to me, and even when she was ill left her alone for whole days together. She cries about it ; she misses you, and what hurts her most of all is that you don't notice it. Now, at a moment like this, you have left her alone for my sake. Yes, she'll be ill to-morrow because of it. And how could you leave her ? Go back to her at once. . . ."

"I should not have left her but . . "

"Yes, I know. I begged you to come, myself. But now go."

"I will, but of course I don't believe a word of it."

"Because it's all so different from other people. Remember her story, think it all over and you will believe it. She has not grown up as you and I did."

I got home late, however. Alexandra Semyonovna told me that again Nellie had, as on the previous evening, been crying a great deal and "had fallen asleep in tears," as before.

"And now I'm going, Ivan Petrovitch, as Filip Filippovitch told me. He's expecting me, poor fellow."

I thanked her and sat down by Nellie's pillow. It seemed

dreadful to me myself that I could have left her at such a moment. For a long time, right into the night, I sat beside her, lost in thought. . . . It was a momentous time for us all.

But I must describe what had been happening during that fortnight.

CHAPTER V

AFTER the memorable evening I had spent with Prince Valkovsky at the restaurant, I was for some days in continual apprehension on Natasha's account. "With what evil was that cursed prince threatening her, and in what way did he mean to revenge himself on her?" I asked myself every minute, and I was distracted by suppositions of all sorts. I came at last to the conclusion that his menaces were not empty talk, not mere bluster, and that as long as she was living with Alyosha, the prince might really bring about much unpleasantness for her. He was petty, vindictive, malicious, and calculating, I reflected. It would be difficult for him to forget an insult and to let pass any chance of avenging it. He had in any case brought out one point, and had expressed himself pretty clearly on that point: he insisted absolutely on Alyosha's breaking off his connexion with Natasha, and was expecting me to prepare her for the approaching separation, and so to prepare her that there should be "no scenes, no idyllic nonsense, no Schillerism." Of course, what he was most solicitous for was that Alyosha should remain on good terms with him, and should still consider him an affectionate father. This was very necessary to enable him the more conveniently to get control of Katya's money. And so it was my task to prepare Natasha for the approaching separation. But I noticed a great change in Natasha; there was not a trace now of her old frankness with me; in fact, she seemed to have become actually mistrustful of me. My efforts to console her only worried her; my questions annoyed her more and more, and even vexed her. I would sit beside her sometimes, watching her. She would pace from one corner of the room to the other with her arms folded, pale and gloomy, as though oblivious of everything, even forgetting that I was there beside her. When she happened to look at me (and she even avoided my eyes), there was a gleam of impatient vexation in her face, and she turned away quickly. I realized that she was perhaps herself revolving some plan of her own for the approaching separation, and how could she think of it without pain and bitterness ? And I was convinced that she had already made up her mind to the separation. Yet I was worried and alarmed by her gloomy despair. Moreover sometimes I did not dare to talk to her or try to comfort her, and so waited with terror for the end.

As for her harsh and forbidding manner with me, though that worried me and made me uneasy, yet I had faith in my Natasha's heart. I saw that she was terribly wretched and that she was terribly overwrought. Any outside interference only excited vexation and annoyance. In such cases, especially, the intervention of friends who know one's secrets is more annoying than anything. But I very well knew, too, that at the last minute Natasha would come back to me, and would seek comfort in my affection.

Of my conversation with the prince I said nothing, of course ; my story would only have excited and upset her more. I only mentioned casually that I had been with the prince at the countess's and was convinced that he was an awful scoundrel. She did not even question me about him, of which I was very glad ; but she listened eagerly to what I told her of my interview with Katya. When she heard my account of it she said nothing about her either, but her pale face flushed, and all that day she seemed especially agitated. I concealed nothing about Katya, and openly confessed that even upon me she had made an excellent impression. Yes, and what was the use of hiding it ? Natasha would have guessed, of course, that I was hiding something, and would only have been angry with me. And so I purposely told her everything as fully as possible, trying to anticipate her questions, for in her position I should have felt it hard to ask them ; it could scarcely be an easy task to inquire with an air of unconcern into the perfections of one's rival.

I fancied that she did not know yet that the prince was insisting on Alyosha's accompanying the countess and Katya into the country, and took great pains to break this to her so as to soften the blow. But what was my amazement when Natasha stopped me at the first word and said that there was no need to comfort her and that she had known of this for the last five days.

" Good heavens ! " I cried, " why, who told you ? "
" Alyosha ! "
" What ? He has told you so already ? "

"Yes, and I have made up my mind about everything, Vanya," she added, with a look which clearly, and, as it were, impatiently warned me not to continue the conversation.

Alyosha came pretty often to Natasha's, but always only for a minute; only on one occasion he stayed with her for several hours at a time, but that was when I was not there. He usually came in melancholy and looked at her with timid tenderness; but Natasha met him so warmly and affectionately that he always forgot it instantly and brightened up. He had taken to coming to see me very frequently too, almost every day. He was indeed terribly harassed and he could not remain a single moment alone with his distress, and kept running to me every minute for consolation.

What could I say to him? He accused me of coldness, of indifference, even of ill-feeling towards him; he grieved, he shed tears, went off to Katya's, and there was comforted.

On the day that Natasha told me that she knew that Alyosha was going away (it was a week after my conversation with the prince) he ran in to me in despair; embraced me, fell on my neck, and sobbed like a child. I was silent, and waited to see what he would say.

"I'm a low, abject creature, Vanya," he began. "Save me from myself. I'm not crying because I'm low and abject, but because through me Natasha will be miserable. I am leaving her to misery . . . Vanya, my dear, tell me, decide for me, which of them do I love most, Natasha or Katya?"

"That I can't decide, Alyosha," I answered. "You ought to know better than I . . ."

"No, Vanya, that's not it; I'm not so stupid as to ask such a question; but the worst of it is that I can't tell myself. I ask myself and I can't answer. But you look on from outside and may see more clearly than I do. . . . Well, even though you don't know, tell me how it strikes you?"

"It seems to me you love Katya best."

"You think that! No, no, not at all! You've not guessed right. I love Natasha beyond everything. I can never leave her, nothing would induce me; I've told Katya so, and she thoroughly agrees with me. Why are you silent? I saw you smile just now. Ech, Vanya, you have never comforted me when I've been too miserable, as I am now. . . . Good-bye!"

He ran out of the room, having made an extraordinary impression on the astonished Nellie, who had been listening to our conversation in silence. At the time she was still ill, and was lying in bed and taking medicine. Alyosha never addressed her, and scarcely took any notice of her on his visits.

Two hours later he turned up again, and I was amazed at his joyous countenance. He threw himself on my neck again and embraced me.

"The thing's settled!" he cried, "all misunderstandings are over. I went straight from you to Natasha. I was upset, I could not exist without her. When I went in I fell at her feet and kissed them; I had to do that, I longed to do it. If I hadn't I should have died of misery. She embraced me in silence, crying. Then I told her straight out that I loved Katya more than I love her."

"What did she say?"

"She said nothing, she only caressed me and comforted me— me, after I had told her that! She knows how to comfort one, Ivan Petrovitch! Oh, I wept away all my sadness with her—I told her everything. I told her straight out that I was awfully fond of Katya, but however much I loved her, and whomever I loved, I never could exist without her, Natasha, that I should die without her. No, Vanya, I could not live without her, I feel that; no! And so we made up our minds to be married at once, and as it can't be done before I go away because it's Lent now, and we can't get married in Lent, it shall be when I come back, and that will be the first of June. My father will allow it, there can be no doubt of that. And as for Katya, well, what of it! I can't live without Natasha, you know. . . . We'll be married, and go off there at once to Katya's. . . ."

Poor Natasha! What it must have cost her to comfort this boy, to bend over him, listen to his confession and invent the fable of their speedy marriage to comfort the naïve egoist. Alyosha really was comforted for some days. He used to fly round to Natasha's because his faint heart was not equal to bearing his grief alone. But yet, as the time of their separation grew nearer, he relapsed into tears and fretting again, and would again dash round to me and pour out his sorrow. Of late he had become so bound up with Natasha that he could not leave her for a single day, much less for six weeks. He was fully convinced, however, up to the very last minute, that he was only leaving her for six weeks and that their wedding would take place on his return. As for Natasha, she fully realized that her whole life was to be transformed, that Alyosha would never come back to her, and that this was how it must be.

The day of their separation was approaching. Natasha was ill, pale, with feverish eyes and parched lips. From time to time she talked to herself, from time to time threw a rapid and searching glance at me. She shed no tears, did not answer my questions, and quivered like a leaf on a tree when she heard Alyosha's ringing voice; she glowed like a sunset and flew to meet him; kissed and embraced him hysterically, laughed . . . Alyosha gazed at her, asking with anxiety after her health, tried to comfort her by saying that he was not going for long, and that then they would be married. Natasha made a visible effort, controlled herself, and suppressed her tears. She did not cry before him.

Once he said that he must leave her money enough for all the time he was away, and that she need not worry, because his father had promised to give him plenty for the journey. Natasha frowned. When we were left alone I told her I had a hundred and fifty roubles for her in case of need. She did not ask where the money came from. This was two days before Alyosha's departure, and the day before the first and last meeting between Natasha and Katya. Katya had sent a note by Alyosha in which she asked Natasha's permission to visit her next day, and at the same time she wrote to me and begged me, too, to be present at their interview.

I made up my mind that I would certainly be at Natasha's by twelve o'clock (the hour fixed by Katya) regardless of all obstacles; and there were many difficulties and delays. Apart from Nellie, I had for the last week had a great deal of worry with the Ichmenyevs.

Anna Andreyevna sent for me one morning, begging me to throw aside everything and hasten to her at once on account of a matter of urgency which admitted of no delay. When I arrived I found her alone. She was walking about the room in a fever of agitation and alarm, in tremulous expectation of her husband's return. As usual it was a long time before I could get out of her what was the matter and why she was in such a panic, and at the same time it was evident that every moment was precious. At last after heated and irrelevant reproaches such as "Why didn't I come, why did I leave her all alone in her sorrow?" so that "Goodness knows what had been happening in my absence," she told me that for the last three days

Nikolay Sergeyitch had been in a state of agitation "that was beyond all description."

"He's simply not like himself," she said, "he's in a fever, at night he prays in secret on his knees before the ikons. He babbles in his sleep, and by day he's like some one half crazy. We were having soup yesterday, and he couldn't find the spoon set beside him; you ask him one thing and he answers another. He has taken to running out of the house every minute, he always says ' I'm going out on business, I must see the lawyer,' and this morning he locked himself up in his study. ' I have to write an important statement relating to my legal business,' he said. Well, thinks I, how are you going to write a legal statement when you can't find your spoon? I looked through the keyhole though: he was sitting writing, and he all the while crying his eyes out. A queer sort of business statement he'll write like that, thinks I. Though maybe he's grieving for our Ichmenyevka. So it's quite lost then! While I was thinking that, he suddenly jumped up from the table and flung the pen down on the table; he turned crimson and his eyes flashed, he snatched up his cap and came out to me. ' I'm coming back directly, Anna Andreyevna,' he said. He went out and I went at once to his writing-table. There's such a mass of papers relating to our lawsuit lying there that he never lets me touch it. How many times have I asked him: ' Do let me lift up those papers, if it's only for once, I want to dust the table ' ' Don't you dare !' he shouts, and waves his arms. He's become so impatient here in Petersburg and so taken to shouting. So I went up to the table and began to look what paper it was he had been writing. For I knew for a fact he had not taken it with him but had thrust it under another paper when he got up from the table. And here, look, Ivan Petrovitch, dear, what I have found."

And she gave me a sheet of note-paper half covered with writing but so blotted that in some places it was illegible.

Poor old man! From the first line one could tell what and to whom he was writing. It was a letter to Natasha, his adored Natasha. He began warmly and tenderly, he approached her with forgiveness, and urged her to come to him. It was difficult to make out the whole letter, it was written jerkily and unevenly, with numerous blots. It was only evident that the intense feeling which had led him to take up the pen and to write the first lines, full of tenderness, was quickly followed by other emotions. The old man began to reproach his daughter, describing her wickedness in the bitterest terms, indignantly reminding her of her obstinacy, reproaching her for heartlessness in not having once, perhaps, considered how she was treating her father and mother. He threatened her with retribution and a curse for her pride, and ended by insisting that she should return home promptly and submissively, "and only then perhaps after a new life of humility and exemplary behaviour in the bosom of your family we will decide to forgive you," he wrote. It was evident that after the first few lines he had taken his first generous feeling for weakness, had begun to be ashamed of it, and finally, suffering from tortures of wounded pride, he had ended in anger and threats. Anna Andreyevna stood facing me with her hands clasped, waiting in an agony of suspense to hear what I should say about the letter.

I told her quite truly how it struck me, that is that her husband could not bear to go on living without Natasha, and that one might say with certainty that their speedy reconciliation was inevitable, though everything depended on circumstances. I expressed at the same time my conjecture that probably the failure of his lawsuit had been a great blow and shock to him, to say nothing of the mortification of his pride at the prince's triumph over him, and his indignation at the way the case had been decided. At such a moment the heart cannot help seeking for sympathy, and he thought with a still more passionate longing of her whom he had always loved more than anyone on earth. And perhaps too he might have heard (for he was on the alert and knew all about Natasha) that Alyosha was about to abandon her. He might realize what she was going through now and how much she needed to be comforted. But yet he could not control himself, considering that he had been insulted and injured by his daughter. It had probably occurred to him that she would not take the first step, that possibly she was not thinking of him and felt no longing for reconciliation. "That's what he must have thought," I said in conclusion, "and that's why he didn't finish his letter, and perhaps it would only lead to fresh mortification which would be felt even more keenly than the first, and might, who knows, put off the reconciliation indefinitely . . ."

Anna Andreyevna cried as she listened to me. At last, when I said that I had to go at once to Natasha's, and that I was late, she started, and informed me that she had forgotten the *chief* thing. When she took the paper from the table she had upset the ink over it. One corner was indeed covered with ink, and the old lady was terribly afraid that her husband would find out from this blot that she had been rummaging among his papers when he was out and had read his letter to Natasha. There were good grounds for her alarm; the very fact that we knew his secret might lead him through shame and vexation to persist in his anger, and through pride to be stubborn and unforgiving.

But on thinking it over I told my old friend not to worry herself. He had got up from his letter in such excitement that he might well have no clear recollection of details and would probably now think that he had blotted the letter himself. Comforting Anna Andreyevna in this way, I helped her to put the letter back where it had been before, and I bethought me to speak to her seriously about Nellie. It occurred to me that the poor forsaken orphan whose own mother had been cursed by an unforgiving father might, by the sad and tragic story of her life and of her mother's death, touch the old man and move him to generous feelings. Everything was ready; everything was ripe in his heart; the longing for his daughter had already begun to get the upper hand of his pride and his wounded vanity. All that was needed was a touch, a favourable chance, and that chance might be provided by Nellie. My old friend listened to me with extreme attention. Her whole face lighted up with hope and enthusiasm. She began at once to reproach me for not having told her before; began impatiently questioning me about Nellie and ended by solemnly promising that she would of her own accord urge her husband to take the orphan girl into their house. She began to feel a genuine affection for Nellie, was sorry to hear that she was ill, questioned me about her, forced me to take the child a pot of jam which she ran herself to fetch from the store-room, brought me five roubles, thinking I shouldn't have enough money for the doctor, and could hardly be pacified when I refused to take it, but consoled herself with the thought that Nellie needed clothes, so that she could be of use to her in that way. Then she proceeded to ransack all her chests and to overhaul all her wardrobe, picking out things she might give to the orphan.

I went off to Natasha's. As I mounted the last flight of the staircase, which, as I have said, went round in a spiral, I noticed at her door a man who was on the point of knocking, but hearing my step he checked himself. Then, after some hesitation he apparently abandoned his intention and ran downstairs. I came upon him at the turn of the stairs, and what was my astonishment when I recognized Ichmenyev. It was very dark on the stairs even in the daytime. He shrank back against the wall to let me pass ; and I remember the strange glitter in his eyes as he looked at me intently. I fancied that he flushed painfully. But anyway he was terribly taken aback, and even overcome with confusion.

"Ech, Vanya, why, it's you!" he brought out in a shaky voice. "I've come here to see some one . . . a copying-clerk . . . on business . . . he's lately moved . . . somewhere this way . . . but he doesn't live here it seems . . . I've made a mistake . . . good-bye."

And he ran quickly down the stairs.

I decided not to tell Natasha as yet of this meeting, but to wait at any rate till Alyosha had gone and she was alone. At the moment she was so unhinged that, though she would have understood and have realized the full importance of the fact, she would not have been capable of taking it in and feeling it as she would do at the moment of the last overwhelming misery and despair. This was not the moment.

I might have gone to the Ichmenyevs' again that day and I felt a great inclination to do so. But I did not. I fancied my old friend would feel uncomfortable at the sight of me. He might even imagine that my coming was the result of having met him. I did not go to see them till two days later , my old friend was depressed, but he met me with a fairly unconcerned air and talked of nothing but his case.

"And I say, who was it you were going to see so high up, when we met, do you remember—when was it ?—the day before yesterday, I fancy," he asked suddenly, somewhat carelessly, though he avoided looking at me.

"A friend of mine lives there," I answered, also keeping my eyes turned away.

"Ah! And I was looking for my clerk, Astafyev ; I was told it was that house . . . but it was a mistake. Well, as I was just telling you . . . in the Senate the decision . . ." and so on, and so on.

He positively crimsoned as he turned the subject.

I repeated all this to Anna Andreyevna the same day, to cheer her up. I besought her among other things not to look at him just now with a significant air, not to sigh, or drop hints ; in fact, not to betray in any way that she knew of this last exploit of his. My old friend was so surprised and delighted that at first she would not even believe me. She, for her part, told me that she had already dropped a hint to Nikolay Sergeyitch about the orphan, but that he had said nothing, though till then he had always been begging her to let them adopt the child. We decided that next day she should speak to him openly, without any hints or beating about the bush. But next day we were both in terrible alarm and anxiety.

What happened was that Ichmenyev had an interview in the morning with the man who had charge of his case, and the latter had informed him that he had seen the prince, and that, though the prince was retaining possession of Ichmenyevka, yet, "*in consequence of certain family affairs,*" he had decided to compensate the old man and to allow him the sum of ten thousand roubles. The old man came straight from this visit to me, in a terrible state of excitement, his eyes were flashing with fury. He called me, I don't know why, out of my flat on to the stairs and began to insist that I should go at once to the prince and take him a challenge to a duel.

I was so overwhelmed that for a long time I could not collect my ideas. I began trying to dissuade him. But my old friend became so furious that he was taken ill. I rushed into the flat for a glass of water, but when I came back I found Ichmenyev no longer on the stairs.

Next day I went to see him, but he was not at home. He disappeared for three whole days.

On the third day we learnt what had happened. He had hurried off from me straight to the prince's, had not found him at home and had left a note for him. In his letter he said he had heard of the prince's intentions, that he looked upon them as a deadly insult, and on the prince as a low scoundrel, and that he therefore challenged him to a duel, warning him not to dare decline the challenge or he should be publicly disgraced.

Anna Andreyevna told me that he returned home in such a state of perturbation and excitement that he had to go to bed. He had been very tender with her, but scarcely answered her questions, and was evidently in feverish expectation of something. Next morning a letter came by the post. On reading it he had cried out aloud and clutched at his head. Anna Andreyevna was numb with terror. But he at once snatched up his hat and stick and rushed out.

The letter was from the prince. Drily, briefly, and courteously he informed Ichmenyev that he, Prince Valkovsky, was not bound to give any account to anyone of what he had said to the lawyer, that though he felt great sympathy with Ichmenyev for the loss of his case, he could not feel it just for the man who had lost a case to be entitled to challenge his rival to a duel by way of revenge. As for the " public disgrace " with which he was threatened, the prince begged Ichmenyev not to trouble himself about it, for there would be, and could be, no public disgrace, that the letter would be at once sent to the proper quarter, and that the police would no doubt be equal to taking steps for preserving law and order.

Ichmenyev with the letter in his hand set off at once for the prince's. Again he was not at home, but the old man learnt from the footman that the prince was probably at Count Nainsky's. Without wasting time on thought he ran to the count's. The count's porter stopped him as he was running up the staircase. Infuriated to the utmost the old man hit him a blow with his stick. He was at once seized, dragged out on to the steps and handed over to a police officer, who took him to the police station. The count was informed. When the prince, who was present, explained to the old profligate that this was Ichmenyev, the father of the charming young person (the prince had more than once been of service to the old count in such enterprises) the great gentleman only laughed and his wrath was softened. The order was given that Ichmenyev should be discharged. But he was not released till two days after, when (no doubt by the prince's orders) Ichmenyev was informed that the prince had himself begged the count to be lenient to him.

The old man returned home in a state bordering on insanity, rushed to his bed and lay for a whole hour without moving. At last he got up, and to Anna Andreyevna's horror announced that he should curse his daughter for ever, and deprive her of his fatherly blessing.

Anna Andreyevna was horrified, but she had to look after the old man, and, hardly knowing what she was doing, she waited upon him all that day and night, wetting his head with vinegar, and putting ice on it. He was feverish and delirious. It was past two o'clock in the night when I left them. But next morning Ichmenyev got up, and he came the same day to me to take Nellie home with him for good. I have already described his scene with Nellie. This scene shattered him completely. When he got home he went to bed. All this happened on Good Friday, the day fixed for Katya to see Natasha, and the day before Alyosha and Katya were to leave Petersburg. I was present at the interview. It took place early in the morning, before Ichmenyev's visit, and before Nellie ran away the first time.

CHAPTER VI

ALYOSHA had come an hour before the interview to prepare Natasha. I arrived at the very moment when Katya's carriage drew up at the gate. Katya was accompanied by an old French lady, who after many persuasions and much hesitation had consented at last to accompany her. She had even agreed to let Katya go up to Natasha without her, but only on condition that Alyosha escorted her, while she remained in the carriage. Katya beckoned to me, and without getting out of the carriage asked me to call Alyosha down. I found Natasha in tears. Alyosha and she were both crying. Hearing that Katya was already there, she got up from the chair, wiped her eyes, and in great excitement stood up, facing the door. She was dressed that morning all in white. Her dark brown hair was smoothly parted and gathered back in a thick knot. I particularly liked that way of doing her hair. Seeing that I was remaining with her Natasha asked me, too, to go and meet the visitor.

"I could not get to Natasha's before," said Katya as she mounted the stairs. "I've been so spied on that it's awful. I've been persuading Mme. Albert for a whole fortnight, and at last she consented. And you have never once been to see me, Ivan Petrovitch! I couldn't write to you either, and I don't feel inclined to. One can't explain anything in a letter. And how I wanted to see you. . . . Good heavens, how my heart is beating . . ."

"The stairs are steep," I answered.

"Yes . . . the stairs . . . tell me, what do you think, won't Natasha be angry with me?"

"No, why?"

"Well . . . why should she after all? I shall see for myself directly. There's no need to ask questions."

I gave her my arm. She actually turned pale, and I believe she was very much frightened. On the last landing she stopped to take breath; but she looked at me and went up resolutely.

She stopped once more at the door and whispered to me. "I

shall simply go in and say I had such faith in her that I was not afraid to come. . . . But why am I talking, I'm certain that Natasha is the noblest creature. Isn't she ?"

She went in timidly as though she were a culprit, and looked intently at Natasha, who at once smiled at her. Then Katya ran swiftly to her, seized her hand and pressed her plump little lips to Natasha's. Then without saying a word to Natasha, she turned earnestly and even sternly to Alyosha and asked him to leave us for half an hour alone.

"Don't be cross, Alyosha," she added, "it's because I have a great deal to talk about with Natasha, of very important and serious things, that you ought not to hear. Be good, and go away. But you stay, Ivan Petrovitch. You must hear all our conversation."

"Let us sit down," she said to Natasha when Alyosha had left the room. "I'll sit like this, opposite you. I want to look at you first"

She sat down almost exactly opposite Natasha, and gazed at her for some minutes. Natasha responded with an involuntary smile.

"I have seen your photograph already," said Katya. "Alyosha showed it to me."

"Well, am I like my portrait ?"

"You are nicer," said Katya earnestly and decisively. "And I thought you would be nicer."

"Really ? And I keep looking at you. How pretty you are !"

"Me ! How can you . . . ! You darling !" she added, taking Natasha's hand with her own, which trembled, and both relapsed into silence, gazing at each other.

"I must tell you, my angel," Katya broke the silence, "we have only half an hour to be together; Mme. Albert would hardly consent to that, and we have a great deal to discuss. . . . I want . . . I must . . Well, I'll simply ask you—do you care very much for Alyosha ?"

"Yes, very much."

"If so . . . if you care very much for Alyosha . . . then . . . you must care for his happiness too," she added timidly, in a whisper.

"Yes. I want him to be happy . . ."

"Yes. . . . But this is the question—shall I make him happy ? Have I the right to say so, for I'm taking him away from you. If you think, and we decide now that he will be happier with you, then . . . then . . ."

"That's settled already, Katya dear. You see yourself that it's all settled," Natasha answered softly, and she bowed her head. It was evidently difficult for her to continue the conversation.

Katya, I fancy, was prepared for a lengthy discussion on the question which of them would make Alyosha happy and which of them ought to give him up. But after Natasha's answer she understood that everything was settled already and there was nothing to discuss. With her pretty lips half opened, she gazed with sorrow and perplexity at Natasha, still holding her hand.

"And you love him very much ?" Natasha asked suddenly.

"Yes ; and there's another thing I wanted to ask you, and I came on purpose : tell me, what do you love him for exactly ?"

"I don't know," answered Natasha, and there was a note of bitter impatience in her voice.

"Is he clever ; what do you think ?" asked Katya.

"No, I simply love him . . ."

"And I too. I always feel somehow sorry for him."

"So do I," answered Natasha.

"What's to be done with him now ? And how he could leave you for me I can't understand !" cried Katya. "Now that I've seen you I can't understand !"

Natasha looked on the ground and did not answer. Katya was silent for a time, and then getting up from her chair she gently embraced her. They embraced each other and both shed tears. Katya sat on the arm of Natasha's chair still holding her in her embrace, and began kissing her hands.

"If you only knew how I love you !" she said, weeping. "Let us be sisters, let us always write to one another . . . and I will always love you. . . . I shall love you so . . . love you so . . ."

"Did he speak to you of our marriage in June ?" asked Natasha.

"Yes. He said you'd consented. That's all just . . . to comfort him, isn't it ?"

"Of course."

"That's how I understood it. I will love him truly, Natasha, and write to you about everything. It seems as though he will soon be my husband ; it's coming to that ; and they all say so. Darling Natasha, surely you will go . . . home now ?"

Natasha did not answer, but kissed her warmly in silence.

"Be happy!" she said.

"And ... and you ... and you too!" said Katya.

At that moment the door opened and Alyosha came in. He had been unable to wait the whole half-hour, and seeing them in each other's arms and both crying, he fell on his knees before Natasha and Katya in impotent anguish.

"Why are you crying?" Natasha said to him. "Because you're parting from me? But it's not for long. Won't you be back in June?"

"And then your marriage," Katya hastened to add through her tears, also to comfort Alyosha.

"But I can't leave you, I can't leave you for one day, Natasha. I shall die without you. . . . You don't know how precious you are to me now! especially now!"

"Well, then, this is what you must do," said Natasha, suddenly reviving; "the countess will stay for a little while in Moscow, won't she?"

"Yes, almost a week," put in Katya.

"A week! Then what could be better: you'll escort her to Moscow to-morrow; that will only take one day and then you can come back here at once. When they have to leave Moscow, we will part finally for a month and you will go back to Moscow to accompany them."

"Yes, that's it, that's it . . . and you will have an extra four days to be together, anyway," said Katya, enchanted, exchanging a significant glance with Natasha.

I cannot describe Alyosha's rapture at this new project. He was at once completely comforted. His face was radiant with delight, he embraced Natasha, kissed Katya's hands, embraced me. Natasha looked at him with a mournful smile, but Katya could not endure it. She looked at me with feverish and glittering eyes, embraced Natasha, and got up to go. At that moment the Frenchwoman appropriately sent a servant to request her to cut the interview short and to tell her that the half-hour agreed upon was over.

Natasha got up. The two stood facing one another, holding hands, and seemed trying to convey with their eyes all that was stored up in their souls.

"We shall never see each other again, I suppose," said Katya.

"Never, Katya," answered Natasha.

"Well, then, let us say good-bye!"

They embraced each other.

"Do not curse me," Katya whispered hurriedly, "I'll . . . always . . . you may trust me . . . he shall be happy. . . . Come, Alyosha, take me down!" she articulated rapidly, taking his arm.

"Vanya," Natasha said to me in agitation and distress when they had gone, "you follow them . . . and don't come back. Alyosha will be with me till the evening, till eight o'clock. But he can't stay after. He's going away. I shall be left alone; come at nine o'clock, please!"

When at nine o'clock, leaving Nellie with Alexandra Semyonovna (after the incident with the broken cup), I reached Natasha's, she was alone and impatiently expecting me. Mavra set the samovar for us. Natasha poured me out tea, sat down on the sofa and motioned me to come near her. "So everything is over," she said, looking intently at me. Never shall I forget that look.

"Now our love, too, is over. Half a year of life! And it's my whole life," she added, gripping my hands.

Her hand was burning. I began persuading her to wrap herself up and go to bed.

"Presently, Vanya, presently, dear friend. Let me talk and recall things a little. I feel as though I were broken to pieces now . . . to-morrow I shall see him for the last time at ten o'clock, for the last time!"

"Natasha, you're in a fever. You'll be shivering directly. . . . Do think of yourself."

"Well, I've been waiting for you now, Vanya, for this half-hour, since he went away. And what do you think I've been thinking about? What do you think I've been wondering? I've been wondering, did I love him? Or didn't I? And what sort of thing our love was? What, do you think it's absurd, Vanya, that I should only ask myself that now?"

"Don't agitate yourself, Natasha."

"You see, Vanya, I decided that I didn't love him as an equal, as a woman usually loves a man. I loved him like . . . almost like a mother. . . . I even fancy that there's no love in the world in which two love each other like equals. What do you think?"

I looked at her with anxiety, and was afraid that it might be the beginning of brain-fever. Something seemed to carry her away. She seemed to be impelled to speech. Some of her words were quite incoherent, and at times she even pronounced them indistinctly. I was very much alarmed.

"He was mine," she went on. "Almost from the first time I met him I had an overwhelming desire that he should be *mine*, *mine* at once, and that he should not look at anyone, should not know anyone but me. . . . Katya expressed it very well this morning. I loved him, too, as though I were always sorry for him . . . I always had an intense longing, a perfect agony of longing when I was alone that he should be always happy, awfully happy. His face (you know the expression of his face, Vanya), I can't look at it without being moved; *no one else* has such an expression, and when he laughs it makes me turn cold and shudder . . . Really ! . . ."

"Natasha, listen . . ."

"People say about him . . . and you've said it, that he has no will and that he's . . . not very clever, like—a—child. And that's what I loved in him more than anything. . . . would you believe it ? I don't know though, whether I loved that one thing; I just simply loved him altogether, and if he'd been different in some way, if he'd had will or been cleverer, perhaps I shouldn't have loved him so. Do you know, Vanya, I'll confess one thing to you. Do you remember we had a quarrel three months ago when he'd been to see that—what's her name— that Minna . . . I knew of it, I found it out, and would you believe it, it hurt me horribly, and yet at the same time I was somehow pleased at it. . . . I don't know why . . . the very thought that he was amusing himself—or no, it's not that— that, like a *grown-up man* together with other *men* he was running after pretty girls, that he too went to Minnas ! I . . . what bliss I got out of that quarrel ; and then forgiving him . . . oh, my dear one ! "

She looked into my face and laughed strangely. Then she sank into thought as though recalling everything. And for a long time she sat like that with a smile on her face, dreaming of the past.

"I loved forgiving him, Vanya," she went on. "Do you know when he left me alone I used to walk about the room, fretting and crying, and then I would think that the worse he treated me the better . . . yes ! And do you know, I always picture him as a little boy. I sit and he lays his head on my knees and falls asleep, and I stroke his head softly and caress him. . . . I always imagined him like that when he was not with me. . . . Listen, Vanya," she added suddenly, "what a charming creature Katya is!"

It seemed to me that she was lacerating her own wounds on purpose, impelled to this by a sort of yearning, the yearning of despair and suffering, . . . and how often that is so with a heart that has suffered great loss.

"Katya, I believe, can make him happy," she went on. "She has character and speaks as though she had such conviction, and with him she's so grave and serious—and always talks to him about such clever things, as though she were grown up. And all the while she's a perfect child herself! The little dear, the little dear! Oh, I hope they'll be happy! I hope so, I hope so!"

And her tears and sobs burst out in a perfect torrent. It was quite half an hour before she came to herself and recovered some degree of self-control.

My sweet angel, Natasha! Even that evening in spite of her own grief she could sympathize with my anxieties, when, seeing that she was a little calmer, or, rather, wearied out, thinking to distract her mind I told her about Nellie. We parted that evening late. I stayed till she fell asleep, and as I went out I begged Mavra not to leave her suffering mistress all night.

"Oh . . . for the end of this misery," I cried as I walked home. "To have it over quickly, quickly! Any end, anyhow, if only it can be quick!"

Next morning at nine o'clock precisely I was with her again. Alyosha arrived at the same time . . . to say good-bye. I will not describe this scene, I don't want to recall it. Natasha seemed to have resolved to control herself, to appear cheerful and unconcerned, but she could not. She embraced Alyosha passionately, convulsively. She did not say much to him, but for a long while she looked intently at him with an agonizing and almost frantic gaze. She hung greedily on every word he uttered, and yet seemed to take in nothing that he said. I remember he begged her to forgive him, to forgive him for his love, and for all the injury he had done her, to forgive his infidelities, his love for Katya, his going away . . . he spoke incoherently, his tears choked him. He sometimes began suddenly trying to comfort her, saying that he was only going away for a month, or at the most five weeks; that he would be back in the summer, when they would be married, and that his father would consent, and above all that the day after to-morrow he would come back from Moscow, and then they would have four whole days together again, so now they were only being parted for one day. . . .

It was strange! He fully believed in what he said, and that he would certainly return from Moscow in two days. . . . Why then was he so miserable and crying?

At last eleven o'clock struck. It was with difficulty I persuaded him to go. The Moscow train left exactly at midday. There was only an hour left. Natasha said afterwards that she did not remember how she had looked at him for the last time. I remember that she made the sign of the cross over him, kissed him, and hiding her face in her hands rushed back into the room. I had to see Alyosha all the way downstairs to his carriage, or he would certainly have returned and never have reached the bottom.

"You are our only hope," he said, as we went downstairs. "Dear Vanya! I have injured you, and can never deserve your love; but always be a brother to me; love her, do not abandon her, write to me about everything as fully, as minutely as possible, write as much as you can. The day after to-morrow I shall be here again for certain; for certain; for certain! But afterwards, when I go away, write to me!"

I helped him into his carriage.

"Till the day after to-morrow," he shouted to me as he drove off. "For certain!"

With a sinking heart I went upstairs, back to Natasha. She was standing in the middle of the room with her arms folded, gazing at me with a bewildered look, as though she didn't recognize me. Her coil of hair had fallen to one side; her eyes looked vacant and wandering. Mavra stood in the doorway gazing at her, panic-stricken.

Suddenly Natasha's eyes flashed.

"Ah! That's you! You!" she screamed at me. "Now you are left alone! You hate him! You never could forgive him for my loving him. . . . Now you are with me again! He's come to comfort me again, to persuade me to go back to my father, who flung me off and cursed me. I knew it would be so, yesterday, two months ago. . . . I won't, I won't. I curse them, too. . . . Go away! I can't bear the sight of you! Go away! Go away!"

I realized that she was frantic, and that the sight of me roused her anger to an intense pitch, I realized that this was bound to be so, and thought it better to go. I sat down on the top stair outside and—waited. From time to time I got up, opened the door, beckoned to Mavra and questioned her. Mavra was in tears.

An hour and a half passed like this. I cannot describe what I went through in that time. My heart sank and ached with an intolerable pain. Suddenly the door opened and Natasha ran out with her cape and hat on. She hardly seemed to know what she was doing, and told me herself afterwards that she did not know where she was running, or with what object.

Before I had time to jump up and hide myself, she saw me and stopped before me as though suddenly struck by something. " I realized at all once," she told me afterwards, " that in my cruelty and madness I had actually driven you away, you, my friend, my brother, my saviour! And when I saw that you, poor boy, after being insulted by me had not gone away, but were sitting on the stairs, waiting till I should call you back, my God! if you knew, Vanya, what I felt then! It was like a stab at my heart. . . ."

"Vanya, Vanya!" she cried, holding out her hands to me. "You are here!"

And she fell into my arms.

I caught her up and carried her into the room. She was fainting! "What shall I do?" I thought. "She'll have brain-fever for certain!"

I decided to run for a doctor; something must be done to check the illness. I could drive there quickly. My old German was always at home till two o'clock. I flew to him, begging Mavra not for one minute, not for one second, to leave Natasha, and not to let her go out. Fortune favoured me. A little later and I should not have found my old friend at home. He was already in the street, just coming out of his house, when I met him. Instantly I put him in my cab, before he had time to be surprised, and we hastened back to Natasha.

Yes, fortune did favour me! During the half-hour of my absence something had happened to Natasha which might have killed her outright if the doctor and I had not arrived in the nick of time. Not a quarter of an hour after I had gone Prince Valkovsky had walked in. He had just been seeing the others off and had come to Natasha's straight from the railway station. This visit had probably been planned and thought out by him long before. Natasha told me that for the first minute she was not even surprised to see the prince. "My brain was in a whirl," she said.

He sat facing her, looking at her with a caressing and pathetic expression.

"My dear," he said, sighing, "I understand your grief; I know how hard it must be for you at this moment, and so I felt it my duty to come to you. Be comforted, if you can, if only that by renouncing Alyosha you have secured his happiness. But you understand that better than I, for you resolved on your noble action . . ."

"I sat and listened," Natasha told me, "but at first I really did not understand him. I only remember that I stared and stared at him. He took my hand and began to press it in his. He seemed to find this very agreeable. I was so beside myself that I never thought of pulling my hand away."

"You realized," he went on, "that by becoming Alyosha's wife you might become an object of hatred to him later on, and you had honourable pride enough to recognize this, and make up your mind . . . but—I haven't come here to praise you. I only wanted to tell you that you will never, anywhere, find a truer friend than me! I sympathize with you and am sorry for you. I have been forced to have a share in all this against my will, but —I have only done my duty. Your excellent heart will realize that and make peace with mine. . . . But it has been harder for me than for you—believe me."

"Enough, prince," said Natasha, "leave me in peace."

"Certainly, I will go directly," he answered, "but I love you as though you were my own daughter, and you must allow me to come and see you. Look upon me now as though I were your father and allow me be of use to you."

"I want nothing. Leave me alone," Natasha interrupted again.

"I know you are proud. . . . But I'm speaking sincerely, from my heart. What do you intend to do now? To make peace with your parents? That would be a good thing. But your father is unjust, proud and tyrannical; forgive me, but that is so. At home you would meet now nothing but reproaches and fresh suffering. But you must be independent, and it is my obligation, my sacred duty to look after you and help you now. Alyosha begged me not to leave you but to be a friend to you. But besides me there are people prepared to be genuinely devoted to you. You will, I hope, allow me to present to you

Count Nainsky. He has the best of hearts, he is a kinsman of ours, and I may even say has been the protector of our whole family. He has done a great deal for Alyosha. Alyosha has the greatest respect and affection for him. He is a very powerful man with great influence, an old man, and it is quite possible for a girl, like you, to receive him. I have talked to him about you already. He can establish you, and, if you wish it, find you an excellent position . . . with one of his relations. I gave him a full and straightforward account of our *affair* long ago, and I so enlisted his kind and generous feelings that now he keeps begging me to introduce him to you as soon as possible. . . . He is a man who has a feeling for everything beautiful, believe me—he is a generous old man, highly respected, able to recognize true worth, and indeed, not long ago he behaved in a most generous way to your father in a certain case."

Natasha jumped up as though she had been stung. Now, at last, she understood him.

"Leave me, leave me at once!" she cried.

"But, my dear, you forget, the count may be of use to your father too . . ."

"My father will take nothing from you. Leave me!" Natasha cried again.

"Oh, how unjust and mistrustful you are! How have I deserved this!" exclaimed the prince, looking about him with some uneasiness. "You will allow me in any case," he went on, taking a large roll out of his pocket, "you will allow me in any case to leave with you this proof of my sympathy, and especially the sympathy of Count Nainsky, on whose suggestion I am acting. This roll contains ten thousand roubles. Wait a moment, my dear," he said hurriedly, seeing that Natasha had jumped up from her seat angrily. "Listen patiently to everything. You know your father lost a lawsuit against me. This ten thousand will serve as a compensation which . . ."

"Go away!" cried Natasha, "take your money away! I see through you! Oh, base, base, base man!"

Prince Valkovsky got up from his chair, pale with anger.

Probably he had come to feel his way, to survey the position, and no doubt was building a great deal on the effect of the ten thousand roubles on Natasha, destitute, and abandoned by every one. The vile and brutal man had often been of service to Count Nainsky, a licentious old reprobate, in enterprises of the kind. But he hated Natasha, and realizing that things were not going smoothly he promptly changed his tone, and with spiteful joy hastened to insult her, that he might anyway *not have come for nothing.*

"That's not the right thing at all, my dear, for you to lose your temper," he brought out in a voice quivering with impatience to enjoy the effect of his insult, "that's not the right thing at all. You are offered protection and you turn up your little nose. . . . Don't you realize that you ought to be grateful to me ? I might have put you in a penitentiary long ago, as the father of the young man you have led astray, but I haven't done it, he-he-he ! "

But by now we had come in. Hearing the voices while still in the kitchen, I stopped the doctor for a second and overheard the prince's last sentence. It was followed by his loathsome chuckle and a despairing cry from Natasha. "Oh, my God ! " At that moment I opened the door and rushed at the prince.

I spat in his face, and slapped him on the cheek with all my might. He would have flung himself upon me, but seeing that there were two of us he took to his heels, snatching up the roll of notes from the table. Yes, he did that. I saw it myself. I threw after him the rolling-pin, which I snatched from the kitchen table. . . . When I ran back into the room I saw the doctor was supporting Natasha, who was writhing and struggling out of his arms as though in convulsions. For a long time we could not soothe her ; at last we succeeded in getting her to bed ; she seemed to be in the delirium of brain-fever.

"Doctor, what's the matter with her ? " I asked with a sinking heart.

"Wait a little," he answered, "I must watch the attack more closely and then form my conclusions . . . but speaking generally things are very bad. It may even end in brain-fever . . . But we will take measures however. . . ."

A new idea had dawned upon me. I begged the doctor to remain with Natasha for another two or three hours, and made him promise not to leave her for one minute. He promised me and I ran home.

Nellie was sitting in a corner, depressed and uneasy, and she looked at me strangely. I must have looked strange myself.

I took her hand, sat down on the sofa, took her on my knee, and kissed her warmly. She flushed.

"Nellie, my angel ! " I said to her, " would you like to be our salvation ? Would you like to save us all ? "

She looked at me in amazement.

"Nellie, you are my one hope now! There is a father, you've seen him and know him. He has cursed his daughter, and he came yesterday to ask you to take his daughter's place. Now she, Natasha (and you said you loved her), has been abandoned by the man she loved, for whose sake she left her father. He's the son of that prince who came, do you remember one evening, to see me, and found you alone, and you ran away from him and were ill afterwards . . . you know him, don't you? He's a wicked man!"

"I know," said Nellie, trembling and turning pale.

"Yes, he's a wicked man. He hates Natasha because his son Alyosha wanted to marry her. Alyosha went away to-day, and an hour later his father went to Natasha and insulted her, and threatened to put her in a penitentiary, and laughed at her. Do you understand me, Nellie?"

Her black eyes flashed, but she dropped them at once.

"I understand," she whispered, hardly audibly.

"Now Natasha is alone, ill. I've left her with our doctor while I ran to you myself. Listen, Nellie, let us go to Natasha's father. You don't like him, you didn't want to go to him. But now let us go together. We'll go in and I'll tell them that you want to stay with them now and to take the place of their daughter Natasha. Her father is ill now, because he has cursed Natasha, and because Alyosha's father sent him a deadly insult the other day. He won't hear of his daughter now, but he loves her, he loves her, Nellie, and wants to make peace with her. I know that. I know all that! That is so. Do you hear, Nellie?"

"I hear," she said in the same whisper.

I spoke to her with my tears flowing. She looked timidly at me.

"Do you believe it?"

"Yes."

"So I'll go in with you, I'll take you in and they'll receive you, make much of you and begin to question you. Then I'll turn the conversation so that they will question you about your past life; about your mother and your grandfather. Tell them, Nellie, everything, just as you told it to me. Tell them simply, and don't keep anything back. Tell them how your mother was abandoned by a wicked man, how she died in a cellar at Mme. Bubnov's, how your mother and you used to go about the streets begging, what she said, and what she asked you to do when she was dying. . . . Tell them at the same time about your grandfather, how he wouldn't forgive your mother, and how she sent you to him just before her death, how she died. Tell them everything, everything! And when you tell them all that, the old man will feel it all, in his heart, too. You see, he knows Alyosha has left her to-day and she is left insulted and injured, alone and helpless, with no one to protect her from the insults of her enemy. He knows all that. . . . Nellie, save Natasha! Will you go?"

"Yes," she answered, drawing a painful breath, and she looked at me with a strange, prolonged gaze. There was something like reproach in that gaze, and I felt it in my heart.

But I could not give up my idea. I had too much faith in it. I took Nellie by the arm and we went out. It was past two o'clock in the afternoon. A storm was coming on. For some time past the weather had been hot and stifling, but now we heard in the distance the first rumble of early spring thunder. The wind swept through the dusty streets.

We got into a droshky. Nellie did not utter a word all the way, she only looked at me from time to time with the same strange and enigmatic eyes. Her bosom was heaving, and, holding her on the droshky, I felt against my hand the thumping of her little heart, which seemed as though it would leap out of her body.

CHAPTER VII

THE way seemed endless to me. At last we arrived and I went in to my old friends with a sinking at my heart. I did not know what my leave-taking would be like, but I knew that at all costs I must not leave their house without having won forgiveness and reconciliation.

It was by now past three. My old friends were, as usual, sitting alone. Nikolay Sergeyitch was unnerved and ill, and lay pale and exhausted, half reclining in his comfortable easy-chair, with his head tied up in a kerchief. Anna Andreyevna was sitting beside him, from time to time moistening his forehead with vinegar, and continually peeping into his face with a questioning and commiserating expression, which seemed to worry and even annoy the old man. He was obstinately silent, and she dared not be the first to speak. Our sudden arrival surprised them both. Anna Andreyevna, for some reason, took fright at once on seeing me with Nellie, and for the first minute looked at us as though she suddenly felt guilty.

"You see, I've brought you my Nellie," I said, going in. "She has made up her mind, and now she has come to you of her own accord. Receive her and love her. . . ."

The old man looked at me suspiciously, and from his eyes alone one could divine that he knew all, that is that Natasha was now alone, deserted, abandoned, and by now perhaps insulted. He was very anxious to learn the meaning of our arrival, and he looked inquiringly at both of us. Nellie was trembling, and tightly squeezing my hand in hers she kept her eyes on the ground and only from time to time stole frightened glances about her like a little wild creature in a snare. But Anna Andreyevna soon recovered herself and grasped the situation. She positively pounced on Nellie, kissed her, petted her, even cried over her, and tenderly made her sit beside her, keeping the child's hand in hers. Nellie looked at her askance with curiosity and a sort of wonder. But after fondling Nellie and making her sit beside her, the old lady did not know what to do next and began looking at me with naïve expectation. The old man frowned, almost suspecting why I had brought Nellie. Seeing that I was noticing his fretful expression and frowning brows, he put his hand to his head and said:

"My head aches, Vanya."

All this time we sat without speaking. I was considering how to begin. It was twilight in the room, a black storm-cloud was coming over the sky, and there came again a rumble of thunder in the distance.

"We're getting thunder early this spring," said the old man. "But I remember in '37 there were thunderstorms even earlier."

Anna Andreyevna sighed.

"Shall we have the samovar?" she asked timidly, but no one answered, and she turned to Nellie again.

"What is your name, my darling?" she asked.

Nellie uttered her name in a faint voice, and her head drooped lower than ever. The old man looked at her intently.

"The same as Elena, isn't it?" Anna Andreyevna went on with more animation.

"Yes," answered Nellie.

And again a moment of silence followed.

"Praskovya Andreyevna's sister had a niece whose name was

Elena; and she used to be called Nellie, too, I remember," observed Nikolay Sergeyitch.

"And have you no relations, my darling, neither father nor mother?" Anna Andreyevna asked again.

"No," Nellie jerked out in a timid whisper.

"I'd heard so, I'd heard so. Is it long since your mother died?"

"No, not long."

"Poor darling, poor little orphan," Anna Andreyevna went on, looking at her compassionately.

The old man was impatiently drumming on the table with his fingers.

"Your mother was a foreigner, wasn't she? You told me so, didn't you, Ivan Petrovitch?" the old lady persisted timidly.

Nellie stole a glance at me out of her black eyes, as though begging me to help her. She was breathing in hard, irregular gasps.

"Her mother was the daughter of an Englishman and a Russian woman; so she was more a Russian, Anna Andreyevna. Nellie was born abroad."

"Why, did her mother go to live abroad when she was married?"

Nellie suddenly flushed crimson. My old friend guessed at once that she had blundered, and trembled under a wrathful glance from her husband. He looked at her severely and turned away to the window.

"Her mother was deceived by a base, bad man," he brought out suddenly, addressing Anna Andreyevna. "She left her father on his account, and gave her father's money into her lover's keeping; and he got it from her by a trick, took her abroad, robbed and deserted her. A good friend remained true to her and helped her up to the time of his death. And when he died she came, two years ago, back to Russia, to her father. Wasn't that what you told us, Vanya?" he asked me abruptly.

Nellie got up in great agitation, and tried to move towards the door.

"Come here, Nellie," said the old man, holding out his hand to her at last. "Sit here, sit beside me, here, sit down."

He bent down, kissed her, and began softly stroking her head. Nellie was quivering all over, but she controlled herself. Anna Andreyevna with emotion and joyful hope saw how her Nikolay Sergeyitch was at last beginning to take to the orphan.

"I know, Nellie, that a wicked man, a wicked, unprincipled man ruined your mother, but I know, too, that she loved and honoured her father," the old man, still stroking Nellie's head, brought out with some excitement, unable to resist throwing down this challenge to us.

A faint flush suffused his pale cheeks, but he tried not to look at us.

"Mother loved grandfather better than he loved her," Nellie asserted timidly but firmly. She, too, tried to avoid looking at anyone.

"How do you know?" the old man asked sharply, as impulsive as a child, though he seemed ashamed of his impatience.

"I know," Nellie answered jerkily. "He would not receive mother, and . . . turned her away. . . ."

I saw that Nikolay Sergeyitch was on the point of saying something, making some reply such as that the father had good reason not to receive her, but he glanced at us and was silent.

"Why, where were you living when your grandfather wouldn't receive you?" asked Anna Andreyevna, who showed a sudden obstinacy and desire to continue the conversation on that subject.

"When we arrived we were a long while looking for grandfather," answered Nellie; "but we couldn't find him anyhow. Mother told me then that grandfather had once been very rich, and meant to build a factory, but that now he was very poor because the man that mother went away with had taken all grandfather's money from her and wouldn't give it back. She told me that herself."

"Hm!" responded the old man.

"And she told me, too," Nellie went on, growing more and more earnest, and seeming anxious to answer Nikolay Sergeyitch, though she addressed Anna Andreyevna, "she told me that grandfather was very angry with her, and that she had behaved very wrongly to him; and that she had no one in the whole world but grandfather. And when she told me this she cried. . . . 'He will never forgive me,' she said when first we arrived, 'but perhaps he will see you and love you, and for your sake he will forgive me.' Mother was very fond of me, and she always used to kiss me when she said this, and she was very much afraid of going to grandfather. She taught me to pray for grandfather, and she used to pray herself, and she told me a great deal of how she used to live in old days with grandfather, and how grandfather used to love her above everything. She used to play the piano to him and read to him in the evening, and grandfather used to kiss her and give her lots of presents. He used to give her everything; so that one day they had a quarrel on mother's nameday, because grandfather thought mother didn't know what present he was going to give her, and mother had found out long before. Mother wanted earrings, and grandfather tried to deceive her and told her it was going to be a brooch, not earrings; and when he gave her the earrings and saw that mother knew that it was going to be earrings and not a brooch, he was angry that mother had found out and wouldn't speak to her for half the day, but afterwards he came of his own accord to kiss her and ask her forgiveness."

Nellie was carried away by her story, and there was a flush on her pale, wan little cheek. It was evident that more than once in their corner in the basement the mother had talked to her little Nellie of her happy days in the past, embracing and kissing the little girl who was all that was left to her in life, and weeping over her, never suspecting what a powerful effect these stories had on the frail child's morbidly sensitive and prematurely developed feelings.

But Nellie seemed suddenly to check herself. She looked mistrustfully around and was mute again. The old man frowned and drummed on the table again. A tear glistened in Anna Andreyevna's eye, and she silently wiped it away with her handkerchief.

"Mother came here very ill," Nellie went on in a low voice. "Her chest was very bad. We were looking for grandfather a long time and we couldn't find him; and we took a corner in an underground room."

"A corner, an invalid!" cried Anna Andreyevna.

"Yes . . . a corner . . ." answered Nellie. "Mother was poor. Mother told me," she added with growing earnestness, "that it's no sin to be poor, but it's a sin to be rich and insult people, and that God was punishing her."

"It was in Vassilyevsky Island you lodged? At Mme. Bubnov's, wasn't it?" the old man asked, turning to me, trying to throw a note of unconcern into his question. He spoke as though he felt it awkward to remain sitting silent.

"No, not there. At first it was in Myestchansky Street," Nellie answered. "It was very dark and damp there," she added after a pause, "and mother got very ill there, though she was still walking about then. I used to wash the clothes for her, and she used to cry. There used to be an old woman living there, too, the widow of a captain; and there was a retired clerk, and he always came in drunk and made a noise every night. I was dreadfully afraid of him. Mother used to take me into her bed and hug me, and she trembled all over herself while he used to shout and swear. Once he tried to beat the captain's widow, and she was a very old lady and walked with a stick. Mother was sorry for her, and she stood up for her; the man hit mother, too, and I hit him. . . ."

Nellie stopped. The memory agitated her; her eyes were blazing.

"Good heavens!" cried Anna Andreyevna, entirely absorbed in the story and keeping her eyes fastened upon Nellie, who addressed her principally.

"Then mother went away from there," Nellie went on, "and took me with her. That was in the daytime. We were walking about the streets till it was quite evening, and mother was walking about and crying all the time, and holding my hand. I was very tired. We had nothing to eat that day. And mother kept talking to herself and saying to me: ' Be poor, Nelly, and when I die don't listen to anyone or anything. Don't go to anyone, be alone and poor, and work, and if you can't get work beg alms, don't go to *him*.' It was dusk when we crossed a big street; suddenly mother cried out, ' Azorka! Azorka!' And a big dog, whose hair had all come off, ran up to mother, whining and jumping up to her. And mother was frightened; she turned pale, cried out, and fell on her knees before a tall old man, who walked with a stick, looking at the ground. And the tall old man was grandfather, and he was so thin and in such poor clothes. That was the first time I saw grandfather. Grandfather was very much frightened, too, and turned very pale, and when he saw mother kneeling before him and embracing his feet he tore himself away, pushed mother off, struck the pavement with his stick, and walked quickly away from us. Azorka stayed behind and kept whining and licking mother, and then ran after grandfather and took him by his coat-tail and tried to pull him back. And grandfather hit him with his stick. Azorka was going to run back to us, but grandfather called to him; he ran after grandfather and kept whining. And mother lay as though she were dead; a crowd came round and the police came. I kept calling out and trying to get mother up. She got up, looked round her, and followed me. I led her home. People looked at us a long while and kept shaking their heads."

Nellie stopped to take breath and make a fresh effort. She was very pale, but there was a gleam of determination in her eyes. It was evident that she had made up her mind at last to tell *all*. There was something defiant about her at this moment.

"Well," observed Nikolay Sergeyitch in an unsteady voice, with a sort of irritable harshness. "Well, your mother had injured her father, and he had reason to repulse her."

"Mother told me that, too," Nellie retorted sharply; "and as she walked home she kept saying 'that's your grandfather, Nellie, and I sinned against him; and he cursed me, and that's why God has punished me.' And all that evening and all the next day she kept saying this. And she talked as though she didn't know what she was saying. . . ."

The old man remained silent.

"And how was it you moved into another lodging?" asked Anna Andreyevna, still crying quietly.

"That night mother fell ill, and the captain's widow found her a lodging at Mme. Bubnov's, and two days later we moved, and the captain's widow with us; and after we'd moved mother was quite ill and in bed for three weeks, and I looked after her. All our money had gone, and we were helped by the captain's widow and Ivan Alexandritch."

"The coffin-maker, their landlord," I explained.

"And when mother got up and began to go about she told me all about Azorka."

Nellie paused. The old man seemed relieved to turn the conversation to the dog.

"What did she tell you about Azorka?" he asked, bending lower in his chair, so as to look down and hide his face more completely.

"She kept talking to me about grandfather," answered Nellie; "and when she was ill she kept talking about him, and as soon as she began to get better she used to tell me how she used to live. . . . Then she told me about Azorka, because some horrid boys tried once to drown Azorka in the river outside the town, and mother gave them some money and bought Azorka. And when grandfather saw Azorka he laughed very much. Only Azorka ran away. Mother cried; grandfather was frightened and promised a hundred roubles to anyone who would bring back Azorka. Two days after, Azorka was brought back. Grandfather gave a hundred roubles for him, and from that time he got fond of Azorka. And mother was so fond of him that she used even to take him to bed with her. She told me that Azorka had been used to performing in the street with some actors, and knew how to do his part, and used to have a monkey riding on his back, and knew how to use a gun and lots of other things. And when mother left him, grandfather kept Azorka with him and always went out with him, so that as soon as mother saw Azorka in the street she guessed at once that grandfather was close by."

The old man had evidently not expected this about Azorka, and he scowled more and more. He asked no more questions.

"So you didn't see your grandfather again?" asked Anna Andreyevna.

"Yes, when mother had begun to get better I met grandfather again. I was going to the shop to get some bread. Suddenly I saw a man with Azorka; I looked closer and saw it was grandfather. I stepped aside and squeezed up against the wall. Grandfather looked at me; he looked so hard at me and was so terrible that I was awfully afraid of him, and walked by. Azorka remembered me, and began to jump about me and lick my hands. I went home quickly, looked back, and grandfather went into the shop. Then I thought, 'he's sure to make inquiries,' and I was more frightened than ever, and when I went home I said nothing to mother for fear she should be ill again. I didn't go to the shop next day; I said I had a headache; and when I went the day after I met no one; I was terribly frightened so that I ran fast. But a day later I went, and I'd hardly got round the corner when grandfather stood before me with Azorka. I ran and turned into another street and went to the shop a different way; but I suddenly came across him again, and was so frightened that I stood quite still and couldn't move. Grandfather stood before me and looked at me a long time and afterwards stroked my head, took me by the hand and led me along, while Azorka followed behind wagging his tail. Then I saw that grandfather couldn't walk properly, but kept leaning on his stick, and his hands were trembling all the time. He took me to a stall at the corner of the street where gingerbread and apples were sold. Grandfather bought a gingerbread cock and a fish, and a sweetmeat, and an apple; and when he took the money out of his leather purse, his hands shook dreadfully and he dropped a penny, and I picked it up. He gave me that penny and gave me the gingerbread, and stroked me on the head ; but still he said nothing, but walked away.

"Then I went to mother and told her all about grandfather, and how frightened I had been of him at first and had hidden from him. At first mother didn't believe me, but afterwards she was so delighted that she asked me questions all the evening, kissed me and cried ; and when I had told her all about it she told me for the future not to be afraid of him, and that grandfather must love me since he came up to me on purpose. And she told me to be nice to grandfather and to talk to him. And next day she sent me out several times in the morning, though I told her that grandfather never went out except in the evening. She followed me at a distance, hiding behind a corner. Next day she did the same, but grandfather didn't come ; and it rained those days, and mother caught a bad cold coming down to the gate with me, and had to go to bed again.

"Grandfather came a week later, and again bought me a gingerbread fish and an apple, and said nothing that time either. And when he walked away I followed him quietly, because I had made up my mind beforehand that I'd find out where grandfather lived and tell mother. I walked a long way behind on the other side of the street so that grandfather didn't see me. And he lived very far away, not where he lived afterwards and died, but in another big house in Gorohovoy Street, on the fourth storey. I found out all that, and it was late when I got home. Mother was horribly frightened, for she didn't know where I was. When I told her she was delighted again and wanted to go to see grandfather next day. The next day she began to think and be afraid, and went on being afraid for three whole days, so she didn't go at all. And then she called me and said, 'Listen, Nellie, I'm ill now and can't go, but I've written a letter to your grandfather ; go to him and give him the letter. And see, Nellie, how he reads it, and what he says, and what he'll do ; and you kneel down and kiss him and beg him to forgive your mother.' And mother cried dreadfully and kept kissing me, and making the sign of the cross and praying ; and she made me kneel down with her before the ikon, and though she was very ill she went with me as far as the gate, and when I looked round she was still standing watching me go. . . .

"I went to grandfather's and opened the door ; the door had no latch. Grandfather was sitting at the table eating bread and potatoes; and Azorka stood watching him eat and wagging his tail. In that lodging, too, the windows were low and dark and there, too, there was only one table and one chair. And he lived alone. I went in, and he was so frightened that he turned white and began to tremble. I was frightened, too, and didn't say a word. I only went up to the table and put down the letter. When grandfather saw the letter he was so angry that he jumped up, lifted his stick and shook it at me; but he didn't hit me, he only led me into the passage and pushed me. Before I had got down the first flight of stairs he opened the door again and threw the letter after me without opening it. I went home and told mother all about it. Then mother was ill in bed again. . . ."

CHAPTER VIII

At that moment there was a rather loud peal of thunder; and heavy raindrops pattered on the window-panes. The room grew dark. Anna Andreyevna seemed alarmed and crossed herself. We were all startled.

"It will soon be over," said the old man, looking towards the window. Then he got up and began walking up and down the room.

Nellie looked askance at him. She was in a state of extreme abnormal excitement. I saw that, though she seemed to avoid looking at me.

"Well, what next?" asked the old man, sitting down in his easy-chair again.

Nellie looked round timidly.

"So you didn't see your grandfather again?"

"Yes, I did. . . ."

"Yes, yes! Tell us, darling, tell us," Anna Andreyevna put in hastily.

"I didn't see him for three weeks," said Nellie, "not till it was quite winter. It was winter then and the snow had fallen. When I met grandfather again at the same place I was awfully pleased . . . for mother was grieving that he didn't come. When I saw him I ran to the other side of the street on purpose that he might see I ran away from him. Only I looked round and saw that grandfather was following me quickly, and then ran to overtake me, and began calling out to me, 'Nellie, Nellie!'

And Azorka was running after me. I felt sorry for him and I stopped. Grandfather came up, took me by the hand and led me along, and when he saw I was crying, he stood still, looked at me, bent down and kissed me. Then he saw that my shoes were old, and he asked me if I had no others. I told him as quickly as I could that mother had no money, and that the people at our lodging only gave us something to eat out of pity. Grandfather said nothing, but he took me to the market and bought me some shoes and told me to put them on at once, and then he took me home with him, and went first into a shop and bought a pie and two sweetmeats, and when we arrived he told me to eat the pie; and he looked at me while I eat it, and then gave me the sweetmeats. And Azorka put his paws on the table and asked for some pie, too; I gave him some, and grandfather laughed. Then he took me, made me stand beside him, began stroking my head, and asked me whether I had learnt anything and what I knew. I answered him, and he told me whenever I could to come at three o'clock in the afternoon, and that he would teach me himself. Then he told me to turn away and look out of the window till he told me to look round again. I did as he said, but I peeped round on the sly and I saw him unpick the bottom corner of his pillow, and take out four roubles. Then he brought them to me and said, ' That's only for you.' I was going to take them, but then I changed my mind and said, ' If it's only for me I won't take them.' Grandfather was suddenly angry, and said to me, ' Well, do as you please, go away.' I went away, and he didn't kiss me.

"When I got home I told mother everything. And mother kept getting worse and worse. A medical student used to come and see the coffin-maker; he saw mother and told her to take medicine.

"I used to go and see grandfather often. Mother told me to. Grandfather bought a New Testament and a geography book, and began to teach me; and sometimes he used to tell me what countries there are, and what sort of people live in them, and all the seas, and how it used to be in old times, and how Christ forgave us all. When I asked him questions he was very much pleased, and so I often asked him questions, and he kept telling me things, and he talked a lot about God. And sometimes we didn't have lessons, but played with Azorka. Azorka began to get fond of me and I taught him to jump over a stick and grandfather used to laugh and pat me on the head.

Only grandfather did not often laugh. One time he would talk a great deal, and then he would suddenly be quiet and seem to fall asleep, though his eyes were open. And so he would sit till it was dark, and when it was dark he would become so dreadful, so old. . . . Another time I'd come and find him sitting in his chair thinking, and he'd hear nothing; and Azorka would be lying near him. I would wait and wait and cough, and still grandfather wouldn't look round. And so I'd go away. And at home mother would be waiting for me. She would lie there, and I would tell her everything, everything, so that night would come on while I'd still be telling her and she'd still be listening about grandfather: what he'd done that day, and what he'd said to me, the stories he had told and the lessons he'd given me. And when I told her how I'd made Azorka jump over a stick and how grandfather had laughed, she suddenly laughed, too, and she would laugh and be glad for a long time and make me repeat it again and then begin to pray. And I was always thinking that mother loved grandfather so much and grandfather didn't love her at all, and when I went to grandfather's I told him on purpose how much mother loved him and was always asking about him. He listened, looking so angry, but still he listened and didn't say a word. Then I asked him why it was that mother loved him so much that she was always asking about him, while he never asked about mother. Grandfather got angry and turned me out of the room. I stood outside the door for a little while; and he suddenly opened the door and called me in again; and still he was angry and silent. And afterwards when we began reading the Gospel I asked him again why Jesus Christ said 'Love one another and forgive injuries' and yet he wouldn't forgive mother. Then he jumped up and said that mother had told me that, put me out again and told me never to dare come and see him again. And I said that I wouldn't come and see him again anyhow, and went away. . . . And next day grandfather moved from his lodgings. . . ."

"I said the rain would soon be over; see it is over, the sun's come out . . . look, Vanya," said Nikolay Sergeyitch, turning to the window.

Anna Andreyevna turned to him with extreme surprise, and suddenly there was a flash of indignation in the eyes of the old lady, who had till then been so meek and overawed. Silently she took Nellie's hand and made her sit on her knee.

"Tell me, my angel," she said, "I will listen to you. Let the hard-hearted . . ."

She burst into tears without finishing. Nellie looked questioningly at me, as though in hesitation and dismay. The old man looked at me, seemed about to shrug his shoulders, but at once turned away.

"Go on, Nellie," I said.

"For three days I didn't go to grandfather," Nellie began again; "and at that time mother got worse. All our money was gone and we had nothing to buy medicine with, and nothing to eat, for the coffin-maker and his wife had nothing either, and they began to scold us for living at their expense. Then on the third day I got up and dressed. Mother asked where I was going. I said to grandfather to ask for money, and she was glad, for I had told mother already about how he had turned me out, and had told her that I didn't want to go to him again, though she cried and tried to persuade me to go. I went and found out that grandfather had moved, so I went to look for him in the new house. As soon as I went in to see him in his new lodging he jumped up, rushed at me and stamped; and I told him at once that mother was very ill, that we couldn't get medicine without money, fifty kopecks, and that we'd nothing to eat. . . . Grandfather shouted and drove me out on to the stairs and latched the door behind me. But when he turned me out I told him I should sit on the stairs and not go away until he gave me the money. And I sat down on the stairs. In a little while he opened the door, and seeing I was sitting there he shut it again. Then after a long time he opened it again, saw me and shut it again. And after that he opened it several times and looked out. Afterwards he came out with Azorka, shut the door and passed by me without saying a word. And I didn't say a word, but went on sitting there and sat there till it got dark."

"My darling!" cried Anna Andreyevna, "but it must have been so cold on the staircase!"

"I had on a warm coat," Nellie answered.

"A coat, indeed! . . . Poor darling, what miseries you've been through! What did he do then, your grandfather?"

Nellie's lips began to quiver, but she made an extraordinary effort and controlled herself.

"He came back when it was quite dark, and stumbled against me as he came up, and cried out, 'Who is it?' I said it was

I. He must have thought I'd gone away long ago, and when he saw I was still there he was very much surprised and for a long while he stood still before me. Suddenly he hit the steps with his stick, ran and opened his door, and a minute later brought me out some coppers and threw them to me on the stairs.

" 'Here, take that!' he cried. 'That's all I have, take it and tell your mother that I curse her.' And then he slammed the door. The money rolled down the stairs. I began picking it up in the dark. And grandfather seemed to understand that he'd thrown the money about on the stairs, and that it was difficult for me to find it in the dark; he opened the door and brought out a candle, and by candlelight I soon picked it up. And grandfather picked some up, too, and told me that it was seventy kopecks altogether, and then he went away. When I got home I gave mother the money and told her everything; and mother was worse, and I was ill all night myself and next day, too, I was all in a fever. I was angry with grandfather. I could think of nothing else; and when mother was asleep I went out to go to his lodging, and before I got there I stopped on the bridge, and then *he* passed by. . . ."

"Arhipov," I said. "The man I told you about, Nikolay Sergeyitch—the man who was with the young merchant at Mme. Bubnov's and who got a beating there. Nellie saw him then for the first time. . . . Go on, Nellie."

" I stopped him and asked him for some money, a silver rouble. He said, 'A silver rouble?' I said, 'Yes.' Then he laughed and said, 'Come with me.' I didn't know whether to go. An old man in gold spectacles came up and heard me ask for the silver rouble. He stooped down and asked me why I wanted so much. I told him that mother was ill and that I wanted as much for medicine. He asked where we lived and wrote down the address, and gave me a rouble note. And when the other man saw the gentleman in spectacles he walked away and didn't ask me to come with him any more. I went into a shop and changed the rouble. Thirty kopecks I wrapped up in paper and put apart for mother, and seventy kopecks I didn't put in paper, but held it in my hand on purpose and went to grandfather's. When I got there I opened the door, stood in the doorway, and threw all the money into the room, so that it rolled about the floor.

" 'There, take your money!' I said to him. 'Mother doesn't

want it since you curse her.' Then I slammed the door and ran away at once."

Her eyes flashed, and she looked with naïve defiance at the old man.

"Quite right, too," said Anna Andreyevna, not looking at Nikolay Sergeyitch, and pressing Nellie in her arms. "It served him right. Your grandfather was wicked and cruel-hearted...."

"Hm!" responded Nikolay Sergeyitch.

"Well, what then, what then?" Anna Andreyevna asked impatiently.

"I left off going to see grandfather and he left off coming to meet me," said Nellie.

"Well, how did you get on then—your mother and you? Ah, poor things, poor things!"

"And mother got worse still, and she hardly ever got up," Nellie went on, and her voice quivered and broke. "We had no more money, and I began to go out with the captain's widow. She used to go from house to house, and stop good people in the street, too, begging; that was how she lived. She used to tell me she wasn't a beggar, that she had papers to show her rank, and to show that she was poor, too. She used to show these papers, and people used to give her money for that. She used to tell me that there was no disgrace in begging from all. I used to go out with her, and people gave us money, and that's how we lived. Mother found out about it because the other lodgers blamed her for being a beggar, and Mme. Bubnov herself came to mother and said she'd better let me go to her instead of begging in the street. She'd been to see mother before and brought her money, and when mother wouldn't take it from her she said why was she so proud, and sent her things to eat. And when she said this about me mother was frightened and began to cry; and Mme. Bubnov began to swear at her, for she was drunk, and told her that I was a beggar anyway and used to go out with the captain's widow; and that evening she turned the captain's widow out of the house. When mother heard about it she began to cry; then she suddenly got out of bed, dressed, took my hand and led me out with her. Ivan Alexandritch tried to stop her, but she wouldn't listen to him, and we went out. Mother could scarcely walk, and had to sit down every minute or two in the street, and I supported her. Mother kept saying that she would go to grandfather and that I was to take her there, and by then it was quite night. Suddenly we came into a big street; there a lot of carriages were waiting outside one of the houses, and a great many people were coming out, there were lights in all the windows and one could hear music. Mother stopped, clutched me, and said to me then, ' Nellie, be poor, be poor all your life; don't go to *him* whoever calls you, whoever comes to you. You might be there, rich and finely dressed, but I don't want that. They are cruel and wicked, and this is what I bid you : remain poor, work, and ask for alms, and if anyone comes after you say " I won't go with you ! " ' That's what mother said to me when she was ill, and I want to obey her all my life," Nellie added, quivering with emotion, her little face glowing; " and I'll work and be a servant all my life, and I've come to you, too, to work and be a servant. I don't want to be like a daughter. . . ."

" Hush, hush, my darling, hush ! " cried Anna Andreyevna, clasping Nellie warmly. " Your mother was ill, you know, when she said that."

" She was out of her mind," said the old man sharply.

" What if she were ! " cried Nellie, turning quickly to him. " If she were out of her mind she told me so, and I shall do it all my life. And when she said that to me she fell down fainting."

" Merciful heavens ! " cried Anna Andreyevna. ." Ill, in the street, in winter ! "

" They would have taken us to the police, but a gentleman took our part, asked me our address, gave me ten roubles, and told them to drive mother to our lodging in his carriage. Mother never got up again after that, and three weeks afterwards she died. . . ."

" And her father ? He didn't forgive her after all then ? " cried Anna Andreyevna.

" He didn't forgive her," answered Nellie, mastering herself with a painful effort. " A week before her death mother called me to her and said, ' Nellie, go once more to your grandfather, the last time, and ask him to come to me and forgive me. Tell him in a few days I shall be dead, leaving you all alone in the world. And tell him, too, that it's hard for me to die. . . .' I went and knocked at grandfather's door. He opened it, and as soon as he saw me he meant to shut it again, but I seized the door with both hands and cried out to him :

" ' Mother's dying, she's asking for you, come along.' But he pushed me away and slammed the door. I went back to mother, lay down beside her, hugged her in my arms and said nothing. Mother hugged me, too, and asked no questions."

At this point Nikolay Sergeyitch leant his hands heavily on the table and stood up, but after looking at us all with strange, lustreless eyes, sank back into his easy-chair helplessly. Anna Andreyevna no longer looked at him. She was sobbing over Nellie. . . .

"The last day before mother died, towards evening she called me to her, took me by the hand and said:

"'I shall die to-day, Nellie.'

"She tried to say something more, but she couldn't. I looked at her, but she seemed not to see me, only she held my hand tight in hers. I softly pulled away my hand and ran out of the house, and ran all the way to grandfather's. When he saw me he jumped up from his chair and looked at me, and was so frightened that he turned quite pale and trembled. I seized his hand and only said:

"'She's just dying.'

"Then all of a sudden in a flurry he picked up his stick and ran after me; he even forgot his hat, and it was cold. I picked up his hat and put it on him, and we ran off together. I hurried him and told him to take a sledge because mother was just dying, but grandfather only had seven kopecks, that was all he had. He stopped a cab and began to bargain, but they only laughed at him and laughed at Azorka; Azorka was running with us, and we all ran on and on. Grandfather was tired and breathing hard, but he still hurried on, running. Suddenly he fell down, and his hat fell off. I helped him up and put his hat on, and led him by the hand, and only towards night we got home. But mother was already lying dead. When grandfather saw her he flung up his hands, trembled, and stood over her, but said nothing. Then I went up to my dead mother, seized grandfather's hand and cried out to him:

"'See, you wicked, cruel man. Look! . . . Look!'

"Then grandfather screamed and fell down as though he were dead. . . ."

Nellie jumped up, freed herself from Anna Andreyevna's arms, and stood in the midst of us, pale, exhausted, and terrified. But Anna Andreyevna flew to her, and embracing her again cried as though she were inspired.

"I'll be a mother to you now, Nellie, and you shall be my child. Yes, Nellie, let us go, let us give up these cruel, wicked people. Let them mock at people; God will requite them. Come, Nellie, come away from here, come!"

I have never, before or since, seen her so agitated, and I had never thought she could be so excited. Nikolay Sergeyitch sat up in his chair, stood up, and in a breaking voice asked:

"Where are you going, Anna Andreyevna?"

"To her, to my daughter, to Natasha!" she exclaimed, drawing Nellie after her to the door.

"Stay, stay! Wait!"

"No need to wait, you cruel, cold-hearted man! I have waited too long, and she has waited, but now, good-bye! . . ."

Saying this, Anna Andreyevna turned away, glanced at her husband, and stopped petrified. Nikolay Sergeyitch was reaching for his hat, and with feeble, trembling hands was pulling on his coat.

"You, too! . . . You coming with us, too!" she cried, clasping her hands in supplication, looking at him incredulously as though she dared not believe in such happiness.

"Natasha! Where is my Natasha? Where is she? Where's my daughter?" broke at last from the old man's lips. "Give me back my Natasha! Where, where is she?"

And seizing his stick, which I handed him, he rushed to the door.

"He has forgiven! Forgiven!" cried Anna Andreyevna.

But the old man did not get to the door. The door opened quickly and Natasha dashed into the room, pale, with flashing eyes as though she were in a fever. Her dress was crumpled and soaked with rain. The handkerchief with which she had covered her head had slipped on to her neck, and her thick, curly hair glistened with big raindrops. She ran in, saw her father, and falling on her knees before him, stretched out her hands to him.

CHAPTER IX

But he was already holding her in his arms!

He lifted her up like a child and carried her to his chair, sat her down, and fell on his knees before her. He kissed her hands and her feet, he hastened to kiss her, hastened to gaze at her as though he could not yet believe that she was with him, that he saw and heard her again—her, his daughter, his Natasha.

Anna Andreyevna embraced her, sobbing, pressed her head to her bosom and seemed almost swooning in these embraces and unable to utter a word.

"My dear! . . . My life! . . . My joy! . . ." the old man exclaimed incoherently, clasping Natasha's hands and gazing like a lover at her pale, thin, but lovely face, and into her eyes which glistened with tears. "My joy, my child!" he repeated, and paused again, and with reverent transports gazed at her. "Why, why did you tell me she was thinner?" he said, turning to us with a hurried, childlike smile, though he was still on his knees before her. "She's thin, it's true, she's pale, but look how pretty she is! Lovelier than she used to be, yes, even lovelier!" he added, his voice breaking from the joyful anguish which seemed rending his heart in two.

"Get up, father! Oh, do get up," said Natasha. "I want to kiss you, too. . . ."

"Oh, the darling! Do you hear, Annushka, do you hear how sweetly she said that."

And he embraced her convulsively.

"No, Natasha, it's for me, for me to lie at your feet, till my heart tells me that you've forgiven me, for I can never, never deserve your forgiveness now! I cast you off, I cursed you; do you hear, Natasha, I cursed you! I was capable of that! . . . And you, you, Natasha, could you believe that I had cursed you! She did believe it, yes, she did! She ought not to have believed it! She shouldn't have believed it, she simply shouldn't! Cruel little heart! why didn't you come to me? You must have known I should receive you. . . . Oh, Natasha, you must remember how I used to love you! Well, now I've loved you all this time twice as much, a thousand times as much as before. I've loved you with every drop of my blood. I would have torn my heart out, torn it into shreds and laid it at your feet. Oh! my joy!"

"Well, kiss me then, you cruel man, kiss me on my lips, on my face, as mother kisses me!" exclaimed Natasha in a faint, weak voice, full of joyful tears.

"And on your dear eyes, too! Your dear eyes! As I used to, do you remember?" repeated the old man after a long, sweet embrace. "Oh, Natasha! Did you sometimes dream of us? I dreamed of you almost every night, and every night you came to me and I cried over you. Once you came as a little thing, as you were when you were ten years old and were just beginning to have music lessons, do you remember ? I dreamed you came in a short frock, with pretty little shoes on, and red little hands . . . she used to have such red little hands then, do you remember, Annushka ?—she came up to me, sat on my knee and put her arms round me. . . . And you, you bad girl ! You could believe I cursed you, that I wouldn't have welcomed you if you'd come ? Why, I . . . listen, Natasha, why, I often went to see you, and your mother didn't know, and no one knew ; sometimes I'd stand under your windows, sometimes I'd wait half a day, somewhere on the pavement near your gate, on the chance of seeing you in the distance if you came out ! Often in the evening there would be a light burning in your window ; how often I went to your window, Natasha, only to watch your light, only to see your shadow on the window-pane, to bless you for the night. And did you bless me at night, did you think of me ? Did your heart tell you that I was at the window ? And how often in the winter I went up your stairs, and stood on the dark landing listening at your door, hoping to hear your voice. Aren't you laughing ? Me curse you ? Why, one evening I came to you ; I wanted to forgive you, and only turned back at the door. . . . Oh, Natasha !"

He got up, lifted her out of the chair and held her close, close to his heart.

"She is here, near my heart again ! " he cried. " Oh Lord, I thank Thee for all, for all, for Thy wrath and for Thy mercy ! . . . And for Thy sun which is shining upon us again after the storm ! For all this minute I thank Thee ! Oh, we may be insulted and injured, but we're together again, and now the proud and haughty who have insulted and injured us may triumph ! Let them throw stones at us ! Have no fear, Natasha. . . . We will go hand in hand and I will say to them, ' This is my darling, this is my beloved daughter, my innocent daughter whom you have insulted and injured, but whom I love and bless for ever and ever ! ' "

"Vanya, Vanya," Natasha cried in a weak voice, holding out her hand to me from her father's arms.

Oh, I shall never forget that at that moment she thought of me and called to me !

"Where is Nellie ? " asked the old man, looking round.

" Ah, where is she ? ' cried his wife. " My darling ! We're forgetting her ! "

But she was not in the room. She had slipped away

unnoticed into the bedroom. We all went in. Nellie was standing in the corner behind the door, hiding from us in a frightened way.

"Nellie, what's the matter with you, my child?" cried the old man, trying to put his arm round her.

But she bent on him a strange, long gaze.

"Mother, where's mother?" she brought out, as though in delirium. "Where is my mother?" she cried once more, stretching out her trembling hands to us.

And suddenly a fearful, unearthly shriek broke from her bosom; her face worked convulsively, and she fell on the floor in a terrible fit.

EPILOGUE

LAST RECOLLECTIONS

It was the beginning of June. The day was hot and stifling; it was impossible to remain in town, where all was dust, plaster, scaffolding, burning pavements, and tainted atmosphere. . . . But now—oh joy!—there was the rumble of thunder in the distance; there came a breath of wind driving clouds of town dust before it. A few big raindrops fell on the ground, and then the whole sky seemed to open and torrents of water streamed upon the town. When, half an hour later, the sun came out again I opened my garret window and greedily drew the fresh air into my exhausted lungs. In my exhilaration I felt ready to throw up my writing, my work, and my publisher, and to rush off to my friends at Vassilyevsky Island. But great as the temptation was I succeeded in mastering myself and fell upon my work again with a sort of fury. At all costs I had to finish it. My publisher had demanded it and would not pay me without. I was expected *there*, but, on the other hand, by the evening I should be free, absolutely free as the wind, and that evening would make up to me for the last two days and nights, during which I had written three and a half signatures.

And now at last the work was finished. I threw down my pen and got up, with a pain in my chest and my back and a heaviness in my head. I knew that at that moment my nerves were strained to the utmost pitch, and I seemed to hear the last words my old doctor had said to me:

"No, no health could stand such a strain, because it's impossible."

So far, however, it had been possible! My head was going round, I could scarcely stand upright, but my heart was filled with joy, infinite joy. My novel was finished and, although I owed my publisher a great deal, he would certainly give me something when he found the prize in his hands—if only fifty roubles, and it was ages since I had had so much as that. Freedom and money! I snatched up my hat in delight, and with my manuscript under my arm I ran at full speed to find our precious Alexandr Petrovitch at home.

I found him, but he was on the point of going out. He, too, had just completed a very profitable stroke of business, though not a literary one, and as he was at last escorting to the door a swarthy-faced Jew with whom he had been sitting for the last two hours in his study, he shook hands with me affably, and in his soft pleasant bass inquired after my health. He was a very kind-hearted man, and, joking apart, I was deeply indebted to him. Was it his fault that he was all his life only a publisher? He quite understood that literature needs publishers, and understood it very opportunely, all honour and glory to him for it!

With an agreeable smile he heard that the novel was finished and that therefore the next number of his journal was safe as far as its principal item was concerned, and wondered how I could ever *end* anything and made a very amiable joke on the subject. Then he went to his iron strong-box to get me the fifty roubles he had promised me, and in the meantime held out to me another thick, hostile journal and pointed to a few lines in the critical column, where there were a few words about my last novel.

I looked: it was an article by "Copyist." He neither directly abused me nor praised me, and I was very glad. But "Copyist" said among other things that my works generally "smelt of sweat"; that is, that I so sweated and struggled over them, so worked them up and worked them over, that the result was mawkish.

The publisher and I laughed. I informed him that my last story had been written in two nights, and that I had now written three and a half signatures in two days and two nights, and if only "Copyist," who blamed me for the excessive laboriousness and solid deliberation of my work, knew that!

"It's your own fault though, Ivan Petrovitch," said he. "Why do you get so behindhand with your work that you have to sit up at night?"

Alexandr Petrovitch is a most charming person, of course, though he has one particular weakness—that is, boasting of his literary judgment, especially before those whom he suspects of knowing him through and through. But I had no desire to discuss literature with him; I took the money and picked up my hat. Alexandr Petrovitch was going to his villa on the Island, and hearing that I, too, was bound for Vassilyevsky, he amiably offered to take me in his carriage.

"I've got a new carriage," he said; "you've not seen it. It's very nice."

We set off. The carriage was certainly delightful, and in the early days of his possession of it Alexandr Petrovitch took particular pleasure in driving his friends in it and even felt a spiritual craving to do so.

In the carriage Alexandr Petrovitch several times fell to criticizing contemporary literature again. He was quite at his ease with me, and calmly enunciated various second-hand opinions which he had heard a day or two before from literary people whom he believed in and whose ideas he respected. This led him sometimes to repeat very extraordinary notions. It sometimes happened, too, that he got an idea wrong or misapplied it, so that he made nonsense of it. I sat listening in silence, marvelling at the versatility and whimsicality of the passions of mankind. "Here's a man," I thought to myself, "who might make money and has made it; but no, he must have fame, too, literary fame, the fame of a leading publisher, a critic!"

At the actual moment he was trying to expound minutely a literary theory which he had heard three days before from me myself, which he had argued against then, though now he was giving it out as his own. But such forgetfulness is a frequent phenomenon in Alexandr Petrovitch, and he is famous for this innocent weakness among all who know him. How happy he was then holding forth in his *own* carriage, how satisfied with his lot, how benign! He was maintaining a highly cultured, literary conversation, even his soft, decorous bass had the note of culture. Little by little he drifted into liberalism, and then passed to the mildly sceptical proposition that no honesty or modesty was possible in our literature, or indeed in any other, that there could be nothing but "slashing at one another," especially where the system of signed articles was prevalent. I reflected to myself that Alexandr Petrovitch was inclined to regard every honest and sincere writer as a simpleton, if not a fool, on account of his very sincerity and honesty. No doubt such an opinion was the direct result of his extreme guilelessness.

But I had left off listening to him. When we reached Vassilyevsky Island he let me get out of the carriage, and I ran to my friends. Now I had reached Thirteenth Street; here was their little house. Seeing me Anna Andreyevna shook her finger at me, waved her hand, and said " Ssh ! " to me, to be quiet.

"Nellie's only just fallen asleep, poor little thing!" she whispered to me hurriedly. "For mercy's sake, don't wake her ! But she's very worn, poor darling ! We're very anxious about her. The doctor says it's nothing for the time. One can get nothing out of your doctor. And isn't it a shame of you, Ivan Petrovitch ! We've been expecting you ! We expected you to dinner. . . . You've not been here for two days ! "

"But I told you the day before yesterday that I shouldn't be here for two days," I whispered to Anna Andreyevna. "I had to finish my work. . . ."

"But you know you promised to be here to dinner to-day ! Why didn't you come ? Nellie got up on purpose, the little angel !—and we put her in the easy-chair, and carried her in to dinner. 'I want to wait for Vanya with you,' she said ; but our Vanya never came. Why, it'll soon be six o'clock ! Where have you been gadding, you sinner ? She was so upset that I didn't know how to appease her. . . . Happily, she's gone to sleep, poor darling. And here's Nikolay Sergeyitch gone to town, too (he'll be back to tea). I'm fretting all alone. . . . A post has turned up for him, Ivan Petrovitch ; only when I think it's in Perm it sends a cold chill to my heart. . . ."

"And where's Natasha ? "

"In the garden, the darling ! Go to her. . . . There's something wrong with her, too. . . . I can't make her out. . . . Oh, Ivan Petrovitch, my heart's very heavy ! She declares she's cheerful and content, but I don't believe her. Go to her, Vanya, and tell me quietly what's the matter with her. . . . Do you hear ? "

But I was no longer listening to Anna Andreyevna. I was running to the garden. The little garden belonged to the house. It was twenty-five paces long and as much in breadth, and it was all overgrown with green. There were three old spreading trees, a few young birch-trees, a few bushes of lilac and of honeysuckle ; there was a patch of raspberries in the corner, two beds of strawberries, and two narrow, winding paths crossing the garden both ways. The old man declared with delight that it would soon grow mushrooms. The great thing was that Nellie was fond of the garden and she was often carried out in the easy-chair on to the garden path. Nellie was by now the idol of the house.

But now I came upon Natasha. She met me joyfully, holding out her hands. How thin she was, how pale! She, too, had only just recovered from an illness.

"Have you quite finished, Vanya?" she asked me.

"Quite, quite! And I am free for the whole evening."

"Well, thank God! Did you hurry? Have you spoilt it?"

"What could I do? It's all right though. My nerves get strung up to a peculiar tension by working at such a strain; I imagine more clearly, I feel more vividly and deeply, and even my style is more under my control, so that work done under pressure always turns out better. It's all right. . . ."

"Ah, Vanya, Vanya! . . ."

I had noticed that of late Natasha had been keeping a jealous and devoted watch over my literary success and reputation. She read over everything I had published in the last year, was constantly asking me about my plans for the future, was interested in every criticism, was angry at some; and was desperately anxious that I should take a high place in the literary world. Her desire was expressed so strongly and insistently that I was positively astonished at her feeling.

"You'll simply write yourself out, Vanya," she said to me. "You're overstraining yourself, and you'll write yourself out; and what's more, you're ruining your health. S. now only writes a novel a year, and N. has only written one novel in ten years. See how polished, how finished their work is. You won't find one oversight."

"Yes, but they are prosperous and don't write up to time; while I'm a hack. But that's no matter! Let's drop that, my dear. Well, is there no news?"

"A great deal. In the first place a letter from *him*."

"Again?"

"Yes, again."

And she gave me a letter from Alyosha. It was the third she had had since their separation. The first was written from Moscow, and seemed to be written in a kind of frenzy. He informed her that things had turned out so that it was impossible for him to come from Moscow to Petersburg, as they had planned at parting. In the second letter he announced that he was coming to us in a few days to hasten his marriage to Natasha, that this was settled and that nothing could prevent it. And yet it was clear from the whole tone of the letter that he was in despair, that outside influences were weighing heavily upon him, and that he did not believe what he said. He mentioned among other things that Katya was his Providence and she was his only support and comfort. I eagerly opened this third letter.

It covered two sheets of paper and was written disconnectedly and untidily in a hurried, illegible scrawl, smudged with ink and tears. It began with Alyosha's renouncing Natasha, and begging her to forget him. He attempted to show that their marriage was impossible, that outside, hostile influences were stronger than anything, and that, in fact, it must be so; and that Natasha and he would be unhappy together because they were not equals. But he could not keep it up, and suddenly abandoning his arguments and reasoning, without tearing up or discarding the first half of his letter, he confessed that he had behaved criminally to Natasha, that he was a lost soul, and was incapable of standing out against his father, who had come down to the country. He wrote that he could not express his anguish, admitted among other things that he felt confident he could make Natasha happy, began to prove that they were absolutely equals and obstinately and angrily refuted his father's arguments; he drew a despairing picture of the blissful existence that might have been in store for them both, himself and Natasha, if they had married; cursed himself for his cowardice, and said farewell for ever! The letter had been written in distress; he had evidently been beside himself when he wrote. Tears started to my eyes. Natasha handed me another letter from Katya. This letter had come in the same envelope as Alyosha's, though it was sealed up separately. Somewhat briefly, in a few lines, Katya informed Natasha that Alyosha really was much depressed, that he cried a great deal and seemed in despair, was even rather unwell, but that *she* was with him and that he would be happy. Among other things, Katya endeavoured to persuade Natasha not to believe that Alyosha could be so quickly comforted, and that his grief was not serious. "He will never forget you," added Katya; "indeed, he never can forget you, for his heart is not like that. He loves you immeasurably; he will always love you, so that if he ever ceased to love you, if he ever left off grieving at the thought of you I should cease to love him for that, at once. . . ."

I gave both letters back to Natasha ; we looked at one another and said nothing ; it had been the same with the other two letters ; and in general we avoided talking of the past, as though this had been agreed upon between us. She was suffering intolerably, I saw that, but she did not want to express it even before me. After her return to her father's house she had been in bed for three weeks with a feverish attack, and was only just getting over it. We did not talk much either of the change in store for us, though she knew her father had obtained a situation, and that we had soon to part. In spite of that she was so tender to me all that time, so attentive, and took such interest in all that I was doing ; she listened with such persistence, such obstinate attention, to all I had to tell her about myself that at first it rather weighed upon me ; it seemed to me that she was trying to make up to me for the past. But this feeling soon passed off. I realized that she wanted something quite different, that it was simply that she loved me, loved me immensely, could not live without me and without being interested in everything that concerned me ; and I believed that no sister ever loved a brother as Natasha loved me. I knew quite well that our approaching separation was a load on her heart, that Natasha was miserable ; she knew, too, that I could not live without her ; but of that we said nothing, though we did talk in detail of the events before us.

I asked after Nikolay Sergeyitch.

"I believe he'll soon be back," said Natasha ; "he promised to be in to tea."

"He's still trying to get that job ? "

"Yes ; but there's no doubt about the job now ; and I don't think there's really any reason for him to go to-day," she added, musing. "He might have gone to-morrow."

"Why did he go then ? "

"Because I got a letter. . . . He's so ill over me," Natasha added, "that it's really painful to me, Vanya. He seems to dream of nothing but me. I believe that he never thinks of anything except how I'm getting on, how I'm feeling, what I'm thinking. Every anxiety I have raises an echo in his heart. I see how awkwardly he sometimes tries to control himself, and to make a pretence of not grieving about me, how he affects to be cheerful, tries to laugh and amuse us. Mother is not herself either at such moments and doesn't believe in his laugh either, and sighs. . . . She's so awkward . . . an upright soul," she added with a laugh. "So when I got a letter to-day he had to run off at once to avoid meeting my eyes. I love him more than myself, more than anyone in the world, Vanya," she added, dropping her head and pressing my hand, "even more than you. . . ."

We had walked twice up and down the garden before she began to speak.

"Masloboev was here to-day and yesterday, too," she said.

"Yes, he has been to see you very often lately."

"And do you know why he comes here? Mother believes in him beyond everything. She thinks he understands all this sort of thing so well (the laws and all that), that he can arrange anything. You could never imagine what an idea is brewing in mother! In her heart of hearts she is very sore and sad that I haven't become a princess. That idea gives her no peace, and I believe she has opened her heart to Masloboev. She is afraid to speak to father about it and wonders whether Masloboev couldn't do something for her, whether nothing could be done through the law. I fancy Masloboev doesn't contradict her, and she regales him with wine," Natasha added with a laugh.

"That's enough for the rogue! But how do you know?"

"Why, mother has let it out to me herself . . . in hints."

"What about Nellie? How is she?" I asked.

"I wonder at you, Vanya. You haven't asked about her till now," said Natasha reproachfully.

Nellie was the idol of the whole household. Natasha had become tremendously fond of her, and Nellie was absolutely devoted to her. Poor child! She had never expected to find such friends, to win such love, and I saw with joy that her embittered little heart was softening and her soul was opening to us all. She responded with painful and feverish eagerness to the love with which she was surrounded in such contrast to all her past, which had developed mistrust, resentment, and obstinacy. Though even now Nellie held out for a long time; for a long time she intentionally concealed from us her tears of reconciliation and only at last surrendered completely. She grew very fond of Natasha, and later on of Nikolay Sergeyitch. I had become so necessary to her that she grew worse when I stayed away. When last time I parted from her for two days in order to finish my novel I had much ado to soothe her . . . indirectly, of course. Nellie was still ashamed to express her feelings too openly, too unrestrainedly.

She made us all very uneasy. Without any discussion it was

THE INSULTED AND INJURED 329

tacitly settled that she should remain for ever in Nikolay Sergeyitch's family; and meantime the day of departure was drawing nearer, and she was getting worse and worse. She had been ill from the day when I took her to Nikolay Sergeyitch's, the day of his reconciliation with Natasha, though, indeed, she had always been ill. The disease had been gradually gaining ground before, but now it grew worse with extraordinary rapidity. I don't understand and can't exactly explain her complaint. Her fits, it is true, did occur somewhat more frequently than before, but the most serious symptom was a sort of exhaustion and failure of strength, a perpetual state of fever and nervous exhaustion, which had been so bad of late that she had been obliged to stay in bed. And, strange to say, the more the disease gained upon her, the softer, sweeter and more open she became with us. Three days before, as I passed her bedside, she held out her hand to me and drew me to her. There was no one in the room. She had grown terribly thin; her face was flushed, her eyes burned with a glow of fever. She pressed me to her convulsively, and when I bent down to her she clasped me tightly round the neck with her dark-skinned little arms, and kissed me warmly, and then at once she asked for Natasha to come to her. I called her; Nellie insisted on Natasha sitting down on the bed, and gazed at her. . . .

"I want to look at you," she said. "I dreamed of you last night and I shall dream of you again to-night. . . . I often dream of you . . . every night. . . ."

She evidently wanted to say something; she was overcome by feeling, but she did not understand her own feelings and could not express them. . . .

She loved Nikolay Sergeyitch almost more than anyone except me. It must be said that Nikolay Sergeyitch loved her almost as much as Natasha. He had a wonderful faculty for cheering and amusing Nellie. As soon as he came near her there were sounds of laughter and even mischief. The sick girl was as playful as a little child, coquetted with the old man, laughed at him, told him her dreams, always had some new invention and made him tell her stories, too; and the old man was so pleased, so happy, looking at his "little daughter, Nellie," that he was more and more delighted with her every day.

"God has sent her to us to make up to us all for our suffering," he said to me once as he left Nellie at night, after making the sign of the cross over her as usual.

In the evenings, when we were all together (Masloboev was there, too, almost every evening), our old doctor often dropped in. He had become warmly attached to the Ichmenyevs. Nellie was carried up to the round table in her easy-chair. The door was opened on to the verandah. We had a full view of the green garden in the light of the setting sun, and from it came the fragrance of the fresh leaves and the opening lilac. Nellie sat in her easy-chair, watching us all affectionately and listening to our talk; sometimes she grew more animated, and gradually joined in the conversation, too. But at such moments we all usually listened to her with uneasiness, because in her reminiscences there were subjects we did not want touched upon. Natasha and I and the Ichmenyevs all felt guilty and recognized the wrong we had done her that day when tortured and quivering she had been forced to tell us all her story. The doctor was particularly opposed to these reminiscences and usually tried to change the conversation. At such times Nellie tried to seem as though she did not notice our efforts, and would begin laughing with the doctor or with Nikolay Sergeyitch.

And yet she grew worse and worse. She became extraordinarily impressionable. Her heart was beating irregularly. The doctor told me, indeed, that she might easily die at any moment.

I did not tell the Ichmenyevs this for fear of distressing them. Nikolay Sergeyitch was quite sure that she would recover in time for the journey.

"There's father come in," said Natasha, hearing his voice. "Let us go, Vanya."

. . . . .

Nikolay Sergeyitch, as usual, began talking loudly as soon as he had crossed the threshold. Anna Andreyevna was gesticulating at him. The old man subsided at once, and seeing Natasha and me began with a hurried air telling us in a whisper of the result of his expedition. He had received the post he was trying for and was much pleased.

"In a fortnight we can set off," he said, rubbing his hands and anxiously glancing askance at Natasha.

But she responded with a smile and embraced him so that his doubts were instantly dissipated.

"We'll be off, we'll be off, my dears!" he said joyfully. "It's only you, Vanya, leaving you, that's the rub. . . ." (I may add that he never once suggested that I should go with them, which, from what I know of his character, he certainly would have done . . . under other circumstances . . . that is, if he had not been aware of my love for Natasha.)

"Well, it can't be helped, friends, it can't be helped! It grieves me, Vanya; but a change of place will give us all new life. . . . A change of place means a change of *everything!*" he added, glancing once more at his daughter.

He believed that and was glad to believe it.

"And Nellie?" said Anna Andreyevna.

"Nellie? Why . . . the little darling's still poorly, but by that time she'll certainly be well again. She's better already, what do you think, Vanya?" he said, as though alarmed, and he looked at me uneasily, as though it was for me to set his doubts at rest.

"How is she? How has she slept? Has anything gone wrong with her? Isn't she awake now? Do you know what, Anna Andreyevna, we'll move the little table out on to the verandah, we'll take out the samovar; our friends will be coming, we'll all sit there and Nellie can come out to us. . . . That'll be nice. Isn't she awake yet? I'll go in to her. I'll only have a look at her. I won't wake her. Don't be uneasy!" he added, seeing that Anna Andreyevna was making signals to him again.

But Nellie was already awake. A quarter of an hour later we were all sitting as usual round the samovar at evening tea.

Nellie was carried out in her chair. The doctor and Masloboev made their appearance. The latter brought a big bunch of lilac for Nellie, but he seemed anxious and annoyed about something.

Masloboev, by the way, came in almost every evening. I have mentioned already that all of them liked him very much, especially Anna Andreyevna, but not a word was spoken among us about Alexandra Semyonovna. Masloboev himself made no allusion to her. Anna Andreyevna, having learned from me that Alexandra Semyonovna had not yet succeeded in becoming his *legal* wife, had made up her mind that it was impossible to receive her or speak of her in the house. This decision was maintained, and was very characteristic of Anna Andreyevna. But for Natasha's being with her, and still more for all that had happened, she would perhaps not have been so squeamish.

Nellie was particularly depressed that evening and even preoccupied. It was as though she had had a bad dream and was brooding over it. But she was much delighted with Masloboev's present, and looked with pleasure at the flowers which we put in a glass before her.

"So you're very fond of flowers, Nellie," said the old man. "Just wait," he said eagerly. "To-morrow . . . well, you shall see. . . ."

"I am fond of them," answered Nellie, "and I remember how we used to meet mother with flowers. When we were out *there*" ("out there" meant now abroad) "mother was very ill once for a whole month. Heinrich and I agreed that when she got up and came for the first time out of her bedroom, which she had not left for a whole month, we would decorate all the rooms with flowers. And so we did. Mother told us overnight that she would be sure to come down to lunch next day. We got up very, very early. Heinrich brought in a lot of flowers, and we decorated all the rooms with green leaves and garlands. There was ivy and something else with broad leaves, I don't know the name of, and some other leaves that caught in everything, and there were big white flowers and narcissus—and I like them better than any other flower—and there were roses, such splendid roses, and lots and lots of flowers. We hung them all up in wreaths or put them in pots, and there were flowers that were like whole trees in big tubs; we put them in the corners and by mother's chair, and when mother came in she was astonished and awfully delighted, and Heinrich was glad. . . . I remember that now. . . ."

That evening Nellie was particularly weak and nervous. The doctor looked at her uneasily. But she was very eager to talk. And for a long time, till it was dark, she told us about her former life out *there;* we did not interrupt her. She and her mother and Heinrich had travelled a great deal together, and recollections of those days remained vivid in her memory. She talked eagerly of the blue skies, of the high mountains with snow and ice on them, which she had seen and passed through, of the waterfalls in the mountains; and then of the lakes and valleys of Italy, of the flowers and trees, of the villagers, of their dress, their dark faces and black eyes. She told us about various incidents and adventures with them. Then she talked of great towns and palaces, of a tall church with a dome, which was suddenly illuminated with lights of different colours; then of a hot, southern town with blue skies and a blue sea. . . . Never had Nellie talked to us with such detail of what she remembered. We listened to her with intense interest. Till then we had heard only of her experiences of a different kind, in a dark, gloomy town, with its crushing, stupefying atmosphere, its pestilential air, its costly palaces, always begrimed with dirt, with its pale dim sunlight, and its evil, half-crazy inhabitants, at whose hands she and her mother had suffered so much. And I pictured how on damp, gloomy evenings in their filthy cellar, lying together on their poor bed, they had recalled past days, their lost Heinrich, and the marvels of other lands. I pictured Nellie alone, too, without her mother, remembering all this, while Mme. Bubnov was trying by blows and brutal cruelty to break her spirit and force her into a vicious life. . . .

But at last Nellie felt faint, and she was carried indoors Nikolay Sergeyitch was much alarmed and vexed that we had let her talk so much. She had a sort of attack or fainting-fit. She had had such attacks several times. When it was over Nellie asked earnestly to see me. She wanted to say something to me alone. She begged so earnestly for this that this time the doctor himself insisted that her wish should be granted, and they all went out of the room.

"Listen, Vanya," said Nellie, when we were left alone. "I know they think that I'm going with them, but I'm not going because I can't, and I shall stay for the time with you. I wanted to tell you so."

I tried to dissuade her; I told her that the Ichmenyevs loved her and looked on her as a daughter; that they would all be very sorry to lose her. That, on the other hand, it would be hard for her to live with me; and that, much as I loved her, there was no hope for it—we must part.

"No, it's impossible!" Nellie answered emphatically; "for I often dream of mother now, and she tells me not to go with them but to stay here. She tells me that I was very sinful to leave grandfather alone, and she always cries when she says that. I want to stay here and look after grandfather, Vanya."

"But you know your grandfather is dead, Nellie," I answered, listening to her with amazement.

She thought a little and looked at me intently.

"Tell me, Vanya, tell me again how grandfather died," she said. "Tell me all about it, don't leave anything out."

I was surprised at this request, but I proceeded to tell her the story in every detail. I suspected that she was delirious, or at least that after her attack her brain was not quite clear.

She listened attentively to all I told her, and I remember how her black eyes, glittering with the light of fever, watched me intently and persistently all the while I was talking. It was dark by now in the room.

"No, Vanya, he's not dead," she said positively, when she had heard it all and reflected for a while. "Mother often tells me about grandfather, and when I said to her yesterday, 'but grandfather's dead,' she was dreadfully grieved; she cried and told me he wasn't, that I had been told so on purpose, and that he was walking about the streets now, begging 'just as we used to beg,' mother said to me; 'and he keeps walking about the place where we first met him, and I fell down before him, and Azorka knew me. . . .'"

"That was a dream, Nellie, a dream that comes from illness, for you are ill," I said to her.

"I kept thinking it was only a dream myself," said Nellie, "and I didn't speak of it to anyone. I only wanted to tell you. But to-day when you didn't come and I fell asleep I dreamed of grandfather himself. He was sitting at home, waiting for me, and was so thin and dreadful; and he told me he'd had nothing to eat for two days, nor Azorka either, and he was very angry with me, and scolded me. He told me, too, that he had no snuff at all, and that he couldn't live without it. And he did really say that to me once before, Vanya, after mother died, when I went to see him. Then he was quite ill and hardly understood anything. When I heard him say that to-day, I thought I would go on to the bridge and beg for alms, and then buy him bread and baked potatoes and snuff. So I went and stood there, and then I saw grandfather walking near, and he lingered a little and then came up to me, and looked how much I'd got and took it. 'That will do for bread,' he said; 'now get some for snuff.' I begged the money, and he came up and took it from me. I told him that I'd give it him all, anyway, and not hide anything from him. 'No,' he said, 'you steal from me. Mme. Bubnov told me you were a thief; that's why I shall never take you to live with me. Where have you put that other copper?' I cried because he didn't believe me, but he wouldn't listen to me and kept shouting, 'You've stolen a penny!' And he began to beat me there on the bridge, and hurt me. And I cried very much. . . . And so I've begun to think, Vanya, that he must be alive, and that he must be walking about somewhere waiting for me to come."

I tried once more to soothe her and to persuade her she was

wrong, and at last I believe I succeeded in convincing her. She said that she was afraid to go to sleep now because she would dream of her grandfather. At last she embraced me warmly.

"But anyway, I can't leave you, Vanya," she said, pressing her little face to mine. "Even if it weren't for grandfather I wouldn't leave you."

Every one in the house was alarmed at Nellie's attack. I told the doctor apart all her sick fancies, and asked him what he thought of her state.

"Nothing is certain yet," he answered, considering. "So far I can only surmise, watch, and observe; but nothing is certain. Recovery is impossible, anyway. She will die. I don't tell them because you begged me not to, but I am sorry and I shall suggest a consultation to-morrow. Perhaps the disease will take a different turn after a consultation. But I'm very sorry for the little girl, as though she were my own child. . . . She's a dear, dear child! And with such a playful mind!"

Nikolay Sergeyitch was particularly excited.

"I tell you what I've thought of, Vanya," he said. "She's very fond of flowers. Do you know what? Let us prepare for her to-morrow when she wakes up a welcome with flowers such as she and that Heinrich prepared for her mother, as she described to-day. . . . She spoke of it with such emotion. . . ."

"I dare say she did," I said. "But emotion's just what's bad for her now."

"Yes, but pleasant emotion is a different matter. Believe me, my boy, trust my experience; pleasurable emotion does no harm; it may even cure, it is conducive to health."

The old man was, in fact, so fascinated by his own idea that he was in a perfect ecstasy about it. It was impossible to dissuade him. I questioned the doctor about it, but before the latter had time to consider the matter, Nikolay Sergeyitch had taken his cap and was running to make arrangements.

"You know," he said to me as he went out, "there's a hot-house near here, a magnificent shop. The nurserymen sell flowers; one can get them cheap. It's surprising how cheap they are, really! . . . You impress that on Anna Andreyevna, or else she'll be angry directly at the expense. . . . So, I tell you what. . . . I tell you what, my dear boy, where are you off to now? You are free now, you've finished your work, so why need you hurry home? Sleep the night here, upstairs in the attic; where you slept before, do you remember? The bedstead's there and the mattress just as it was before; nothing's been touched. You'll sleep like the King of France. Eh? Do stay. To-morrow we'll get up early. They'll bring the flowers, and by eight o'clock we'll arrange the whole room together. Natasha will help us. She'll have more taste than you and I. Well, do you agree? Will you stay the night?"

It was settled that I should stay the night. Nikolay Sergeyitch went off to make his arrangements. The doctor and Masloboev said good-bye and went away. The Ichmenyevs went to bed early, at eleven o'clock. As he was going, Masloboev seemed hesitating and on the point of saying something, but he put it off. But when after saying good night to the old people I went up to my attic, to my surprise I found him there. He was sitting at the little table, turning over the leaves of a book and waiting for me.

"I turned back on the way, Vanya, because it's better to tell you now. Sit down. It's a stupid business, you see, vexatiously so, in fact—"

"Why, what's the matter?"

"Why, your scoundrel of a prince flew into a rage a fortnight ago; and such a rage that I'm angry still."

"Why, what's the matter? Surely you're not still on terms with the prince?"

"There you go with your 'what's the matter?' as though something extraordinary had happened. You're for all the world like my Alexandra Semyonovna and all these insufferable females! ... I can't endure females. ... If a crow calls it's 'what's the matter?' with them."

"Don't be angry."

"I'm not a bit angry; but every sort of affair ought to be looked at reasonably, and not exaggerated ... that's what I say."

He paused a little, as though he were still feeling vexed with me. I did not interrupt him.

"You see, Vanya," he began again, "I've come upon a clue. That's to say, I've not really come upon it, and it's not really a clue But that's how it struck me ... that is, from certain considerations I gather that Nellie ... perhaps ... well, in fact, is the prince's legitimate daughter."

"What are you saying?"

"There you go roaring again, 'what are you saying?' So

that one really can't say anything to people like this!" he shouted, waving his hand frantically. "Have I told you anything positive, you feather-head? Did I tell you she's been *proved to be* the prince's legitimate daughter? Did I, or did I not?"

"Listen, my dear fellow," I said to him in great excitement. "For God's sake don't shout, but explain things clearly and precisely. I swear I shall understand you. You must realize how important the matter is, and what consequences. . . ."

"Consequences, indeed, of what? Where are the proofs? Things aren't done like that, and I'm telling you a secret now. And why I'm telling you I'll explain later. You may be sure there's a reason for it. Listen and hold your tongue and understand that all this is a secret. . . . This is how it was, you see. As soon as the prince came back from Warsaw in the winter, before Smith died, he began to go into this business. That is, he had begun it much earlier, during the previous year. But at that time he was on the look-out for one thing, and later he was on the look-out for something else. What mattered was that he'd lost the thread. It was thirteen years since he parted from Nellie's mother in Paris, and abandoned her, but all that time he had kept an incessant watch on her, he knew that she was living with Heinrich, whom Nellie was talking about to-day; he knew she had Nellie, he knew she was ill; he knew everything, in fact, but then he suddenly lost the thread. And this seems to have happened soon after the death of Heinrich, when she came to Petersburg. In Petersburg, of course, he would very soon have found her, whatever name she went by in Russia; but the thing was that his agents abroad misled him with false information, informing him that she was living in an out-of-the-way little town in South Germany. They deceived him through carelessness. They mistook another woman for her. So it went on for a year or more. But during the previous year the prince had begun to have doubts; certain facts had led him even earlier to suspect that it was not the right woman. Then the question arose: where was the real lady? And it occurred to him (though he'd nothing to go upon) to wonder whether she were not in Petersburg. Inquiries were being made meanwhile abroad, and he set other inquiries on foot here; but apparently he did not care to make use of the official channels, and he became acquainted with me. He was recommended to me: he was told this and that about me, that I took up detective work as an amateur, and so on, and so on. . . . Well, so he explained the business to me; only vaguely, damn the fellow; he explained it vaguely and ambiguously. He made a lot of mistakes, repeated himself several times; he represented facts in different lights at the same time. . . . Well, as we all know, if you're ever so cunning you can't hide every track. Well, of course, I began, all obsequiousness and simplicity of heart, slavishly devoted, in fact. But I acted on a principle I've adopted once for all, and a law of nature, too (for it is a law of nature), and considered in the first place whether he had told me what he really wanted, and secondly whether, under what he had told me, there lay concealed something else he hadn't told me. For in the latter case, as probably even you, dear son, with your poetical brain, can grasp, he was cheating me: for while one job is worth a rouble, say, another may be worth four times as much; so I should be a fool if I gave him for a rouble what was worth four. I began to look into it and make my conjectures, and bit by bit I began to come upon traces; one thing I'd get out of him, another out of some outsider, and I'd get at a third by my own wits. If you ask me what was my idea in so doing, I'll answer, well, for one thing that the prince seemed somewhat too keen about it; he seemed in a great panic about something. For after all, what had he to be frightened of? He'd carried a girl off from her father, and when she was with child he had abandoned her. What was there remarkable in that? A charming, pleasant bit of mischief, and nothing more. That was nothing for a man like the prince to be afraid of! Yet he was afraid. . . . And that made me suspicious. I came on some very interesting traces, my boy, through Heinrich, among other things. He was dead, of course, but from one of his cousins (now married to a baker here, in Petersburg) who had been passionately in love with him in old days, and had gone on loving him for fifteen years, regardless of the stout papa baker to whom she had incidentally borne eight children; from this cousin, I say, I managed by means of many and various manœuvres to learn an important fact, that Heinrich, after the German habit, used to write her letters and diaries, and before his death he sent her some of his papers. She was a fool. She didn't understand what was important in the letters, and only understood the parts where he talked of the moon, of 'mein lieber Augustin,' and of Wieland, too, I believe. But I got hold of the necessary facts, and through those letters I hit on a new clue. I found out, too, about Mr. Smith, about the money filched from him by his daughter, and about the prince's getting hold of that money ; at last, in the midst of exclamations, rigmaroles, and allegories of all sorts, I got a glimpse of the essential truth ; that is, Vanya, you understand, nothing positive. Silly Heinrich purposely concealed that, and only hinted at it ; well, and these hints, all this taken together, began to blend into a heavenly harmony in my mind. The prince was legally married to the young lady. Where they were married, how, when precisely, whether abroad or here, the whereabouts of the documents—is all unknown. In fact, friend Vanya, I've torn my hair out in despair, searching for them in vain ; in fact, I've hunted day and night. I unearthed Smith at last, but he went and died. I hadn't even time to get a look at him. Then, through chance, I suddenly learned that a woman I had suspicions of had died in Vassilyevsky Island. I made inquiries and got on the track. I rushed off to Vassilyevsky, and there it was, do you remember, we met ? I made a big haul that time. In short, Nellie was a great help to me at that point. . . ."

"Listen," I interrupted, "surely you don't suppose that Nellie knows ?"

"What ?"

"That she is Prince Valkovsky's daughter ?"

"Why, you know yourself that she's the prince's daughter," he answered, looking at me with a sort of angry reproach. "Why ask such idle questions, you foolish fellow ? What matters is not simply that she's the prince's daughter, but that she's his *legitimate* daughter—do you understand that ? . . ."

"Impossible !" I cried.

"I told myself it was 'impossible' at first. But it turns out that it *is possible* and in all probability is *true*."

"No, Masloboev, that's not so, your fancy is running away with you !" I cried. "She doesn't know anything about it, and what's more she's his illegitimate daughter. If the mother had had any sort of documentary evidence to produce, would she have put up with the awful life she led here in Petersburg, and what's more, have left her child to such an utterly forlorn fate ? Nonsense ! It's impossible !"

"I've thought the same myself ; in fact, it's a puzzle to me to this day. But then, again, the thing is that Nellie's mother was the craziest and most senseless woman in the world. She was an extraordinary woman ; consider all the circumstances, her romanticism, all that star-gazing nonsense in its wildest and craziest form. Take one point : from the very beginning she dreamed of something like a heaven upon earth, of angels; her love was boundless, her faith was limitless, and I'm convinced that she went mad afterwards, not because he got tired of her, and cast her off, but because she was deceived in him, because he was *capable* of deceiving her and abandoning her, because her idol was turned into clay, had spat on her, and humiliated her. Her romantic and irrational soul could not endure this transformation, and the insult besides. Do you realize what an insult it was ? In her horror and, above all, her pride, she drew back from him with infinite contempt. She broke all ties, tore up all her papers, spat upon his money, forgetting that it was not her money, but her father's, refused it as so much dirt in order to crush her seducer by her spiritual grandeur, to look upon him as having robbed her, and to have the right to despise him all her life. And very likely she said that she considered it a dishonour to call herself his wife. We have no divorce in Russia, but *de facto* they were separated, and how could she ask him for help after that ! Remember that the mad creature said to Nellie on her death-bed, ' Don't go to him ; work, perish, but don't go to him, whoever may try to take you.' So that even then she was dreaming that she would be sought out, and so would be able once more to avenge herself by crushing the seeker with her contempt. In short, she fed on evil dreams instead of bread. I've got a great deal out of Nellie, brother ; in fact, I get a good deal still. Her mother was ill, of course, in consumption ; that disease specially develops bitterness and every sort of irritability, yet I know for certain, through a crony of the woman Bubnov's, that she did write to the prince, yes, to the prince, actually to the prince. . . ."

"'She wrote ! And did he get the letter ? " I cried.

" That's just it. I don't know whether he did or not. On one occasion Nellie's mother approached that crony. (Do you remember that painted wench ? Now she's in the penitentiary.) Well, she'd written the letter and she gave it to her to take, but didn't send it after all and took it back. That was three weeks before her death. . . . A significant fact; if once she brought herself to send it, even though she did take it back, she might have sent it again—I don't know ; but there is one reason for believing that she really did not send it, for the prince, I fancy, only found out for *certain* that she had been in Petersburg, and where she'd been living, after her death. He must have been relieved!"

"Yes, I remember Alyosha mentioned some letter that his father was very much pleased about, but that was quite lately, not more than two months ago. Well, go on, go on. What of your dealings with the prince?"

"My dealings with the prince? Understand, I had a complete moral conviction, but not a single positive proof, *not a single one*, in spite of all my efforts. A critical position! I should have had to make inquiries abroad. But where?—I didn't know. I realized, of course, that there I should have a hard fight for it, that I could only scare him by hints, pretend I knew more than I really did. . . ."

"Well, what then?"

"He wasn't taken in, though he was scared; so scared that he's in a funk even now. We had several meetings. What a leper he made himself out! Once in a moment of effusion he fell to telling me the whole story. That was when he thought I knew all about it. He told it well, frankly, with feeling—of course he was lying shamelessly. It was then I took the measure of his fear for me. I played the simpleton one time to him, and let him see I was shamming. I played the part awkwardly—that is awkwardly on purpose. I purposely treated him to a little rudeness, began to threaten him, all that he might take me for a simpleton, and somehow let things out. He saw through it, the scoundrel! Another time I pretended to be drunk. That didn't answer either—he's cunning. You can understand that, Vanya. I had to find out how far he was afraid of me; and at the same time to make him believe I knew more than I did."

"Well, and what was the end of it?"

"Nothing came of it. I needed proofs and I hadn't got them. He only realized one thing, that I might make a scandal. And, of course, a scandal was the one thing he was afraid of, and he was the more afraid of it because he had begun to form ties here. You know he's going to be married, of course?"

"No."

"Next year. He looked out for his bride when he was here last year; she was only fourteen then. She's fifteen by now, still in pinafores, poor thing! Her parents were delighted. You can imagine how anxious he must have been for his wife to die. She's a general's daughter, a girl with money—heaps of money! You and I will never make a marriage like that, friend Vanya.... Only there's something I shall never forgive myself for as long as I live!" cried Masloboev, bringing his fist down on the table. "That he got the better of me a fortnight ago ... the scoundrel!"

"How so?"

"It was like this. I saw he knew I'd nothing positive to go upon; and I felt at last that the longer the thing dragged on the more he'd realize my helplessness. Well, so I consented to take two thousand from him."

"You took two thousand!"

"In silver, Vanya; it was against the grain, but I took it. As though such a job were worth no more than two thousand! It was humiliating to take it. I felt as though he'd spat upon me. He said to me: 'I haven't paid you yet, Masloboev, for the work you did before.' (But he had paid long ago, the hundred and fifty roubles we'd agreed upon.) 'Well, now I'm going away; here's two thousand, and so I hope *everything's* settled between us.' So I answered, 'Finally settled, prince,' and I didn't dare to look into his ugly face. I thought it was plainly written upon it, 'Well, he's got enough. I'm simply giving it to the fool out of good-nature!' I don't remember how I got away from him!"

"But that was disgraceful, Masloboev," I cried. "What about Nellie!"

"It wasn't simply disgraceful... it was criminal... it was loathsome. It was... it was... there's no word to describe it!"

"Good heavens! He ought at least to provide for Nellie!"

"Of course he ought! But how's one to force him to? Frighten him? Not a bit of it; he won't be frightened; you see, I've taken the money. I admitted to him myself that all he had to fear from me was only worth two thousand roubles. I fixed that price on myself! How's one going to frighten him now?"

"And can it be that everything's lost for Nellie?" I cried, almost in despair.

"Not a bit of it!" cried Masloboev hotly, starting up. "No, I won't let him off like that. I shall begin all over again, Vanya. I've made up my mind to. What if I have taken two thousand? Hang it all! I took it for the insult, because he cheated me, the rascal; he must have been laughing at me. He cheated me and laughed at me, too! No, I'm not going to let myself be laughed at. . . . Now, I shall start with Nellie, Vanya. From things I've noticed I'm perfectly sure that she has the key to the whole situation. She knows *all*—all about it! Her mother told her. In delirium, in despondency, she might well have told her. She had no one to complain to. Nellie was at hand, so she told Nellie. And maybe we may come upon some documents," he added gleefully, rubbing his hands. "You understand now, Vanya, why I'm always hanging about here? In the first place, because I'm so fond of you, of course; but chiefly to keep a watch on Nellie; and another thing, Vanya, whether you like it or not, you must help me, for you have an influence on Nellie! . . ."

"To be sure I will, I swear!" I cried. "And I hope, Masloboev, that you'll do your best for Nellie's sake, for the sake of the poor, injured orphan, and not only for your own advantage."

"What difference does it make to you whose advantage I do my best for, you blessed innocent? As long as it's done, that's what matters! Of course it's for the orphan's sake, that's only common humanity. But don't you judge me too finally, Vanya, if I do think of myself. I'm a poor man, and he mustn't dare to insult the poor. He's robbing me of my own, and he's cheated me into the bargain, the scoundrel. So am I to consider a swindler like that, to your thinking? Morgen früh!"

. . . . .

But our flower festival did not come off next day. Nellie was worse and could not leave her room.

And she never did leave that room again.

She died a fortnight later. In that fortnight of her last agony she never quite came to herself, or escaped from her strange fantasies. Her intellect was, as it were, clouded. She was firmly convinced up to the day of her death that her grandfather was calling her and was angry with her for not coming, was rapping with his stick at her, and was telling her to go begging to get bread and snuff for him. She often began crying in her sleep, and when she waked said that she had seen her mother.

Only at times she seemed fully to regain her faculties. Once we were left alone together. She turned to me and clutched my hand with her thin, feverishly hot little hand.

"Vanya," she said, "when I die, marry Natasha."

I believe this idea had been constantly in her mind for a long time. I smiled at her without speaking. Seeing my smile she smiled, too; with a mischievous face she shook her little finger at me and at once began kissing me.

On an exquisite summer evening, three days before her death, she asked us to draw the blinds and open the windows in her bedroom. The windows looked into the garden. She gazed a long while at the thick, green foliage, at the setting sun, and suddenly asked the others to leave us alone.

"Vanya," she said in a voice hardly audible, for she was very weak by now, "I shall die soon, very soon. I should like you to remember me. I'll leave you this as a keepsake." (And she showed me a little bag which hung with a cross on her breast.) "Mother left it me when she was dying. So when I die you take this from me, take it and read what's in it. I shall tell them all to-day to give it to you and no one else. And when you read what's written in it, go to *him* and tell him that I'm dead, and that I haven't forgiven him. Tell him, too, that I've been reading the Gospel lately. There it says we must forgive all our enemies. Well, I've read that, but I've not forgiven *him* all the same; for when mother was dying and still could talk, the last thing she said was: 'I curse him.' And so I curse him, not on my own account but on mother's. Tell him how mother died, how I was left alone at Mme. Bubnov's; tell him how you saw me there, tell him all, all, and tell him I liked better to be at Mme. Bubnov's than to go to him. . . ."

As she said this, Nellie turned pale, her eyes flashed, her heart began beating so violently that she sank back on the pillow, and for two minutes she could not utter a word.

"Call them, Vanya," she said at last in a faint voice. "I want to say good-bye to them all. Good-bye, Vanya!"

She embraced me warmly for the last time. All the others came in. Nikolay Sergeyitch could not realize that she was dying; he could not admit the idea. Up to the last moment he refused to agree with us, maintaining that she would certainly get well. He was quite thin with anxiety; he sat by Nellie's bedside for days and even nights together. The last night he didn't sleep at all. He tried to anticipate Nellie's slightest wishes, and wept bitterly when he came out to us from her, but he soon began hoping again that she would soon get well. He filled her room with flowers. Once he bought her a great bunch of exquisite white and red roses; he went a long way to get them and bring them to his little Nellie. . . . He excited her very much by all this. She could not help responding with her whole heart to the love that surrounded her on all sides. That evening, the evening of her good-bye to us, the old man could not bring himself to say good-bye to her for ever. Nellie smiled at him, and all the evening tried to seem cheerful; she joked with him and even laughed. . . . We left her room, feeling almost hopeful, but next day she could not speak. And two days later she died.

I remember how the old man decked her little coffin with flowers, and gazed in despair at her wasted, little face, smiling in death, and at her hands crossed on her breast. He wept over her as though she had been his own child. Natasha and all of us tried to comfort him, but nothing could comfort him, and he was seriously ill after her funeral.

Anna Andreyevna herself gave me the little bag off Nellie's neck. In it was her mother's letter to Prince Valkovsky. I read it on the day of Nellie's death. She cursed the prince, said she could not forgive him, described all the latter part of her life, all the horrors to which she was leaving Nellie, and besought him to do something for the child.

"She is yours," she wrote. "She is *your* daughter, *and you know* that she is *really your daughter*. I have told her to go to you when I am dead and to give you this letter. If you do not repulse Nellie, perhaps then I shall forgive you, and at the judgment day I will stand before the throne of God and pray for your sins to be forgiven. Nellie knows what is in this letter. I have read it to her. I have told her *all;* she knows *everything, everything.* . . ."

But Nellie had not done her mother's bidding. She knew all, but she had not gone to the prince, and had died unforgiving.

When we returned from Nellie's funeral, Natasha and I went out into the garden. It was a hot, sunny day. A week later they were to set off. Natasha turned a long, strange look upon me.

"Vanya," she said, "Vanya, it was a dream, you know."

"What was a dream?" I asked.

"All, all," she answered, "everything, all this year. Vanya, why did I destroy your happiness?"

And in her eyes I read:

"We might have been happy together for ever."

PRINTED AT
THE BALLANTYNE PRESS
LONDON & EDINBURGH

A LIST OF CURRENT FICTION

PUBLISHED BY

WILLIAM HEINEMANN

AT 21 BEDFORD ST., LONDON, W.C

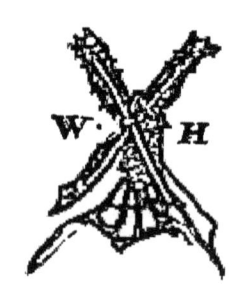

MR HEINEMANN will always be pleased to send periodically particulars of his forthcoming publications to any reader who desires them. In applying please state whether you are interested in works of Fiction, Memoirs, History, Art, Science, etc.

MR. WILLIAM HEINEMANN'S NEW FICTION

WHEN GHOST MEETS GHOST
by WILLIAM DE MORGAN   6/-

"The plot of Mr. De Morgan's novel is distinctly original . . . but what matters the plot in a masterpiece of character-drawing? There are several characters here whom it is delightful to sit and think about after closing the book. . . . Into the gradual evolution of these fine traits Mr. De Morgan puts all the subtlety of his art."

Author of
JOSEPH VANCE   IT NEVER CAN HAPPEN
ALICE-FOR-SHORT   AGAIN
AN AFFAIR OF DISHONOUR   SOMEHOW GOOD
A LIKELY STORY

VANDOVER AND THE BRUTE
by FRANK NORRIS   6/-

Author of "The Octopus," etc.

"An extraordinarily penetrative study and certainly enhances the collective value of Frank Norris' work."
—*Times.*

"One of the most moving stories of a man's moral decay that I have read since Mr. Maxwell's haunting story, 'In Cotton Wool' . . . undeniably impressive and interesting."
—*Tatler.*

THE MAN OF IRON
by RICHARD DEHAN   6/-

"We do not know any contemporary English novelist who would have conjured up a livelier, more effective picture of the famous dinner of three at which Bismarck initiated war by altering his royal master's message so that what 'sounded like a parley' became a fanfare of defiance. Excellent, too, are the characterization and comedy in the author's sketches of the Prussian mobilization and transport of troops."—*Athenæum.*

21 BEDFORD STREET, LONDON, W.C.

MR. WILLIAM HEINEMANN'S NEW FICTION

THE COST OF WINGS
by RICHARD DEHAN 6/-

"Richard Dehan has collected in this volume twenty-six clever short stories. They are all well designed, brightly—now and then, perhaps, over brightly written, and the authoress has a very clear conception of the value of the climax; she can keep her secret, if necessary, to the last line of her tale."—*Evening News*.

BY THE SAME AUTHOR
THE HEADQUARTER RECRUIT
6/-

"There is real truth and pathos in the 'Fourth Volume,' originality in 'The Tribute of Offa,' and pith in nearly all of them."—*Times*.

"There is not one of the tales which will fail to excite, amuse, entertain, or in some way delight the reader."
—*Liverpool Daily Post*.

BETWEEN TWO THIEVES
(New Edition) 2/- net

"The book is really an amazing piece of work. Its abounding energy, its grip on our attention, its biting humour, its strong, if sometimes lurid word painting have an effect of richness and fullness of teeming life, that sweeps one with it. What an ample chance for praise and whole-hearted enjoyment. The thing unrols with a vividness that never fails."—*Daily News and Leader*.

THE DOP DOCTOR
(Now in its 18th Edition). 2/- net

"Pulsatingly real—gloomy, tragic, humorous, dignified, real. The cruelty of battle, the depth of disgusting villainy, the struggles of great souls, the irony of coincidence, are all in its pages. . . . Who touches this book touches a man. I am grateful for the wonderful thrills 'The Dop Doctor' has given me. It is a novel among a thousand."—*The Daily Express*.

21 BEDFORD STREET, LONDON, W.C.

MR. WILLIAM HEINEMANN'S NEW FICTION

THE FREELANDS
by JOHN GALSWORTHY 6/-

"A sincere, powerful, and humane study of the modern English Countryside."—*Daily News.*

Author of

A MAN OF PROPERTY	COUNTRY HOUSE
THE ISLAND PHARISEES	FRATERNITY
THE PATRICIAN	THE INN OF TRANQUILLITY
A MOTLEY	MOODS, SONGS & DOGGERELS
THE DARK FLOWER	

OF HUMAN BONDAGE
by W. SOMERSET MAUGHAM 6/-

"The only novel of the year in which we can take cover from the sad, swift thoughts which sigh and whine about our heads in war time."—*Morning Post.*

"We have never read a cleverer book."—*Outlook.*

A LADY OF RUSSIA
by ROBERT BOWMAN 6/-

"Those who are interested in Russian life—and who is not?—should read the book for themselves. The author knows his subject and writes graphically about it, and his contrasts are powerful."—*Pall Mall Gazette.*

---

21 BEDFORD STREET, LONDON, W.C.

MR. WILLIAM HEINEMANN'S NEW FICTION

THE PERFECT WIFE
by JOSEPH KEATING   6/-

"It is all written in the gayest, happiest spirit of light comedy . . . the whole thing is cleverly and entertainingly done . . . the story holds you interested and amused throughout."—*The Bookman.*

"It is a pure comedy . . . it makes excellent and exciting and humorous reading. There is plenty of good character-drawing to boot, and the writing is simple and effective and often witty. . . . Mr. Keating has written a very entertaining story, and we are grateful to him."
—*Daily Chronicle.*

THE MILKY WAY
by F. TENNYSON JESSE   6/-

"A light-hearted medley, the spirit and picturesqueness of which the author cleverly keeps alive to the last act."
—*Times Literary Supplement.*

"A book of youth and high spirits! That is the definition of this altogether delightful 'Milky Way' . . . this wholly enchanting 'Viv,' her entourage . . . as gay and irresponsible as herself. . . . Miss Tennyson Jesse has great gifts; skill and insight, candour, enthusiasm, and a pleasant way of taking her readers into her confidence . . . the final impression is that she enjoyed writing her book just as much as this reviewer has enjoyed reading it."
—*Daily Mail.*

THE REWARD OF VIRTUE
by AMBER REEVES   6/-

"There is cleverness enough and to spare, but it is . . . a spontaneous cleverness, innate, not laboriously acquired. . . . The dialogue . . . is so natural, so unaffected, that it is quite possible to read it without noticing the high artistic quality of it. . . . For a first novel Miss Reeves's is a remarkable achievement; it would be a distinct achievement even were it not a first novel."
—*Daily Chronicle.*

21 BEDFORD STREET, LONDON, W.C.

MR. WILLIAM HEINEMANN'S NEW FICTION

THE BUSINESS OF A GENTLEMAN
by H. N. DICKINSON 6/-

Author of "Keddy," "Sir Guy and Lady Rannard," etc.

"His tale is undoubtedly refreshing. He is obviously sincere. . . . His whole book is a plea for the personal responsibility of all landowners and employers of labour. Distinctly this is a novel to be read, for it is the work of one who has the courage of conviction, and who thinks for himself."—*Standard*

"Mr. H. N. Dickinson's new novel is one of the most humorous books we have met with for a long time. 'The Business of A Gentleman' is a satire on that grandmotherly legislation which seeks to regulate the lives of the poor—their amusements, their morals, their family and the upbringing of their children. . . . Wittily written with an atmosphere of laughter, touched with pungent satire, we cordially recommend this clever novel."
—*Everyman.*

BRUNEL'S TOWER
by EDEN PHILLPOTTS 6/-

"Time and again Mr. Phillpotts has given us proof of his wonderful keenness and observation and of the loving care with which he gives expression to it. But there has never been a finer instance of it than in the exquisite descriptions in this story of the potter in all the stages of his work. One could read 'Brunel's Tower' for that alone, even if there were no other interests in it. It is a beautifully told story and there is something austere in the style, though exquisitely sensitive. It is the master potter at work."—*Pall Mall Gazette.*

21 BEDFORD STREET, LONDON, W.C.

MR. WILLIAM HEINEMANN'S NEW FICTION

THE MERCY OF THE LORD
by FLORA ANNIE STEEL   6/-

Mrs. Steel's ever-delightful pen is here employed in giving us pictures as it were from her experience—stories of India, stories of the Highlands, quick impressions of modern life—each a rounded, well-defined tale, written with so sane a touch, with so pleasant a mind behind them that she makes the strongest appeal to her public.

Author of

A PRINCE OF DREAMERS	MISS STUART'S LEGACY
THE FLOWER OF FORGIVE-NESS	ON THE FACE OF THE WATERS
FROM THE FIVE RIVERS	THE POTTER'S THUMB
THE HOSTS OF THE LORD	RED ROWANS
IN THE GUARDIANSHIP OF GOD	A SOVEREIGN REMEDY
	VOICES IN THE NIGHT
IN THE PERMANENT WAY	and other stories.
KING ERRANT	

THE STEPPE AND OTHER STORIES
by ANTON TCHEKOV   6/-

On account of his simplicity, his tender humour, and his power of delineating character, Tchekov holds a very high place in Russian literature. In this volume, which contains longer and more important stories than any which have hitherto appeared in English, he portrays with peculiar fidelity the resignation and patient idealism which is so characteristic of the Russian spirit.

"These tales have not only the simplicity of genius, but give a most remarkable insight into the Russian character."—*Globe*.

21 BEDFORD STREET, LONDON, W.C.

MR. WILLIAM HEINEMANN'S NEW FICTION

THE HOUSE IN DEMETRIUS ROAD
by J. D. BERESFORD — 6/-

This story is the study of a mysterious man, a man of undoubted mental force, subtly and skilfully written. The three chief characters, Greg, the mystery, Mary, his sister-in-law, and Martin Bond, are real and living; the medley of something like genius, cunning, weakness of will and force of personality in Greg being extraordinarily well depicted.

BY THE SAME AUTHOR

GOSLINGS — 6/-

"Many of the scenes of his book will live long in the imagination. The book is packed with such striking episodes, which purge the intellect, if not always the soul, with pity and terror and wonder. Mr. Beresford has, in fact, proved once again that, even if he may appear somewhat unsympathetic on the emotional side, he has an intellectual grasp as strong and as sure as that of any living novelist."—*Morning Post.*

JOHN CHRISTOPHER:
I. Dawn and Morning.   II. Storm and Stress.
III. John Christopher in Paris
IV. The Journey's End
by ROMAIN ROLLAND — each 6/-

Translated by GILBERT CANNAN. Author of "Little Brother," etc.

" A noble piece of work, which must, without any doubt whatever, ultimately receive the praise and attention which it so undoubtedly merits. . . . There is hardly a single book more illustrative, more informing and more inspiring . . . than M. Romain Rolland's creative work, 'John Christopher.'"—*The Daily Telegraph.*

21 BEDFORD STREET, LONDON, W.C.

MR. WILLIAM HEINEMANN'S NEW FICTION

VEILED LIFE
by Mrs. GOLDIE   6/-

This charming story, which is remarkable for its clearness of conception, simplicity of writing, and restraint, opens in life below stairs; but soon, not without shadow and not without sunshine, broadens into the larger life of the world, with its ups and downs, its cruel passions and its saving pleasures.

"It is of the liveliest interest . . . a very able study."—*Bookman.*

"The story has real and unusual merit."—*Publishers' Circular.*

THE LIFE MASK   6/-
by the Author of "He Who Passed."

"A highly remarkable novel, with a plot both striking and original, and written in a style quite distinctive and charming."

"Seldom, if ever, has a tale given me so genuine a surprise or such an unexpectedly creepy sensation."
Punch.

HE WHO PASSED
To M. L. G.   6/-

"As a story, it is one of the most enthralling I have read for a long time. . . . Six—seven o'clock struck—half-past-seven—and yet this extraordinary narrative of a woman's life held me absolutely enthralled. . . . I forgot the weather; I forgot my own grievances; I forgot everything, in fact, under the spell of this wonderful book. . . . In fact the whole book bears the stamp of reality from cover to cover. There is hardly a false or strained note in it. It is the ruthless study of a woman's life. . . . If it is not the novel of the season, the season is not likely to give us anything much better."—*The Tatler.*

ALSO POPULAR EDITION, 2/- NET.

21 BEDFORD STREET, LONDON, W.C.

MR. WILLIAM HEINEMANN'S NEW FICTION

STORIES OF INDIA
by ROSE REINHARDT ANTHON 6/-

"In her 'Stories of India' Miss Rose Reinhardt Anthon has given us a remarkable book ... wonderfully stimulating to the imagination. The stories are told with a quaint compelling charm, and their directness and simplicity are infinitely refreshing to the jaded mind of the reviewer, tired by the trivialities of much modern fiction."
—*Everyman*.

"The stories will be appreciated for their novelty and freshness, and for the insight they afford into the Indian mind."—*Academy*.

"The stories are always picturesque and pointed. They interest apart from their elusive and charming suggestions of deep and hidden truth ... and the book has a fine flavour of mythology."—*Scotsman*.

THE ISLAND
by ELEANOR MORDAUNT 6/-

Author of "The Cost of It," "The Garden of Contentment," etc.

This charming volume of stories shows the whole range of this author's talents. It is a book that will be bought and read by all admirers of the "Garden of Contentment," and they should not be disappointed, for it is full of the spirit which has made this author so popular.

BY THE SAME AUTHOR.

LU OF THE RANGES 6/-

"Miss Eleanor Mordaunt has the art, not only of visualizing scenes with such imminent force that the reader feels the shock of reality, but of sensating the emotions she describes. A finely written book, full of strong situations."—*Everyman*.

21 BEDFORD STREET, LONDON, W.C.

MR. WILLIAM HEINEMANN'S NEW FICTION

YES
by MARY AGNES HAMILTON 6/-

"There is a poignancy of human and artistic feeling in the book which gives distinction to the style and easily leads us captive."—*Pall Mall Gazette.*

"To the solid merits of a story worth the telling the author adds the advantage of sound feeling and a genuine gift of humour. Our verdict on 'Yes' is complete concurrence."—*Bookman.*

The GARDEN WITHOUT WALLS
by CONINGSBY DAWSON 6/-

". . . work of such genuine ability that its perusal is a delight and its recommendation to others a duty. . . . It is a strong book, strong in every way, and it is conceived and executed on a large scale. But long as it is, there is nothing superfluous in it; its march is as orderly and stately as the pageant of life itself . . . and it is a book, too, that grows on you as you read it . . . and compels admiration of the talent and skill that have gone to its writing and the observation and reflection that have evolved its philosophy of life."—*Glasgow Herald.*

A COUNTRY HOUSE COMEDY
by DUNCAN SWANN 6/-

"A vivid picture of society in some of its phases, a picture evidently drawn from close observation and actual experience, and pervaded throughout with a delicate humour, keen satire, and racy cynicisms which make the whole book exceptionally well worth reading."—
Bookseller.

UNTILLED FIELD
by GEORGE MOORE 6/-

"A thing of quite exquisite art. . . . Each of the fourteen stories in the book will be read with enjoyment by every lover of good literature and every student of national types . . . admirable volume."—*Observer.*

21 BEDFORD STREET, LONDON, W.C.

MR. WILLIAM HEINEMANN'S NEW FICTION

THE SHUTTLE
by Mrs. HODGSON BURNETT
Author of "The Secret Garden," etc.   (New Edition) **2/- net**

"Now and then, but only now and then, a novel is given to English literature that takes its place at once and without dispute among the greater permanent works of fiction. Such a novel is 'The Shuttle.' Breadth and sanity of outlook, absolute mastery of human character and life, bigness of story interest place Mrs. Hodgson Burnett's new book alongside the best work of George Eliot, and make one keenly aware that we are in danger of forgetting the old standards and paying too much homage to petty work. The dignity and strength of a great novel such as this put to the blush all but a very few English storytellers."—*Pall Mall Gazette.*

THE WEAKER VESSEL
by E. F. BENSON   **6/-**

"Among the writers of the present day who can make fiction the reflection of reality, one of the foremost is Mr. E. F. Benson. From the very beginning the interest is enchained."—*Daily Telegraph.*

JUGGERNAUT	*THE LUCK OF THE VAILS
*ACCOUNT RENDERED	*MAMMON & CO.
AN ACT IN A BACKWATER	*PAUL
*THE ANGEL OF PAIN	THE PRINCESS SOPHIA
*THE BOOK OF MONTHS	*A REAPING
*THE CHALLONERS	THE RELENTLESS CITY
*THE CLIMBER	*SCARLET AND HYSSOP
THE HOUSE OF DEFENCE	*SHEAVES
*THE IMAGE IN THE SAND	

Each Crn. 8vo.   Price 6/-.

Those volumes marked * can also be obtained in the Two Shilling net Edition, and also the following volumes

THE OSBORNES   THE VINTAGE   DODO

⁎ "The Book of Months" and "A Reaping" form one volume in this Edition.

21 BEDFORD STREET, LONDON, W.C.

MR. WILLIAM HEINEMANN'S NEW FICTION

THE WOMAN THOU GAVEST ME
by HALL CAINE 6/-

"The filling in of the story is marked by all Mr. Hall Caine's accustomed skill. There is a wealth of varied characterisation, even the people who make but brief and occasional appearances standing out as real individuals, and not as mere names. . . . In description, too, the novelist shows that his hand has lost nothing of its cunning. . . . Deeply interesting as a story—perhaps one of the best stories that Mr. Hall Caine has given us—the book will make a further appeal to all thoughtful readers for its frank and fearless discussion of some of the problems and aspects of modern social and religious life."
—*Daily Telegraph.*

"Hall Caine's voice reaches far; in this way 'The Woman Thou Gavest Me' strikes a great blow for righteousness. There is probably no other European novelist who could have made so poignant a tale of such simple materials. In that light Mr. Hall Caine's new novel is his greatest achievement."—*Daily Chronicle.*

Other NOVELS of HALL CAINE
(of which over 3 million copies have been sold).

"These volumes are in every way a pleasure to read. Of living authors, Mr. Hall Caine must certainly sway as multitudinous a following as any living man. A novel from his pen has become indeed for England and America something of an international event."—*Times.*

Author of

THE BONDMAN 6/-, 2/-, 7d. net.	THE ETERNAL CITY 6/-, 2/-
CAPT'N DAVEYS HONEY-MOON 2/-	THE MANXMAN 6/-, 2/-
	THE PRODIGAL SON 6/-
MY STORY 6/-, 2/- net.	THE SCAPEGOAT 6/-, 7d. net.
THE WHITE PROPHET 6/-	THE CHRISTIAN 6/-, 2/-

21 BEDFORD STREET, LONDON, W.C.

MR. WILLIAM HEINEMANN'S NEW FICTION

KATYA
by FRANZ DE JESSEN (2nd Impression) 6/-

"To a certain number of readers in this country the writings of M. de Jessen are known as those of a brilliant war correspondent and traveller, a man who has kept tryst with danger and adventure in many lands. This is the first time that he has appeared in England, at any rate, as a writer of fiction. His novel, 'Katya,' possesses a threefold value: in the first place he has woven into it, in very intimate fashion, some of the tragic and exciting happenings that took place in Russian and Balkan lands some dozen and less years ago; secondly, the story itself is one of intense human interest; and lastly, it gives as brilliant and true a picture of modern Russian life as any that one can remember in a recent work of fiction."
—*Morning Post.*

WHAT A WOMAN WANTS
by Mrs. HENRY DUDENEY 6/-

"High as has always been our opinion of Mrs. Dudeney's work, she has certainly never written anything to compare in interest with 'What a Woman Wants.' The narrative and description are vivid, the thought is impressive, and the character of Christmas Hamlyn has been drawn with great power and with all the author's peculiar skill. . . . Her work is admirably well done."—*Standard.*

SMALL SOULS
by LOUIS COUPERUS 6/-
Translated by ALEXANDER TEIXEIRA DE MATTEOS.

"We most cordially hope the reception will justify the translation of all four, for the taste of the first makes us hunger for the others. . . . A master of biting comedy, a psychologist of rare depth and finesse, and a supreme painter of manners."—*Pall Mall Gazette.*

---

21 BEDFORD STREET. LONDON, W.C.

MR. WILLIAM HEINEMANN'S NEW FICTION

NEW NOVELS FOR 1915.

THE IMMORTAL GYMNAST
By MARIE CHER

CARFRAE'S COMEDY
By GLADYS PARRISH

OLD DELABOLE
By EDEN PHILLPOTTS

THE PUSH ON THE S.S. "GLORY"
By FREDERICK NIVEN
Illustrated by FRED HOLMES

THE BOTTLE FILLERS
By EDWARD NOBLE

MUSLIN
By GEORGE MOORE

THE LITTLE ILIAD
By MAURICE HEWLETT
Illustrated by Sir PHILIP BURNE-JONES

BEGGARS ON HORSEBACK
By F. TENNYSON JESSE

LATER LIVES
By LOUIS COUPERUS

21 BEDFORD STREET, LONDON, W.C.

MR. WILLIAM HEINEMANN'S NEW FICTION

THE NOVELS OF DOSTOEVSKY

Translated by CONSTANCE GARNETT
Cr. 8vo, 3/6 net each

"By the genius of Dostoevsky you are always in the presence of living, passionate characters. They are not puppets, they are not acting to keep the plot in motion. They are men and women—I should say you can hear them breathe—irresistibly moving to their appointed ends."—*Evening News*.

I. THE BROTHERS KARAMAZOV
II. THE IDIOT
III. THE POSSESSED
IV. CRIME AND PUNISHMENT
V. THE HOUSE OF THE DEAD
VI. INSULTED AND INJURED

Other volumes to follow

THE NOVELS OF LEO TOLSTOY

Translated by CONSTANCE GARNETT

ANNA KARENIN	3/6 net
WAR AND PEACE	3/6 net
THE DEATH OF IVAN ILYVITCH	3/6 net

"Mrs. Garnett's translations from the Russian are always distinguished by most careful accuracy and a fine literary flavour."—*The Bookman*.

"Mrs. Garnett's translation has all the ease and vigour which Matthew Arnold found in French versions of Russian novels and missed in English. She is indeed so successful that, but for the names, one might easily forget he was reading a foreign author."
—*The Contemporary Review*.

21 BEDFORD STREET, LONDON, W.C.